A MILITARY EDUCATION

SILKEN DALLIANCE

John Ogden

Silken Dalliance

The sequel to *On Fire*
and the second book in the trilogy
A Military Education

Thorntons
Faringdon

First published in Great Britain in 2009 by

Thorntons

The Old Barn, Walnut Court, Faringdon SN7 7JH

Typeset in Plantin 10.5 on 14 by Jenni Navratil Graphic Art and Design, Oxford
Printed by the MPG Books Group in the UK

A catalogue record for this book is available from The British Library.

ISBN 978 0 85455 040 1

Now all the youth of England are on fire
And silken dalliance in the wardrobe lies:

William Shakespeare
Henry V, Act Two

For Naomi

I am not I. You are not she or he.
They are not they.

Nor is a pound sterling a pound. The 1953 pound
would be worth at least £35 today and in those days
there were about 12 Deutschmarks to the pound.

Contents

1

Change of command, in which we find
our new colonel wanting.

'So, Miles, what do you make of our new colonel?'

Jasper Knox asked me the question that was on everyone's mind.

We were sitting on our horses at the edge of the forest that stretched away behind us twenty miles to the border with East Germany, the Iron Curtain. Below us lay the barracks where the battalion had arrived three weeks before. Beyond, lying in the plain beside the river, was the great medieval university town mercifully untouched by the war. The barracks and the town were to be our home for the next two years; the border our responsibility to patrol and protect against the imminent threat of invasion by Soviet Russia.

It was the early 1950s. Western Germany was recovering rapidly after the war. We were part of the British Army of the Rhine, one of the four occupying armies. As I looked down at the town I thought how serene and inviting it looked, how much it promised, how good life could be here. But there was the niggling question Jasper had just asked.

'Come on, Miles, what do you think?'

For the last two years, most of them on active service in Korea, Guy Surtees had commanded us. He had been everything you could wish for in a commanding officer. He had had the good fortune to take over a well trained battalion and had made it into an effective fighting force. We worshipped him and would have followed him anywhere. His tour of command over, he had brought us to Germany and, after ten days, had handed over to Dennis Parker Brown.

Colonel Dennis had the reputation of being a brilliant staff officer and had been serving as such in Germany. Clever and a scholar, on arrival he seemed a little unrelaxed, a trifle on edge, his good humour rather forced. Maybe that was natural in one who had just assumed command of a battalion that had recently been in action but it was not what we were used to. He was the opposite of Colonel Guy. It would take some time for us to settle to him, and he to us.

'Why the silence? Mourning Colonel Guy?' asked Jasper.

Yes, I was mourning Colonel Guy. He had been a great influence. I had grown up under him and hated losing him.

'Well I couldn't see what you all saw in Guy Surtees. All he did since I joined in England four months ago was go racing.'

Jasper Knox had not been with us in Korea. Newly commissioned, he had joined us when we came home to England. His father had been in the regiment, as had mine. We had known each other as children and at school, though he was four years my junior. He was shorter than me, lightly built, lithe, and a born horseman. He had beautiful hands and dark wavy hair. He spoke with a slight drawl. We had taken to riding together since he joined us.

'I can only take your silence as disapproval,' he continued. 'I like Colonel Dennis. I think he's rather sweet. He's a good horseman. I never saw Colonel Guy on a horse, only betting on them. Colonel Dennis is just the soldier for Germany. He knows the form here. The battalion's living on its laurels and we need to change. He'll be good for us. I suppose one day, Miles, you'll tell me what went on in Korea. You're all so secretive about it. Come on now. Wake up. Race you back to barracks.'

Jasper picked up his reins, wheeled his horse and started off. I took a last look at the promise of all that lay before me. How could our new colonel spoil it?

All this, of course, was a long time ago now. The Second World War, only eight years over, still dominated our thoughts, much as we were trying to adapt to the cold war with Soviet Russia and all that meant. These were austere years in England. Stationed in Germany we seemed to be comparatively well off. In many ways the early 1950s were closer to the 1930s than to the 1960s. Britain still had an empire and a large army to protect it. It was a different world, especially the small regimental world in which we lived.

I write this from memory. Memory can mislead, I know. So I have talked to many who were, consulted the records and looked through some letters written at the time; I want to record, once and for all, what really happened all those years ago in Germany. Was Colonel Dennis as wicked and deranged as many of us came to believe? Was Adam Hare as bad an influence on the young as many thought? Or were we at fault that they behaved as they did? I want to know. And to know I must go back and re-live those days.

I lost the race back to barracks. Jasper was walking his horse in a circle waiting for me at the entrance. Together we walked our horses past the guard at the gate, acknowledging his salute, and on past battalion headquarters. The barracks were well laid out and, to us, modern. They had been built in the 1930s for Hitler's *Wehrmacht*. Five rows of buildings ran across and down the hill, with the parade grounds on which we also played sports between them. The buildings at the top lay just under the forest; those at the bottom just above the town. The stables were at the bottom not far from the officers' mess. We turned right and walked our horses slowly down.

A horsebox stood outside the stables. Out of this Corporal O'Reilly, the head groom, was coaxing a horse down the plank.

'Who's this, Corporal?' Jasper asked.

'Why, he's the colonel's horse, Red Ember. And about time too. The fucking driver lost his way or he'd have been here long ago and

I could have gone for my tea. Now, my beauty, come on down.'

'Yes, he looks a beauty.'

'No question there.'

'Does he go?'

'Does he go, Sir? Why Red Ember goes like the wind. There's no stopping him.'

'Wins races, then?'

'First, second, third, he's always up there. Now, gentlemen, let me get him into his box. Whistler can attend to you.' He raised his voice. 'Whistler, where the fucking hell are you?'

We watched O'Reilly walk Red Ember into his box. I could feel Jasper's excitement. He followed him with his eyes until Red Ember was out of sight. Whistler, short and dirty, ambled out of the stables. We dismounted and led our horses into their boxes. As soon as we'd finished stabling them we had a closer look at Red Ember. He was smaller than he had at first appeared and sturdier.

'Would you like to ride him, Jasper?' said a voice close behind us.

I turned round and saluted. Jasper continued to appraise Red Ember. Seconds passed.

'Yes,' he finally said, 'I would, Colonel.'

He turned round slowly, looked the colonel in the eye and saluted him.

Lieutenant Colonel Dennis Parker Brown was short, thin and wiry. Crinkly blond hair, going grey round the ears, showed under his hat. He was a handsome man and must have been exceptionally good looking when young. His uniform fitted him closely. Between the pockets of his tunic hung a gold watch chain. On the little finger of his left hand he wore a signet ring, which I later noticed he often played with when beginning to lose his temper. He was very dapper and had an attractive smile.

'So you shall, Jasper. They tell me you're a fine horseman. When I'm too busy to ride him you must exercise him for me. I was on my way to the mess but wanted to check that he was all right. Have you seen our polo ponies? Yes? Of course, several of them are Horace Belcher's. I arranged to buy the rest from the 25th Lancers when they left Germany. If you've finished stabling your horses let's go and have a drink.'

The officers' mess was an easy walk from the stables. Within minutes we were entering the main door of the mess, a converted barrack block with three main storeys. The officers' rooms were on the ground and second floors. Between them, on the first floor, were the reception rooms. Some of the mess staff lived in the attics. We climbed the stairs to the first floor and, leaving our hats and belts in the cloakroom, entered the anteroom together.

Wide, long and light, the room was furnished with leather armchairs and sofas arranged in groups. Just inside the door was a large table covered with several magazines and some English newspapers. The walls were white and that over the fireplace was covered by 19th century prints of battle scenes, massed together. On the others hung oil paintings: a large oil of the regiment charging the Old Guard at Waterloo by Lady Butler; portraits by Wilkie, Etty and Winterhalter; military scenes by Frith and Tissot; and a portrait by Constable of the colonel who had commanded us at Waterloo. Silver lamps with red shades stood on occasional tables besides silver rose bowls and cups. On the red carpet were scattered some Persian rugs. The room gave an air of confidence and comfort. Colonel Dennis surveyed it with pride.

'When I knew I was to command this battalion,' he said, 'I went to the depot to claim the mess possessions. Do you know most of them were still in the cases we packed them in when we went to France in 1939? I remembered them because I had overseen the packing. Of course,' he said, looking at me, 'you took the silver with you to Hong Kong though I always thought that rather dangerous. Now we've got everything together again we can settle down to some proper regimental soldiering.'

At that moment Corporal Cheke, the mess barman, came in. We all asked for whisky and soda.

'What do you mean by proper regimental soldiering, Colonel?' asked Jasper.

'Doing all the things we used to do before the war. Entertaining, of course. Horses, polo, shooting. Winning the competitions. BAOR is a competitive command. And then of course there's military efficiency. We've a testing day tomorrow with the visit of General Boot.'

The next day, Wednesday, Major General Boot, our divisional commander was visiting us, coming to welcome us to his command. We regarded it an important occasion and had been preparing for it for weeks.

'How did you think today's rehearsal went?' I asked.

'Too well. Things shouldn't go too well at a dress rehearsal. The men get over confident. It's the time to turn up the weaknesses and irregularities. I was rather surprised at how few there were.'

'That's because we've some wonderful NCOs.'

'I can see that. I hope the officers aren't relying on them too much. BAOR is a different game from Korea. I know what you did in Korea but it was trench warfare. Here, in an armoured division, we've got to be mobile, alert, and fast. Of course you, Jasper, were not in Korea. Those that were have a lot to re-learn.'

Some figures appeared at the door. First came Dermot Lisle. Well built and dark, he had an engaging manner and an air of gaiety. He had won a DSO in Korea commanding a company, and an MC in Italy in the Second World War. He was an Olympic shot and regarded as a future commanding officer, possibly a general. Following him were Ben Wildbore and Burgo Howard, who had been in Korea too. Ben was a company second in command, slender and a bon viveur. He often had a cigarette drooping out of the corner of his mouth. He had been mentioned in despatches. Burgo was blond and blue eyed, and noted for his penetrating look. He had won an MC. They were both pentathletes. They looked hot and were dressed as if they had been fencing. Following them was Corporal Cheke with three silver goblets of beer.

'Ah, Dermot, Ben, Burgo, good evening. We're just discussing the challenges of BAOR.'

'You've got to guide us here, Colonel. We're fortunate to have you command us with all your BAOR experience,' said Dermot.

'I shall. I shall.'

'Some of us are finding ourselves being pulled in too many directions already. I've just come from the pistol range, but I'd have liked to have been riding with Miles and Jasper or fencing with Ben and Burgo. There seem to be too many opportunities, too many things to do, too little time to do them in.'

'Yes, so I see. I'll soon acclimatize you to the pace here. We may have to be clearer about who does what.'

He said this kindly, but with scrutiny. Dermot, Ben and Burgo were being appraised. They, in turn, were appraising Colonel Dennis.

'Will you be joining us for dinner, Colonel?' asked Ben.

'No. In fact I think it best for a colonel to live out of the mess and leave it to the unmarried officers like you, even though I'm a bachelor again. I like eating luncheon here. That way I can get to know you better. I'm dining with the Stanhopes so I must be going. I trust you are all prepared for tomorrow?'

He nodded to each of us and strode out of the anteroom. Algy Stanhope was second in command to Colonel Dennis. He had joined us in England when we had returned from Korea. We had quickly grown to admire him and to love his wife, Olivia.

'What,' asked Dermot, looking at me with a grin, 'are the challenges of BAOR?'

'Being mobile, alert and fast in an armoured division.'

'Oh dear, oh dear. Even in the mess before dinner,' said Ben.

He flopped into an armchair and we all sat down round him.

'Who knows where the mess big game rifles are?' asked Ben. 'The ones we didn't take to Korea. I'm sure we had them in Hong Kong though we didn't use them. The colonel has asked me, as president of the mess committee, for a list and location of all the mess possessions including the sporting rifles and shotguns. He's amazing at detail and remembers item by item what there was before the war. He didn't find the rifles at the depot when he reclaimed all the mess possessions.'

'They're in three long cases in the silver room still to be un-packed from Hong Kong,' said Burgo who was responsible for the mess silver.

'Good. Let's unpack them tomorrow. Now what are the arrangements for this evening?'

'Because of the parade tomorrow, pretty frugal,' said Jasper. 'Soup, goulash, and Welsh rarebit. Tomorrow's lunch will be asparagus, trout, and strawberries.' As the youngest regular officer, Jasper had drawn the short straw to be responsible for messing.

'And after dinner?'

'Perhaps a game of chance to prepare us for the morrow?' said Burgo.

'Let's all pray we're prepared for tomorrow.'

A bugle call echoed up the stairs of the mess into the ante-room.

'Half-hour dress. Just time for the other half,' said Burgo.

About twenty of us sat down to dinner. At one end of the room stood the cased colours in front of a large signed photograph of the young queen. At the opposite end was a full-length portrait of George IV by Lawrence. George IV had been the great patron of the regiment. As Prince Regent, at one of the early Waterloo dinners given by the Duke of Wellington, he had turned to General Lord Lynedoch and said, 'I'll tell you this, Lynedoch. I don't think the Duke would have toppled Boney without that regiment of light infantry of yours.' To which Lord Lynedoch replied, 'Sir, you do me the greatest honour. May I return the honour by proposing you make the regiment your own.' 'What! The Prince Regent's Regiment of Light Infantry? I like it. I'll have the Horse Guards command my new regiment to be with me in Brighton immediately.'

One evening at Brighton, after the Prince Regent had become king, the colonel and some of the officers went to the Theatre Royal, occupying the stalls. As soon as the performance began the crowd in the gallery started to pelt them with vegetables and eggs.

The officers drew their swords and cleared the theatre. Returning, they discovered George IV in a box with Mrs Fitzherbert. The king had entered quietly as the play began and the crowd had recognised him immediately. The officers then realised that the crowd had been pelting the king not them. The king, mistaking the officers' action for loyalty, was delighted with them and knighted the colonel on the spot. When Lord Lynedoch suggested to the king that he might like to rename the regiment 'The King's Light Infantry' the king replied, 'No, no, Lynedoch. I've king's regiments to take me from Brighton to John O'Groats, but there's only one Prince Regent's Light Infantry. I'll tell you what. My Prince Regent's shall not drink the loyal toast except when I'm present.' And that custom we observe to this day.

We were not an old regiment. We'd been raised in the French revolutionary wars as light infantry and trained under Sir John Moore. Proud of this, we still observed Moore's methods and ideals and felt elitist about it. We were one of the few infantry regiments in the army still to have two battalions.

In the middle of the long wall hung the portrait, also by Lawrence, of our original patron, General Lord Lynedoch. Alongside it hung a portrait of Field Marshal Viscount Wolseley, our colonel-in-chief at the end of the nineteenth century. In those days, as General Sir Garnet Wolseley, he was known as 'our only general' and had earned a reputation for conducting his campaigns perfectly. The regiment still used the expression 'All Sir Garnet' to indicate that something was perfectly organised or arranged.

Along the centre of the rosewood dining table were three silver candelabra standing between four silver vases. These had been given to the regiment by the Prince Regent. It was the tradition of the mess only to have these seven pieces of silver on the mess table when dining informally as we were that evening.

In those days we used to dine informally on Mondays, Tuesdays, Thursdays, and Fridays. Informal dress meant you could wear whatever formal dress you wished: black tie, number one dress or mess kit. Most of the officers were wearing number one dress, a dark green tunic that buttoned up to the neck with silver buttons. A few were wearing dinner jackets. Three were wearing mess kit, a dark green bum-freezer that buttoned only at the neck, faced with a blue silk collar. Beneath it was a blue silk waistcoat, gleaming with a long line of tiny silver buttons. Dark green was our privilege as a light infantry regiment, blue facings our right as a royal regiment. This informality of dress was reached partly by preference, partly by prudence. Half the officers present were national service second lieutenants. All had number one dress. None had mess kit, as it was expensive and therefore unjustified for a short period of service. Not all wanted to wear dinner jackets, for in those days we still wore starched shirts and wing collars with a black bow tie.

Ben Wildbore sat at the head of the table as president of the mess committee. Harry Fox, a national service officer and orderly officer of the day, sat at the bottom. I was sitting at Ben Wildbore's end of the table next to Finbar O'Connell, our regimental medical officer. Finbar and I were sharing a bottle of Piesporter Michelsberg. Opposite me was Burgo Howard, drinking whisky that was brought to him by Corporal Cheke in a little silver decanter with a decanter of water. Burgo leant forward a little.

'Many cases of VD yet, Doctor?' he asked.

'I'm delighted to say, none,' replied Finbar.

'What odds would you give for a case by the end of the week?'

'One case is unlikely but possible. A bad bet for me. But I'll give you five pounds to one there'll be fewer than five by the end of the month.'

'Not bad odds. I could write it in the betting book as accidental injuries.'

'That's a crass bet,' intervened Ben.

'Why, Ben?'

'Don't you know that Finbar's been round the town with Provost Serjeant Feard and the town's medical officer visiting all the brothels, examining all the girls and issuing them with French letters.'

'That true, Finbar?' demanded Burgo.

'It's my duty to try and protect the darling lads. I'm doing my best.'

'Have you told the colonel?'

'The colonel suggested it. I mean Colonel Guy did as soon as we arrived.'

'Does Colonel Dennis know?'

'I've had no reason to mention it to him.'

'I wonder how he'll react when he learns.'

'There's no reason for him to learn from anyone. The VD rate in BAOR is high. He'll have one of the lowest rates in the division. He'll be delighted.'

'I wouldn't be too sure about that,' said Burgo.

'What do you think of the Piesporter, Finbar?' I asked.

'Interesting. Not sure I'd want to drink it every night, though. What about some red wine?'

'Yesterday I went down to the wine merchants in the town with Harry Fox. His father's a wine merchant. They only had German wine so we bought some Rhine wine and some Moselle but nothing red. The German red wine is rather thin and sweet and you wouldn't enjoy it.'

'Haven't the NAAFI got some claret?' asked Burgo.

'Yes, we've tried them. Not much choice and it would be good to have claret the other regiments haven't. By the way, anyone know how far we are from the Frogs?' I asked.

'The French Zone is one to two hours' motoring away,' said Ben.

'*They'll* have some decent burgundy and claret. Couldn't we go and see them?'

'Ask Dermot.'

'Why Dermot?'

'As intelligence officer Dermot is meant to liaise with our neighbouring allies.'

'He's too engrossed talking to Harry Fox. Let's tackle him after dinner.'

'What did you think of the goulash?' asked Jasper, looking round the table.

'You're certainly feeding us well, far better than in England. Are you going to hit us for a fortune for this food?' enquired Finbar, who, being a captain and a doctor, was well paid but was always careful with his money.

'Karl, our German mess caterer, looks after it all. He wants no more than we were spending in England. There could be a trick somewhere, but I'm not rushing to find out what it is. Whenever I challenge Karl on the price of something he's says it's the exchange rate. We can live here very well with twelve Deutschmarks to the pound.'

'Miles, have you had a look at that restaurant someone recommended? What was it called?' asked Burgo.

'The Lucullus. Yes, Harry looked in after the wine merchants. He said it looked promising, the owner was friendly, and he's ordered a table for six for Saturday night.'

Dinner was coming to a close. The mess serjeant, Colour Serjeant Tom Body, MM, who had two long rows of medal ribbons on his large chest, had overseen the mess servants clearing the table. Decanters of port and Madeira were circulating. Not many were tempted. We still never drank the sovereign's health. Once the decanters had circulated the custom was to smoke if you wanted and then leave the table at will. Some continued to sit and drink. Others left for the anteroom, billiards room, or card room. In view of the general's visit on the following day most were clearly opting for a quiet evening. I didn't feel like gambling. I wanted to talk to Dermot Lisle about whether he had made contact with the French Army, but he was still deep in conversation. So I left and, remembering I hadn't read the day's papers, made for the anteroom and settled in a comfortable chair with the airmail edition of *The Times*.

'Hello Miles. Good dinner?'

Val Portal had entered the anteroom and was approaching, dressed in a dinner jacket. He hadn't been in Korea and had taken over as adjutant when we returned to England. He was thin and tall. Many of us thought him a little too openly ambitious.

'Not bad. What about you? You played truant tonight.'

'Dined with Brigadier Popham, the British resident in the town.'

'Meet anyone new?'

'Professor Hoffnung and Frau Professor Hoffnung and their very plain daughter Fräulein Ilse Hoffnung. Also a beautiful Turkish girl. They all spoke English.'

'Interesting?'

'You'll meet them. They'll be invited to our party.'

'When's that?'

'Soon.'

'Enigmatic as ever, Val. Discretion itself. I admire you.'

'Stop being facetious.'

'What's Miles being facetious about?' asked Dermot, who had joined us.

'My attempts at discretion.'

'Miles was born curious. Aren't you drinking?'

'One whisky and then I'm going to bed,' said Val.

'I'll ring the bell.'

'Have you made contact with the Frogs yet, Dermot?' I asked.

'I'm going to see them next week. I'll need an interpreter. My French isn't good enough.'

'Take Harry Fox,' I said. 'He speaks fluent French and German. You should have heard him at the wine merchants.'

'What do you want from the Frogs?'

'Do you think they'd let us have some decent claret and burgundy? It's difficult to buy in the town. We can't drink Riesling all the time. The German red wines are pretty dire.'

'We can ask. What about the NAAFI?'

'Not much choice and no bargains.'

'That's a good idea, Miles,' said Val. 'The colonel will approve. He wants to cultivate our allies. When they come to dinner he'll want to flatter them with some decent claret.'

'Val, are you going to be a bachelor adjutant and live in the mess, or is your wife joining you?' I asked.

'Jennifer is joining me next week. I'm only in the mess temporarily. Now I'm for bed.'

As Val left, Corporal Cheke came in with the night tray of drinks, which suggested that many were having an early night and that Cheke was retiring too. We refreshed our glasses.

'Tell me, Dermot, why are you intelligence officer?' I asked him.

'What do you mean?'

'In Korea you were a major and commanded a company. Now you are a captain commanding the intelligence section.'

'I was only a temporary major, remember. When Horace Belcher rejoined he took my place. He's senior to me. Colonel Guy was deeply apologetic and suggested I take on the intelligence role. He explained that, as we are out on a limb here on the flank of BAOR and in a pivotal position with our allies, it would be an interesting and independent job, especially with the war room and all the top secret plans that have to be kept up to date. He said it would only be for a few months until I go to the Staff College in the autumn.'

'You're going?'

'I'm on the short list for a place. Colonel Guy recommended me and I have the backing of the colonel of the regiment.'

'That's very good news.'

'Colonel Dennis has to support the recommendation too, of course. Dennis Parker Brown is trouble, Miles. Keep out of his way as far as you can. Unfortunately I have to see him every day.'

'I do wish I didn't find Colonel Dennis so different from Colonel Guy and so difficult to understand.'

'He's very easy to understand,' said Jasper, who had come into the anteroom without our noticing and was standing behind my chair, 'experienced BAOR hand, a horseman, and civilized. He likes to be comfortable - just look at this room. Proud of the regiment as he remembers it and bored with all the posturing of how good you all were in Korea. He wants to move on. He's a visionary.

I'm going to bed. I want to be fresh as the morning dew for the general's parade tomorrow. I'm not going to let Colonel Dennis down. Good night.'

'That young officer,' said Dermot, when Jasper had left the room, 'is headstrong. He needs watching.'

'I am watching. He's all keyed up and desperately wants to take part. You know, Dermot, it's not easy joining a battalion that has just come out of action. Not for him.'

'Not for the colonel either.'

The next day, Wednesday, General Boot was due to arrive at 11 o'clock. At 10.30 the massed bugles played Light Division assembly, a call the regiment had first used in the Peninsular War. We marched on to the parade ground and formed up in five divisions, each about one hundred strong. From the right in order of division were W, X, and Y companies, the three rifle companies. As we were under strength, Z company was training company and not on parade. The members of headquarter company that were not on administrative duties made up the fourth division. Finally, on the left as the fifth division came support company, comprising the anti-tank, assault pioneer, machine gun and mortar platoons. I was the battalion machine gun officer and therefore with support company.

Having paraded and been inspected by the colonel, we stood at ease. The colonel took his position in front of us all; immediately behind him was the colour party. Jasper was carrying the regimental colour, a dark blue silk flag bearing the regiment's insignia and battle honours embroidered in silver and gold. The officers stood in front of their companies and the serjeants stood behind theirs. We all wore battle dress, the khaki serge uniform that the army had adopted during the Second World War, with boots and gaiters. Everyone, both officers and men, also wore the dark green beret which as a regiment we had adopted at the end of the war and had continued to wear since. The officers wore revolvers in holsters on the left side of their webbing belts. The other ranks carried rifles, with cased bayonets on their left hips. About half wore the two Korean War medals. Nearly one hundred wore other medals too. We looked a compact, experienced, close-knit and uniform outfit.

The general arrived two minutes early. As he stepped on to the dais in front of the parade the colonel gave the command 'General Salute Present Arms'. The parade, as one man and in one continuous movement, came to attention, advanced fifteen paces in quick time and presented arms, the officers saluting, whereupon the band struck up the General Salute and Jasper lowered the regimental colour to the ground with a wide sweep of his arm. Most regiments would have made these drill movements on several commands and in several steps. Being light infantry we made all the steps on one command. It made for rapid movements. The movement we had just performed was spectacular. It always came as a surprise to those who hadn't seen it done before.

Then the colonel brought the parade back to attention, marched forward and reported to the general: 'I have the honour to report the Second Battalion the Prince Regent's Regiment of Light Infantry is present, correct and ready for your inspection General, Sir.'

While the general inspected us the band played. The bandmaster had chosen some popular numbers including 'Baby, It's cold outside,' 'Home cooking' and 'On a slow boat to China,' all favourites of those who had been in Korea.

Then we formed into line and, colour flying, double-marched past the general. Only a handful of regiments in the army did a double-march past and we were very proud of it. It was another spectacular sight, done to the 'Keel Row'.

The general then addressed us:

'Lieutenant Colonel Parker Brown, officers, warrant officers, non-commissioned officers, and men of the Second Battalion the Prince Regent's Light Infantry. I come here today to welcome you to the First Armoured Division. It's a great pleasure for me to do this. I fought alongside you in the war, at Dunkirk, in North Africa, in Sicily, and in Italy. I know your great reputation is justified. And now you come here having enhanced it fighting in Korea. You will find the British Army of the Rhine is playing on a different field from the one you have just left. But the discipline and bearing you display to me on parade today will stand you well here. I therefore expect you, under my command, not only to maintain but enhance your great reputation.'

A profound silence followed. Colonel Dennis seemed to hesitate over his next word of command. Then he called the battalion to attention, marched forward and asked permission for the battalion to march off. We made our final march past in quick time to our regimental quick march 'The Trojans'. This had been adopted after the Crimean War when some officers had been in Paris and by chance had seen a performance of Berlioz's great opera. They felt the tune of the Trojan march and the theme of the Trojans' battles and voyages fitted the regiment well. There had followed some discussion whether they should use a tune composed by a Frenchman. The bandmaster transposed the tune for band and bugles with some stirring bugle fanfares. The colonel of the day said, 'Who'd know it was by a Frenchman? I like it.' 'The Trojans' became one of our nicknames. Often, when in a tight corner, a soldier might say, 'Who'd be a fucking Trojan?' to get a laugh.

So we marched off at 140 paces to the minute, 500 strong and, as far as I could see, without a false step or note.

In front of our company lines we dismissed. Serjeant Whettingsteel, my platoon serjeant, and I marched up to the garages where our Oxford carriers were kept, the armoured tracked vehicles in which we carried our Vickers machine guns and ammunition.

'How do you think that went, Sir?'

'As good a parade as I ever remember. The band and bugles were terrific.'

'That's what I thought. The colonel will be pleased.'

Serjeant Whettingsteel's elder brother was our company serjeant major. They were known as Big Steel and Little Steel. Both were six foot, Little Steel the thinner and taller. Big Steel was ahead of us.

The general, accompanied by Colonel Dennis, our adjutant Val Portal, and the general's aide-de-camp, was touring the barracks starting with support company at the top. He went up to Big Steel, recognising the North African and Italian stars among his medals. They chatted about those years, one old soldier to another.

'Now, Serjeant Major, how's your equipment?'

The general knew he'd get closer to the truth from an experienced serjeant major than from any of us.

'As well as can be expected, Sir.'

'Go on.'

'Well, the carriers need constant attention and the machine guns look as if they've been in service since the Great War.'

'Yes. We're doing what we can. There's a new jeep coming out called a champ. It's a specially designed cross-country vehicle, can swim rivers too. They say it's a marvellous little job. A real champ. You'll be getting them soon.'

The general went on with his tour round the companies, looked in at the cookhouse, had a drink with the serjeants in their mess and ended at the officers' mess. Lunch went well and was enjoyable. Afterwards, outside the mess, we made a line for the general as he walked to his staff car. He turned to Colonel Dennis and, in everyone's hearing, said, 'I congratulate you, Colonel, on the fine battalion of which you have taken command. I've never had a battalion arrive in this division in a smarter condition than yours.'

That evening before dinner in the mess there was champagne in silver goblets. Val Portal came into the anteroom last.

'Unusually late at the adjutant's office tonight, aren't you Val?' I asked. 'Hasn't battalion headquarters let up a little after the triumph of the morning?'

Val called for a double whisky.

'What makes you think it was a triumph?'

'Well don't try and tell me it wasn't. Colonel Dennis must be delighted.'

'He's livid,' said Val.

'He's what?'

'He's furious.'

'Why? What on earth for?'

'It all went too well. Then the general congratulated him "on the fine battalion of which you have taken command" in front of all of us.'

'So what?'

'Look. If things hadn't gone so well the general would have taken Colonel Dennis to one side and said to him in private that he could see that the colonel had work to do to lick us into shape. And the colonel would then lick us into shape. At the next inspection the general would say, "Well done, Parker Brown, well done" and Colonel Dennis would get all the credit. As it went today the battalion gets the credit, as does the *last* commanding officer. Colonel Dennis can't claim the credit after only commanding for ten days. We started practising for this parade in England under Colonel Guy. Colonel Dennis is seething.'

'So?'

'So he's called a battalion exercise for Friday.'

'Friday? Friday? We haven't done any company exercises yet. Half the vehicles are in workshop. No one will know what to do. Isn't he going to have a dry run first?'

'No. The colonel says we have to learn to move fast in an armoured division and there's nothing like a live exercise to see how people perform.'

'It will be a disaster.'

'I'm late because I've been getting out the orders for the exercise.'

'Disaster.'

'What also niggled the colonel was the programme the band played while the general was inspecting the companies on parade. Horace Belcher, as band president, got one hell of a rocket. The band has been forbidden to play "Baby, It's cold outside", "Home cooking" and "On a slow boat to China" ever again.'

2

A disastrous exercise, in which our new colonel finds us wanting, ends in a Lucullan evening.

The exercise was a disaster. Some misread maps, vehicles broke down, and wireless sets refused to work. Few reached their objectives on time and several never reached them at all. Many failed to rendezvous with their ration trucks. In the afternoon it began to rain. The men became dispirited, the NCOs became irritated, and the officers exasperated. Those acting as umpires were the only ones to retain any good humour, delighting in pointing out errors. The rain became heavier. In mid-afternoon the exercise was called off and a dejected battalion returned to barracks in dribs and drabs. The last vehicle was pulled into barracks by the recovery vehicle after midnight.

Spiritless, the battalion mustered for first parade the following morning, Saturday. News came there was to be a meeting of officers at midday in the officers' mess. By five to twelve we had all assembled, rather subdued, in the anteroom. Promptly at noon Colonel Dennis entered the room. We all stood up.

'Please be seated, gentlemen,' he said. He was wearing breeches, boots and spurs. Everyone else was wearing battledress. In silence he surveyed the room with an air of confidence I had not seen in him before.

'Gentlemen, I do not wish to dwell on the sad performance of yesterday's exercise. I have already debriefed the company commanders who have their instructions what to do.' He looked round the room with a tight smile. 'I thought this morning would be a good opportunity to review some of the points I've noticed since I took over command and to give you some direction on where I want to go.

'You came here with a great record. That doesn't count for anything in this command. In an armoured division we have to be mobile, alert, and fast. Yesterday we were none of these things. I cannot overstress how, as a battalion, we have to change. Accurate map reading, first class vehicle maintenance, faultless wireless handling and procedure, and dash are the order of the day. Every officer must take this on board and ensure that his NCOs and men know this too.

'Next is the matter of what I like to term military efficiency. The battalion may provide a fine spectacle on the parade ground. I have yet to see that reflected in the day-to-day routine. Officers are leaving too much to the NCOs, delegating too much. Officers must direct change themselves. The relationship between officers and NCOs is too relaxed, leading to slackness. I've observed officers not being correctly saluted and not returning salutes correctly. I appreciate it is the custom for officers to wear berets and, in most respects, to dress as the men, and I accept that is the correct dress on exercises. In barracks I want officers to wear service dress hats so that you stand apart from the men. A distinction must be drawn. I also encourage regular officers, and any national service officers who are prepared to make the outlay, to wear service dress on Saturday mornings, as I do today, to help set a new example.

'The pace here is a fast one. You have been slow to adapt to it. As a battalion we must set priorities on what to do, and what not to do. This battalion, under my command, is going to excel on exercise, and excel in sport. I have decided on the sports we will pursue and win. I will be talking to each of you to tell you what I expect of you. Shooting, football, cross-country running, pentathlon and steeplechase will be the battalion's priorities in that order. These we shall win. All other sports will be secondary. Except polo. I expect the officers to mount two polo teams. We've some way to go to retrieve our pre-war reputation on the polo field but we shall.

'To sum up. This battalion has to learn to be mobile, alert, and fast to be at the forefront of the First Armoured Division. I require a high degree of military efficiency to achieve this.

'We also have to play our part socially. Three weeks today we shall hold our first cocktail party, followed by a day of polo. We shall invite the other units in the division, representatives from the town and university, and some local landowners. The Germans are our allies. I must stress this. Our allies. I expect every officer to carry out his social duties impeccably. That is all, gentlemen.'

He left the room immediately.

We broke into groups.

'Can you imagine Colonel Guy talking to us like that?'

'Or any other colonel?'

'He set up that exercise to humiliate us.'

'He certainly did that.'

'Did you notice his triumphant look?'

'Did I.'

'What about cricket?'

'Forget cricket.'

'Corporal Cheke.'

'Where's Corporal Cheke?'

'Here, Sir.'

'Gin and tonic.'

'Double gin and tonic.'

'No, bring a jug of martini.'

'Bring two jugs of martini.'

'Yes, martinis, martinis. And not too much martini.'

'Very good, gentlemen.'

We broke into smaller groups. I found myself next to Jasper. He turned to me and, in a low voice, said, 'I think Colonel Dennis was absolutely right. That's what I call leadership. He's asked me to exercise Red Ember next week. And he's given me permission to wear service dress with breeches whenever I want. My priorities, he told me, will be polo and steeplechasing.'

That evening in the anteroom Burgo said, 'Let's have one more sharpener before we go to the Lucullus.'

'While you're doing that I'll go and get my car round from the garage,' said Ben.

'I'll get mine round too,' said Harry.

Ben had a 1938 Talbot, green and black. It could do 50 to 60 miles an hour. Harry had a new Ford Consul which he'd bought tax free for export when he knew he was coming out to Germany. On the autobahn he could drive it along at seventy for miles.

'Captain Wildbore and Mr Fox are at the front door,' announced Corporal Cheke a few minutes later.

Burgo and Finbar joined Ben. Jasper and I joined Harry. Down the hill into the town we motored, through narrow streets and out into the town square where we parked in front of the *Rathaus*.

'Must try the *Ratskeller*, one day,' said Harry. 'They generally have good, plain German scoff and none the worse for that.'

'One day. Tonight I'm looking forward to a Lucullan feast,' said Jasper.

'Well you'll get one here,' said Harry as we walked down a side street and entered an unimposing door. A red carpeted and red walled corridor took us in to a plush hall off which several rooms led. At first sight I thought we had entered a fancy, rather grand brothel. But then I saw there were tables and chairs where the beds and chaises longues might have been. Herr Schwarz, the owner, greeted us in perfect English and led us through to a room at the back. We were clearly being placed discreetly out of the way.

The restaurant was fairly full. As I passed one of the rooms I had a shock, which I knew was going to happen sometime. I saw Horace Belcher, who commanded headquarter company. With him was Kitty, his wife. Kitty and I had grown up together and she was my oldest friend. She was a great beauty and great fun. When I had been aide-de-camp to Ivan Blessington, the governor

of Hong Kong, Kitty had come to stay with the Blessingtons as
Sonia Blessington, my cousin, was her godmother. Kitty and I
had fallen in love and, when I went to Korea, we had had an understanding that we would wait for each other. Then, suddenly,
she had married Horace Belcher, which had stunned me. I still
couldn't understand why. She had broken my heart.

Horace was a considerable horseman and rich. He could behave
outrageously and, prejudiced as I was, I was not the only one
to think him a fool. They were dining with the Trenches. Jack
Trench, whom Burgo had nicknamed Trench Foot, commanded
W company. He was a martinet and not a popular officer. He had
behaved badly in Korea and we were not friends. None of us really
knew his new wife Julia, who was much younger than Jack.

'While we interrogate the *Speisekarte* let's start with a bottle of
Sekt,' said Ben.

'What's the *Speisekarte*?'

'The menu.'

'What's *Sekt*?'

'Champagne,' replied Harry. 'We'd be better advised, Ben, to
start with a dry Rheingau. You need to be a little pissed or desperate to drink German champagne. Herr Ober, what about the
Johannisberger 49?'

'An excellent choice, Herr Fox.'

'Better make it two bottles, then,' said Ben.

The menus were handed round. They were naturally written
in German.

'What are *Schnecken*?'

'Snails.'

'I've never had snails.'

'Pure garlic.'

'What's *Schweineschnitzel Jägerart*?'

'Pork chop huntsman's style.'

'What would that be like?'

'Have it and see.'

'I'm going to have Tournedos Rossini.'

'So am I.'

'Me too.'

'Harry, ask them if they've got any caviar.'

'What about some foie gras?'

'You'll get foie gras with your Tournedos Rossini, you fool.'

It took some time to order. A third bottle of Johannisberger was called for. By the time the food came most of us had drunk half a bottle each. The food was delicious. We went on drinking Johannisberger until the meat came when we switched to burgundy, a Clos Vougeot 45.

'How come the Lucullus can provide a delicious burgundy and yet we can't buy any in the town?' asked Ben.

'The merchants in the town only really know about German wine,' Harry answered. 'Herr Schwartz was probably in France during the war and could have made good contacts with the vineyards in Burgundy. He probably imports it himself.'

'Why burgundy and so little Bordeaux?' asked Burgo.

'Look at the map. Burgundy is accessible to Germany. Bordeaux is a sea journey.'

We drank more Clos Vougeot.

'Pretty good restaurant this,' said Burgo.

'Not quite as good as the Savoy Grill,' said Ben.

'Nowhere's as good as the Savoy Grill,' drawled Jasper.

'I'm not so sure,' Harry answered. 'In its German way the food is every bit as good. It's the wine list that's different. The Savoy Grill can't match the German wines on the list here. And the Lucullus doesn't begin to compete on the French wines.'

'So we're destined to drink white wine here?' said Ben.

'When in Rome,' said Jasper.

'I've never understood why one should do what the locals do,' interrupted Burgo. 'We English have studiously avoided going native for centuries. We may have to drink Riesling and burgundy here at the Lucullus but let's get some decent claret in the mess.'

'Hear, hear.'

'There's a challenge for you, Miles.'

'Why, oh why do you all go on so about claret?' said Jasper.

'If you'd been locked away in Hong Kong and Korea for nearly four years you'd be banging on about more than claret,' said Burgo.

'Maybe it's time for coffee,' said Finbar.

Everyone looked a little flushed. We had drunk seven bottles. Jasper was slurring his words and was a little wild eyed. Harry was the least flushed. I'd noticed he had sipped while we had drunk.

'What about a postprandial?' said Burgo.

'They won't have any port worth drinking,' said Harry.

'I was thinking of liqueurs or cognac or a kirsch, which I rather fancy.'

The waiter put bottles on the table so that we could take our pick. We all had a liqueur.

I went to have a pee. On my return I purposely passed the room in which the Belchers and the Trenches were dining. I couldn't resist it. The Trenches were standing up as if ready to leave. Kitty was still sitting. Horace was leaning forward over the table, his head a few inches above the tablecloth and his right hand clutching a full glass.

'We'll take you both home, Kitty,' Jack Trench was saying, 'take you home now.'

'Horace won't move until he's finished the wine, there's half a bottle left.'

'Really, Kitty, he's a disgrace. We must go.'

'You know perfectly well what Horace is like. Dennis Parker Brown gave him a dressing down again this morning and he took it badly. It was inevitable he'd get drunk this evening. You shouldn't have come out with us if you weren't prepared to face the consequences.'

'I am facing up to the consequences. We're all going home together now.'

'Be practical, he won't move.' Horace's face dropped a little closer to the table.

'We're going then. Come on, Julia.'

'We can't leave them like this,' said Julia.

'Oh yes we can,' replied Jack, 'Horace's behaviour is outrageous. That's it.'

I let the Trenches walk out. Jack barely acknowledged me. I walked in.

'Oh, Miles, how lovely. The Trenches have been perfectly beastly. Julia is rather fun but Jack is a prig. Everyone knows how Horace drinks himself into a stupor. He'll be fine in the morning. Will you help and take us home?'

'Yes, Kitty, I'll take you both home. I've got to talk to you. How long will it take Horace to finish the wine and pass out?'

'Not long. So silly of the Trenches. But nice for me.' She gave me a shy but wonderful smile. At that moment Horace's head hit the table and his glass went for a Burton. He was drinking white wine so it didn't look too obvious by the time Kitty and I had done a little clearing up.

I returned to our table. The liqueur bottles were noticeably emptier.

'Harry,' I said, 'Horace Belcher is pissed out of his mind and the Trenches have buggered off. Come and help me get him into his car. I'll drive them home. Kitty can't manage on her own. I can see you might have problems with Jasper. No need to wait for me to come back.' Jasper looked none too well. He was rocking forwards and backwards over the table.

Harry and I carried Horace out of the restaurant. We held his arms tightly round our necks. He wasn't too heavy. We dumped him on to the back seat of his Bentley and he started snoring straight away.

'How are you going to get him out?' Harry asked.

'We won't. He'll sleep the night there,' said Kitty.

'Are you sure you wouldn't like me to come with you?'

'Don't worry,' I said, 'you look after Jasper.'

I got in the car behind the wheel, with Kitty beside me. We motored off in silence. After a bit Kitty said, 'How are you, Miles?'

'I'm fine,' I said.

There was another long silence.

'Do you hate me, Miles?'

'I just can't understand why you married Horace.'

'Couldn't you guess?'

'How could I guess? I was absolutely baffled. It didn't make any sense. And Horace, of all people.'

'Horace came to my rescue.'

'Why did you need rescuing? We agreed to wait for each other. I hadn't been in Korea three months before you got married.'

'I was going to have a baby.'

'A baby? What, Horace's baby?'

'Don't be silly.'

'Whose baby then?'

'Your baby, darling.'

'Mine? Mine? Oh, Kitty, why didn't you tell me?'

'How could I? You were in Korea. It was my fault. I didn't know what to do. I didn't want to lose it. I wanted to have your baby. I couldn't have an abortion. Anyhow, I didn't know how, in Hong Kong, living in Government House. I couldn't tell anyone. I couldn't tell Sonia. I thought the only thing to do was to get married. Horace courted me. I let him. I used him. It seemed the only answer at the time. I was desperate.'

'Do you love Horace?'

'Good heavens, no. I admired his horsemanship. I thought I could cure him of drinking. Now, the only thing we have in common is horses, and his drinking is worse than ever.'

'What happened to the baby?'

'I had a miscarriage in Singapore, where we went after we were married. I'm not sure whether Horace guessed the baby wasn't his. I was miserable and I went back to England. I rejoined Horace when he came to Germany. Can you guess why?'

'You married him. I suppose you wanted to be with him.'

'No, I wanted to be with you, to see you again.'

'How could you? You didn't even write to me about it. Sonia had to tell me you were marrying Horace.'

'I was at my wits' end. I didn't know how to tell you, and I didn't know what you really felt. I sensed I had made you agree that we would wait for each other. I wasn't sure of you, I wasn't sure you'd survive Korea. I know I behaved badly but I didn't see what else I could do.'

We had arrived at the Belchers' house. Horace was in a deep sleep, snoring on the back seat.

'What now?' I said.

'We'll leave Horace where he is. He'll wake up at dawn and come in. He'll be fine in the morning. Come into the house with me.'

I followed Kitty into the house and we went into a sitting room.

'Would you like a drink?' she said.

'Have you any brandy?'

'Horace has some Remy Martin in that cupboard. Why don't you pour some for yourself?'

'What about you?'

'I'm not going to drink any more.'

We sat down in two armchairs that faced each other across the fireplace. I sipped my brandy.

'Can you see the situation I was in?'

'Yes, but I wish you'd shared it with me.'

'What could you have done?'

'I'm not sure.'

We sat there in silence while I thought about what I could have done. Asked for compassionate leave, gone to Hong Kong and married Kitty? Would I have been able or allowed to do it?

'Why didn't you go back to England?' I said.

'What would I have done there'

'You could have had the baby and we could have married on my return.'

'I don't think my father would have understood, or your mother. And how did I know you would survive?'

More silence.

'What are you thinking of doing now?' I said.

'I made my bed and I've got to lie in it. But I love you, Miles. I always have.'

Sitting opposite me she looked incredibly beautiful and sad. I got up and took her in my arms.

'Oh my darling,' she said, 'I can't believe this is happening.'

3

Adam Hare joins us and we go on border patrol.

'Orders, Sir.'

Big Steel was standing in front of me in the machine gun platoon stores. He had walked smartly in and saluted with considerable flourish. Ah, I thought, the serjeants' mess has been given the message about saluting, too. The platoon was cleaning the machine guns, the parts of which lay in neat rows across the floor. I was sitting on the floor with Little Steel stripping a faulty machine gun lock to check what was wrong with it. One or two heads looked up. Big Steel read from a flimsy paper he had in his hand:

> 'One section Machine Gun Platoon to support 5 Platoon X Company on border patrol. Patrol to be under command Captain D. Lisle, Intelligence Officer. Lieutenant M. Player to report to Battalion Headquarters for orders at 1100 hours. Signed V. Portal, Captain and Adjutant.'

'It's ten hundred hours now, Sir.'

Handing the lock to Little Steel I stood up.

'When's the patrol?'

'Two days' time.'

'How long?'

'Two days.'

'Short notice isn't it?'

'Better ask battalion headquarters that, Sir.'

'They must have known before this.'

'Battalion headquarters moves in wondrous ways. X company serjeant major tells me he's known for over a week.'

'Why do you think they want a machine gun section?'

'Don't question your luck, Sir. It'll be good for the lads to get out of barracks and meet some nice country fräuleins and not the trash they've been poking in the town here.'

There were a few sniggers from the floor.

'Silence you nignogs on the floor there while I speak to your officer.'

Little Steel stood up. 'Why,' he said, 'don't you ask if the whole platoon can go.'

'Yes,' said Big Steel, 'we'll keep an eye on the stores while you're away.'

'Are all the carriers on the road? Isn't that chancing our luck? Remember the battalion exercise when two broke down?'

'Only temporarily, Sir. We mended them. We didn't have to get the recovery truck to tow us in,' said Little Steel.

'Worth trying, Sir,' said Big Steel.

'Let's see. I'll go and talk to Captain Lisle.'

The intelligence section worked in two rooms on the first floor of battalion headquarters. Dermot Lisle was sitting at a large table studying a map of the border. No one else was around.

'Hello, Miles. Thought you'd be dropping in. So you've heard about the border patrol?'

'Why such short notice and why the machine guns?'

'Colonel Dennis has had second thoughts. He wants to make a stronger impression and thinks a few carriers would add clout. He believes you're mechanically sound and your carriers won't break down like the mortars and the anti-tank guns did.'

'Little does he know. We had two breakdowns but we managed to repair them ourselves. Can I bring the whole platoon?'

'For what reason?'

'I'm going to disappoint half the platoon otherwise.'

'I can ask.'

Together we went down to the adjutant's office. The other interested parties were already there, including Jasper Knox who commanded 5 platoon and Jack Trench his company commander.

'Miles, why are you wearing a beret?' asked Val. 'You know the colonel's wishes.'

'You can't work on a carrier in a flat hat.'

'H'm. I trust that's not an emendation of the truth. I think you'd all better leave your hats in my office. We don't want to get off on the wrong foot.'

We filed into the colonel's office and sat down. Colonel Dennis nodded at each of us in turn with a genial grin.

'Before I ask Captain Lisle to give out his orders,' he said, 'I want to emphasise that, as this is the first border patrol the battalion has been ordered to carry out, we must make an impressive show not just for the Russians and East Germans across the border but for the West Germans in the villages and towns you patrol. On the final day the patrol will end up on the boundary between the British and American zones of occupation and will perform a liaison ceremony with the 101st Armored Cavalry Regiment of the US Army. That's why the machine guns in their carriers will be present as our armour. We must make an impression on the Yanks, too. The band and bugles will join that parade. They will be wearing number one dress and officers going as spectators should wear service dress. I must also emphasise that the West Germans are our allies and the men must be on their best behaviour. Now, Captain Lisle, continue.'

Dermot gave out his orders. There were a few questions. Then Dermot said, 'Colonel, you have emphasised the need to make an impression. I would like to propose both sections of the machine gun platoon take part, one to lead, and one to bring up the rear. They'll make us look a stronger fighting force.'

Colonel Dennis turned to the quartermaster. 'Have we fuel to do this?'

'Yes, Colonel.'

'Miles, are you prepared and are all your carriers on the road?'

'Yes, Colonel.'

'Val, any reason why they can't?'

'No, Colonel.'

'Then agreed, Dermot.'

He continued. 'I shall not be able to visit you or take part in your parade with the Americans. I have to attend a commanding officers' conference at BAOR Headquarters. Major Stanhope will represent me at the parade. That is all, gentlemen. Mr Player, would you stay a minute.'

What now, I thought. He looked at my none too clean denim overalls. I tried to hide my dirty hands.

'I'm pleased with the way you've involved yourself in leading your platoon. I can see you've been cleaning your carriers yourself. Good example.'

'I've just come from cleaning the machine guns, Colonel.'

'Even better. Now I'm talking to all officers about priorities. I want you to concentrate on shooting and be No 2 to Dermot Lisle.'

'I'm already officer in charge of hockey and was hoping to play cricket.'

'Hockey we will resume in the winter and I want you to continue to run it. Cricket is to be an occasional game. The BAOR training season doesn't allow time to build a first class cricket team and we have no grass playing fields here. We have to be practical. We have some excellent shots in the battalion, good enough to win the divisional rifle meeting. That's what I aim to do and that's what I want you to do.'

'Do you want me to play polo?'

'I've thought of that. Good of you to volunteer. But I want you to concentrate on shooting. You'll have to take it over when Dermot Lisle leaves us.'

That relieved me. I like shooting. After what Dermot had said I thought playing polo might bring me too close to the colonel. Someone had probably told him that I was only a moderate horseman.

'Very good, Colonel.'

'I knew you would see it that way.'

I got up to leave.

'One other thing. We've a new officer who's joined us today, Adam Hare. He's just come down from Oxford. He's a full lieutenant and replaces one of the casualties you had in Korea. As senior subaltern I expect you to be his mentor. He'll be in X company but I think it would be a good idea for him to go as a supernumerary on the border patrol. You can get to know him and start him on the right lines.'

Back in the adjutant's office I asked Val, 'Who's Adam Hare?'

'The colonel seems rather keen on him. Has he asked you to keep on eye on him?'

'He's ordered me to get him off on the right lines. Any regimental connections?'

'None. In fact no connections of any sort as far as I can see.'

Back in the machine gun platoon stores the four machine guns were standing on their tripods fully assembled. As I walked in I could smell how clean they were. The sweet scent of rifle oil hung lightly in the air. Private Crabbe, the storeman, was guarding them.

'They've all gone up to the carrier lines, Sir. As soon as they heard the whole platoon was for border patrol Serjeant Whettingsteel took them off. The guns are "All Sir Garnet" and the broken lock is mended. I was told to stay here until you returned.'

'How did Serjeant Whettingsteel know we are all to go?'

'Serjeant major told him. Said the orderly room had signalled him.'

'Lock the stores, Crabbe, and come up to the carrier lines with me.'

As Crabbe and I walked up to the carrier lines together I thought the colonel was going to have a struggle to stop the NCOs running the battalion. And I prayed he would fail.

Walking up the stairs in the mess before lunch I saw a strange officer standing at the top.

'I'm Adam Hare.'

He was tall, well built and florid. He had red hair and a physical presence in a slightly caddish way.

'How d'you do, I'm Miles Player.'

'Oh good, you're the senior lieutenant. The colonel said I could learn a lot from you. I'm glad to be here in Germany out of stingy, socialist England. Are you all having a lot of fun?'

'I wouldn't describe it exactly as that yet.'

'I'm sure it will be.'

I took off my beret and belt and went into the cloakroom next to the anteroom to hang them up and clean my filthy hands. He followed me. Hands washed, I went to the *pissoirs*. He stood at the one next to mine.

'I suppose,' he said looking at me sideways, 'you've got a coat of arms and a family house like all the others.'

What an odd thing to say, I thought, what a very odd thing to say. What a strange fellow to say that.

'Well, yes, I suppose so.'

'Well I haven't. I hope I'm going to fit in here.'

'I don't think anyone worries too much about that sort of thing any longer. The regiment is the family, the depot the family home.'

'I liked the depot. It had rather a good cellar.'

'Better than here.'

'We'll have to change that.'

By this time we were in the anteroom. I introduced him to Dermot Lisle.

'This is Adam Hare, just joined. He's to come on the border patrol.'

'So the colonel told me. Welcome Adam, it's good to have you with us. Do you shoot?'

'I was taken shooting at the depot and enjoyed it. Cricket's really my game.'

Val joined us.

'Dermot, we must organise a boar shoot when the season comes. Brigadier Popham said he'd help arrange it.'

'We must tackle him at the party.'

'He's given us a list of German landowners to ask as well as people from the town and university.' Then turning to Adam he said, 'You went to Oxford. Do you know anyone at the university here?'

'The university here has an excellent reputation for mathematics and the physical sciences. I'm a classicist. I don't speak German. I suppose I could converse in Latin.'

'*Arma virumque cano,*' said Colonel Dennis, who had just entered the room.

'*Troiae qui primus ab oris,*' replied Adam.

'Hare, it's very good to have another Oxford man in the mess, and a Latinist too.' Turning to Val he said, 'I want to bring up to date General Flaxman's monograph on the mess possessions now that we've assembled them all here. It was written in the thirties. Hare can assist, he's a scholar. It will familiarise him with our history and traditions. We can make a start, now that Ben has shown me the missing sporting rifles. Hare, come and talk to me about it.'

General Flaxman had commanded the battalion in India in the 1930s. In the Second World War he commanded large formations in North Africa and Italy. Now, as General Sir John Flaxman, he was colonel of the regiment. He had seen us off at Harwich on our departure for Germany and had promised to visit us. He was well liked by the regiment to which he was dedicated. Colonel Dennis, I thought, obviously wants to keep in with him.

'Hadn't we better tell Ben Wildbore as mess president?' said Val.

'Yes. Where is he?'

'He's already gone into lunch.'

'Let's join him then.'

We walked along the hall to the dining room.

'Wasn't that Virgil?' asked Dermot.

'Yes. The first line of the Aeneid.'

'Of arms and the man I sing... '

'That's it. Who first from the coasts of Troy...'

'Is he a bit of a creep?'

'The colonel likes him.'

'So what!'

'He seems to be the colonel's protégé.'

'Bugger that. It's us he's got to fit in with.'

'Yes, it's not the best of introductions.'

Two days later the patrol left barracks promptly at half past eight. Dermot Lisle led in his jeep. He wasn't taking chances with anyone else's map reading. Then followed, in order, No 1 machine gun section in its two carriers, the machine guns visible on their mountings; me in my jeep; Jasper, sitting in front of his 3 ton truck with 5 platoon; the two carriers of No 2 machine gun section; and finally Little Steel in his carrier. Adam Hare was sitting in the back of my jeep.

When we reached the bottom of the hill we turned left, skirted the town and drove north-east towards the border. We climbed slowly out of the valley into a lovely upland landscape that rolled ahead of us. We motored through several small villages, timbered and old, that nestled in the uplands untouched by war. Then, just before a village clearly larger than the others, we pulled up. Dermot got out of his jeep and greeted a man in a dark blue uniform standing with some Germans wearing blue green uniform.

'Who's that?' asked Adam.

'He's our guide. Mr Forrester from the British Frontier Inspection Service. The others are from the *Bundesgrenschutz*, the West German frontier police. They're here to see we don't make fools of ourselves and that we observe frontier etiquette. The last thing anyone wants is a frontier incident.'

'A frontier incident?'

'Shooting.'

'Haven't we got live ammunition?'

'Yes, but it's only to be used on the say-so of Mr Forrester, and the *Bundesgrenschutz* officer, and Dermot jointly, and they'll never give it.'

'The Russians shoot all the time, don't they?'

'Now and again, but we don't.'

We were moving again. Through the village we turned a corner and there before us lay the border. A ploughed strip, heavily fenced with barbed wire, cut a broad swathe through the fields and woods. The wire was bent on heavy timbers, 15 foot high. Every few hundred yards stood a 20-foot tower similar to the towers we had seen in newsreels of prisoner of war camps. The road now ran along the border, sometimes within a hundred yards, sometimes half a mile away. The patrol motored slowly along because the carriers could only do 15 to 20 miles an hour. We came to another village where Jasper disembarked his platoon, formed them up, and marched smartly through it at a fast pace. The carriers followed, the men looking straight ahead. The few Germans around ignored us. Across the border we were being observed through binoculars by two East German policemen. Jasper re-embarked his men and we motored on.

'Here we are on the edge of the world and it couldn't be more peaceful,' said Adam.

'What made you join the army, Adam? Looking for excitement?'

'Not necessarily. The army has a sense of order and routine which I admire. I like closed institutions. They may demand conformity in return for security and privilege but they protect one. I like that.'

'Don't you have any ambition?'

'Oh, yes, I'd like to be a general. Chief of the Imperial General Staff is probably beyond me but I wouldn't mind being Major General Sir Adam Hare.'

'I'd like that, too. My father was a general. But they say you're a scholar. Why didn't you try something in that line?'

'I have to admit I did. It was suggested that a fellowship might be possible depending on my thesis. Trouble was I had such a good time I somehow failed to write a word. In retrospect, rather a good decision. I think I'm going to enjoy the regiment far more than the senior common room.'

'And why the regiment? Do you have connections?'

'I thought it would be fun to be the Prince Regent's own.'

'That's an old joke. How did you manage to get in?'

'Before I went up to Oxford I'd done my national service with the gunners: not too much fun there, I can tell you. When I said to my tutor I was thinking of becoming a regular soldier he recommended me to Colonel Dennis who'd been at my college before the war.'

'You wouldn't have got in if we hadn't had losses in Korea.'

'Yes, I realise I'm lucky. I'm conscious of wearing dead men's boots.'

I started to think about those dead men but Korea seemed so far away.

'Has anyone told you about our day to day customs?'

'Not yet.'

'We try to observe pre-war manners. All officers are considered to be equal in the mess except the colonel to whom we show due deference so we address him as "Colonel". All other officers address each other by their surnames or christian names, but wait for someone senior to you to use your christian name before you use his.'

'That's not unlike Oxford.'

'Old fashioned it may be, but it works.'

'I feel at home already.'

'But on parade you address any officer senior to you as "Sir".'

'I understand that.'

'Now to saluting. Always salute the colonel when you see him. Field officers, that is majors, you salute first time you see them in the morning. Not after that. If in doubt it's best to salute the second in command whenever you see him but he doesn't expect it. You should remember to salute an officer senior to you if you enter his office though no one is too particular about that except our present adjutant.'

'That's clear enough.'

'The important thing about saluting is the way you return salutes from other ranks. The colonel is keen on that. Not stiffly like Marines or loosely like the Brigade of Guards but properly, with an open hand, out of respect to him saluting you.'

We were coming into another village.

'Anything else you think I should know?'

'Yes. Always, always remember the men come first. Field Marshal Slim said that, as a platoon commander, you have the opportunity to know your men better than their mothers do and to love them as much. We believe that, too.'

After following our routine in several villages we found an open space out of sight of the border where we laagered for lunch. We parked the carriers in a circle round the soft vehicles as if we were about to be attacked by a band of Apaches. Little Steel supervised digging a latrine. The platoon serjeant of 5 platoon handed out the haversack rations and the officers congregated round Dermot's jeep. Jasper's soldier servant produced a light picnic for us from the officers' mess: pieces of chicken, egg sandwiches and cherries. Glasses and a bottle of hock came out of a box, then a bottle of port.

Jasper opened a gold cigarette case and offered it to Adam.

'Egyptian or Virginian?'

Adam took an Egyptian. Jasper then offered the case to me. I took it and looked at the inscription on the inside of the lid.

To General Sir Jasper Knox GCB GCMG GCVO
from the Officers of the Prince Regent's Light Infantry
in grateful recognition of his great services as
Colonel of the Regiment.
18 June 1908

'My great grandpa, given him on his retirement as colonel of the regiment. I'm lucky to have it. My grandfather had it when he was killed at Ypres. My father had it when he was killed at Dunkirk. Somehow it was rescued. My mother gave it to me the day I was commissioned. I mean to have it when I'm a general or when I get killed. Now I must go and see how my men are getting on.'

The afternoon was a repeat performance of the morning. A little before five o'clock we arrived at the farm where we were to spend the night. We parked the vehicles in a laager in the farmyard, which was surrounded on four sides by large half-timbered barns with steep roofs. The X company colour serjeant had already arrived with the company stores truck. On it were hay boxes, large insulated containers, carrying a hot evening meal, as well as the day's mail, beer, and the heavy packs with personal gear and blankets. The vehicles were re-fuelled and weapons cleaned and inspected. 5 platoon had a foot inspection. Orders were given out, and repeated, including fire precautions and the disposal of cigarettes. A guard rota was agreed between the two platoons and the first sentries were posted. By the time all this was done it was seven o'clock. Then the men settled down to prepare their kit for the morning and relax.

Inspections and administration over, the officers moved to the farmhouse where Mr Forrester had made arrangements for us to have dinner: soup, ham and sauerkraut, strawberries and cream washed down with local Pils. It was a good farmhouse dinner, everyone agreed, and well worth the five Deutschmarks a head we had to pay for it.

'Rather tame today, wasn't it?' asked Adam.

'This border is one of the most peaceful places in the world,' replied Forrester.

'Never an incident?'

'Not since I've been here which is over two years now.'

'No wonder the colonel isn't visiting us,' said Jasper.

'There's another reason for that,' said Dermot. 'The frontier reminds him of prison camp.'

'Prison camp?'

'Didn't you know he was a prisoner for the last year and a half of the war? The barbed wire and the towers bring it all back to him. That's why he speaks such good German. But he's still sore about being captured at Anzio.'

'Were you there?'

'I was a platoon commander in North Africa. Then we landed in Sicily, then in Italy. Algy Stanhope was my company commander. He'd won his first DSO in North Africa. Colonel Dennis was a company commander too. Then we went into Anzio. The British and American armies hadn't been able to break through the German line in Italy, so the idea was to land behind them, cut them off and capture Rome. I was looking forward to that. The landing was easy, totally unopposed, hardly a German in sight. We marched inland and then we got orders to stop and dig in. We couldn't understand it. I still can't. The general got cold feet. Within 48 hours the Germans had amassed more troops than we'd landed. Only then were we ordered to break through. They were too strong for us and started to push us back into the sea. It was touch and go and Anzio became one of the most vicious battles of the war. We held our ground, but only just. The casualties were appalling. The colonel was killed, Dennis Parker Brown and two other officers were captured and Algy took over. That's when he won his second DSO and I became adjutant. Algy commanded the battalion for the rest of the war and won a third DSO. Colonel Dennis spent the rest of the war as a prisoner. He doesn't like wire or towers.'

'Does he like Algy?'

Dermot paused. He seemed to be wondering if he should go on.

'I don't really think so. They say they are great friends. But Colonel Dennis is ambitious and he can't really forgive Algy for stealing the limelight. As he's senior to Algy he would have got command in Italy and won a DSO, with any luck, if he hadn't been captured. As it is, Algy won three in addition to the MC he won at Dunkirk.'

By 8 o'clock the next day the patrol was lined up ready to move off. Adam Hare accompanied me as I inspected the machine gun platoon.

'Trouble with Cookson's carrier, Sir,' reported Little Steel. 'He's working on it now. If anyone will get it going he will. It's the fuel pump and it'll take him some time.'

'We don't want to leave him behind alone, Serjeant,' I said. 'You've a map haven't you, and you know the morning's programme? Good. You stay with Cookson. Follow on once the carrier is repaired. You'll catch us up before we get to the town. The parade is timed for 1100 hours. If you don't make that then rendezvous at the *Gasthaus* on the far side of the town where we're to meet up after the parade. If you don't make that rendezvous then we'll come back and rescue you.'

'Very good, Sir.'

I reported what I'd done to Dermot and the patrol moved off in the same order as the previous day and with Adam in the back of my jeep.

'Tell me about Dermot Lisle.' said Adam.

'What do you want to know?'

'How he won his DSO.'

'In Korea he played the pivotal part in an attack and then in defending a hill we had taken. Quite hairy.'

'What was Korea like?'

'The First World War.'

'In what way?'

'It became a static war while we were there. So it was trench warfare, heavy shelling, massive Chinese attacks, lots of patrolling, extreme weather, and too many casualties. And we felt a long way away, lost in a remote land, not totally clear why we were there or what we were fighting for.'

'How long were you there?'

'Seventeen months.'

'What was Hong Kong like?'

'Great fun.'

'I'd like to have been there, not Korea.'

'You'd have had no choice.'

'Where do you think we'll go after Germany?'

'We've only just arrived.'

'I think I'm going to enjoy Germany from what little I've seen. It seems far preferable to being in England.'

'I haven't lived in England since I was commissioned five years ago.'

'It's not much different: rationing, shortages, and the country seems to be broke.'

I turned to my driver who was a national serviceman.

'What do you think, Catchpole?'

'I'd rather be in England than here, Sir.'

'Why's that?'

'The army's not so bad and I get on with my mates. It's just not the same as being at home. I miss the girl friend and I want to get on with my trade.'

'That's understandable. Trouble is there's still a war even if it is a cold one. Look at us here patrolling the frontier. It's got to be done.'

We had arrived at the outskirts of a village. Jasper debussed his platoon, marched through the village and we followed. Then we all motored on.

'Tell me about the colonel and the other officers,' said Adam.

'*Pas devant les enfants,*' I replied.

'Quite so.'

We motored on in silence to another village, performed the same ceremony, and continued on. No one took any notice of us. As we neared the town at which we were to meet the Americans Dermot pulled off the road to the verge, stopped the column, got out of his jeep and walked down the line of vehicles.

'Miles,' he said when he came to us, 'we'll stop here for fifteen minutes to rest and brush up. We've a little time in hand and I thought this a pleasant spot.'

We were in the open, away from the woods but quite sheltered

in a dip and the border was out of sight. We got out and stretched
our legs. Most smoked.

'So, tell me about the colonel,' said Adam.

'I've only known him for days.'

'You must know something about him.'

'You seem to have hit it off with him.'

'Hasn't everyone? He seems genial enough.'

'He doesn't seem to have much time for those of us who were
in Korea.'

'What about Major Trench?'

'Yes, he appears to have taken to Trench Foot, probably because Colonel Guy is said to have given him an adverse report
and recommended his return to the paras.'

'What's Trench like?'

'He's over ambitious and a creep. I'd watch him carefully if I
were you.'

At that moment two carriers hove into view. Little Steel and
Cookson rejoined us.

'Adam,' I said, 'when we get to the town I propose you join the
spectators. Find Algy Stanhope and stay with him.'

Crowds greeted us as we drove into the border town. The local
police guided us in. When we got to the town square the crowd
was six deep and people were leaning out of every window that
commanded a view. The band and bugles were already there playing 'Lili Marlene' as we drove in. No wonder there were crowds.
Standing beside the band was Algy Stanhope, deep in conversation
with an American colonel. Jack Trench was with them. Algy and
Trench were wearing service dress.

I led the carriers in and drew up on one side of the square. On
my command the platoon dismounted smartly and stood in front
of the carriers. Then 5 platoon, led by Dermot and Jasper, marched
in and took up a position in front of us facing into the square. A
minute later the American patrol drove slowly into the square in
their jeeps and dismounted opposite 5 platoon. They were wearing

yellow scarves and white belts. They presented arms. Five platoon presented arms and Dermot, Jasper and I saluted. The band played the Star-Spangled Banner followed by the national anthem. The crowd cheered and clapped. The Americans remounted their jeeps and drove out of the square. We followed.

There must have been over a hundred all told at the *Gasthaus*.

'You in Korea?' said the American lieutenant looking at our medal ribbons.

'Yes, were you?'

'Too darned right, I was. Where were you?'

'On the Han River to begin, then on the Imjin. And you?'

'We went all the way to the Yalu on the Chinese border and back. I was one of the lucky ones not to get caught.'

I left Dermot talking to him as I'd spotted Adam with Trench Foot across the room and Trench looked as though he was working himself up into a bait. As I approached I heard Trench raise his voice.

'Lieutenant Hare, I say again you are incorrectly dressed. The commanding officer said specifically that spectators were to wear service dress and here you are in battledress and a beret.'

'I'm not here as a spectator,' said Adam, 'I'm a supernumerary.'

'Don't split hairs and argue with me.'

'I'm not arguing, I'm merely stating a fact.'

'You're a disgrace and I'll report you to the adjutant.'

'What's the problem, Jack?' I said as I came up to them.

'It's got nothing to do with you.'

'The colonel asked me to look after Adam Hare so it must have something to do with me.'

'Hare is in my company and is my responsibility. Go away.'

'That may be, but today he is attached to me and I'd like to know what he's done because it may be my responsibility too'

'You impertinent little puppy. How dare you speak to me like that.'

'Abuse me if you wish but what is it that Adam has done?'

'You know perfectly well that spectators were ordered to wear service dress.'

'Adam is *not* a spectator. He has been on border patrol for two days with me and is correctly dressed for that. Or would you like the second in command to decide?'

'Damn you, Player,' said Trench and strode off.

'Well, well,' said Adam, 'what a display of military hysteria. Are all the company commanders like that?'

'Only Trench. I can never understand how he got into the regiment.'

'Quite a brute.'

'You see what I mean. I'll have drawn his sting, not you. He'll hate me even more now but do be careful yourself.'

4

We entertain but the colonel disapproves of the stakes.

The day for the party arrived. Returning to the mess late in the morning I found Olivia Stanhope, Kitty Belcher, and Julia Trench arranging flowers. There were to be flowers at the entrance to the mess, in the hall, the anteroom, the dining room, and the ladies' room. The last was a separate set of rooms on the first floor of the mess, recently converted so that ladies could be entertained there. For the party the reception rooms would be open to everyone. Normally ladies got no further into the mess than the ladies' room.

'How beautiful you're making it look,' I said.

Olivia looked up and smiled. 'Oh, Miles, you've arrived just in time. Could you ask Colour Serjeant Body for some help in moving these vases?'

'I'll do it. I've finished for the morning.'

We went into the anteroom and I moved the vases under Olivia's instructions.

'How are you settling down, Olivia?'

'I was doing fine until Dennis Parker Brown told me, as senior wife, it was my responsibility to organise the wives. It's the last thing they want. "What sort of organising?" I asked. "Don't ask me," he replied, "it's your duty to see they have things to keep them occupied. Otherwise there'll be trouble." What do you think, Miles?'

'Why don't you ask them?'

'Exactly. I've arranged for them all to have a coffee morning next Wednesday. I expect they'll either be too polite to say anything and say nothing at all; or they'll be so polite they'll ask for a long list of things to do, which I'll organise and then no one will come. Dennis keeps on harping back to the thirties and what we did before the war. "Proper peacetime soldiering," he says. Women nowadays are much more independent and self-sufficient. The war saw to that. Will you come and hold my hand on Wednesday morning? Algy says he'll have nothing to do with it.'

'I can't. Wouldn't it be best to have only women there?'

'I just thought having a younger officer there might contain their wilder thoughts. Suppose they want to learn to shoot. How do I handle that?'

'You tell me and I'll organise it. And if I'm not there they won't be prompted to ask.'

'Perhaps I could ask Harry Fox. He's such a nice young man and I understand he speaks German.'

'They'll all fall for him. Beware.'

'Yes, I suppose you're right. I'll have to do it myself.'

Kitty came in.

'Olivia, how lovely you've made the room. Hello, Miles darling. I see you've chosen to help Olivia and not me.'

'Olivia asked me.'

'Have you finished with Miles, Olivia? I need help in the dining room.'

'Of course, Kitty.'

I followed Kitty to the dining room.

'I hope I'll see you tonight, darling,' she said.

'Oh Kitty!'

'It worked the other night.'

'Kitty, it was wonderful. But we must be sensible. And aren't you putting up some of the guests?'

'Not now. Dennis Parker Brown has decided to put them up instead. That rat Jack Trench has probably told him Horace can't be trusted not to get terribly drunk. So you'll be able to take me home.'

'People will start to talk.'

'I couldn't give a damn what anyone thinks.'

'I don't think Colonel Dennis would turn a blind eye if he knew.'

'It's no business of his.'

'You may not be, but Horace is, and so am I. He'd have me transferred to the First Battalion or the Aden Protectorate Levies if he knew.'

'You don't love me.'

'I adore you. You know I do. But we're in a hopeless position.'

'You two finished?' Olivia was standing in the doorway. 'Colour Serjeant Body is asking if we've finished. He wants to have the table laid. Come and have a look at what Julia and Ben Wildbore have done in the ladies' room.'

Ben Wildbore was the president of the mess committee partly because it was his turn and partly because he loved to do it, especially arranging parties. The ladies' room was more than just one room. There was a hall, a sitting room, a cloakroom, and a dining room with its own pantry. Julia and Ben had turned the dining room into a nightclub. The windows had been blacked out, the lighting dimmed, and a small dance floor of polished wood laid down.

'After the party,' said Ben, 'I thought we might have a little fun. Some of the guests are staying the night so we will have to go on entertaining them. Supper won't be enough. A little soft shoe shuffling will be good for all of us. We haven't had a proper party with the wives since we left Hong Kong two years ago. And Julia's got some snazzy records.'

'Oh, what fun!' said Kitty.

'What will Colonel Dennis say?' I asked.

'It's up to us to decide on the entertainment in the mess. Anyhow, he said to make it into a special evening. Show them how we can entertain.'

'He'll approve. As long as it's good clean fun,' said Olivia.
In the dark, Kitty looked at me and rolled her eyes.

During the afternoon the guests who were staying the night began
to arrive. Some of the regiments we had invited were stationed miles
away. It was the custom in BAOR to put up guests after a party.
Colonel Dennis had known this, of course. We had asked officers
from all the regiments and corps in the division. The first to arrive
were from the divisional armoured car regiment of the Household
Cavalry. Then came officers, some bringing their wives, from a
sister Light Infantry regiment, from our nearest neighbours The
Borderers, from a Rifle Regiment, and from the 5th Hussars and
the 19th Lancers. The last two had brought their polo ponies for
the next day's game. We had been especially careful to ask the
Divisional Engineer Regiment and our Royal Artillery battery, as
well as the Service and Ordnance Corps and the Electrical and
Mechanical Engineers who supported us; we would be working
closely with them all and it was essential to make friends with them.
Colonel Dennis knew whom to ask. He was good at that. About
a dozen single officers would be staying in the mess. Some of us
had agreed to lend our rooms and double up for the night. The
married officers would be putting up those guests who brought
wives. It promised to be a long and enjoyable evening.

The party started at 6 p.m. with the band and bugles sounding
retreat. This took place on the lower parade ground in front of
the officers' mess, where chairs had been placed for our guests.
The serjeants' mess too were having a party. Most of the battalion
turned out to watch. By the time the band and bugles marched on
to the square the four sides were crowded with spectators. The
ceremony was good theatre and moving. To end, twenty buglers
sounded the last post. The sound must have been heard in the
town. As the band and bugles marched off, a great cheer rose from
the crowd. The party had started well.

Our guests then moved into the mess and up into the anteroom
to be greeted by trays of cocktails: white ladies, manhattans, dry

martinis and sherry. Colonel Dennis fell deep into conversation with the *Burgermeister*, while Olivia, who also spoke German, was engaging the *Frau Burgermeister*. Brigadier Popham beckoned and introduced me to the von Sengers. Andreas von Senger spoke perfect English; to all intents he appeared to be English.

'Do you live nearby?' I asked.

'In the forest to the east. The border cuts across our land, so we've lost half of it. We still have good shooting. Will you come and shoot boar with us and bring some of your friends? We have a good stock of deer too.'

'I'd very much like to do that.'

'Now what have you seen since you arrived?' asked Elizabeth von Senger. 'Have you discovered the Harz Mountains yet?'

I was conscious of Kitty and Harry talking behind me. Their voices intermingled with ours.

'…that was kind of you to help look after Horace at the Lucullus the other night…'

'It's wonderful there at all times of year.'

'…I was only too happy to help…'

'Of course our town is too small to have an opera house.'

'…You must come and have a meal with us one evening…'

'Hanover has a good opera house and isn't too far.'

'…I'd love to do that…'

'Have you found the Lucullus Restaurant yet?'

'…How old are you…'

'Yes we think it's rather good.'

'…I'm nineteen…'

'Not as good as your Savoy Grill.'

'…You look much older…'

'You know England well?'

'…I'd like to go on talking to you, Kitty, but I'm under orders to look after our guests and I'm worried about those three standing alone in the corner…'

'In my three years at Cambridge I was able to get round a bit.'

'…What a good host you are…'

'Of course London in the thirties was the most enjoyable city in Europe.'

'…Would you dance with me later…'

'What about Paris and Budapest?'

'…Of course…'

'They were fun, too. Our German cities, especially Berlin, were dismal.'

Dermot joined us and engaged the von Sengers' attention. I was able to turn round. Harry was now in the corner talking to a German couple and a very plain young woman. They, I thought, must be the Hoffnungs. I was still looking for Kitty when Brigadier Popham brought up an exotic girl, dark and tall. 'Rana,' he said, 'I want you to meet Lieutenant Player. He's the senior subaltern here and fought alongside the Turkish Brigade in Korea. I'm sure he'll have some stories to tell you about your brave countrymen.'

'I'm so glad to meet you, Lieutenant Player. You're giving a wonderful party.'

'It's lovely to meet you. But please call me Miles.'

'Miles? Latin for a soldier? How apt. Do you enjoy being a soldier?'

'Very much, and a regiment is like a family. It's a world of its own.'

'I'm not sure I can understand that. My father is a general. I don't think the regimental system in our army can be quite like yours. I hope you will tell me more about it.'

'Does your name have a meaning?'

'In Turkish it's taken for granted as it's a name. It's rather embarrassing in English. Don't laugh. It means beautiful.'

She gave me a beautiful smile.

'What foresight your parents had. And your English is beautiful too.'

'I had an English nanny. I am here at the university to perfect my German, which is more useful than English in Turkey. But I like to speak English and I hope I will see more of you.'

She gave me another beautiful smile.

'Will you introduce us?' said Kitty.

They looked each other up and down and seemed to take an instant dislike to each other. Kitty was looking exquisite in an elegant dress which accentuated her wonderful figure. Brigadier Popham appeared at my elbow and whisked Rana away.

'So you've started on Harry already.'

'O good, I've made you jealous. I'm not going to give up on you, Miles.'

'You know it's impossible.'

'I suppose you fancy that Turkish houri.'

'She's not married.'

'You won't get far with her.'

'Kitty, we're playing with fire.'

'I'm a soldier's daughter. I'm not afraid of fire.'

'Kitty, you're married to Horace.'

At that moment there was a shout of laughter from the far corner of the room.

'Just look at Horace now,' said Kitty, 'getting pissed already. He's found some Germans who are keen to play polo. He'll be dead drunk by midnight.'

'I love you Kitty. I always have. But what can we do?'

'We can start again.'

'We've already discussed that. It's impossible. What about Horace? What about the army?'

'Bugger Horace. Bugger the army.'

'You're being impractical.'

'I love you, Miles darling, and I think you're being damned selfish.'

'What's Miles being selfish about?' asked Olivia who joined us.

'He's all eyes for that Turkish houri and doesn't want to talk to us any more.'

'She *is* very beautiful. Miles, Algy wants you to meet the people he's talking to. Come on, Kitty, let's go and flirt with the Household Cavalry. I see an old flame.'

The party was going exceedingly well. Even Colonel Dennis seemed relaxed and pleased. Perhaps we'd have to admit he did know a thing or two about BAOR. And perhaps he'd give us the credit for organising a good party. But I couldn't enjoy it.

The von Sengers came up to me. 'We have to go. A most excellent party. We've been talking to Captain Lisle. He's going to bring you to our next shooting party.' Later Rana came past me on her way out. 'It was wonderful to meet you,' she said. 'Brigadier Popham has promised to arrange for us to meet again. Thank you for a delightful party.'

Only the military guests who were staying the night were left. We all went into the dining room where a splendid buffet supper was on the table. Groups began to form. Burgo, Finbar, Jasper, and Adam had collected some young officers from the other regiments at one end of the room. At the other, Algy had collected the more senior married officers with their wives. In between there were small, animated groups. Colonel Dennis was sitting with Brigadier Popham and the colonel from the 19th Lancers. Everyone had found a niche.

Supper finished, Burgo's group went off to the card room where he had arranged a game of roulette. Others went to play billiards. A few sat in the anteroom, smoking and talking. Most went down to the ladies' room where Ben Wildbore had opened his nightclub.

I joined the group playing roulette. After half an hour I had lost a pound and decided to leave. I didn't feel lucky and I always think if you don't win quickly at roulette you're unlikely to win at all. Besides I was in a miserable mood and wanted to see what was going on in Ben's nightclub.

Quite a throng had gathered in the sitting room, chattering away. The lights were dimmed and about half a dozen couples were dancing. The gramophone was playing a record of Fred Astaire singing 'Cheek to Cheek' and some of the couples were dancing cheek to cheek. Julia and Jack Trench were dancing very close. Olivia was dancing with Brigadier Popham but not close. Kitty was holding Harry close but not too close. Then, in the far corner, I could just discern Horace dancing. At first I thought he was dancing alone. As my eyes got used to the dark I could see that he was dancing with an upturned broom, his cheek crushed against the brush. His eyes were closed, his feet were shuffling slowly and he was crooning the words of the song. Every now and again he kissed the brush.

'Don't you think it time Kitty took Horace home?' said Ben Wildbore.

'Kitty couldn't get him into the Bentley.'

'Colonel Dennis will explode if he sees Horace dancing with a broomstick.'

'Horace is just being Horace.'

'That may be but he's in enough trouble as it is. The colonel only puts up with him because he's the best polo player we've got.'

'Let him be.'

'Can't risk it. You'd better drive them home.'

'I drove them home the other night.'

'Then you can do it again.'

'Oh Ben, can't you get someone else to do it?'

'Well, I'll ask Harry to.'

'All right then, I'll do it.' The music stopped and no one left the floor. The next record dropped on to the turntable, Fred Astaire singing 'A Fine Romance'.

'Kitty,' I said, 'will you dance with me?'

'Friendly, darling?'

'Yes, friendly.'

'I'm dancing with Harry.'

'My turn, Harry,' I said.

We started dancing.

'Where's your Turkish houri? Have you deserted her already like you've deserted me?'

'She went home hours ago. And now I'm going to take you and Horace home.'

'What's Horace up to?'

'He's dancing with a broom.'

She giggled.

'Where? I must see.'

'In the corner.'

'He's rather good at it, isn't he? Bloody fool.'

'Yes, but now it's time to go home.'

'Oh, lucky me.'

So I drove them home in their Bentley. Horace was very drunk but not yet insensible. With my help he stumbled on to the sofa in the sitting room and passed out. I went upstairs with Kitty and stayed half the night.

When, before breakfast on Sunday, I returned Horace's Bentley he was up, pink faced, and dressed for polo with not a sign of a hangover. He had remarkable powers of recovery.

'Kitty's still asleep. I've left her a note saying you will collect her for lunch. I hope you will be so kind. I'll come and breakfast in the mess with you.' So we drove back to the barracks talking about the day.

We were to field two teams against the two cavalry regiments that had come with their ponies. The matches were to be friendly but organised as a mini knock out tournament. It would be the first time our teams had played against another regiment.

Breakfast was muted. Burgo, to play in our second team, was trying to liven it up by interesting the others in a bet.

'You don't have much faith in yourselves.'

'A fiver we'll win,' said a 5th Hussar.

'Done,' said Burgo.

'I'll take that too,' said a 19th Lancer.

'Excellent,' said Burgo. Turning to me he said in a low voice, 'I'm trying to recover my confiscated winnings from last night. I'll explain later.'

There were two matches in the morning. The first was between our second team and the 5th Hussars. We lost. They were clearly superior and Colonel Dennis, who had captained our second team, rode off looking black. But he'd been looking black all morning. As the second game was about to start Horace, who was playing in it, reminded me to go and collect Kitty.

'How lovely of you to come and fetch me, darling,' she said as she gave me her cheek to kiss. She was in her dressing gown. 'I've just made some coffee. I expect you need some. That was rather too exciting a night. I'm really hooked on you. How much time have we got before we have to go?'

'Kitty, to do what we did once is forgivable. To do it twice is careless. For us to go on would be madness.'

'You're not going to give me that drivel?'

'It's not drivel, it's practical good sense. We're both playing with fire.'

'You said you adored me.'

'I do.'

'Take me up to my bedroom now and show me.'

'No.'

'Yes, darling, now.'

'Can't you see how dangerous this is for us all?'

'All I can see is you and I'm in love with you.' She let her dressing gown fall open.

'Please, Kitty, please go upstairs and get dressed. It's broad daylight. Everyone's waiting for us. They'll be sitting down to lunch in half an hour. Please.'

Kitty looked at me. Her smile faded.

'You bastard, you don't love me at all. You never did.'

She slapped my face and ran up the stairs.

Ten minutes later she came down. She had been crying.

'I don't know what got into me. Very silly. I'm sorry, darling. Oh, what a mess I've got us into. Let's go.'

We drove to the polo ground in silence. Kitty worked on her face.

Burgo met us. 'Horace beat the 19th Lancers and I've won a fiver.'

Kitty went off to find Horace. Burgo and I went to the drinks tent.

'What happened to you last night?' Burgo asked me.

'After I'd lost a quid to your bank at roulette I felt my luck was out so I went down to Ben Wildbore's nightclub. Horace was dancing with a broom. Ben thought Colonel Dennis would have a fit if he saw Horace so drunk. Kitty was getting pissed too. Ben asked me to take them home. Horace passed out when we got there.'

'And Kitty?'

'Oh Burgo, don't ask. It's impossible. You know how I loved Kitty. She still loves me. What can I do?'

'Do you still love her?'

'Yes.'

'Then go for it.'

'It would be a disaster for all three of us.'

'I've never fallen in love. When I do I'll let love take its course, whatever the consequences.'

'You've got money, Burgo. You can do what you want.'

'I'd have more money if last night hadn't been such a farce.'

'You hinted at something at breakfast.'

Adam joined us.

'Adam, tell Miles about the farce last night.'

'Burgo and I were doing quite well with the bank. Some of our guests were down, nothing too much. Dermot and Val were down too. Finbar was up, of course. Also the engineer major, which was good. We wanted him to win. Then Colonel Dennis, who'd been playing billiards, looked in all bonhomie. "Five shillings worth of chips, Adam," he said. "That all, colonel?" I asked. "Isn't that enough to play?" "Oh yes, of course." He lost them pretty quickly by plastering the table. When he'd lost them all he watched for a bit and began to realise there was some fairly sophisticated betting. Finbar was winning consistently on *noir* and *impair* and had a huge pile of chips. Then Jasper won a *carré* and *tranversale* and I had to push across a big pile of chips. Colonel Dennis twigged the play was quite high. He beckoned to Val to follow him out of the room. After a bit Val returned looking crestfallen. He announced that the colonel felt, in view of the polo today, that it was time to close the game. Worse to come. As some of the guests, he said, had had the misfortune to lose sizeable sums, all the winnings and losses would be scaled down so that no one would win or lose more than a pound. The colonel couldn't allow our guests to depart with empty pockets.'

'I can understand Colonel Dennis's point of view,' I said. 'I've seen the stakes scaled down before so that no one gets hurt. But not quite like that.'

'It was a farce,' said Burgo. 'Mind you, some of our guests looked gratified. Not the engineer major. He'd made a tenner and it was cut down to a quid. Not a happy bunny. The colonel will rue that. Bloody farce. All Adam and I were allowed to win was a quid each. Should have been fifty lovely oncers. The man's an interfering lunatic. Colonel Guy never interfered like that.'

The final between Horace's team and the 5th Hussars started immediately after lunch as the visiting teams had a long way to get home. From the start it was clear that the teams were evenly matched except for one player who was everywhere and dominated the game. Chukka after chukka he came on with fresh ponies and never faltered. His determination and skill were unequalled. He was as hard on himself as he was on his ponies. His team worked well with him but it was Horace who won the game.

After they'd dismounted we crowded round to congratulate them.

Kitty went up to Horace. 'Not now,' he said as he brushed her aside and walked on to be congratulated by the colonel. Olivia put her arm round Kitty. I turned away and found myself with Burgo and Adam, who said, 'Let's go and have a drink.'

We sat outside the tent drinking Pimms.

'I've won ten pounds today,' said Burgo, 'on two unscientific bets that I knew I'd lose and only took to save our faces. It makes up a little bit for last night. Little does the colonel know. If he did he'd probably make me give the lolly back.'

'The more I know the man the less I know him.' I said.

'For all his forced good humour,' said Adam, 'the poor man's an introvert. He's complex and rather interesting. You should have a more open mind, Burgo, and try to see the world from his point of view.'

'What, pray, is his point of view?'

'Consider his position. A lonely man, divorced, wife has the children, forced to live as a bachelor, scourged by being captured in the war, doing his best in his own terms to lead a largely hostile tribe. He must know he's not much liked. But he has a set of standards that he believes to be right and to which he believes we should adhere. I'm not saying for one moment that I accept them. Far from it. But if we're going to have a good time here we need to be seen to pay him lip service. After all, he is our anointed leader. What he really needs is love. We all need love, he more than anyone. And he doesn't get any. I'm going to give him love.'

5

The Colonel claims everything goes to plan.

'The north German plain is intersected by several rivers, and these rivers are the keys to attack and defence. An attacking army must force these river lines and a defending army must hold them. We do not want to develop a defensive mentality. Attack is the best form of defence, so our next exercise will be attacking across a river.'

Colonel Dennis gave out his orders meticulously and precisely. No one could be in any doubt about what he had to do. There was little room for individual initiative. Colonel Dennis even had a reserve hot cocoa ration that was to be distributed on his command only. In his orders he placed the machine gun sections and the mortar sections under command of X and Y companies. He instructed Burgo Howard – who commanded the mortars – and me to attach ourselves to battalion headquarters as his personal liaison officers. As we broke up Dermot Lisle beckoned to Burgo and me to follow him. We joined him in his office.

'The colonel's intention is that you should work alongside me. I'm not entirely sure why. He probably anticipates problems with the rifle companies making a balls-up and the company commanders not telling him what they're up to, so he wants you to keep him informed of what's happening by sending you out as his eyes.'

'You mean like Monty's liaison officers?' I asked.

'That sort of thing. It seems quite unnecessary to me, really overdoing it. But that's what's in his mind, I think.'

'Why us?' asked Burgo.

'He knows your NCOs are competent and can get by without you. Apart from the river crossing it's quite a simple exercise.'

'That's just what he said he didn't want us to do. Delegate.'

'There may be other reasons. Maybe he wants to get to know you better. You two are senior lieutenants. You, Miles, are the next in line for promotion. Val can't go on as adjutant forever. I go to Staff College in the autumn.'

'Is that fixed?'

'Not finally. Any day now.'

'Doesn't he know I was intelligence officer in Korea?' I asked.

'Yes, and that's probably why he wants you to be a liaison officer today. You know how the battalion works. Remember, he's always got more than one reason for everything he does.'

'Thanks for telling us,' said Burgo.

Since the first battalion exercise we had made great improvements in map reading and wireless procedure. Most of the vehicles were running reliably. We were settling down to our role. There was even a little of the old elan back.

The battalion motored out to the assembly area in the training grounds 45 miles away. Because of the imagined air threat – we couldn't count on air superiority against the Russians as we had against the Luftwaffe – we had to move well dispersed. This meant we moved in packets of about five vehicles, each a hundred yards apart, with each packet well apart from that preceding and following it. Once out of the barracks the battalion vehicles were stretched out over five to ten miles, the last vehicle of all being 20 to 30 minutes behind the first. To ensure that we kept to the route the regimental police had marked it with small traffic signs and, as we progressed, they dashed up and down it on their motorcycles, setting out the signs, and then recovering them to set them out again further up the route. The men sitting in the back of the trucks used to watch out for each policeman to pass and then made bets on when he'd pass again.

We arrived in the assembly area, a large wood about two miles from the river we were to cross, where we were to await further orders to move up to the river on foot. Here, too, we were to meet the engineer squadron, which would bring the assault craft and bridging equipment we needed to get across the river. The far river bank was defended by a battalion of the Borderers, another infantry battalion in the division, acting as the enemy.

I motored up to the area of the wood allocated to battalion headquarters to find Burgo Howard already there. He and his driver were camouflaging their jeep by spreading a huge net over it. Catchpole, my driver, drove our jeep under a tree and then we camouflaged the jeep in the same way. Burgo and I walked across to a large truck that served as battalion headquarters in the field, also heavily camouflaged. The inside was fitted out as an office with maps on the walls and a lot of signal equipment. Val Portal and Dermot Lisle were inside it trying to look busy.

'Good, you've arrived. Everything's "All Sir Garnet",' said Val. 'The colonel's going to recce the river. He wants you, Burgo, to accompany him and Dermot. You, Miles, are to liaise with the engineer squadron, commanded by Major Skidmore. You remember him, he came to our party. They're due in their assembly area any time now. Remember we've got wireless silence until the assault across the river starts. We don't want the enemy to pick up our signals and know we're here. You're to go and check Major Skidmore has arrived and knows his orders, and then report to the colonel who's setting up his tactical headquarters here.' He pointed to a spot on the map in front of him. 'You'd better take a despatch rider with you in case of problems. There shouldn't be any but you never know. Talk to Serjeant Feard. He's out there somewhere.'

Serjeant Feard, the provost serjeant known to all as Geordie Feard, was with his jeep, also camouflaged, checking the signs in his trailer.

'Could you let me have a despatch rider, Serjeant Feard,' I asked, 'I need him for an hour or two.'

'Can't do that, Sir. Haven't got one to spare.'

'Adjutant's orders, Serjeant. I have to go and liaise with the engineer squadron.'

'That's another matter, Sir. Why didn't you tell me that in the first place? You've no idea how many officers try and wheedle a despatch driver out of me. Now let's see. You'd better take Croucher, he's free at the moment.'

I returned to my jeep on the back of Croucher's motorbike. Catchpole my driver, who looked after me, was already removing the camouflage net.

'Mr Howard said we were moving out, so I thought I'd get the bleeder off. Not so easy single handed.'

We stowed it tightly on the canopy of the jeep.

The engineer squadron was to assemble in another wood about a mile away. I found the entrance already marked with an engineer squadron sign. We pulled in, re-camouflaged the jeep and waited. Half an hour went by, then an hour. No engineers came. I sent Croucher back to battalion headquarters to report. He returned with a message to ask if I was sure I was in the right place. I checked the map again, checked the sign and sent Croucher back to say I was. The sun was going down the sky and Catchpole decided it was time to brew up a pot of tea. One of the advantages of having vehicles, as we had in the machine gun platoon, was we could carry equipment we could not possibly carry on foot. Catchpole and I had made ourselves comfortable for such an exercise as this. We had a small stove, reserve rations, sleeping gear, a tent, and our personal packs all stored carefully in the jeep with a few special goodies. By the time Croucher got back Catchpole had tea and biscuits ready and was question-ing whether it wasn't time to make a proper meal. Croucher delivered the same message: were we really in the right place? I was now getting a little worried whether we were or not. The engineer sign was still there and they must have put it there. As I was deliberating what to reply a despatch driver drove up and inspected the sign. I beckoned him across.

'What's your unit?'

'125 Bridging Squadron Royal Engineers.'

'What are you doing?'

'I'm checking the route for the squadron.'

'Where is the squadron? We've been expecting you for nearly two hours.'

'Squadron won't be here till after dark, Sir. Major Skidmore never moves the squadron by day, always by night. Standing orders. Too many enemy aircraft about to risk it.' He half looked up at the sky and then roared off back down the road as if pursued by a squadron of fighter planes.

I sent Croucher back to Battalion Headquarters to tell them.

The sky was getting overcast. It began to rain, a constant drizzle. That wasn't in Colonel Dennis's orders. By this time Catchpole was cooking a meal on our stove. We couldn't complain.

Croucher returned, followed by a jeep out of which Burgo jumped.

'You're just in time for some scoff,' I said.

'No time for that. Oh well, if you insist. Smells good. Give some to Croucher first, he's soaked. I'm pretty wet, too. What is it?'

'Curried snake and beans,' said Catchpole.

'Delicious.'

Catchpole had erected a canopy to the side of the jeep. We all sat under it and ate.

'How did your recce go?' I asked.

'Hilarious. Dermot had had some of his section observing the far bank to locate the enemy positions. They gave a very clear report, all too clear, so Colonel Dennis didn't believe a word of it and made me swim the river to check.'

'In your clothes?'

'I walked half a mile upstream, stripped off and swam across with one arm, holding my clothes above my head with the other. On the other side I put them back on with a white armband to show I was an umpire. Dermot's observers had been spot on. No one on the other side challenged me and I swam back in the same way.'

'You're barmy.'

'It was rather invigorating.'

'What did the colonel say?'

'He said it was good pentathlon training.'

'You'd better have some pudding, Sir, after all that exertion. And here's a little brandy in your tea,' said Catchpole.

'What now?' I asked Burgo.

'You're to go and join the colonel. I'll show you on the map where everyone is. It was all going quite well until this hold-up with the boats. All the timings have been put back two hours. I'm to stay here until the boats arrive and then lead them up to the companies by the river. I know where they are. We're to keep wireless silence until the assault across the river starts. Any more pudding?'

'All gone, sir. Tinned cheese and hard tack biscuits?'

'Yes, please. You'd better cut along fairly soon. The colonel's getting a bit fractious over the delay. He needs comforting. I don't think he gets on that well with Dermot and he's always questioning everything Dermot says or does. Trouble is, Dermot is generally right.'

We packed up, a little wet but warm inside. I wondered what I would have done if the colonel had asked me to swim the river.

It was almost dark and still drizzling. We motored without lights, very slowly. After a bit we were waved down by a regimental policeman and told where to park. Soldiers in huddled groups were standing or lying around. They were wearing their groundsheets as capes, the capes glistening with the rain dripping off the trees. Dermot loomed out of the dark.

'The colonel's driving me nuts. You'd better go and report to him. If he's talkative, stay. If not, join me over here. Use your judgement.'

I walked on and saluted the colonel.

'Miles, any news of the engineers?'

'No more than I've already sent. They were still to arrive when I left Burgo at their assembly area.'

'Can't understand why Major Skidmore is being so intransigent over moving in daylight. This was never mentioned at the briefing. And he came to our party.'

I thought it best to be silent over that.

'I'd better bring you up to date,' said the colonel. 'W company is forward ready to hold our bank of the river and support our crossing. X company will assault left, Y company right. Once they've established a bridgehead we'll get the bridge built. The anti-tank guns will be first across. We should all be in position on the other side by dawn, but it will be tight. At least we've still got surprise on our side. The enemy will be wondering when the attack's coming but the men are getting wet and bored. They've been assembled here for four hours. I've got the reserve of cocoa to cheer them up. You always need to keep something up your sleeve. Clear so far?'

'Yes, colonel.'

'I suppose you're wondering why I want you and Burgo to act as liaison officers? Well I want the company commanders to con-centrate on carrying out my orders and seeing that their platoons achieve their objectives. I don't want them worrying about hav-ing to report back to me. When we attack, you and Burgo will be with the company commanders and I'll rely on you giving me an accurate report on what's going on. That way the company com-mander is able to give his full attention to the attack and I get an independent view of what's happening.'

He didn't seem to want to talk any more. I slipped away and rejoined Dermot.

'It's bad enough being me but I'm glad I'm not Major Skidmore,' said Dermot.

'I wonder if he's delayed on purpose? Burgo and Adam said he didn't take kindly to the scaling down of the roulette stakes.'

'True enough. He was muttering about being diddled when he left. Oh dear!'

'Tell me what happened when you went to see the Frogs with Harry Fox. You did go, didn't you?'

'We went earlier in the week. It was quite a drive. We should have stayed the night but they weren't that friendly. They perked up when I delivered the invitation to the "Allied Dinner" Colonel Dennis is arranging for the end of the month.'

'I haven't heard about that.'

'Colonel Dennis doesn't want to announce it until he knows all our allies – as he calls them – can come. He's asked the commanding officers of two French Regiments and two American Regiments. The band has been ordered to perfect the Marseillaise and the Star-Spangled Banner, and put on a French and American programme.'

'Did you get any decent wine out of them?'

'They seemed very co-operative. Anything we wanted, at a price. They produced two bottles which Harry asked if we could taste. That disconcerted them a bit but we all had a glass of wine. Lots of sucking and gurgling and knowing looks. I thought it pretty ordinary but Harry waxed lyrical over it. I couldn't quite understand everything he said but it was approval, and he'd let them know how much we'd like to buy of each. That pleased them. On the way back Harry asked me what I thought of the wine. I said I was surprised he had said what he had. Harry said it was Algerian wine which they'd bottled themselves, and we shouldn't touch it. I asked him how he was going to get out of buying some. He said we should write and thank them but we'd found, after all, we could buy what we needed locally and would not deprive them of their excellent wine.'

'Has he found some locally?'

'Not that I know. I thought he would have discussed that with you.'

'Now I understand. He left me a note to say he's come to some agreement with Herr Schwarz at the Lucullus. Which Americans are coming to the dinner?'

'Colonel Smiley from the 101st Armored Cavalry, and one other I'm going to ask as soon as this exercise is over.'

'I liked the look of Colonel Smiley.'

'He and Algy Stanhope are old friends from Anzio. I remember him well. He's a good man.'

'Will Algy command next?'

'Nothing's been said as Colonel Dennis has only just taken over but I gather that's the idea. He probably would have already if he wasn't so young.'

'I can't wait.'

Someone nudged my arm. Colonel Dennis's driver was standing just beside me. I wondered how long he'd been there.

'Commanding Officer's compliments and he'd like you both to join him.'

We walked across.

'If we don't get news of the engineers in the next five minutes,' Colonel Dennis said, 'we'll have to put everything back another hour. Dermot, prepare the necessary orders.'

'All the company commanders are here, Colonel. That will be straightforward,' said Dermot.

'Miles, stay with me,' said the colonel.

When Dermot had gone Colonel Dennis began to muse.

'The big question is when to release the reserve cocoa. If the engineers don't arrive within the next five minutes I think I'll release it. That will soften another delay. On the other hand we may have to face an even longer delay. Damn Major Skidmore, he's ruining my exercise. Perhaps it's best to release it now. Yes, I'll release it now and take the risk. Miles, go and tell the company commanders they can release the cocoa.'

Dermot was now standing in a group with the company commanders; Ben Wildbore was there as an acting company commander with Jack Trench and the others. I joined them. They all looked at me.

'The colonel says that if the engineers aren't here within the next five minutes you are to release the reserve cocoa to the men.'

'What?' said Jack Trench.

'The colonel wants the men to have the reserve cocoa if we have to put the timings back another hour. He's authorised its release'

'But Miles,' said Ben Wildbore, 'we released that hours ago.'

'It was only to be released on the commanding officer's orders,' I said.

'Don't be silly. It's all gone.'

One or two began to laugh.

'What shall I tell the colonel?'

'Tell him it's as good as done.'

More laughter.

'Didn't he get his?' Ben asked.

Laughter again.

'He's missed the boat.'

Several guffawed.

'What's going on, Miles? What's that about the boat? Have you given out my orders about the cocoa?' The colonel, presumably attracted by the laughter, had joined us.

'Yes, Colonel.'

'Well, gentlemen?'

There was quite a silence. Colonel Dennis fixed his eyes on Ben Wildbore.

Finally Ben spoke. 'Your orders have been anticipated, Colonel. The cocoa has been released.'

'Anticipated? My orders have been anticipated? I specifically said that only I could order the release of the reserve cocoa ration. How dare you? Explain yourself.'

Colonel Dennis was fiddling with his signet ring. Ben Wildbore was getting the full blast now. No one stepped in to help him.

'We didn't want to trouble you, Colonel. It seemed a straight-forward and minor decision.'

'Minor decision, indeed! It was my idea and my prerogative. How dare you gainsay my orders? Have you all done this?'

Another silence. Everyone nodded.

'What disloyalty! You will learn, gentlemen, that I will not tolerate disloyalty. Not from anyone.'

He stood there glaring. No one moved or spoke. A dim rumble began to be heard in the distance. Dermot was the first to speak.

'The engineers, Colonel.'

'All timings stand,' barked the colonel and strode towards the sound of the trucks. Dermot and I followed him.

The engineer column took some minutes to arrive. Dermot and I thought it best to keep mum. Colonel Dennis was silent. I wondered if he felt better for having re-asserted his authority over the company commanders.

The engineer column was led by two jeeps. As they came up to us Burgo jumped out of the first. Colonel Dennis went up to the second jeep and flashed his torch straight at the person in the passenger seat.

'Put that bloody light out,' said Major Skidmore. 'Do you want to blind me? Put it out.'

'This is Colonel Parker Brown. Major Skidmore, you are late. Disgracefully late.'

'I'm following divisional standing orders. The engineer bridging squadron is only to move by night. Do you want chapter and verse?'

'That may be, but it was dropped for this exercise.'

'By whose authority?'

'By mine.'

'Since when have you the authority to change divisional standing orders? You may be able to change the rules in your battalion, as I noticed the other night, but not in my squadron.'

'We'll see about that,' said Colonel Dennis. 'Now let's get on with the exercise. My men have been waiting in the rain for far too long.'

There was some discussion about how the trucks with the assault boats were to be disposed. Then the engineer column divided and the trucks were led slowly away to the companies they were to support.

Colonel Dennis turned to Dermot, Burgo and me.

'Burgo, you go with X company and Miles, you go with Y. As soon as your company is established across the river, report back immediately so that we get Major Skidmore building his bridge. I want that bridge built as fast as possible. Dermot, you stay with me. I can see we're in for a difficult night and, with this delay, anything could go wrong now.'

It was still raining.

Colonel Dennis was unnecessarily pessimistic. The river crossing went perfectly. The assault started dead on the new time. Admittedly this was in the early hours of the morning, hours later than originally planned, but surprise had been maintained. The enemy didn't start to fire until the companies reached the far bank, rushed the enemy positions, and took them without difficulty. The enemy withdrew. The engineers built the bridge in record time. Well before dawn the anti-tank carriers led the rest of the battalion across the river. Dermot set up tactical headquarters on the far bank and Burgo and I rejoined him. When dawn began to break, the rain had stopped, the companies were well dug in and all the vehicles camouflaged. As the sun climbed over the horizon, the enemy counter-attacked. Despite advancing with the sun behind them, half blinding us, they were easily repelled. The umpires appeared and declared that we had held our position and that the exercise was over. The quartermaster serjeants arrived with breakfast and a tot of rum. It had not been too bad a night, after all.

Having visited the companies with Burgo, Colonel Dennis returned in a very genial mood. 'I'm delighted with the battalion this morning,' he said. 'It's in good spirits and everyone has done well. Dermot, send out a signal of congratulations. And draw up a plan for the return to barracks. We must maintain this level of efficiency until we're safely back.'

He was even courteous to Major Skidmore and thanked him for his support.

After breakfast we were lighting up cigarettes when we were joined by the commanding officer and adjutant of the Borderers who had been acting as the enemy.

'You won fair and square, Dennis, you old rascal,' their colonel said. 'We were expecting you to attack as soon as night fell. When you didn't we decided you'd put it off till dawn. We couldn't see or hear you. You caught us on the hop attacking in the middle of the night, like that.'

'All in the plan,' replied Colonel Dennis, 'a well thought out and rehearsed tactical manoeuvre. We made a thorough reconnaissance and knew your exact positions. Thought we'd catch you asleep and we did.'

Dermot and Major Skidmore exchanged surprised looks. Then they both laughed incredulously. We all laughed.

General Boot appeared out of nowhere with his ADC and the brigadier.

'I must congratulate you both,' he said addressing Colonel Dennis and the commanding officer of the Borderers, 'on a successful exercise. Your counter attack,' he said to the Borderer colonel, 'was well planned and executed. But honours go to the Prince Regent's with their skilfully timed assault across the river. Well done, Dennis. I can see you've got a fine all round battalion. True Trojans.'

As we packed up to return to barracks I said to Burgo, 'Colonel Dennis hates it when things don't go to plan. But wasn't that a surprise when he claimed it had and then took all the credit for the timing of the assault?'

'Just like Monty.'

'Very quick on his feet.'

'Perhaps he's better than we think.'

'And perhaps Jasper's right. Maybe he's just the colonel we need in BAOR, knowing all the tricks of the trade.'

'I wonder what Major Skidmore will say when he gets back to division? Colonel Dennis claimed all the glory for the battalion and none to the engineers.'

'Yes, I expect the general will get to hear what really happened, one way or another.'

6

Allies to dinner

'What are we going to eat and drink?' asked Ben Wildbore. 'The colonel wants it to be a memorable evening in every way.'

'Difficult to satisfy American and Frenchmen with the same menu,' said Jasper. 'In fact, I'd say it was impossible.'

'Why not one course for the Yanks and then one for the Frogs, and so on?' said Burgo.

'Let's leave it to Karl to do his best,' said Jasper.

'Good idea. And drink?' asked Ben.

'I've bought some burgundy from Herr Schwarz,' Harry replied. 'We'll start with Rhine wine. This is Germany. We'll end with port. I found some Offley's Boa Vista '37 at the NAAFI. Quite amazing. And we'll have Madeira, brandy and cigars.'

'Good. I want the details to clear with Colonel Dennis the day after tomorrow. He loves detail, lots of detail.'

'What about entertainment?' asked Burgo.

'No gambling. That's not on for this occasion,' replied Ben.

'I would have thought roulette perfect for after dinner.'

'The colonel's given strict instructions he wants no gambling on this occasion.'

'Surely the Americans will want to play poker?'

'No gambling. Can't you think of anything else, Burgo?'

'The colonel's got no right to instruct us what to do in the mess. In the mess he's just another officer, even if he is the most senior.'

'You don't have to instruct me on how we behave in the mess, Burgo. We've got to be practical. You can gamble to your heart's content when the colonel's not present. But not at his special dinner for our allies.'

'Then won't the band be enough entertainment? Aren't the guests going home afterwards? I haven't heard any arrangements for putting them up for the night.'

'Colonel Dennis thinks some mess games might amuse them,' said Ben.

'Oh no,' said Jasper.

'How uncivilized,' said Burgo.

'Which ones?' I asked.

'He favours high cocklelorum, splosh and mess rugger,' said Ben, 'and he wants you and Burgo to organise them.'

'I resign,' said Burgo.

'No you don't. And the colonel also wants speeches and toasts.'

'Speeches and toasts?' we all said in unison.

'We never have speeches or toasts,' said Burgo.

'On this occasion he wants us to toast the President of the United States and the President of France. And, just once, as it's a very special occasion and our guests will expect it, he says, we will toast the Queen.'

'You'll have a mutiny,' I said.

'No, we won't. It's merely a simple courtesy for our guests.'

'I'm going on leave,' said Burgo.

'All leave is cancelled.'

'The French never toast their President,' said Harry.

'Well Colonel Dennis wants us to.'

'You'd better warn him. They toast *La France*. They might take it amiss otherwise.'

'Look,' said Burgo, 'it's just not us. We never do these things.'

'I concede that speeches and toasts are unusual, but we do play games sometimes. Admit it,' said Ben.

'It depends on the guests and how much everyone has drunk. It's always spontaneous, not planned,' I said.

'We'll have had plenty to drink I hope,' replied Ben. 'Can't you see the colonel wants to put on a show?'

'The French will think us mad and the Yanks will think us decadent.'

'We are.'

'But is that how we want to be seen?' I asked.

'That's all for the moment. Let me have the details. I'm glad you're being so understanding and co-operative. Now why don't you all go and have a drink and leave me alone to make some notes?'

He lit another cigarette and blew smoke rings at us.

'And ask Corporal Cheke to bring me a gin and tonic.'

We, the mess committee, had been sitting in the mess office, a tiny room at the end of the corridor on the first floor of the mess. It was just before lunch.

'Come on,' said Burgo. 'I need a brandy to recover. It's unbelievable.'

We left Ben to his notes and walked down the corridor to the anteroom.

'The man's a maniac,' said Burgo.

'Ben's only doing his job as mess president,' said Jasper.

'No, no. Not Ben, the colonel.'

Corporal Cheke was walking towards us with a gin and tonic on a silver salver. He had anticipated Ben's request. 'Captain Wildbore still in the mess office, gentlemen? I've got his preprandial for him.'

'Yes,' said Burgo, 'and, Corporal Cheke, bring me a double horse's neck.'

As we ordered drinks, Algy came up the stairs into the hall. We all walked into the anteroom together. Between the centre windows had been placed a low, late-Victorian rosewood bookcase. Adam Hare was putting books into it with Tom Body, the mess serjeant, helping him.

'What's this, Adam?' I asked.

'Colonel Dennis asked me to bring up to date General Flaxman's monograph on the mess possessions. The general included a bookcase and a list of books. Colonel Dennis said if they weren't here they must still be at the depot and sent for them. They've just arrived. The colonel said the bookcase was always kept in the anteroom before the war. Ben Wildbore said put it here. Odd lot of books.'

I looked at them. There was a set of the *Badminton Library* and a set of the *Lonsdale Library, Jack Mytton* by Nimrod, *Kelly's Directory of the Titled, Landed and Official Classes 1939, Handley Cross* and other novels by Surtees, *Burke's Landed Gentry 1937, Burke's Peerage 1930, The Prince Regent's Light Infantry: The First Hundred Years*, a set of the 1911 edition of *Encyclopaedia Britannica*, and *The Blue and Green: The Prince Regent's Light Infantry in the Great War*. There were also about fifty green leather bound books. I picked up the top one.

'Those look interesting,' said Adam. 'Regimental Journals going back to 1890, which appears to be the first volume. The one you're looking at is 1940 and seems to be the last one.'

'It's the last journal to be bound,' said Algy. He pronounced 'journal' as if were spelt 'jawnal'. 'It's time we had the later ones bound and added to these.'

I opened the one in my hands at a page of photographs.

'Algy, is this you?'

'Let me see. Yes, that's the officers of the Second Battalion in France in 1940, just before Dunkirk. I was the adjutant. I remember it being taken.'

We all looked at the young adjutant Algy.

'What's that hat you're wearing?' asked Harry.

'It's a field service hat. We called them fore and aft caps. We all wore them then. The soldiers wore khaki ones and the officers and warrant officers green ones.'

'How elegant,' said Adam.

'I've got one somewhere,' chipped in Burgo. 'We used to wear them in Hong Kong.'

'Why don't we still wear them?' asked Harry.

'Why not, Algy?'

'I can't see why not. We always did.'

'Colonel Dennis, too?'

'Look. Here's a photo of Colonel Dennis wearing one,' said Adam.

We all drew closer to peer at a photograph of Colonel Dennis, then a captain, wearing a fore and aft cap.

'I'm getting one,' said Harry.

'I'm going to find mine,' said Burgo. 'Colonel Dennis said he wanted us to wear service dress hats to stand apart from the men. Well, you can do that with a fore and aft cap. I'll wear mine this afternoon if I can find it. What do you say, Algy?'

'I wouldn't dream of advising you on your sartorial problems.'

We all laughed and went into lunch.

That afternoon Colonel Dennis was holding a sports conference at which those of us in charge of a game or sport had to report on progress. A timetable of events was to be agreed, final priorities were to be decided, and any problems or clashes ironed out. I was waiting in the adjutant's office when Burgo came in. He had found his fore and aft cap, dusted it, and was wearing it. It was made from a handsome dark green moleskin. On the front was a dark blue, almost black, bobble on which there sat a miniature regimental badge: a stringed silver bugle surmounted by a crown.

'What's that on your head?' asked Val.

'I thought everyone could recognise a fore and aft cap,' said Burgo.

'Why are you wearing it?'

'It's much more comfortable than any other hat we wear and it needs an airing. I haven't worn it since Hong Kong.'

'I suggest you take it off before we go into the colonel's office.'

'Why? Colonel Dennis said he wanted us to wear flat hats so

we "stood apart from the men". His exact words. A fore and aft cap does it as well.'

As we went into the colonel's office I noticed Burgo take off his cap. He sat down and placed it on his lap.

'Where shall we start?' said the colonel looking round. His eye fell on Algy. 'Football, I think.'

There was a long discussion on football training. Then we moved to cross-country running. Burgo reported. We missed out polo. The first team continued to be successful but Horace Belcher was away on a course. Then we came to shooting. The divisional small arms meeting was due to be held on our range as soon as we returned from the next exercise. We hadn't had much time for practice, so far. Dermot wanted the team to be excused from the next battalion training exercise in favour of shooting practice. Colonel Dennis did not. He argued that we had some outstanding shots but that many held key positions in the battalion and could not therefore be excused from the exercise, which was to be training to co-operate with tanks, a tricky operation that was to take a week.

'If you'll not excuse the team from the whole exercise may I have them for the last two days?' asked Dermot.

'That doesn't make any sense. If we need them for armoured training we need them the whole time. The last two days will be the culmination of the training when we'll exercise as a battalion group with tanks.'

'Colonel, we do need to practise for the team events.'

'You'll have to do it before the exercise.'

'I know the Household Cavalry are moving down here while we're on exercise to train on our range.'

'They probably haven't got anything better to do. Can they shoot?'

'They're the major competition. They have some very good shots and they'll have got their eyes in.'

'You're saying that to try and persuade me. No, I've made up my mind, Dermot. You've got some very good shots too and you're going to win. I'm not going to excuse the team from armoured training. That's final. Now pentathlon. Ben?'

Ben reported on his team, the training they'd been doing and the date of the pentathlon trials. Colonel Dennis had been a pentathlete in his time. He asked some shrewd questions which Ben answered well. The meeting closed.

'Burgo, what's that you've got on your lap?'

'A fore and aft cap, Colonel.'

'Where did you get it?'

'Jermyn Street. I last wore it in Hong Kong.'

Colonel Dennis got up from behind his desk and walked round until he stood in front of Burgo. He leant down, picked up the cap, examined it inside and out, studied the badge and then placed it carefully on the centre of Burgo's head.

'Elegant, Burgo. I used to wear one myself.'

As we walked away from Battalion Headquarters I said to Burgo, 'You didn't expect that, did you?'

'Say what you like about Colonel Dennis, he's clever.'

We walked on down to the officers' mess. Within a month, half the officers were wearing fore and aft hats, including Algy. I never saw Colonel Dennis in one.

In the anteroom we found Jasper and Adam. Adam was standing next to a side table, on which there were plates of sandwiches and cakes, helping himself to tea. Jasper was lying on a sofa playing with his dog, a red setter called Kaiser. Karl had found him abandoned in the town. Kaiser was highly strung, even for a red setter, and kept running away.

'Decided on the menu for the great dinner, Jasper?' Burgo asked.

'Karl has. He's proposed Beef Wellington preceded by lobster bisque and sole Veronique. I've been telling him how to make angels on horseback. The Germans don't know about savouries.'

'Beef Wellington? Interesting insult to the French,' said Adam.

'There, Kaiser, I told you so. We'll have to think again. Kaiser and I are off to exercise Red Ember in a moment. Are you coming Miles?'

'No, I can't.'

'You haven't been riding at all recently'

'Blame the colonel's priorities. I'm spending little enough time as it is on the shooting team. Haven't you got anyone to go with?'

'Kitty Belcher said she'd come. Horace is away, still. She's bought a rather good steeplechaser. And she's bringing Julia Trench. Harry Fox is coming too. What about you, Adam?'

'Horses are good for betting not for riding. I'm going to put the final touch to my revision of the Flaxman monograph. I'm showing it to Colonel Dennis tomorrow.'

'Well I'd better get going. Come on Kaiser, no friends here.'

Jasper, Kaiser and Adam left the room.

'Adam's all right, you know,' said Burgo. 'I've seen a bit of him in the Silver Room doing his research into the mess possessions to update Flaxman. He's quick and bright and can tell a good story. He'll be an asset. We should ask him down to the Lucullus with us.'

'You're very easily swayed, Burgo. I must go to the pistol range.'

'So you weren't just looking for an excuse not to go riding with Kitty?'

Burgo looked at me knowingly.

'It's getting difficult. She keeps on sending me messages. They've increased since Horace has been away.'

'You must have known what you were in for?'

'It all happened again on the spur of the moment. Just like that.'

'You should enjoy it.'

'Olivia's asked me to dinner on Saturday. She's also asked Harry Fox. Kitty's bound to be there. Olivia can't not ask her with Horace away. They're quite close.'

'Perhaps she wants to protect Kitty by having you together in her house so she can keep an eye on both of you. Then you won't be able to do anything. After all Kitty lives virtually next door to Olivia.'

'Burgo, is everyone talking about it?'

'Not everyone. Do you still love her?'

'I'm infatuated.'

'Why not let it rip?'

'Think of the consequences.'

'You look miserable. You should be happy.'

'Being in love always makes me miserable.'

Saturday night came, and Harry and I motored down to the Stanhope's in his car. He was quite excited about dining with them.

'Who else is going to be there?' he asked.

'Olivia hasn't told me. She'll want it to be a surprise.'

It was. Kitty was there as I thought she would be. But Olivia had also asked Rana Selzuk and the von Sengers as well as the Pophams. We sat down ten. The Sengers were treated as the senior guests and seated on the right of the host and hostess. Harry sat between Mrs Popham and Kitty, and I sat between Elizabeth Senger and Rana on the opposite side of the table. The meal was good, the wine liberal. We all talked to our right and left and, when the pudding came, the conversation became general.

Olivia appeared to have Kitty under control. Kitty was staying with the Stanhopes, having moved in the day Horace had left for his course, and would not move back until he returned. Olivia was keeping her occupied morning, noon, and night. The only time Kitty was out of Olivia's sight seemed to be when she was exercising the ponies.

'Miles,' said Kitty, 'why don't you come and help exercise the ponies like Harry does?'

'I'm trying to train the shooting team and there's just not time to do both.'

'Oh Miles,' said Olivia, 'some of the wives want to learn to shoot. We must talk about that soon.'

'Some of the wives want to learn to ride,' said Kitty, 'I'll need some help there.'

'I ride,' said Rana. 'I'd like to help you.'

Kitty looked surprised. Not, I thought, quite the answer she was expecting. Everyone was rather surprised.

'Well, yes, that would be nice,' said Kitty.

'I can shoot, too,' said Rana.

'With a shotgun?' asked Kitty.

'Yes, and with a rifle. I've shot a boar. My father wanted me to be a boy. I'm his only child, so he brought me up as a boy. That's why I'm here at the university getting the education his son would have had. I'd love to have some shooting.'

'I can only arrange target shooting with pistol or rifle,' I said.

'When' asked Algy, 'does boar shooting start in Germany?'

'In the autumn,' replied von Senger, 'and you must all come. I insist.'

'I think' said Olivia, 'it's time for the ladies to retire.'

We all rose and the ladies left. The men moved to sit round Algy, who produced some cigars.

'Unusual girl, Rana' said Algy.

'Her mother died when she was very young,' said Brigadier Popham. 'You know her father was a general, don't you? He never married again though I gather he had mistresses. So Rana was brought up in a man's world. She's fascinated by your regiment, and she wants to learn all about you to tell her father. He's one of the few Turks who still have vast estates. Fancy shooting boar in Turkey for the rest of your life, Miles?'

They all laughed.

'I hear, Algy, that your regiment's got a big dinner planned and I've not been asked.'

'For once, Brigadier, I'm afraid not. Dennis Parker Brown is having a getting-to-know-the-allies evening. He's asked some of the commanding officers from neighbouring American and French regiments. We're all to be on our best behaviour.'

'That doesn't sound like my territory. I'm here strictly to look after your relations with the Germans. How do you think that's going, von Senger?'

'You have a saying in England that "time cures everything". This is the first time since the war that I've dined in an English house. Your party was the first time I'd been in your barracks. I rejoice at that. But it's taking a long time to repair the damage.'

We were all silent.

He went on. 'We were hijacked, as the Americans say. But we fell in with it.'

'The enemy was Hitler and his entourage, not Germany,' said Algy. 'Our enemy now is Russia. Soon there'll be a German army again. You are our allies now and we must all pull together. This is what Dennis's dinner is starting, re-laying the foundations of entente. You will be at the next.'

'It sounds,' said von Senger, 'as if it will be an interesting evening.'

The 'Misalliance Dinner', as it came to be known, was held the following Thursday. The guests had all been asked to stay the night and all had refused. Someone should have thought that strange but none questioned it. Dedicated soldiers, we thought.

As this was a formal occasion we were all dressed in our dark green number one dress but without medals. Dinner was at eight. By half past seven we were gathered in the anteroom in good time for our guests. Two young officers were standing at the entrance to the mess ready to receive. Colonel Smiley of the US Armored Cavalry, who had witnessed the border patrol parade, arrived first, shortly followed by Colonel Hammer, the commanding officer of an American infantry regiment. Each asked for a whisky and soda. Colonel Smiley fell in with Algy and Ben Wildbore collared Colonel Hammer. The rest of us waited for the Frenchmen. Our glasses were refilled, but still no Frenchmen. At eight o'clock a French colonel arrived. Tall and aloof, he looked round the room as if wondering why he was there and whether there was anyone worth talking to. Colonel Dennis greeted him

but it soon became clear that his English was limited. Harry Fox
was pushed forward and tried to get him into conversation. The
French colonel looked Harry up and down, saw him to be young
and without medal ribbons on his chest and looked round the
room again searching for someone of his own rank to talk to. He
spotted Colour Serjeant Body with his two rows of medal ribbons and considerable stature standing by the door. Serjeants, in
their number one dress, only wore chevrons on their right arm.
As Tom's right arm was hidden from the Frenchman, he looked
like an officer. The Frenchman moved across and started talking
to him. Harry Fox followed and was able to translate for them
both. Tom Body, flattered, spoke up well. He was the same height
as the Frenchman and a good conversationalist with a fund of
military stories. They got on well. It was well past eight when
the second French colonel arrived. Led in by a young officer, he
was presented to Colonel Dennis, Algy and the two American
colonels. For a soldier he was short and fat. He looked round
the room and spotted the tall French colonel. He shuddered,
drew himself up as tall as he could, and stared. The tall French
colonel saw the short French colonel, broke off talking to Tom
Body, and blanched.

'This,' said Adam in my ear, 'is going to be interesting.'

I saw Algy say something to Ben Wildbore who beckoned to
Serjeant Body. Immediately a gong was struck and Tom Body
announced in a stentorian voice, 'Gentlemen, dinner is served.'
This somewhat surprised the tall Frenchman whom Algy took by
the arm and led out of the room following Colonel Dennis with
Colonel Hammer. The band, seated in the wide corridor outside
the dining room, played 'The Entrance of Queen Dido' from *The
Trojans* as we all filed along into the dining room. After a Latin
grace, Colonel Dennis sat down in the centre of one side of the table
with Colonel Hammer on his right and the short French colonel
on his left. Opposite was Algy who had the tall French colonel on
his right and Colonel Smiley on his left, so the two Frenchmen
were sitting opposite each other.

The meal had little resemblance to that proposed by Jasper and Karl. Colonel Dennis had decided that roast beef should be the main course preceded by cold artichoke soup and a quiche Lorraine because, he said, the soup and the quiche Lorraine would please the French, and the beef, traditionally English, would please the Americans. We ended with devils on horseback, prunes wrapped in bacon. I was sitting between Burgo and Adam someway down the table.

If the food appeared a little unimaginative, the wine was good and it flowed. There was a lot of noise with thirty-five people in the room and the band playing tunes from *South Pacific, Annie Get Your Gun* and an arrangement from Offenbach.

I wouldn't have paid much attention to what was going on in the middle of the table if Adam hadn't nudged me and said, 'Something going wrong there.' So I watched and could see enough to realise it was not all that happy.

The short French colonel, on Colonel Dennis's left, was not having fun. He tucked into the soup and the burgundy when it arrived, but he refused the German wine and the quiche Lorraine. He left half the beef on his plate and was clearly baffled by the devil on horseback. He tried talking to Colonel Dennis once, but Colonel Dennis seemed more interested in talking to Colonel Hammer. Colonel Dennis's French was elementary so he had placed Harry Fox on the other side of the Frenchman, but Harry had little luck in getting the Frenchman to talk.

The meal ended, the table was cleared, and port and Madeira circulated, as did brandy and cigars. Burgo started to light a cigar until I nudged him hard in the ribs. Then Colonel Dennis rose and we all fell silent. It was too late to mutiny. Colonel Dennis began to speak. 'It is a great honour for us this evening to welcome our distinguished allies.' Every now and again he stopped to let Harry translate. 'We stand here together on the frontier of the free world to guard our nations against the menace of Soviet Russia. Together we successfully defeated the tyranny of Hitler. Together we remain united to combat the tyranny of Stalin. We are fresh to this new frontier. We delight in knowing we have such staunch allies in you. We hope to forge lasting friendships with you as comrades-in-arms.'

He went on in this vein for three or four minutes until he invited everyone to stand and drink the health of the Queen. Everyone stood and the band played God Save the Queen. The Americans emptied their glasses. We all sat down. The Americans' glasses were rapidly refilled. Then Colonel Dennis invited everyone to stand again and drink the health of the President of the United States of America. We all stood. The band played The Star-Spangled Banner, the Americans knocked back their glasses, we all sat down, and the Americans' glasses were rapidly refilled. Colonel Dennis stood up again. *'Messieurs, Monsieur Le President de la Republique Française.'* We all stood up but the Frenchmen remained seated. Colonel Dennis looked at them and started to frown. The Americans looked at them, raised their eyebrows, and then looked at each other. Harry Fox whispered furiously. Colonel Dennis looked at him as if to tell him to shut up. The Frenchmen were immovable. Harry Fox whispered louder. Then Colonel Dennis cleared his throat and in a new voice said, *'Messieurs, La France'*. The two Frenchman rose. In loud voices they said *'La France'*, and then sipped at their glasses while the band played the Marseillaise.

'It's only just beginning,' said Adam. 'Look forward to fireworks when we break up.'

Burgo was finally able to light his cigar as the colonel led the guests out into the corridor where the band played the regimental marches and we all shouted and clapped. Then he took them back into the anteroom where he arranged whiskies for them. Quite a lot had already been drunk. The short French colonel whom I had been watching during dinner had drunk far more than he had eaten. Now he slowly pulled himself up to his full five foot six and advanced on the tall French colonel, who was standing by Algy.

'Gaullist,' he hissed.

'Petainist,' spat back the tall French colonel.

'Sale Gaullist.'

'*Vichyist.*'

They stood there spitting vile epithets at each other.

Algy said something to Harry. Harry went up to the short colonel and told him his driver was at the door. The short colonel spat one more insult at the other and, ignoring Colonel Dennis and everyone, made for the door. The tall colonel drained his whisky glass and handed it to Harry asking him to call his driver to the door. Then he went up to Tom Body, thanked him most courteously for the evening and left.

'Strange allies, those French,' said Colonel Smiley. 'In the last war I never could tell whose side they were on.'

We saw quite a lot of the Americans after that. The Frenchmen we never saw again.

7

The Colonel teaches us the importance of training.

'Would you look after Kaiser while I'm in England?' asked Jasper. 'I'm to go on an equitation course. It's the colonel's idea.'

'I'd love to. But surely *you* don't need to go?'

'I'll qualify as an instructor.'

'How on earth did you get a place?'

'Colonel Dennis heard there was a spare place going. The organisers wanted to fill it.'

'Won't you miss the next polo game?'

'Only one. I'll be back in time for the tournament.'

'You'll miss the tank training.'

'Colonel Dennis says we need more expertise in the stables. We can't just rely on Horace. I'm to teach more soldiers to ride when I return.'

'He does have odd priorities. He won't let Dermot and the shooting team off the tank training exercise so we can train for the divisional small arms meeting but you can swan off to England to play with horses. It doesn't make sense.'

'It makes sense to me,' said Jasper, 'but I shall miss Kaiser.'

'Don't worry about Kaiser. I rather love that dog. He's so beautiful and highly-strung. Where is he?'

'He's run away again. I don't think he likes all the time I spend with the horses. He can be a naughty, jealous doggie. He'll be back soon. He likes Karl, especially what Karl gives him to eat.'

Kaiser came back the day Jasper left for England. I moved his basket to my room and Karl and I inspected him. He badly needed a bath and he had canker in both ears. Karl and I took him to the vet in the town. Within a week the canker cleared up and he seemed a less frenetic dog. When the battalion moved out of barracks again to move to the tank training grounds Kaiser sat happily in the back of my jeep. We had become firm friends. The machine gun platoon thought him a fine addition, and one of them was always prepared to exercise him if I couldn't.

The tank training grounds were in the north of West Germany and it took us the whole day to get there. We had a tented camp on the edge of a wood where we spent 10 days. We made ourselves as comfortable as possible; I've known worse camps. Every day we were out training. It was arduous with not much time for pleasure, but nearby was a river where we swam in the evenings. Once, a mobile bath and laundry unit came and everyone was able to have a shower and change into some clean clothes. The men's spirits were kept up as they were fully occupied; training with tanks, on this scale, was something new. In Korea we'd only once had a tank squadron in support of the whole battalion; most of the time we'd only had a troop of four tanks and they had generally been dug in. Now we had a squadron of tanks working with each company. The weather remained fine and settled and there weren't any major balls-ups. Every night I went to bed tired out and slept with Kaiser as my pillow, trying not to think of Kitty.

When Sunday came, the battalion paraded for church service. We hadn't had such a service in the open air since Korea. The band was with us and played the hymns. Five hundred lusty voices sang out. The bandmaster had collected some of the Welshmen and miners with fine voices to form a choir. They sang the *Venite* and the *Jubilate Deo* with great spirit. Even the padre made a short and moving sermon. Whether you believed in God or not, you felt you were part of a spiritual community. Afterwards there was football and swimming. Colonel Dennis had arranged a special Sunday dinner for the men with beer. After that most lazed the day away.

We had asked officers from the regiments we had been training with to drinks before lunch. Several came and some stayed on for lunch. Afterwards Adam said, 'Who'd say yes to a game of chemmy?'

'Good idea,' said Horace.

'I'll play,' said Burgo. Turning to Charles Millington, a 19th Lancer, and Desmond D'eath, a 5th Hussar, he said, 'Stay and join in. Here's a chance to win your money back.'

They laughed and stayed. I joined in too.

Horace was now commanding X company in which Adam and Jasper served. Jasper, of course, was in England. Horace had changed places with Jack Trench. Jack was back in barracks commanding the rear party with Harry Fox and one or two other officers.

So there were six of us playing. Adam had seen that the chemmy shoe and the necessary packs of cards had been brought from the barracks and had probably been waiting for an occasion like this to offer itself. Tom Body was asked to set up a card table. From the speed with which he did this he must have been prepared for it. He also brought in an ice bucket with two bottles of hock, soda water and glasses, clearly on Adam's instructions. Horace lit a cigar and then offered some round. Horace's Nimrodian and Bacchanalian ways had attracted Adam. I'm not sure Horace had yet realised that Adam was an unusual bird to have in the regiment.

'I suggest we start by auctioning the bank. I'll start the bidding at a fiver,' said Adam.

'A tenner,' said Horace as he blew on his cigar to get it going.

'Any other bids?' asked Adam. 'No? Then it's yours, Horace.'

Horace didn't have much luck, either immediately or later. We must have started playing about 3 o'clock. By half past five we had drunk four bottles of hock, had tea and sandwiches, and Horace was calling for whisky and soda. There had been some wild fluctuations in the play but the final tally was against Horace. He had lost consistently and was down £55. Burgo had lost a fiver. Everyone else had won. Charlie Millington was up £12 and Desmond D'eath £15. Adam was up £22 and I was up £11.

'It just so happens that we've brought the bridge book with us,' said Adam. 'The best way to handle this is to put it in the book and settle through mess bills at the end of the month. So, Charlie and Desmond, we'll send you cheques then. Are you happy with that?'

'By far the neatest way,' said Horace.

Charlie and Desmond nodded assent.

Adam entered the amounts in the bridge book. Tom Body came and cleared away the cards and the chemmy shoe. As we broke up, Colonel Dennis came into the tent with Algy and Ben Wildbore and called for tea. He saw the card table and said, 'What about a four at bridge? Algy and Ben, are you game? Good. Who'll join us? Horace?'

Horace was only just sober.

'I've been playing cards all afternoon.'

'Well you'll have your hand in.'

'I haven't any other plans. My luck might change.'

Tom Body brought the cards back and they settled down to play. Burgo, Adam and I saw our guests on their way and decided we would go for a swim as we needed fresh air and exercise. Kaiser came too. By the time I got back to the mess tent to have a drink before Sunday supper the bridge players were breaking up.

'How clever of someone to bring the bridge book,' said Colonel Dennis as Tom Body passed it to Ben. 'That your idea, Ben?'

'No, it was Adam Hare's.'

'So he's got foresight as well as a good mind. He did an excellent job on updating the Flaxman monograph. I'm glad to hear he plays bridge, too. Now, what were the final scores?'

Ben carefully wrote them into the book as Colonel Dennis said, 'Ben and I win eleven shillings and sixpence. Algy and Horace lose ditto.'

'Pass me the book, Ben. I'd like to see who's been playing.'

Ben affected not to hear him.

'Body, hand me the book from Captain Wildbore,' said Colonel Dennis

Tom Body did what he was asked.

'You said you'd been playing this afternoon, Horace. Better luck than this evening?'

'No.'

'Who were you playing with? I see. Burgo, Adam, Miles, and two guests I presume. Six at bridge? How did you manage that? What are these figures? What does £55 mean, Horace? And why six of you?'

'We were playing chemmy.'

'Were you?' said Colonel Dennis thoughtfully.

'What about a drink, Colonel,' said Algy.

Colonel Dennis was silent. He was looking at the book intently and turning back the pages. Then he turned them back again slowly and looked at Horace.

'You lost £55 this afternoon?'

'Yes.'

'And last week you lost £37? That's £92 in all.'

'Not much, Colonel,' said Horace.

'And you, Ben. You seem to gamble too. Last week you won £22?'

'We have some very good games after dinner in the mess. You'd be welcome to join us, Colonel.'

'Would I, indeed?'

'As president of the mess committee I keep an eye on it and see that it doesn't get out of hand.'

'Do you? And you allow officers to win or lose sums equal to a month's pay or more? You don't call that getting out of hand? Horace may be able to afford to lose a year's salary but what about the other officers and the young national service officers?'

'Only those play who can afford to do so, Colonel.'

'Can all the names in this book afford these stakes? I don't be-

lieve you. Algy, I don't like this. We must talk about it. Let's have
that drink now and discuss it after supper.' Apart from the four of
them I was the only person within earshot, settled in a chair and
pretending to read a newspaper. I hadn't read a word.

Supper on Sunday night was an informal meal. I can't remember
what we ate, something very simple like kedgeree followed by
cheese and biscuits. By now, nearly everyone was out of uniform,
even in a tented camp in a training area. We had dressed in uniform for the church parade. As the day wore on we had changed
into what were then regarded as informal plain clothes. Most were
wearing grey flannels with a tweed coat or a regimental blazer. Ties
were *de rigueur* in the evening.

After supper a few sat in a corner of the big tent gossiping. Most
drifted away for an early night. In the morning we were to start
the last exercise: a full-blown battalion exercise with a regiment
of tanks. Colonel Dennis and Algy settled down in the far corner
and started to talk to each other. They kept their voices low. There
was no chance of overhearing them. Kaiser and I left the tent and
started to walk towards our bed. It was a bright clear night. At the
far corner of the tent I stopped to light a cigarette and looked up
to study the stars. Kaiser lay down beside me.

'Aren't you being a little hard, Dennis?' I heard Algy saying.

'You're too soft, Algy. I'm responsible for my officers and I can't
have them gambling a month's pay away.'

'No one's been hurt, Dennis. They're young men out for a
little excitement. Ben's keeping an eye on it. No one's lost more
than he can afford. The main loser seems to be Horace and he
can well afford it.'

'Someone might get hurt. I'm not going to tolerate it.'

'Remember when you were their age? When we were in India
before the war I seem to recall you spent everything you had on
horses. That was a form of high stake gambling.'

'I didn't get into trouble.'

'No one has.'

'Look what happened to Tony Yorke in India. He borrowed so much from the moneylenders he had to resign.'

'That was wild oats. No one could control him. And his father had cut off his allowance. Tony is a much respected Member of Parliament now.'

'The colonel should have controlled him.'

'Maybe, but Tony wasn't cut out to be a soldier. He would have resigned anyway. When war broke out he joined the Navy. Even if the colonel had interfered over Tony he wouldn't have dreamed of stopping everyone gambling as you seem to want to do.'

'I don't want to have a scandal.'

'If one officer gets into trouble you can step in, but I don't see how you can stop them all gambling.'

'They can gamble if they must, but I'm going to control the stakes.'

'They'll think you're treating them like children. They resented you paring down the winnings and losses at our first party when they played roulette. It didn't go down too well with Skidmore, either.'

'They were behaving like children.'

'Far from it. They're behaving adventurously. You are always encouraging them to live life to the full. They're challenging danger. It's good for them if that's what they want to do. Deciding how far you can go in making your bets is a test of the odds and your nerve. It sorts out the weak.'

'You're talking rot, Algy.'

'Just because you don't agree doesn't mean I'm talking rot, Dennis. I think you're in danger of interfering when there's no reason to interfere. They won't understand and they'll resent it. You'll lose their confidence.'

'I sometimes wonder if I have the confidence or loyalty of any of my officers. You never told me, Algy, about that incident on the first border patrol when Adam Hare was dressed incorrectly. That was disloyal.'

'There was no incident to report. Jack Trench was over zealous.

Adam Hare was correctly dressed as he'd been part of the patrol. Trench is a sneak and a bully, full of petty stories.'

'I must have loyalty.'

'You won't have if you do what you're proposing.'

'Damn you, Algy, for telling me what I can do.'

'You asked me for my view and I'm giving it. It's not up to a second in command to tell his commanding officer what to do.'

'I'm sorry. I take that back.'

There was silence. My cigarette had long gone out. Kaiser looked up at me as if to ask if we could go now. I knelt and stroked him. We looked into each other's eyes and I put my fingers to my lips. He understood.

'Algy, you talk to Ben Wildbore. Tell him my views. Tell him that if it gets out of hand I'll come down on him like a ton of bricks. Advise him to cut back on the stakes. I'm relying on you, Algy. If it doesn't work I'll hold you as responsible as the others.'

'That's good of you, Dennis.'

They stopped talking. By now I was sitting on the ground besides Kaiser. He looked up at me again and I began to get up.

'We've got some good young officers if only we could stop these excesses,' said Colonel Dennis.

I sat down again.

'Do you call Horace young?'

'I don't mean Horace. Take Jasper for example. Not unlike his father. Do you remember how brave he was at Dunkirk? That charge in which he was killed to clear the way. I think Jasper's got the same mettle. He's one of the few young officers that doesn't look at me warily.'

'Brave as Jasper's father was, I have always thought that charge was foolhardy and unnecessary. Isn't there a danger of over indulging Jasper? He's been spoilt by his mother all his life and now you seem to be spoiling him by encouraging him to become a second Horace.'

'We need expertise in depth, Algy. We need to develop all the regiment's old skills: pentathlon, shooting, horses, polo. That's what makes good officers with strong nerves.'

'I know that, Dennis. But Jasper's headstrong, like his father was. He'll be twenty-one soon and will come into quite a bit of money, I understand. He'll develop into another Horace if we're not careful.'

'Yes, Horace could be a problem. He drinks too much. It never seems to affect him in the morning. The point about Horace is he's absolutely loyal. I moved him to a rifle company as I thought we were not making the best use of his panache and he'd have more to do to keep him busy.'

'Guy Surtees didn't think much of Horace's panache. He called him a polo stick soaked in whisky. That's why he put him in charge of headquarter company where he couldn't do too much damage.'

'If Guy Surtees said that I feel justified in my decision. I hear Horace's wife is not helping. There's talk about her chasing sub-alterns.'

'Kitty is a darling and may be a bit of a flirt. She has plenty of provocation from Horace. I've not heard anything serious.'

'Nothing about her and Miles Player?'

'They've known each other since childhood. I doubt they're more than just friends.'

'Well, talk has reached me and I'm keeping my ears open. Miles is a good young officer. Pity if he goes off the rails, like his father. I'd have to post him out of the battalion, Horace, too.'

'How can you say Fred Player went off the rails?'

'Didn't you know he had an affair with Verity Knox?'

I must have started for Kaiser looked up and licked my hand. For a moment I lost the train of their conversation. Why had I never guessed that? My father and Jasper's mother? Jasper's father had been killed at Dunkirk. I remembered my father bringing Jasper's mother with him to visit Jasper and me at school. Did that explain some of my parents' constant quarrels? I never really got to know my father as he was away so much during the war and was killed in an aircrash just after he'd been promoted lieutenant general, when I was fifteen.

'Miles,' I heard Algy say and I immediately listened again. 'Miles is a promising officer. So is Burgo. The most promising we have is Dermot though he's hardly young any more.'

'Dermot Lisle? I can't agree with you there. You're prejudiced because he was your adjutant in Italy. I find him too clever. Thinks he has all the answers. Always trying to anticipate me. He takes too many initiatives without consulting me. Guy Surtees recommended him but I just can't see it. He's too easy going and popular with the men. Then there were all those demands for the shooting team to be exempted from coming here so he could train them. I'm watching him carefully.'

'He'll be off to the Staff College in a few months.'

'What makes you so sure about that?'

'Dennis, my last job was as an instructor there. Remember? I've still got friends there. I'm told he's on the list, only awaiting final confirmation.'

'I see. Is that so?'

There was a short silence.

'Then there's Adam Hare. How do you think he's settling down?'

'Adam's unusual. I can't understand why he joined us. He's not cut out to be a soldier. He's amiable, witty, and clever. The soldiers like him. You can see that. Maybe he's too clever, even for us. I sense the gambling has moved to a higher level since he arrived. He's rather louche.'

'Has he money?'

'Seems to have.'

'He strikes me as doing well so far. I think he's got promise and loyalty. I'm thinking of moving him to support company. He'll get more responsibility there.'

'Why don't you let him finish a season's training where he is? You'll get a more consistent view of him. Are there any vacancies in support company?'

'All the senior subalterns are there. When Dermot Lisle leaves there'll be an opportunity to promote one.'

'Who will you promote?'

Kaiser pricked up his ears and I looked round. Someone was leaving the tent and walking our way. We'd better move, I thought, we don't want to be caught here. Kaiser and I rose and walked to our tent. Kaiser slept well. I hardly slept at all.

We were up before reveille and I took Kaiser for a walk along the river. Returning by the machine gun lines I left Kaiser with Cookson while Catchpole came and helped me pack up my kit before I had breakfast. At 8 o'clock the battalion started to move out to an assembly area to start another exercise. My thoughts kept returning to what I'd overheard.

On the Wednesday we returned to barracks. The divisional small arms meeting was to be held on the Friday. Thursday was spent in cleaning weapons and vehicles. At 2 p.m. the shooting team met on the range to make what preparations were possible in the time left. The rear party, left in barracks during the tank training exercises, had prepared the range, pitching tents and putting out signs. Some of the competing teams had been in the barracks for a day or two, practising hard.

'The most important thing we have to do is zero our weapons as accurately as possible,' said Dermot. 'Spend your time zeroing.' He spoke on, giving instructions. The team was experienced. We knew what we had to do, but Dermot gave us confidence and he made it all very clear.

'I'm aiming to finish the zeroing preparations by four o'clock. That should give us plenty of time. At four I'd like to have a practice run through for the falling plates competition. That'll show how well we've zeroed our rifles and remind us how we have to approach that competition.'

The falling plates contest is often the culmination of a shooting meeting. On the bank of the butts are placed two sets of four white plates, each about 9 inches square. Two teams, each of four riflemen, line up on the 300 yards firing point. On the word 'Go' the teams run to the 200 yards firing point and fire at the plates to knock them down. The first team to knock them all down wins. The party in the butts wave a flag in front of the plates the moment the last plate in a set falls. It's the only shooting competition that has a little drama about it and the one that appeals most to spectators.

At 4 o'clock we had finished our zeroing and the falling plates team assembled. Our first team was Dermot, Corporal Rothwell, Little Steel and me, considered to be four of the best rifle shots in the battalion.

'Everyone happy with the zeroing? It looked pretty good to me,' said Dermot. We all nodded.

'The way to approach the falling plates is not to rush it. Don't sprint, just double at a good stride. Then we'll arrive unpuffed on the firing line and be able to shoot well. Take the pace from me. The important thing is to arrive on the point with as near normal breathing as possible so that you can hit your plate with your first shot.'

We all nodded.

For our practice Burgo had formed a second team to compete against us. Both teams lined up on the 300 yard firing point. The plates were up on the bank in the butts. Someone said 'Go'. We all started. One or two of Burgo's team darted off. They were all on the firing point when we still had a few yards to go. As we arrived I saw one of their plates fall. Our team fired as one man. Our flag came up instantly. Burgo's team still had three plates standing.

'If we can do that every time we're in with a good chance,' said Dermot. 'The one practice is enough. No point in doing any more. Well done, everyone. Thank you, Burgo and your team.'

That evening in the officers' mess there was quite a gathering, with officers representing most of the units in the division present. Some of us had had to double up again to make room, and several of our guests had brought their wives, as the meeting was a social occasion. We had decided to have a buffet dinner as there would be too many to sit round the dining room table. Ben Wildbore let it be known it was not an evening for gambling but that we could have a game the following night among ourselves if we wanted. Ben had started to mock our gambling as a way, I believed, of trying to control it. Burgo had some success taking side bets. I spent the evening looking after our guests so I didn't have time to talk to anyone in the regiment, or to Kitty. There was an eve-of-battle tension in the air that made for a sober, considered evening.

By noon the following day we were running neck and neck for the championship with the Household Cavalry. We had won a few of the individual matches but not enough to give us a lead. In the team events the Household Cavalry had won the light machine gun and the sub machine gun matches. We had won the pistol match and some of the rifle matches. The day would be decided by the falling plates competition, the last match that was to take place in the afternoon. This was a bit of a setback for us as we had hoped to end the morning with a clear lead. The falling plates match was notoriously fluky. Spectators and competitors broke for lunch, served in the various mess tents at the back of the range. High excitement was running as the competition was still open. Burgo and Adam were running a covert book. They'd made the Household Cavalry and us joint favourites and were doing a brisk trade.

The falling plates match took a little over half an hour as, with fourteen teams, there had to be four rounds with two byes into the second round. Burgo and Adam had struck the correct odds. We met the Household Cavalry in the final. We had sailed through all our rounds, always arriving last on the firing point. Our competitors generally had one or two plates down before we started firing. Our first volley knocked all our plates down. Our flag always went up first.

A large crowd had gathered, shouting encouragement. Many of my platoon were watching including Catchpole, who had Kaiser on a lead. We paraded on the 300 yard firing point, loaded our rifles and stood easy. The umpire said 'Are you ready?' and then 'Go'. We doubled at a good pace in line with Dermot. The Household Cavalry team raced ahead and gained the firing point first. They shot a plate down, then another. We were on the firing point. A third plate went down. We fired as one. All our plates went down. Our flag was up. But so was the Household Cavalry's flag. It could only have been a difference of a split second. We had lost.

We unloaded our rifles. The umpire inspected them and commiserated with us. Dermot congratulated the winners and we gave them three cheers. Then Dermot drew us together. 'You did everything I asked you to do. You shot brilliantly in every round. You must be proud to have got into the final. It couldn't have been closer.'

In the distance I saw Colonel Dennis striding towards us. Even when he was 50 yards away I could see that he was looking black and fingering his signet ring. We were still standing together as a group when he started to address us from 10 yards.

'What a disgraceful performance. How dare you amble to the firing point. You've let down the battalion. You've let down the regiment. You've let down the light infantry. Beaten by a cavalry regiment. I've never seen anything like it in my life.'

He glared at us.

'May I say something, Colonel?' said Dermot.

'I wouldn't dare say anything if I were you.'

'Colonel, the blame is mine. I gave the orders. The team carried out my orders to the letter. We have had no time to train. We did our best. The fault, if there is a fault, is mine.'

'Well it's a disgrace, Captain Lisle. Report to me in the orderly room at 0900 hours tomorrow.'

He strode off, still fingering his ring. We broke up. Little Steel and Rothwell looked like two sad dogs who had just been beaten. Dermot looked away and walked off slowly towards the officers' mess tent. I turned to Little Steel and Rothwell.

'It's just temporary disappointment on the colonel's part. He won't hold it against you,' I said.

'No,' replied Little Steel, 'but he'll hold it against Captain Lisle. The captain did his best. He's a great shot and a great officer.' He shook his head, saluted and marched smartly off with Rothwell.

When I got to the officers' mess tent Dermot was taking off his shooting equipment in the hallway and hanging it up on a stand. Then he turned round, saw me and tore his beret off, throwing it on the ground.

'Fuck,' he said. 'Fuck. Fuck. Fuck.'

As he sang out the fourth 'fuck' Colonel Dennis walked straight past him and out of the tent.

'Dermot,' I said, 'I'm so sorry. You did your very best. We weren't allowed to train. Even if we had been I don't see how we could have done better in the falling plates. It was the other competitions in which we could have done better.'

'I know, I know. But that won't wash with the colonel. He's not a shot. He doesn't understand shooting. He just thinks I was being idle and too clever. And then he saw me shouting "Fuck" and throwing my beret on the ground.'

Val Portal walked into the hallway.

'Oh dear, Dermot,' he said, 'whatever have you done? Colonel Dennis's out of his mind with anger. He wants to see you now.'

Dermot put his equipment back on and his beret. He followed Val out of the tent. I followed too. Some way away stood Colonel Dennis, smouldering among a large crowd of officers, soldiers and some wives. He turned on Dermot. In front of everyone he shouted, 'You are a disgraceful officer. You have shown disgraceful disloyalty. I will not put up with such disloyalty from you or anyone else. Any further disloyalty and you'll be out of my battalion.'

8

Regimental days

Jasper returned from England in disgrace.

'What happened?' I asked as we moved Kaiser's basket back to Jasper's room.

'I did well, very well. I passed out top. They asked me if I'd like to transfer to the Household Cavalry. The last night I went out to celebrate with two of the other officers. After dinner we went to a rather seedy night club. They were egging me on to have a woman. I got rather drunk. We all did. A fracas started. Not by us, but somehow we got involved. I'm not sure how, but we did. The next thing we knew the police had arrived and we were all in the clink at Bow Street.'

'Doesn't sound like you, Jasper. You usually go to sleep when you get drunk.'

'I just got caught up in it all. After a bit the adjutant from Knightsbridge Barracks arrived. The police serjeant in charge at Bow Street knew him. I think they'd served together. The adjutant got us discharged but my post course leave was stopped and I was sent back here on the next boat. The adjutant was quite nice about it, warned me about seedy night clubs. Not so Colonel Dennis. He gave me a terrible dressing down. I'd let him down. I'd let the regiment down. I'd let the light infantry down. I was disloyal.'

'We've had a bit of that here, lately.'

'How could I have been disloyal? I might have been a fool, but not disloyal. He said he'd have to tell the colonel of the regiment as another regiment had been involved. Next time anything like this happened, he said, he'd put me in front of the general. I was hardly allowed to say a word. And he never acknowledged I'd come top. I don't suppose I'll ever ride Red Ember again.'

'There are other horses,' I said, thinking of Kitty's new hunter. 'Why don't we go riding? You can tell me all about the course and show off your new prowess. Kaiser can come too.'

'I don't want to run into Colonel Dennis again today. Even at school no one ever talked to me like that. I'd have rather been beaten. At least you shook hands afterwards.'

'I always thought that rather bogus.'

'I'll be twenty-one in a few days. That's something to look forward to. I get my trust fund with no trustees to wrangle with any more. I'll buy a horse, maybe two. Yes, let's go riding. What's been happening here?'

On our way out of the mess we ran into Dermot Lisle.

'Just the two I want to see,' said Dermot. Turning to Jasper he said, 'I hear you've been accused of being disloyal. So have I. Don't worry. There'll be a lot more branded like us before the training season's over.'

He grinned at Jasper.

'The 101st Armored Cavalry has invited us to celebrate the Fourth of July with them. Colonel Smiley has asked Colonel Dennis and all the officers and serjeants who were on the first border patrol. He also wants us to take a colour party to take part in their parade. That's you, Jasper.'

'Does the colonel want me to carry the regimental colour?'

'Colonel Dennis doesn't seem to mind who carries the colour as long as he doesn't. He doesn't really like the Americans and he doesn't really want to go. He's left it all to me as I'm responsible for liaison with the Americans. I thought you'd like to carry the colour, Jasper."

'Yes, I would. Thank you, Dermot.'

'We'll wear number one dress. It'll be fun.'

Jasper and I walked on down to the stables.

I told him what had happened at the end of the divisional small arms meeting.

'I feel better already,' said Jasper.

There was quite a crowd at the stables. Kitty was there with her new hunter Vampire. He looked every bit as good a horse as Red Ember. Ben, Burgo, and Little Steel were already mounted.

'What are you up to?' asked Jasper.

'We're training for the pentathlon. Are you coming?' said Ben.

'You only need three in a team.'

'We need a reserve. Come on. Find a horse and follow us.'

'Would you like to ride Vampire?' asked Kitty. 'Go on, I'd love to know what you think of him, Jasper.'

Jasper mounted Vampire and moved off with Ben, Burgo, and Little Steel. I followed on one of the hacks. Then Kitty, Horace, and Harry Fox followed with several others. We were quite a troop as we trotted out of the gates of the barracks and up into the forest.

'Having a lovely summer, darling.'

Kitty had ridden up beside me.

'Not too bad.'

'How's your houri?'

'Houri?'

'That Turkish tart.'

'If you mean Rana, she's not mine. And if you think a houri means a tart, you're mistaken. A houri is a virgin of the Muslim paradise promised as a wife to a believer. I don't qualify.'

'I bet you wish you did. You'd make a wonderful husband for her. Think of all those dusky little Turkish babies she would bear you.'

'I can't afford a wife, Kitty. Why can't we just be friends as we used to be?'

'You abandoned me, Miles. I was having a lousy time with Horace and you left me. Now Horace ignores me. He was quite interested when I bought Vampire. But Vampire is too strong for me and he despises me now, I think. I need you. I love you. Why have you abandoned me?'

'People were talking. Even Colonel Dennis suspected something was going on between us.'

'How on earth did he know? And what did that matter?'

'I overheard a conversation between him and Algy. Algy said he didn't think there was anything in it, that we were just old friends. Colonel Dennis said he was glad to hear that or he would have to post me, and Horace too, out of the battalion, possibly out of the regiment.'

'What a terrible spoilsport that man is. How do you all put up with him? Miles, marry me. I promise I'd be faithful.'

'Kitty, you know that's impossible. I mean marriage. I haven't any money, not the kind of money you've got used to. I'd ruin your life. It would be a regimental scandal. It would ruin both our lives.'

'I thought you'd say that. But I'm yours when you want me, darling.'

There was nothing more I could say. After a while she broke into a canter and rode off to join the party in front of us. She looked incredibly desirable. I felt miserable.

That night, after dinner, we had a game of chemmy to welcome Jasper back. Before we started playing Ben Wildbore said, 'While you were away in England, Jasper, Colonel Dennis looked at the bridge book and got in a bait over the amounts we were playing for. He's let it be known through Algy that he'd like us to play for lower stakes. We discussed this among ourselves. We've decided losses must be kept below £5 and be entered in the bridge book. Lowering the stakes may, I'm told, take much of the interest out of the game for some. If, therefore, a few decide on occasion to play for higher stakes they must settle between themselves and not through the bridge book. A game is automatically a bridge book game unless there is an agreement otherwise. Do you understand?'

'What happened to Colonel Dennis while I was away?'

'He showed his true colours,' said Burgo.

We settled down to play. It was an uneventful evening; we played for two hours and drank a lot of hock and seltzer. No one won or lost much and the winnings and losses went into the bridge book. As Burgo was writing them in Jasper said, 'Next week it's my birthday. I'll be twenty-one. No more trustees. I'm going to give a dinner at the Lucullus and I want you all to come. And I'm not asking Colonel Dennis.'

A few days later the party to go to the Fourth of July celebrations at the 101st US Armored Cavalry assembled outside battalion headquarters. Colonel Dennis led in his staff car, taking Adam with him. By rights he should have taken Dermot who had organised the day and was our liaison with the Americans. Dermot accompanied Algy in Algy's jeep and they took me with them. Then followed another two jeeps with officers and serjeants. Finally Horace came in his Bentley. He commanded X company now, which had provided the first border patrol; he had changed places with Jack Trench. Jasper, with the colour party, had left the day before to take part in the rehearsals for the parade.

The parade was swanky. When the American army wants to show off it can. The 101st Armored Cavalry were all dressed in their yellow scarves, steel helmets and white belts and gaiters. They paraded in their armoured cars, tanks and jeeps and, in perfect ranks, drove past Colonel Smiley on his saluting base, crowded with spectators. Algy sat next to Colonel Smiley, the rest of us sat in the crowd. I couldn't see Colonel Dennis. The regimental colour party, led by Jasper carrying the regimental colour, marched on. The US military band played the 'Keel Row' and the colour party doubled past Colonel Smiley, colour flying. The band, larger than ours and heavy with brass, played the bugle fanfares on trumpets sounding very grand. Then the colour party marched off to 'The Trojans'. We all stood for that and for The Star-Spangled Banner that followed. We broke up and were guided towards tents, pitched next to the parade ground.

Jasper was overseeing the furling of the regimental colour to put it in its casing when Colonel Smiley said, 'I'd like to look at your regimental colour. It's a fine flag.'

Jasper held the staff upright while one of the colour serjeants held the flag out to its full width. It was made of heavy royal blue silk, the three outer edges fringed in gold thread. The staff was topped by a gilded king's crown. In the centre of the flag was a roundel embellished in gold leaves within which was embroidered 'The Prince Regent's Light Infantry' surmounted by a king's crown. On either side of the roundel battle honours were stitched in gold thread and beneath were the regimental mottos: *Cede nullis* and *Nec timor nec spes.*

'Hey, what do they mean, Algy?' asked Colonel Smiley, pointing at the mottoes.

'*Cede nullis* means surrender to none. We adopted it from a French Eagle which we captured at Waterloo.'

'And the second?'

'Neither fear nor hope.'

'Now those are soldier's mottoes I can understand. What about all these names?'

'They're our battle honours. There at the top left is Corunna, the first battle we fought in the Peninsula against Napoleon's armies.'

'Where's Anzio?' said Smiley. 'That was a tight hole, Algy. I'm not sure I'd like to repeat that. You certainly won that one. That deserves to be on your colours.'

'The First and Second World War honours are on the queen's colour which we only carry when a representative of the royal family is present.'

'Let me see what other battles are here. Washington? Why Washington?'

'That's the battle when we beat you and burnt the White House.'

'You what?'

'You know, in the war of 1812. We captured Washington and the president fled. He very kindly left his dinner on the dining table so the regiment ate it and said how thoughtful of the president. Then we burnt the house. Why do you think it's called the White House? Because you had to paint it white to cover up all the parts we'd burnt.'

'Nuts.'

'It's in the history books. We celebrate it as one of our regimental days on August 25th every year.'

'You burned the White House? That's the doggonest tale I ever heard.'

'Then you see Waterloo there to the right. That's when we thrashed Bonaparte on 18th June, 1815. We only just got back in time from fighting you. We celebrate that day too. This year we can't celebrate either on the right day because of exercises. We're going to have a single regimental day later this month. You must come.'

'Hey, fellers,' shouted Colonel Smiley, 'these Limeys burned the White House. Look, it's on their colour. Washington. I'll be damned.'

A crowd began to gather round.

'Yes, these Limeys, The Prince Regent's Light Infantry, say they burned the White House down in the war of 1812. Whad'ya say to that?'

'Maybe it's time they did it again, Colonel.'

There was a roar of laughter and we all went into the tent.

A banquet lay before us. I found myself with Adam.

'What have you done with Colonel Dennis?'

'It's what he's done with himself. There we were, perfectly happy quoting Horace at each other all the way here. As soon as we arrive he becomes semi-hysterical, says he hates the Americans, can't think why he allowed Dermot to accept the invitation, wished he hadn't come, dumped me with a message for Algy, and sped off.'

'How could he? He's unbalanced. All that love you said you'd give him doesn't seem to work, Adam.'

'I think he's envious of the relationship between Algy and

Colonel Smiley. I suspect that when we arrived, he remembered Anzio and all that meant to him. Have you noticed how Algy's got twice the number of medals that Colonel Dennis has. That must rankle too.'

'What did Algy say?'

'He said, "Oh, not again. Thank you, Adam. Now you go and enjoy yourself." '

'What did he mean by "Oh, not again"?'

'That puzzled me for a bit. Do you remember how Colonel Dennis excused himself from the first border patrol saying he had to go to a conference at Rhine Army Headquarters? I think he made it up. There wasn't a conference. He didn't want to meet Smiley. Nor did he today.'

On the morning of his twenty-first birthday Jasper went down into the town with Adam and Harry to organise his dinner party at the Lucullus. Herr Schwarz opened a magnum of Bollinger for them, they told me, which they drank as they discussed the menu. They returned to the mess in a merry mood. There was a lot of laughter at lunch at Jasper's expense as he had received few presents and nothing had arrived from his mother. The mail was erratic and could arrive at any time. The day dragged on for him. He rode with the pentathletes in the afternoon but there was still no mail when he returned and, by the time we were all ready to go to the Lucullus for his birthday treat, he was in a puzzled mood, puzzled that the expected mail from his mother, at least, had not arrived.

'I can't understand it,' he said, sitting in the front of Harry Fox's car on the way down to the town, 'I can't understand why I haven't heard from Mummy. She's always so punctilious about birthdays and she knows the post here is unreliable. It's so unlike her.'

Herr Schwarz met us at the door and showed us into a private room we'd not been in before. There were six of us: Burgo and Adam, Harry and Jasper, Finbar and me.

'This is the best of my rooms,' said Herr Schwarz, and, producing a magnum of Krug, said, 'and this is the best of champagnes.

I wish you, *Herr Leutnant,* the very best of birthdays.'

'There's a limerick about Krug,' said Harry, 'that my father taught me:

> There was a young lady of Ay
> Whose price was exceedingly high.
> Her price to the Yanks
> Was ten thousand francs
> Or a magnum of Krug Extra Dry.'

'Alpha plus,' said Adam.

We drank the magnum and then sat down to a first course of caviare and vodka. Course after course followed, chosen, as far as I could see, by Adam and Herr Schwarz. Bottle after bottle was produced, chosen by Harry and Herr Schwarz. The main topic of conversation was Colonel Dennis.

'He hasn't spoken to me again since he bollocked me on my return,' said Jasper. 'You'd have thought we would have kissed and made up by now.'

'Colonel Dennis doesn't look like a kiss and make up type,' said Burgo.

'That's what worries me. Gosh, Harry, I could drink vodka like this forever.'

'Only have one glass,' said Adam. 'It's lethal, and too much will ruin your dinner.'

'Aren't you imagining it?' said Burgo. 'Maybe it's just because you haven't seen him in the mess. He hasn't been in much lately.'

'I'd like to think that, but Corporal O'Reilly in the stables has made it clear to me that I'm not to ride Red Ember.'

'That's vicious. That's harbouring a grudge,' said Burgo. 'Guy Surtees would reprimand one on occasion but that was the end of it. He would come into the mess afterwards and have a drink with you.'

'He does harbour grudges,' I said. 'Look at the way he's treating Dermot. He's declared war on him. Dermot can do no right in his eyes.'

'It's not going to be much fun if he's declared war on me. Harry, this burgundy is delicious. What is it?'

'Montrachet.'

'I could drink this all night.'

'Wait until you try the Romanée. What'll happen to Dermot? It can't go on as it is,' said Harry.

'Dermot will be all right. He goes to the Staff College in the autumn. He'll be well out of it,' I said.

'I can't go to the Staff College for years,' said Jasper. 'Perhaps I should ask for a transfer?'

'Jasper, you're taking it too seriously. It'll all blow over. He'll find fault with someone else and then he'll forget all about you,' said Finbar.

'I don't want him to forget all about me. I want to ride Red Ember. You're right about this Romanée, Harry. We haven't drunk anything like this before here.'

'It's Romanée St Vivant General Marey Monge. I've no idea who General Marey Monge was, but I thought a general's wine was fit for the occasion.'

'My great grandfather was a general. Do you think I could be?'

'General Jasper. Let's all drink to Jasper becoming a general. General Jasper,' said Burgo.

We all raised our glasses. 'General Jasper,' we said.

'Adam, you said you'd like to be a general,' I said

'Like to be, but going to be is up to the gods. *Dis volentibus.*'

'Do you believe in the gods like the ancients did?' asked Jasper.

'The ancients knew a thing or two. A knowledge of Greece and Rome plays a civilising role in the affairs of man.'

'Tell us.'

'For example, the ancients give us a belief in tolerance. That is, they will teach you not to believe that anyone has a monopoly of the truth as the churches claim, and the communists too. The ancients teach you to believe in reason.'

'Not too much reason, sometimes, in military affairs,' said Burgo.

'Or tolerance,' said Jasper.

'True enough,' said Adam, ' and all the more need for it. Then the ancients will help you to reject enthusiasm and faiths. The more you think about enthusiasm and faiths, the more you realise how blind they can be and how ridiculous the postures they sometimes ask you to adopt.'

'Didn't someone say "nothing great was ever achieved without enthusiasm"?' said Finbar.

'Emerson. That depends on what you consider to be great. A little enthusiasm in itself can be delightful but unbridled enthusiasm leads to all sorts of dangers and excessive behaviour. Look at the Nazis. Or the communists. Remember μηδὲν ἄγαν. Nothing too much. One glass of vodka with the caviare is enough. Two spoils it.'

'I could drink a bottle of General Marey Monge,' said Jasper.

'Under the table you would go,' said Finbar.

'Didn't the ancients invent democracy?' said Burgo.

'There is much good in democracy,' said Adam. 'It gives you freedom and hope. It's the only political form known to man that allows him to dismiss his leaders peacefully. Also, and this is what I think you imply Burgo, it gives a loud voice to fools. The ancients recognised this and prepared accordingly.'

'What about military values?' asked Jasper.

'The ancients admired courage and teach you not to fear death. Either it resembles sleep or it will reveal some new facet of existence that will be a delight to examine. And the ancients admired physical and athletic excellence so necessary to military life.'

'Let's drink to the ancients and military life,' proposed Jasper.

'The ancients and military life,' we all said and drained our glasses.

They were quickly refilled.

'Is Kitty going to let you ride Vampire in the races this winter?' asked Harry.

'Vampire's a lovely horse, maybe better even than Red Ember. But won't Horace want to ride him when it comes to racing him?'

'Horace,' said Burgo, 'isn't a jockey. He's a polo player par excellence. I'm sure Kitty will want you to race Vampire. You're training him with her, aren't you? Besides nobody knows Vampire's form. If you rode him well you'd get the credit. If, on the other hand, you failed to win on Red Ember everyone would blame you'

'Well, that's settled then. I don't think Colonel Dennis will ever ask me to ride Red Ember again.'

'Did he ever say you would race Red Ember?'

'He indicated I would if he wasn't able to. But, no. Now I've got my own money from my trust I'll buy a horse that'll beat both of them. Harry, any of General Monge's burgundy left?'

'Yes, isn't it good?'

'I'd like to drink this every day.'

'You'd soon get bored with it,' said Adam. 'The secret of life is to have a routine of carefully planned changes of pleasures. Drinking the same wine every night is like making love to the same person every night. Why do you think a Turkish sultan, unfettered by Christian ethics, had so many girls in his harem? For variety.'

'Not just girls,' said Burgo. 'Do you know this one?

> 'Then up spoke the King of Siam
> "For fucking I don't give a damn.
> You may think it odd of me
> I far prefer sodomy.
> They call me a bugger. I am."''

'Who taught you that?'

'My father when I was small. We all fell about laughing but none of us had any idea why it was funny.'

'I never really knew my father,' said Jasper.

'Algy said he was a brave and charming man. It was a great misfortune he was killed clearing the way to get to Dunkirk.'

'Algy's been bloody good to me,' said Jasper. 'I'd like to drink a toast to Algy. I can't wait for Algy to command. Come on, everybody, Algy.'

'Algy,' we all said with the last of the Romanée St Vivant.

'Pity Dennis Parker Brown is such a prick,' said Burgo.

'I don't think he's got a prick,' said Harry.

'He's got a prick all right,' said Adam, 'but it never engorges. He's essentially "down penis" about everything. Pleasure is *verboten*. Down Penis Brown is what he is. For short D.P.Brown.'

'D.P. Brown is dead right, Adam,' said Burgo. 'D.P. Brown,' he repeated.

We all chanted, 'D.P.Brown. Down Penis Brown. D.P.Brown.' No one toasted him.

'I thought you were going to give him love, Adam?' said Burgo.

'Yes, he needs love all right. I'm not sure I've got enough, but I'll have to go on trying. We all must.'

'What are we going to drink now, Harry?' asked Jasper.

'Noble rot.'

'Noble rot?'

'Trockenbeerenauslese,' said Harry. 'They pick the grapes when they're ripe and shrivelled. It makes a deliciously sweet wine that will age for years. This wine is as old as you are, Jasper. You'll love it.'

'This wine must be costing a mint,' said Burgo.

'Don't worry about that,' said Jasper, 'I get my trust fund today. I hope it is costing a mint.'

We all drank deeply. The wine was delicious.

'Anyone know this one?' said Burgo:

> 'Then up spoke the Sheik of Algiers
> Who said to his harem, "My dears,
> You may think it odd of me
> I'm giving up sodomy,
> There'll be fucking tonight." Loud cheers.'

'Alpha plus, plus,' said Jasper.

'Do you like fucking, Jasper?' asked Adam.

'Can't say I've done much. Not like you, I expect.'

'I've had my share of boys and girls,' said Adam.

'Very Roman,' said Burgo.

'No, Greek to be accurate,' replied Adam.

'You won't have had much of either here,' said Burgo.

'I'm not without hope.'

'Tell us about the ancients and sex,' said Finbar.

'The ancients delighted in the pleasures of the body and had no inhibitions. How pleasure came was immaterial. Sexual pleasure was to be taken and enjoyed with whoever took one's fancy.'

'I think girls are a distraction,' said Jasper. 'What was it Napoleon said? "Women are the dalliance of the warrior and the occupation of the waster." Time for some brandy.'

'Herr Schwarz has got some Napoleon brandy,' said Harry.

'Which Napoleon?' said Burgo.

'Napoleon the Third. That's old enough. They're all a blend anyway. It's good grand champagne cognac.'

'I'd prefer a marc de Bourgogne,' said Adam.

'You shall have one,' said Jasper. 'Who'd like to end with champagne? What about some Krug? What about this, Harry?'

> 'There was a young lady of Ay
> Whose price was exceedingly high.
> Her price to young Fritz
> For a night at the Ritz
> Was a jeroboam of Krug Extra Dry.'

'Doesn't scan.'

'More.'

'What about this?' said Harry.

> 'There was a young lady of Ay
> Whose price was excessively high.
> Her price to the Boche
> Was oodles of dosh
> And a methuselah of Krug Extra Dry.'

'Something wrong there,' said Burgo.

'Delectable dinner,' said Adam.

'I've never had better,' said Finbar.

'Let's go on to the *Junkernschenke*.'

'Yes, let's take Jasper to the *Junkernschenke* and buy him a woman.'

'That's very generous of you chaps, but I want to get back to barracks to see if anything has arrived from my mother. You go on if you like.'

'Come on, Jasper. A lovely svelte fräulein. Or we might find you a German boy.'

'Find one for yourself, Adam, but not for me. It's my birthday and I decide on treats today. Harry will you drive me back to barracks? Ah, Herr Schwarz, that was a magnificent meal. We couldn't have dined better anywhere. Would you send the bill up to the *Kaserne* for me tomorrow?'

'It will be my pleasure, *Herr Leutnant*. It was wonderful for me to see you young officers enjoying yourselves. It reminded me of my days in France with the panzer grenadiers. Except we always finished our evenings singing marching songs. I am grateful you did not do that at the Lucullus.'

Burgo, Adam, and Finbar went on to the *Junkernschenke*. Harry drove Jasper and me back to barracks.

Corporal Cheke was waiting for us in the mess.

'The mail arrived at battalion headquarters, gentlemen, shortly after you left. I asked the post corporal to bring it over to the mess immediately and not leave it until tomorrow. There are some parcels for you, Mr Knox, and some letters.'

'Corporal, that was so thoughtful of you,' said Jasper. He was beginning to slur his words. He had drunk an enormous amount. 'Can you fix us some champagne while I open my letters?'

'I've put a bottle of Bollinger in an ice bucket in the anteroom with some glasses. Your letters are in your drawer. The parcels are on the hall table.'

Jasper went to the chest of drawers that served as a mailbox for each of us. There were thirty-six drawers, each with a brass plate on which was inscribed an officer's initials and surname.

'Here's one from Mummy and another one from the lawyers. Several more too.'

We walked into the anteroom.

'Miles, do open the champagne and pour some while I read Mummy's letter,' said Jasper as he threw himself into an armchair. I opened the bottle and poured two glasses. There was no one else in the room. I tried handing one to Jasper but he was too engrossed in his mother's letter to notice so I put it on the table beside him. Jasper read the letter, his face rapt and impenetrable. He read the letter again. It took some time. I sipped my champagne. Then he let the letter drop on to the floor and tore open the letter that looked as though it came from the lawyers. He read that through twice, his face still showing not a sign of emotion. Then he lay back in his chair.

'I might have known. Bugger, bugger, bugger, bugger Colonel bloody Down Penis Brown. Read them. Read them both. O bugger.'

I picked up the letter from his mother.

My darling Jasper,

How I wish I could be with you on this twenty-first birthday of yours, my dearest boy. I send you so many hugs and kisses. It is just wonderful for me to know that you are in your father's regiment, following in his footsteps in the British Army of the Rhine where your father served with the regiment after the Great War and doing, from what you say, many of the things he used to do.

Now, darling, I have something to say and I do so wish I didn't have to say it to you on this of all days. You have always been exuberant and adventurous I know, but Colonel Dennis has written to me to say you got into a little trouble when you were in England on your equitation course – is that why you didn't come to see me? I was so disappointed. He said he also thought you were gambling and drinking too much and he had had to have a word with you about the fracas you got yourself into in London. He went on to say that he didn't think you were really ready yet to handle your trust fund yourself and recommended – really quite strongly – that your money should remain in trust for you until he has been able to help you settle down a bit.

It was so good and thoughtful of him to write. Your father never had much time for Dennis – I won't tell you what he used to call him – but Dennis has clearly changed since those days and is really trying to help you and has your best interests at heart. It is so good of him to let you ride Red Ember. From what you say in your letters I realise how much you respect him.

So I went to see Mr Wood at Broadhurst, Wood, and Pope who is your senior trustee. He said there is a clause in your trust deed that states it's up to the trustees whether they hand over your trust when you're twenty-one or later. So I agreed with him to postpone it until we are all sure you are able to handle it wisely.

Dearest Jasper, I know you will be disappointed but you mustn't be. You are still very young though I know you feel very grown up. Mr Wood said he would write to you about your trust and allowance.

Darling, have a wonderful birthday. I enclose a cheque for £25. Do spend it carefully. And do write soon and tell me all your news.

With all my love, Mummy.

The letter from Mr Wood read:

Dear Jasper,

There is a clause in your trust deed that stipulates you are to inherit the capital of your trust fund on your twenty-first or twenty-fifth birthday at the discretion of your trustees. As you are twenty-one this month I write to tell you the trustees' decision.

In consultation with your mother who, I understand, has taken into account the views expressed to her by your commanding officer Lieutenant Colonel Parker Brown, the trustees have decided that it would be best for the trust to remain in force until your twenty-fifth birthday. However, the trustees feel that the trust can well bear increments to your allowance and propose to increase your allowance by £50 each year until you are twenty-five.

I hope you are enjoying the army.

Yours sincerely, Augustus Wood.

'Twenty-five quid from mummy. Fifty quid from my trustees. Will it cover the cost of the dinner? I don't think I'm going to open my parcels. They'll be poisoned too, I wouldn't wonder. Bloody, fucking Down Penis Brown.'

While we were preparing for the regimental day, the pentathlon team left for the Rhine Army pentathlon championship. Ben, Burgo, and Little Steel formed the team, with Jasper as reserve. They didn't really need to take a reserve but Algy thought it would be good for Jasper to stay out of barracks for a bit. He was concerned that Jasper might force a showdown with Colonel Dennis. The news about Jasper's trust fund had been picked up by the officers. Algy thought a week at the pentathlon championship would allow Jasper to cool his heels.

The team returned with honours. They had not won but had come third of the fourteen teams. Burgo had been placed second individually. All the others had come in the top half, so Ben and his team returned to acclaim. Military pentathlon, as it was called, was a series of tasks that might confront a mounted courier under historical battlefield conditions. Besides riding, it comprised gruelling tests in fencing, shooting, swimming and running. Some thought it anachronistic. Most conceded it called for great skill and endurance. Ben, Burgo, Little Steel, and Jasper all returned to barracks with considerable personal kudos.

With all the pressures of the training season and competitive events we hadn't been able to fit in a battalion sports day. It was decided to make 'Waterloo & Washington Day' our sports day. I was to run some of the field events. I needed to clarify some technical points, as I hadn't done this before, and I thought Dermot would know the answers as he knew the answers to most things. So, watching the bustle around me, I walked across the parade ground to Dermot's office in battalion headquarters. I met Dermot storming out of the adjutant's office looking thunderous.

'Dermot?'

'Come up to my office.'

I followed him up the stairs and sat down in his office. He stood at the window, looking out on the town and the great plain beyond.

'A few minutes ago I received official notification from Rhine Army Headquarters that I was to report to division as a Grade III staff officer on Monday next. I couldn't understand it. I went straight to Val, as adjutant, and asked him what on earth it meant. He said, "Hasn't Colonel Dennis told you?" "Told me what?" I said, "I'm due to go to the Staff College in two months' time. Why post me to division?" Val then said he thought the Colonel had told me. He fiddled with some papers in a tray, pulled out one and handed it to me saying "Haven't you seen this?" Here it is, Miles. Read it.'

I took the piece of paper. It was a memorandum from Colonel Dennis to Rhine Army Headquarters.

> Captain Lisle may well have an outstanding record in the field, but my experience of this officer's staff work, while serving me as battalion intelligence officer, leads me to believe that he is not yet ready to attend a Staff College course. I recommend that he be transferred to a division or brigade headquarters as a staff officer third class to gain staff experience, and that his attendance at Staff College be postponed.

I looked at Dermot. He continued to look out of the window.

'I'm going to resign. That's damning. I've never had a report like that. And I'll never live it down. They've given my vacancy to someone else. I know I had one. Algy told me. And now this Machiavellian trick done behind my back. I've no alternative but to resign.'

'Don't do anything until you've talked to Algy.'

'Algy's away. I'm so angry. I'm going to resign.'

'Dermot, don't do anything until you've talked to Algy.'

'What can Algy do? It's all decided. Look, here's my posting order signed major general. What can Algy do?'

'What about the colonel of the regiment?'

'He's no more than a figurehead. Besides Colonel Dennis – what do you all call him now? Down Penis Brown? – Well D. P. Brown has the colonel of the regiment round his little finger. He's a great arse licker is D. P. Brown.'

'Oh Dermot, just wait. There must be something that can be done.'

'No. I could take the humiliation D. P. Brown meted out in the knowledge I was going to Staff College, that I was on the promotion ladder, that I might command the battalion, that one day even, with luck, I might be a general. Not now. Not now. It's resignation time, now. You know,' he said turning towards me with a smile, 'I've been prepared for this. I've had my resignation written out for some time, ever since the divisional small arms meeting. All I've got to do is date it and sign it.'

He opened a drawer in his desk and took out an envelope.

'Don't Dermot. Give it to me.'

'It's no good, Miles. I've no alternative.'

He sat down, opened the envelope and laid the paper on his desk. He took his pen out of his pocket and very carefully wrote in the date and signed the letter. He folded it and put it back in the envelope. Then, with the envelope in his hand he walked to the door. I followed him downstairs. He pushed open the adjutant's door and strode in without saluting, leaving the door ajar so I could see and hear everything that happened.

'Val,' he said, 'here's my letter of resignation.'

'What?' said Val.

'My resignation. I've resigned my commission.'

'You can't do that.'

'That's one thing I can do without your or bloody Down Penis Brown's permission. Do you know that's what they call him? Down Penis Brown. You're no better, Val. When I was adjutant of this battalion I felt it my duty to look after my brother officers and stand up for them.'

'Dermot, you've no idea how difficult it is to be adjutant to Colonel Dennis. I'm doing my best, but Colonel Dennis won't listen to *any* advice.'

'Then, if you've got any guts, you should resign.'

'I can't, Dermot. That would ruin my career.'

'You're beneath contempt, Val. I pity you.'

With that he turned on his heels and strode out of the office. As he passed me he said, 'Come on, Miles. Let's go and have a drink to celebrate my resignation.'

9

Cricket in Berlin

'Are you coming to the Berlin cricket?' asked Burgo.

'Berlin cricket?' replied Adam. 'I must add that to my list of oxymorons. Are we democratising the Berliners by teaching them to play cricket?'

We were drinking preprandials in the anteroom before lunch.

'No, you ass. The British troops in Berlin have an annual cricket week. Algy's been asked to take a team.'

'And D. P. Brown? He's allowed it?'

'Surprisingly, yes,' I said.

'How on earth?'

'Algy and D.P.Brown,' I went on, 'had an almighty row. The day Dermot resigned the word went round the battalion in a flash. When Algy got back from leave that evening he came into the mess to get some whisky. Tom Body said to him that he was very sorry to hear that Dermot had resigned. It was the first Algy had heard. He was very angry. Then, on the Monday, I was in Val's office getting my instructions as duty officer when I overheard this amazing row going on in the colonel's office. There was no mistaking what it was about. My guess is that Colonel Dennis is trying to placate Algy. Besides, he probably wants to see us fall flat on our faces.'

'I see,' said Adam.

'Didn't you bat for your first eleven at school, Adam?' asked Burgo.

'Yes.'

'Well, you're coming then. So is Miles. Algy's asked me to scout around for players. Big Steel will come. He's got sure hands behind the wicket and he can bat, too. Miles has asked Catchpole. He bowled well for the depot when he first joined. Geordie Feard, too.'

'What about Tom Body?' I said. 'He was always good for a few runs.'

'Do you think he'll want to go?'

'You could ask him. Berlin is an attraction in itself. Have you asked Ben Wildbore?'

'Algy has. I've found the cricket gear in the stores. Big Steel is having a net put up on the upper parade ground this afternoon. Algy wants to hold a net practice immediately after guard mounting this evening.'

'What's the wicket in Berlin?' asked Adam.

'Matting. Same as we're going to practise on. We need two more players. Preferably bowlers.'

'What about Jasper?' suggested Adam.

'He doesn't play. It's the Army Polo Championship next week. You won't lure any of them away from that.'

'Harry, then,' said Adam, 'he told me he was a fast bowler.'

'Yes, he'd be an asset.'

'Doesn't Corporal Rothwell play?'

'He used to in Hong Kong. He's got a good eye. That's it then.'

'What about a scorer?'

'Jack Trench is going to score.'

'Oh, no. Why Trench Foot?'

'To keep an eye on us and report back to D.P. Brown.'

'I'm not going.'

'I was only teasing. Brigadier Popham has offered to score. I gather he's got some muckers in Berlin. Algy says he'll give the side some bottom. He's well known in army cricket circles. There're some good teams in Berlin. They've got grass playing fields and play a lot, unlike us.'

After guard mounting, which took place every evening at six, we gathered to practise. Big Steel had erected two nets in the top corner of the upper parade ground under support company lines. Algy, in a pair of grey flannels held up by an MCC tie serving as a belt, was sorting us out.

'I want to see what you can all do. Serjeant Major Whetting-steel and Serjeant Body get padded up. We'll throw some balls at you.'

They were both big men and they could both bat. Neither displayed great style but they had command of the wicket. None of the bowlers got a ball past them. Then Adam and Ben padded up and went in to the nets. Adam was large and stood loosely at the wicket. Catchpole bowled a fast one. Adam, hardly moving, flashed his bat and the ball flew up high over the parade ground and landed in the road below it.

'A six, I think,' said Adam.

'Bugger a six,' said Algy. 'You were caught in the outfield first ball. I want to see what you can do. Catchpole, bowl a decent length.'

Adam settled down and showed he had some good strokes. We all had a go at bowling and batting. Everyone displayed talent at something. Algy went in last. He hadn't been the captain of the army eleven for nothing. He gave a nice display of shots and then called it a day.

'We'll have another practice on Wednesday. Can you all get away? Good. We might not disgrace ourselves. I can see we've the makings of a good team.'

A week later we caught a fast train to Hanover where we were to change on to the Berlin Express. 'Express' was a euphemism. It was a military train and probably the slowest train in Germany. We had an hour or two to spare, as it didn't leave until midnight. We stood in a group with our baggage wondering how to fill in time. We were all in uniform, including Brigadier Popham.

'Any fleshpots hereabouts?' asked Adam

'Well, Sir,' said Tom Body, 'I could show you one or two, but there're too many red caps about with us being in uniform. What we really need is a place for you to have your supper.'

A captain, wearing an armband inscribed 'Railway Transport Officer', came up and saluted Brigadier Popham.

'Are you with the group from the PRLI for Berlin, Sir?'

Brigadier Popham nodded.

'If the officers would come with me, Sir, my corporal will look after the serjeants and the other ranks and the baggage. I'm afraid there's no refreshment car on the train and the facilities here are limited.'

'That's all right,' said Algy, 'we've come prepared.'

We followed the captain into a waiting room. It was clean but basic. A dozen officers were sitting around.

'Not you, staff serjeant,' the captain said to Tom Body.

'I, Sir, am the officers' mess steward and, Sir, I'm a *colour* serjeant. Private Catchpole and I have come to give our officers their supper.'

The captain looked surprised, glanced at Brigadier Popham who nodded his head again, and then withdrew.

Body and Catchpole put some tables together in a corner and, opening up a large hamper, began to lay out a tablecloth and some sandwiches. We sat down.

'Gentlemen,' said Tom Body, 'I can offer you whisky, beer or a glass of hock. And I have some ice.' Catchpole was putting plates and glasses on the table.

'You certainly make yourselves comfortable, Algy,' said Brigadier Popham.

'Any fool can be uncomfortable,' replied Algy, 'as my first serjeant said to me.'

'I'll have whisky, Colour, no ice,' said Popham. 'Where and when was that, Algy?'

'So will I, Body, and I'll have some of your ice. In India. I joined the Second Battalion in Rawalpindi in 1936. If you drank any alcohol in India it was whisky. We even drank whisky at dinner.

There wasn't any wine, partly because it had to be shipped from Europe, partly because it was expensive, but mainly because it didn't suit the climate. Whisky was also thought to be medicinal, that is, good for you. As young officers we didn't drink much in India, not half as much as you all seem to drink now. There were too many things to do. We'd be up at dawn and in bed early. Where were you before the war?'

'I never got to India. I was in Egypt in the thirties. We were completely mechanised and well trained, but we had time to enjoy ourselves. There was very good duck shooting. What did you do in India?'

'There was a lot of football, polo, and cricket, but the colonel encouraged me to shoot. He wouldn't give me forty-eight hours to go poodle faking in Delhi, but he gave me a month to shoot a tiger. You've seen the tiger skins in the mess? Next time you're in I'll show you mine. But the soldiering was simple. We hadn't one lorry. All the transport was drawn by mules and the company commanders were mounted on horses. Fine for keeping law and order or fighting on the frontier, but we couldn't have stopped a single panzer.'

'Did you think we'd lose India?' asked Adam.

'Never crossed our minds.'

'There was talk,' said Popham, 'about self-government but we didn't think it would happen in our lifetime.'

'What's happening to the empire?' asked Adam

'What do you mean?'

'There're trouble spots everywhere. Egypt, Malaya, now Kenya. We had to get out of Palestine.'

'Palestine was only a mandate, not empire. We were always going to leave. It looks as if we are winning now in Malaya. The enemy there is communism. Kenya will soon be under control. The problem there lies with only one tribe, the Kikuyu. There's always been trouble in Egypt, especially over the Suez Canal. You've got to consider each separately, Adam. You can't generalise about the empire.'

'I disagree with you, Brigadier,' said Algy. 'The empire as we knew it has gone. Slowly all these countries will become self-governing within the British Commonwealth. They'll remain red on the map but they'll get the right to rule themselves.'

'Will the army still be needed? I joined the army to see the world,' said Burgo.

'I don't see why not in your lifetime,' said Algy. 'We'll have to protect ourselves and what's left of the empire. The cold war looks as if it's here to stay.'

'Are we here to stay in Germany?' asked Adam.

'Yes, for a long time.'

'I like being in Germany. Life's civilized here,' said Adam.

'That,' said Algy, 'is because you have been enjoying the privileges of an army of occupation which will soon come to an end.'

'What do you think of the idea of a new German army?' asked Burgo.

'It has to happen. The West Germans are our allies now. We couldn't stop the Russians without them.'

'Can we stop the Russians *with* them? Surely the Russians could push us into the Atlantic within a week?'

'We are only a screen to delay them. What stops them is the atom bomb.'

'There do seem to be a lot of problems,' said Adam.

'There always are. There always were,' said Brigadier Popham, 'and they'll keep you on your toes. There never was a golden age. Only in retrospect.'

'Gibbon would agree with that,' said Adam.

'Gentlemen,' said Tom Body, 'the RTO has informed me you may entrain on the Berlin Express. I'd like to pack all these things up. I'll ensure there is whisky on the train for you. It's going to be a hard night. Only the brigadier and Major Stanhope have got sleeping compartments.'

The train was antiquated but not uncomfortable. It left on time and trundled across the British Zone to the frontier. There it stopped for a long time while the British and Russian military police checked the passengers. This was the first time most of us had seen Russian soldiers close to and we were struck by how untidy, dirty and smelly they were. Then the train rattled on across the Russian Zone. The blinds were drawn. We couldn't have seen anything as it was dark. We slept fitfully and were very glad to arrive in Berlin.

Tony Strickland met us. He'd been attached to the battalion in Korea as machine gun officer. Now he was serving with his own light infantry regiment who had invited us to Berlin for the cricket week and were to be our hosts.

'Brigadier Popham?' said Tony, saluting. 'Welcome to Berlin, Sir. Colonel Esdaile sends his apologies for not being able to meet you. There's a bit of a brouhaha. It's to do with the strike in the Russian sector but it won't interfere with the cricket. If you and Major Stanhope take the staff car the driver will take you straight to Colonel Esdaile's residence. I will take the officers to the mess in Charlottenburg. My serjeant will look after the others. How was the journey?'

'Fine,' said Algy, 'but most of the team had to sit up all night.'

'Your first match doesn't start until 11.30. So there's plenty of time for everyone to have a bath and then breakfast.'

Tony led us to some Volkswagens. We sped through the leafy city, its summer clothing screening the still all too apparent evidence of war.

We didn't do too well in our first game against our sister regiment. We won the toss, went in to bat and were all out for 126 by lunchtime. Algy scored 50, Tom Body 27, Burgo 15. The rest of us were pathetic. Adam, opening the batting, was out first ball. By 4 o'clock our opponents had won by six wickets. It was humiliating. Algy was kind, saying we were all tired; he advised an early night. But we were not that tired. We just had not had enough practice and we had never played as a team before. Stumps were drawn early that day.

'Look,' said Burgo to Adam and me at tea, 'I've organised

for a Volkswagen and a driver so we can have a look round
Berlin. Tony Strickland's told me what to see. He says we
can't go into the Russian sector as the Russians have declared
a state of emergency. They've tanks in the streets and barriers
at the border, but we can have a good look round the Western
zones.'

We changed into plain clothes and squeezed into a Volkswagen.
First we went to the Olympic Stadium. Climbing to the top of
the stands we looked down on the empty stadium, which looked
curiously small. Then, motoring through the Tiergarten, freshly
planted with young saplings, we came to the Brandenburg Gate.
We walked up to it and looked at the ruins of the Reichstag. We
could see the barriers set up by the Russians. Afterwards we
motored down the Kurfurstendamm, alongside sleek American
and German cars. The multicoloured neon signs would have put
Piccadilly to shame. Cafes, restaurants and nightclubs stretched
for over a mile. The shops' brilliantly lit windows, well stocked
with goods, were a veritable Aladdin's cave. Behind the Kurfurstendamm there was rubble and ruin. We stopped and had a drink in
a café. Berlin was exciting.

'You've now completed Strickland's "Beginners' Tour of Berlin",'
said Burgo. 'Time to return to barracks.'

'Let's go and find some nightclubs,' said Adam.

'What, now?'

'Yes. The driver will know of some.'

'Nightclubs', said Burgo, 'are for night-time. We've strict instructions from Algy to have an early night. So it's back to barracks
and, if you're good, Adam, and make some runs tomorrow, unlike
your disgraceful performance today, there might be one nightclub
tomorrow night.'

'Algy's already reprimanded me in the nicest possible way about
my duck, so there's no need for you to needle me.'

On the way back in the Volkswagen Adam said, 'I wonder if our
sister regiment play cards?'

'Early bed *is* early bed,' said Burgo.

'Yes, nanny,' replied Adam.

So dinner in the mess and early bed it was.

The match the following day against a Royal Artillery side was another low scoring game though it had a better outcome for us. Algy lost the toss and we took the field. Corporal Rothwell and Harry, our fast bowlers, found a consistent length which they had never found the previous day and dismissed the first four gunner batsmen for 60 runs. Then Sergeant Feard, who bowled with his left arm and could turn the ball either way, took over the bowling with Catchpole at the other end. Between them they got another four wickets in good time. Algy then put Rothwell and Harry on again. The last two wickets fell in the two overs before lunch. We'd dismissed them for 107, less than the runs we'd made the previous day.

Burgo was put into open instead of Adam, dropped to number five. Burgo and Tom Body put on 50 runs until Burgo was caught in the slips. Ben Wildbore and Tom took the score up to 80 when Tom was caught in the slips. Algy and Ben added another 25 runs, taking us to 105 when Ben was clean bowled. Adam came in and struck the winning runs by gently cutting the ball away for four. We had won by seven wickets. Honour was restored.

'The way you cut that winning four shows what a good night's sleep can do,' said Burgo to Adam.

'Not strictly true,' replied Adam.

'Weren't you able to sleep, Adam?' I asked.

'Oh yes, I slept all right, very soundly indeed. But while I was having just one last drink after dinner when you wets had all gone to your rooms for an early night, two of our hosts came into the anteroom, one of whom I'd been at school with, said they were very sorry they had been prevented by their garrison duties from looking after us properly and wondered where we all were. They looked surprised when I said you'd all gone to bed. "Early bed," they said, "on your first night in Berlin? We can't have that. If we cut down to the *Prinz Ruprecht* now we can have some fun and get you back here by midnight." How could I resist? I'm always better for a brandy or two, so I had a very good night's sleep. It was probably the absence of brandy the night we came here that accounted for my poor showing in the match yesterday. I must have a word with Tom Body about the necessity of having a little brandy handy.'

'You went to a *nightclub* last night?' said Burgo.

'Yes.'

'What was it like?'

'Well, if you're good tomorrow and score some runs I might take you there. You'll be in for a surprise or two. But not tonight. Tonight after dinner I'm playing cards with my new chums. You can join us if you like.'

This Burgo and I did. The game was uneventful. Adam's new chums were not high rollers. We got to bed well before midnight after Adam had had a few necessary brandies.

The third match was a long drawn out affair against a Royal Tank Regiment side. They were dogged. We went in to bat first and made runs fast. Burgo and Tom Body started well. Adam, Algy and Big Steel all made fifties. Perhaps Algy should have declared sooner than he did at 3 o'clock, when we had made 235 for 6. Maybe he wanted to give everyone a chance to score. Certainly he was not going to declare without a difficult target for the opposition. So we batted on to the last moment, giving our opponents the three hours that we had had to make their runs.

Runs came slowly. So did wickets. It was soon clear that the Tank Regiment would not make the runs in time and the challenge was, could we bowl them out. Our bowlers were on form and they all took wickets but not quickly enough. When it came to drawing stumps at half past six the RTR were 169 for 8. It was a draw.

'What,' asked Burgo as we had a drink outside the pavilion, 'are the plans for the evening?'

'Seeing how well I played,' said Adam, ' I'm in a generous mood and will take you to the *Prinz Ruprecht* if you organise the transport with your friend Strickland. Ben and Harry want to come too, so that'll make five of us. And we'll have dinner in the mess to save our lolly for other enjoyments.'

Dinner was eaten in an expectant mood. Adam refused to be drawn on the *Prinz Ruprecht* beyond saying that he was sure we would enjoy it because he knew he was going to. Burgo announced it had been too late to arrange the military Volkswagens for the evening and that he had ordered taxis.

By night the Kufurstendamm dazzled. We motored through the Tiergarten and then I lost my bearings. After a while weaving through some dark streets we stopped before a house showing no lights. Adam knocked on a door which opened immediately. We followed him into a dark passage that led into a dimly lit hall. Some women, in fishnet stockings and heavy makeup, were standing around smoking. One of them beckoned us on down some dark stairs and into a large room that was dim and difficult to make out at first. It had a lot of pillars and was lit by table and standard lamps that threw the light down towards the floor. In the middle I could see a dance floor with, at the far side, the instruments and music stands of the band; no musicians were visible. An undertow of noise drew us forwards and we were shown to a far corner where we were seated round a table, Harry and I on a banquette, the others on chairs. Pillars blocked our view to left and right but we could see the dance floor. As my eyes became accustomed to the twilight of the room, I became conscious not so much of the people sitting at other tables but of their eyes moving and darting about.

A man in a dark double-breasted suit asked us what we wanted to drink. He spoke to us in German. There did not seem to be much choice. Harry ordered two bottles of hock and a bottle of brandy.

'Not much action here,' said Burgo.

'Don't be impatient,' replied Adam.

'You should have seen the clubs in Japan.'

'I'm glad I didn't.'

'You would have enjoyed them.'

'I wouldn't have enjoyed Korea.'

'There weren't any night clubs in Korea.'

'Another reason for not enjoying it.'

'Come, Burgo,' I said, 'don't you remember Tom Body's cabaret?'

'Not quite like this,' replied Burgo.

'Tell us,' said Adam.

'Tom Body,' said Ben who had been studying the room carefully, 'when he was pioneer serjeant, had collected a group of young Koreans to help him fetch and carry. They were known as Body's Army. When we came out of the line for Christmas, he organised them into a troupe of entertainers. They were all men, but Koreans are slightly built and many of the men look quite effeminate. He dressed the most effeminate ones up as women, taught them to dance the cancan and called them Body's corps de ballet. He had several shows until the RSM stopped it for over-exciting the soldiers.'

'I would have enjoyed that.'

The drinks arrived on a tray: two bottles of Rheinhessen and a bottle of Remy Martin with glasses. Harry poured the drinks.

'What's the brandy like, Adam?'

'Better than I expected. It tastes like cognac.'

'That's what the bottle says. Let me try a sip.'

Adam pushed his glass across the table.

'Yes,' said Harry, 'it does taste like Remy. I wonder where they got it. Black market from the French Zone, probably. It'll be expensive.'

'Good,' said Adam. 'I hate cheapskate nightclubs. They give you hangovers. Clever Harry. My chums said the club was in the French Zone.'

I looked round the room again. We were clearly the only English people there. The others were not all German. Those at the next table were French. I could just hear their conversation. Further on there were some Americans. Most of the parties were mixed. The women looked well dressed. There was the odd table, like ours, that was all men. The band was assembling. Women in fish net stockings were picking up the instruments. They must have been those we saw upstairs in the hall. They started to play. A tall black girl, similarly dressed, started to sing in a husky voice. A few couples got up to dance.

'What do you make of this place?' I asked Harry.

'In London, nightclubs are either rather grand with people eating expensive meals or they're rather bohemian like the Gargoyle. This is different. More cosmopolitan and I get a strong sense of sin. I'm not sure why.'

'Couldn't we get something to eat if we wanted to?'

'Breakfast later, maybe. Most of the people have probably eaten already like we have. Look, it's beginning to fill up.'

When we had arrived we had passed empty tables. Since the band started, a number of parties had come in and the room, which now looked crowded, was humming loudly. The band was into a second number and the floor was nearly full.

'I'd like to dance,' said Ben. 'Where are the girls?'

'They'll be along when they spot us. We arrived quite early,' said Adam.

At that moment two hostesses, one blond and one brunette, walked up to our table.

'Would you like to make room for two of us?' the blond one asked with a strong American accent. Without waiting for an answer she sat down between Burgo and Adam while the brunette sat next to Ben, who immediately asked her if she would like to dance, and they left for the dance floor.

'I'm Harry. This is Miles. You are sitting between Adam on your left and Burgo on your right.'

'Hello,' she said, 'my name is Gretchen. It's short for Margaret.'

'And your friend?'

'Helen.'

'They're English names.'

'German too. We really have a lot in common.'

'Were you in Berlin during the war?' asked Burgo.

'I was very young.'

'What was it like when the Russians arrived?'

'I'd prefer not to talk about that. Don't any of you want to dance?'

'I'd love to,' said Harry.

They left.

'How old do you think Gretchen is?' asked Burgo.

'Difficult to tell with the make-up in this light.'

'Old enough to have been raped by the Russians?'

'Say she is twenty-one or twenty-two, then she would have been thirteen or fourteen when the Russians came. It depends how mature she looked. Her mother and her elder sisters would certainly have been raped. She could have been. Why do you ask?'

'I don't want to bed a girl who's been raped by a Cossack. I might get a disease.'

'So you're sleeping with someone tonight?'

'Why did we come here? Aren't you?'

The man in the dark double-breasted suit appeared and put a bottle of champagne in an ice bucket on the table with some champagne glasses.

'Who ordered champagne?' said Burgo.

'It's for the girls,' said Adam

'But who ordered it?'

'It comes automatically as soon as you start entertaining tarts at your table. You don't think you're going to get them for nothing?'

Burgo was beginning to look unsettled.

'You *have* brought us to a rum joint.'

'Well, I'm enjoying myself,' said Adam.

Ben returned to the table with Helen, the brunette.

'Ah, *champagne*,' he said. 'Well ordered, Burgo.'

Burgo flinched. Ben poured a glass for Helen, and then one for himself. They toasted each other.

Helen turned to Adam and said, 'Weren't you here last night?'

'You remember?'

'Your red hair. You were here with two different English offic-ers. I hope you're not going to leave early again.'

'Not before I dance with you.'

'Shall we dance now?'

Helen took Adam by the hand and led him away.

'Five of us and two of them. Five into two doesn't go,' said Burgo.

'You're so slow,' I said. 'If you wanted to dance why didn't you ask her? You're not going to land a tart unless you dance with her.'

'I like to get to know someone before I dance with them. I'm not sure I want a tart after all. The only one I really fancy is that black singer and she'll have a protector and I won't get a look in.'

'Not bad champagne. What is it?' said Ben refilling his glass.

'The label says Veuve Clicquot,' I said.

'More black market goods and expensive as hell,' said Burgo.

'Why are you so concerned at the expense?' said Ben. 'It may look pricey in Deutschmarks, but in sterling it'll be peanuts. I'm finding this evening rather amusing. And you are beginning to behave like D.P. Brown. But you have a point. Five into two doesn't go. When the band stops I propose to leave. Late nights are not conducive to scoring runs, and I'd like to score a few runs tomorrow.'

'I'll come with you. If I sit here all evening I'll end up pissed,' I said.

'Who's being a spoilsport now?' asked Burgo.

'We are being practical and we've had some fun,' said Ben.

'Well I suppose I'll have to come with you.'

The band must have been playing for nearly an hour when it finally stopped for a break. Adam and Harry returned to our table with Helen and Gretchen. We all had a drink. Ben said the three of us were leaving. The others seemed quite happy with this. Harry said he'd pick up the bill and we could settle later. We said goodnight. The nightclub had already been asked to arrange for a taxi. The three of us climbed in. As the taxi moved off Ben, who was sitting in the front seat, lit a cigarette, leant back and said, 'I hope those two know what they are doing. The brunette I danced with was a man.'

Burgo started to laugh. He didn't stop until we reached the barracks.

When I came down late for breakfast, the dining room was empty except for Harry and Burgo. Harry, who was halfway through a plate of bacon and eggs, was being cross-questioned by Burgo.

'Did you get to bed?'

'I had a very good night's sleep, thank you, Burgo.'

'I didn't ask how you slept. I was asking if you went to bed with that transvestite.'

'What has that got to do with you?'

'It looked as though you were going to.'

'You owe me forty Deutschmarks for your share of the evening. So do you, Miles.'

'That's extortion.'

'A little over three pounds is very fair for table money and the drinks you had. Adam and I picked up the rest of the bill.'

'I should hope so. How much did they charge you?'

'They charged thirty marks for sitting with us and dancing.'

'And for going to bed?'

'Find out for yourself.'

'Where's Adam?'

'Why should I know? And if you're so keen to know all about it why didn't you pick one of them up?'

'I knew perfectly well what you were in for.'

'Balls.'

After breakfast I followed Harry to his room.

'How would you like the money?' I asked.

'A cheque would do but I'd prefer marks if you've got them.'

I handed him forty marks.

'Do you think we should wake Adam?'

'Let him sleep.'

'He ought to have some breakfast.'

'Too late for that, now.'

'He'll have a dreadful hangover without some.'

'How's yours?'

'Bloody.'

'But you never drink enough to get hangovers.'

'I did last night.'

'How did you leave him?'

'After you left I danced with Helen again. "You want to come to bed with me, don't you?" she said. We were talking in German by that time. And I said, "Yes". She said she couldn't leave until the band stopped at two o'clock, so we went on dancing and drinking. I drank a lot, not as much as Adam. I don't think he cares for dancing. Two o'clock came and we paid the bill. Adam disappeared with Gretchen and I went with Helen. I didn't realise Helen wasn't a woman until we were in bed. It was a bit late then.'

'I'd thought you'd realised. Ben and I had from the start.'

'Why didn't you say something?'

'I thought everyone realised. *Chacun a son gout.*'

'I must say I learned a lot of new German words. I'm going to get a German girl friend. It's the only way to become fluent. Oh God, my head.'

He went to the basin and poured himself a glass of water. He threw in two tablets and watched them fizz.

'This is my second lot of Alka Seltzer.'

A mess servant put his head round the door.

'There's a taxi outside the mess, Sir, with one of your officers in it. He's asleep and we can't wake him up. The driver's creating a bit of a paddy. He was lucky to get past the Regimental Police. They recognised him by his red hair.'

Adam was in the back of the taxi, breathing heavily with his head lolling around. He looked awful. Harry thrust some Deutschmarks into the driver's hand. Then we pulled Adam out, helped him to his room and threw him on his bed.

'What do we do now?' asked Harry. 'He won't be able to stand, let alone hold a bat, and I'm not sure I'll be able to bowl.'

'We wait and see.'

Every morning we had travelled to the cricket ground by bus. It left at 10.15 to give us time to knock up in the nets before the game started. Tony Strickland arranged a Volkswagen for us to leave at 11 o'clock. An extra three quarters of an hour, I thought, might make a difference in trying to get Adam on his feet. At a quarter to eleven we woke him by throwing a jug of water in his face, then we stood him under a shower for five minutes. After he'd shaved and dressed his colouring was still high. Finally he spoke.

'A hair of the dog would help.'

Harry found the barman in the bar and got a double brandy. Adam poured it down in one.

'Better,' he said.

'I think I'd better have one too,' said Harry.

We left for the ground.

Algy had lost the toss. We were fielding.

'What's the matter with Adam?' asked Algy.

'He's a bit dehydrated. He's gone off to find a beer.'

'What's he been drinking?'

'Brandy.'

'Let's hope they mix.'

We walked on to the field, Adam coming out of the pavilion last, belching. Algy set the field. Adam was first slip as usual. Harry was to open the bowling. We were playing the Signals Regiment stationed in Berlin. They were said to be good. Their first batsman took the crease.

'Play,' said the umpire.

Harry ran up and bowled very fast. It was wide on the off side. Big Steel, who was keeping wicket, was unprepared for a wide, lunged for it and missed. Adam put out his left hand, just caught it, but it knocked him over. He threw the ball to Algy who threw it on to Harry. Harry bowled a second ball, very fast again. It was a long hop that shot over the batsman's head, over Big Steel and past Adam who had moved back a little. The ball ran fast to the boundary. The next four balls Harry bowled were just as erratic. The batsman missed two. Then he hit one for four and the next for six.

' I'm sorry Algy. I don't seem to be able to get a length yet.'

'We'll give you a rest Harry. You'd better go and join Adam in the slips.'

Rothwell then bowled well, as did Catchpole and Serjeant Feard. But the signallers were good and made runs. When we broke for lunch they were 170 for 4. Harry had not bowled another over.

'Miles,' said Algy, 'see Adam and Harry have some beer, but slowly. Too much will tip them over the top. This is going to be a long game. And see they eat something.'

After lunch, Algy said to Harry, 'Let's see what you can do now,' and threw him the ball. Harry was more under control. He got a wicket when Big Steel caught a batsman out behind the wicket, and Catchpole and Feard were slowly getting the rest of the wickets when the signallers declared for 232 for 8.

When I got back to the pavilion Adam was already asleep, lying on a bench with a bat for a pillow. Algy took one look at him and said, 'We'll put him in last.'

Burgo and Tom Body opened for us. It was going to be a race against time. We made runs but wickets fell too. In getting to a hundred we lost three wickets. At 145 Algy was caught in the outfield, making our sixth wicket down. He came into the pavilion and told me to wake Adam, pad him up and bowl him some balls in the nets to try and get his eye in. 'And give him a beer, but only one, mind.'

Adam played the balls I bowled him carefully. He seemed steady enough and he was obviously seeing them. 'One more beer,' he said, 'and I'll be fine.'

Our ninth wicket fell at 176. We had to make 57 to win. Catchpole was still at the wicket. He could keep a straight bat but he couldn't score runs. We hadn't a chance.

'You've plenty of time, Adam. No need to rush it,' said Algy as

Adam strolled out to the wicket.

He had a good look round the field, took his crease and waited for the first ball. He left it alone. He left the second ball alone, too. At the third his bat flashed and the ball hit the screens behind the bowler. The next two balls he hit for four. The last ball he glided away for one so he was able to take the next over. He'd scored fifteen runs. There were 42 to win, now. He batted faultlessly and furiously. The Signal's captain changed the bowlers and reset his field. Adam's bat flashed away. In four overs he'd faced every ball and hit 55 runs with only two to win. Adam's bat flashed again and he hit the ball for six over the bowler's head.

'That was close,' said Ben.

'So was Waterloo,' said Algy, and went to clap Adam into the pavilion as he ran off the field.

In the bus on the way back to barracks Burgo turned to Adam and said, 'That was a fine display of fireworks. Did you have to take quite so many chances?'

'When I got to the wicket I suddenly realised I needed a pee. All that beer. So I had to go for runs as fast as I could. I only just got back to the pavilion in time.'

'I congratulate you on the day's performance but not last night's.'

'Yes, that upsets me. That was a cheapskate clip joint after all. I know I shouldn't have mixed brandy and champagne in such quantities but I don't believe they were Remy and Veuve Cliquot. I've done it before but never with that effect. I was so drunk when I got into bed with that tart I couldn't do a thing.'

'I'm glad to hear that.'

'Oh, stop being so bourgeois, Burgo. What was good enough for the Greeks is good enough for me.'

'The Greeks,' said Burgo, 'didn't play cricket.'

10

Army manoeuvres test loyalties.

Summer crept into autumn as we prepared for the annual army manoeuvres. For several days the British Army of the Rhine was to conduct a fantasy battle on the north German plain. All our training since we arrived had been designed to prepare us for this giant exercise. Elements of the Dutch, Danish and Canadian armies were to act as the enemy.

Colonel Dennis had taken a few days' leave. He would return in time for the manoeuvres. Before leaving he had sent for Adam.

'He told me,' said Adam, 'that I was a promising young officer and he wanted me to get wider experience. He said I was to take over as intelligence officer and hinted at even better things soon.'

'You must be pleased,' I said.

'I'm not so sure. You remember in *War and Peace* the Prince tells his son when he goes to the war to keep away from headquarters. I've always thought that good advice. I'll be a little too much under D.P. Brown's eyes for my comfort. You need a quiet life, Miles, for the pursuit of pleasure. The consolation is that I'll have my own jeep. And who knows? Maybe I'll be the next adjutant.'

Algy was in charge of the preparations. He called all the officers into the mess for a briefing.

'I've brought you all together to give you some insights on how to survive Exercise "Grand Repulse" as this year's army manoeuvres are called. These are not orders. They are my impressions on what happens on these manoeuvres from observing them last year, when I was an instructor at the Staff College.

'Let's start with tactics. Early on we will be ordered to take up a position on a river line to serve as a screen. This will not be a defensive position to be held and fought for. It will be a series of listening posts from which to identify the enemy, and to establish where and in what direction he is attacking, and in what strength. Once you have reported enemy movements and been ordered to withdraw, be sure to withdraw swiftly. Don't get cut off and captured. There are no medals in getting captured.'

'Fancy getting captured?' whispered Adam.

'What's that Adam?' said Algy.

'I said I'd got no wish to be captured.'

'Then see that you're not, Adam. Last year the Canadians blindfolded their prisoners, stripped them to their underpants and rolled them in nettles. Now, how best to survive these manoeuvres? The exercise will be long and exhausting: it could result in order, counter order, disorder. Remember, battles never go to plan whatever anyone says to the contrary. In war you'll find you always have to improvise. Look back on your own experience. If we're not careful the men will feel they are being buggered about. So will you. Your job will be to see the men are kept as comfortable and as cheerful as possible. "Endurance," said Napoleon, "is the first quality of the soldier. Courage is but the second." This will be a test of endurance.

'The secret of success will lie in your ability to keep the men's spirits up. Here are some ways to do it. This will be an exercise of movement. When you arrive in a position organise yourselves in a way that you can move out quickly. You'll need to be able to get going with little notice, so reconnoitre your withdrawal route carefully. Second, ensure the soldiers get their scoff regularly and on time. That's not going to be easy, but there are few things worse than an empty stomach. Third, be cheerful yourselves in the face of adversity: as soon as you get pissed off the men will. Personally

I'm going to enjoy the exercise. There will be plenty of opportunity for laughs. Take them. In saying all this I am relying on you to be as professional in the conduct of your business as I know you can be. Does anyone want to ask a question? Now's the time.'

'Can we use gasthauses?' asked Adam.

'Use your intelligence,' said Algy. 'If there's one handy, and its use fits in with the military situation, use it. Do as you would in war. Don't forget to pay for everything you get. And don't get drunk.'

That raised a laugh though Algy had said it with kindness.

'What exactly is the point of these manoeuvres?' asked Burgo.

'To exercise the army in manoeuvring as we might have to if war was declared, and from the top to the bottom. In France in the winter of 1939 and 1940 our division under Monty practised advancing and withdrawing again and again. When Hitler attacked in May 1940 we were able to do it in our sleep. That's why the division got back to Dunkirk almost intact. It was at Dunkirk the army fell to pieces. We hadn't practised for that.'

'How long will we be away?' asked Harry.

'Nearly a week.'

'Will we be getting any new equipment?' asked Ben. 'What about the new jeeps we are supposed to be getting?'

'The champs? Yes, we are getting delivery of a few champs in time for the manoeuvres. Colonel Dennis will have the first, then the company commanders. They appear to be exceptionally sophisticated: they can even swim rivers. Be sure you and your drivers really understand their capabilities and master their technicalities before putting them through their paces.'

'Can I bring Kaiser?' asked Jasper.

'No dogs, no horses, no sweethearts. Anything else? No? Well, there's one last thing I'd like to say. Dermot Lisle will not be with us for army manoeuvres as he leaves for the depot prior to his retirement next week. So I propose we dine him out tomorrow night. Ben, would you arrange a beano?'

'With the greatest pleasure.'

We dispersed.

'What a relief to have Algy giving us a few tips instead of D.P. Brown hectoring us,' said Burgo.

'Rather too laid back, I thought,' said Adam. 'At least he left it up to our discretion whether we could use gasthauses.'

'You won't have time or there won't be any within reach,' said Burgo.

Jasper turned to me. 'Coming riding?'

'Good idea. There's still some time before dusk.'

Horace was already mounted and leading off a string of ponies.

'Oh, Jasper,' said Kitty, 'I'm so glad you've come. You and Vampire are getting on so well I've decided you are to race him this winter. I think you're going to do terribly well and surprise everyone. And I shall be the successful trainer.'

We mounted up and rode out of the barracks into the forest. I found myself riding alongside Kitty.

'How are you, darling?' she said.

'Just fine, thank you Kitty.'

'I don't see anything of you these days.'

'I think that's best, Kitty.'

We rode on.

'I still love you, darling,' she said. 'Won't you marry me?'

'You know that's impossible, Kitty.'

'Nothing's impossible if you want it enough. You're just not a romantic. Everything's possible for a romantic.'

'I'm trying to be realistic. Our lives are at stake.'

'Exactly. And you're so cold and distant about it. You never used to be.'

'It's all so complicated. What are you going to do about Horace?'

'I'm thinking about that.'

We rode on.

'I'll have to make you jealous. Jasper, I think. He's very sweet and what a horseman.'

'Jasper loves horses, not women, not men, not even dogs. Horses. He's in enough trouble with Colonel Dennis as it is. Don't make it worse.'

'He needs solace, then.'

'He's also broke.'

'How so?'

'He spent a fortune on his twenty first-birthday party in expectation of gaining control of his trust fund. Didn't you hear? We all offered to contribute but he wouldn't hear of it, so he's temporarily on the breadline, which adds to his unhappiness. No Lucullus for him.'

'You make me feel I really should comfort him.'

'Comfort him by helping him with his riding. He loves Vampire.'

We rode on in silence.

'Would you be jealous if I comforted him? Even just a bit jealous?'

'Kitty, don't. I'm wildly jealous and miserable.'

'Good. And I won't stop at Jasper.'

'Are you going to seduce everyone?'

'If that's necessary to get you to do something about me, yes. I'd draw the line with D.P. Brown, as I hear you all call him. Horace thinks that rather funny. On second thoughts, maybe not. If he would show a little interest I'm sure I could liven him up. Just think of the power it would give me to be the colonel's mistress. Now, there's a thought.'

She picked up her reins and galloped off to catch up with Jasper.

The following evening we dined Dermot out. He sat on Algy's right in the middle of the table as guest of honour. They were the two most decorated officers in the mess and old comrades in arms. Dermot's resignation had upset Algy as much as it had Dermot. When the port came round, Algy tapped his glass for silence and said, 'I know we don't drink toasts or make speeches. Occasionally

we have to make exceptions and this is such an occasion. Dermot
Lisle has served this regiment with distinction. I ask you to drink
to him and his future, and to wish him that ancient Elizabethan
valediction "God go with you, Captain Lisle".'

We all raised our glasses and said, 'God go with you, Captain
Lisle.'

Dermot looked down at the table. I could see tears in his eyes.

Dinner over, Burgo and I lifted Dermot on to our shoulders.
We carried him out of the dining room and across the corridor
into the billiards room where everyone stood round us singing,
'For he's a jolly good fellow.' Then Burgo and I dumped Dermot
on the floor. He stood up, dusted himself down and said, 'Let's
play splosh.'

Splosh was a form of indoor fives played on a billiard table
between two or more players. A player would hurl a billiard ball
on to the table making it bounce off the cushion into the air. His
opponent would try and catch the ball and hurl it back again. It
was fast and dangerous. Rallies were short. The ball would jump
off the table at odd angles, often hitting a player before he could
catch it. It was a dangerous spectator sport too, as the ball could
fly anywhere to hit someone watching. Dermot and Ben began to
play. This, I thought, is the start of a wild evening. I stood next to
Algy, with my back against the wall, to watch.

A ball hit the wall between us. Time to move, I said to myself,
and edged round the room to get behind the players into a safer
and less exposed position. Algy stayed where he was. He had a
charmed life. In the war he'd been in action as long as anyone
and often in the most dangerous and exposed situations, but he'd
never been hit.

You can't play splosh forever. Someone shouted 'Time for
Crusaders.' A cry of 'pillows, pillows' followed. Dermot climbed
on to Ben's shoulders. Someone gave him a pillow and he cried
'Challenge.' Horace climbed on to the shoulders of one of his
subalterns, shouted 'Challenge' and charged at Dermot, whirling
his pillow. As Horace came up, Ben, as Dermot's horse, side-

stepped and Dermot whacked Horace behind the head and he fell, sprawling on to the floor. 'Challenge,' cried Dermot. Several others challenged Dermot in turn. Feathers flew. Dermot was finally unseated by weight of numbers.

'Roulette,' said someone, 'they're playing roulette.'

We all moved to the card room where a roulette table had been set up and Burgo and Adam were running a bank. Several people were already playing. Almost everyone bought chips. For nearly an hour the play was lively. Then Burgo called, 'Last five throws.' The bets piled on. I cashed in my meagre winnings and went into the anteroom.

Algy and Dermot were alone standing in front of the fireplace, drinking whisky and soda. They beckoned me across.

'Dermot was saying we mustn't forget to take up von Senger's invitation to shoot. When we get back from army manoeuvres I'll ring him. Would you start thinking about a party?'

'I do wish Dermot wasn't leaving us.'

'We all do. But he's made his decision. Only he can decide.'

'What are you going to do, Dermot?' I asked.

'*Force majeure*, I shall farm. My father is pleased. He's getting old, he'll be seventy next year. He didn't marry my mother until after the Great War. He wrote to say he and I had seen enough wars and it was time we should be done with them. "You'll find," he wrote, "there's more to life than soldiering. You've done your time in the regiment and I'm proud of you. Now come and run the farm and I'll make it over to you."'

'It's a wonderful opportunity for you,' said Algy. 'The only constant in life is change. Who knows? Maybe you'll get married and have children like your father.'

'Heaven forbid. I'm a bachelor.'

'Who'll look after you?'

'Carpenter, my soldier servant, I'm buying him out. He'll look after me as he's always done. There'll be openings for other old soldiers of the regiment, too.'

'Careful or we might all apply,' said Algy.

Ben came into the room, lit a cigarette and helped himself from the night tray.

'How did it go, Ben?' asked Algy.

'All within the £5 limit, I'm glad to say, except for one amount. Horace won at last. He won a pony.'

We all laughed.

'Yes, I thought that would amuse you. So I arranged a straight deal between him, Adam and Burgo. Adam will give him a cheque for £25 on his and Burgo's behalf in the morning. After all, they've won a lot of money from him in the past. Time it went back. I think that's all right, don't you?'

'On this occasion, yes. But do watch it. The colonel has an eagle eye for these things and is watching out for irregularities. Dermot, I'm going to leave you now. Come and see me in the morning.'

'Algy, I can't thank you enough for this evening. The mess was as relaxed and fun as it always used to be.'

Algy smiled and said goodnight.

'I'm not going to bed yet,' said Dermot, 'I wouldn't sleep. Stay with me, Miles, as you used to in those nights in Korea. I'm more frightened than I've ever been. I pretend to myself that my life is opening out but I feel it's closing in tonight.'

'Of course I will. What have you been talking to Algy about? Anzio?'

'No. We never talk about that. There's a possibility that he might be made a brevet lieutenant colonel.'

'What's that? I think my father was a brevet major when I was born.'

'Officers on the fast track can be promoted out of sequence to a higher rank by a brevet. It comes in the form of a letter from the War Office. In the old days when promotion was so slow it was a way of accelerating an officer up the ranks. Well, brevet lieutenant colonel still exists. There are about a dozen of them in the army today. You get all the privileges of the rank and the seniority except for the pay. Algy has heard he's been recommended. It would show he's been picked to go to the top, but he's worried how D.P.

Brown would react.'

'He'll be livid.'

'Yes. And it will really turn him against Algy. Algy hasn't said anything but I can see he's getting a hard time from Parker Brown.'

'How does Parker Brown get away with it?'

'He's got a lot of friends on the staff. I also think he's got a protector somewhere high up. He only appears to behave like this in the regiment. A lot of people say it's an inferiority complex to do with the war, what happened at Anzio and being put in the bag. I think it goes deeper than that.'

Colonel Dennis returned from his leave and inspected the battalion, going round every company to gauge how well prepared each was for the manoeuvres. He found things wrong, as he always did, but he found no major faults. While he was away Algy had called the company commanders together, told them it was their responsibility to ensure that their companies were prepared, that they knew what to do, and that he was not going to interfere. Colonel Dennis was a little disconcerted to find even Horace Belcher's company well prepared, but he still found fault with him and gave him a rough ride. He returned to battalion headquarters to find Dermot waiting to say goodbye to him.

'What on earth did he say to you?' I asked Dermot when he got back to the mess. He was leaving that day.

'I had to go to see him. It's the custom on leaving the battalion. And it was too good a chance to miss. He said he'd arranged my posting for my own good and that he couldn't have a disloyal officer in his battalion infecting everyone.'

'What did you say to that?'

'I told him I was proud to have served in the regiment and would always remember it as it had been at Anzio and in Korea.'

'That was brave. You're not short of courage.'

'He screamed, "I'll not have such disloyalty" and ordered me out of his office. I will probably have to walk to the *Bahnhof*.'

'You'll have put him in a vile mood.'

'Far from it. When, after saying goodbye to Algy and to my intelligence section, I left battalion headquarters, D.P. Brown was inspecting his new champ like a schoolboy, all beams and smiles, with Val fawning in attendance.'

The battalion arrived in its assembly area for army manoeuvres intact and without incident. We were well instructed now in the ways of the British Army of the Rhine and in moving across West Germany. The manoeuvres would be our first communion, so to speak, for which Algy had prepared us. We were looking forward to them. We had hardly had time to settle before Burgo and I received orders to hand our platoons over to our serjeants and report to Colonel Dennis.

'I'm going to repeat the way we organised ourselves for our first river crossing exercise,' he said. 'I want you to be my liaison officers again. These manoeuvres will be fast at times and I'll need you to help me to keep control of the battalion. I'm holding an orders group in half an hour. Meanwhile you can go and join Adam at the command vehicle.'

We walked across to find Adam standing outside the battalion headquarters command vehicle. Hidden under a vast camouflage net, it seemed much bigger than it had been. When we walked under the net we realised that a large canopy had been rigged on one side of the vehicle, under which there were deck chairs, made of khaki canvas, and a folding table. Adam was working on a large map that hung on the side of the vehicle.

'Do you like the chairs? I wanted to have them in regimental colours but Val vetoed that. Hang around after the O Group and I'll give you a drink. I can't give you din-dins but I can offer you coffee, sherry, gin or brandy. I haven't been able to manage ice yet. Colonel Dennis doesn't approve of ice. I'm going out of my way to make the colonel more comfortable. He's not said anything but I think he approves. He needs looking after and I'm giving him all the love I can. After all he's looking after me. I'm rather ashamed of some of the things I've said about him and I'll have you know that, in my presence, references to D.P. Brown are *verboten*. Now I must get on with marking up this map.'

We sat down and watched Adam mark his map, a large scale one covering the north west of Germany. At the top right he wrote 'REDLAND' and at the bottom left 'BLUELAND'. Down the map, roughly from north to south, ran a series of rivers, from the Hunte in the east to the Ems in the west, about 80 miles apart. This was to be our battlefield. Adam then drew in a lot of lines from right to left signifying division, brigade, and battalion boundaries. While he was doing this, others began to arrive until the company commanders and the whole orders group were assembled, about ten in all. Colonel Dennis joined us.

'I want to start,' he said, 'by sharing the big picture with you - and be sure you share this with your men so that they know what's going on. Hostilities are imminent and we must expect Redland to cross our border any time in the next 48 hours. The first line of defence is the river line of the Hunte. We are to move up to the Hunte and form a screen along its west bank as soon as we are ordered to. We must avoid any concentrations as we mustn't offer large targets to attract nuclear attack, even if that is unlikely at this stage. Our purpose is to delay the enemy, calculate his strength and direction of attack, but not do more than that. We will then fall back, passing through the next screen on this river line here. The aim is to catch the enemy between rivers and then surround and destroy him. Moving up to the river line and on the river line there will be wireless silence until we are in contact with the enemy. We'll move only by night. That is the broad picture. After I have given out the detailed dispositions you are to brief your men and then, in three hours' time, you are to meet me on the Hunte river to reconnoitre our positions.'

After giving out the detailed dispositions, he sat down. Then Val, as adjutant, and the quartermaster gave their administrative instructions. We broke up.

'One for the road?' said Adam.

'That's generous of you,' said Burgo.

'Oh, I'll see it goes down on your mess bill. Battalion headquarters is not a charity.'

'You surprise me. And what are you going to do on this exercise apart from running a gin joint?'

'I'm sticking close to Colonel Dennis, close as a poodle to meet his every whim.'

'I'll watch that with interest.'

'While you two,' went on Adam, 'will be doing the dirty jobs fit for Korean heroes. Time now to pack up this caravanserai.'

Burgo and I moved off.

'I hope he doesn't come a cropper. He's really quite an eccentric addition,' said Burgo.

The battalion moved up to the river line at dusk. The companies took up their positions and the outposts were posted. The river wound through a valley in such a way that it should have been easy to observe from a line of outposts but, as we arrived, a mist descended, diminishing visibility. I thought it would be easy for an enemy to slip across unseen. We prepared the bridges for demolition. I was liaison officer with Horace Belcher's X company and he decided there was no point in visiting his outposts in the dark. He told everyone to make himself as comfortable as he could. When an umpire arrived and told his operator to turn off his wireless and get some sleep, Horace took the hint there would be no action that night and told everyone to get some rest. The serjeant major said he'd take first turn on duty and we all turned in.

Nothing happened the following day. Horace, the serjeant major, and I went out to inspect the outposts. This took a long time as we had been ordered to move very carefully in daytime. Horace re-sited one or two of the watching points, but there were still gaps an enemy could get through in a mist. The men seemed cheerful enough at this stage. A system had been devised for them to pull back and eat and rest. It was well organised. The day was long with nothing to do except watch. I took a stint, watching with Jasper's platoon, who were in good spirits. There was no sign of life on the far bank.

Night fell. The umpire kept his wireless going so Horace decided we should have a higher level of alertness. Runners were sent out to the outposts to warn them. Nothing happened. The second day on the river dawned and it followed the course of the previous day. Careful routine continued to keep the spirits up. We practised, as far as we could in daylight, a withdrawal. We knew when we had to get out we'd probably have to do it in the dark in a hurry. The day wore on. No signs of movement came from the far bank. On our right was a battalion of the Borderers. I had made contact with them when we first took up our positions. I went across and talked to the company commander. He reported there to be no activity on his front. Night fell, and with it, a wet mist.

The first we knew the enemy was across the river was the breaking of wireless silence. On the left flank, Y company reported it was being infiltrated. Then we heard shooting away to the left. There was still nothing on our front. Then W company, immediately to our left, reported it was being infiltrated. Burgo, who was on the left flank, reported the enemy was pouring through and asked if he could blow the bridges. Colonel Dennis said the picture was not yet clear enough and Burgo was not to blow the bridges. Fifteen minutes later Burgo said he estimated a battalion had broken through and that if he didn't blow the bridges immediately it would be too late. Colonel Dennis said he must be exaggerating: that it wasn't possible for a battalion to cross the river and break through so quickly. W company, in the centre, reported it was being overrun, that the enemy was everywhere and asked to withdraw. Colonel Dennis said he wanted a more detailed report. W company said they couldn't see much in the bad visibility by the river but that the enemy was passing by company headquarters too quickly to count and that they would be on top of battalion tactical headquarters in minutes. Then Colonel Dennis's wireless set went dead.

Burgo continued to call him but could get no reply. I spoke to Burgo. We agreed to blow all the bridges if we still could. All the company commanders said it was time to withdraw and some reported outposts captured. No one could get a reply from Colonel Dennis. Horace gave the order to his company, and it made an orderly withdrawal as arranged. I reported we were withdrawing to the Borderers on our right, who replied that they had been ordered to pull out, too, saying they had been told there was a danger of being outflanked from the left. There was quite a firefight coming from our left now and I guessed that the enemy had concentrated against W and Y companies and were now going for the next river line. Listening to the wireless it sounded as if W and Y companies had been overrun. I didn't hear Burgo's bridges being blown. We blew ours, marched back a mile, found our vehicles, and counted our men on board. Everyone in X company was present. We motored off in withdrawal.

The place specially selected for the battalion check point was deserted. Colonel Dennis and Adam should have been there. I set up the check point, checked Horace's X company through, and waited in the dark. The noise of fighting had stopped but I could hear vehicles. A champ leading some lorries and carriers motored up. It was W company. They had lost a lorry and some men. They had also lost contact with the colonel. I told them to keep going. After a little while Y company came through. They had lost contact with the colonel, too. They were also missing men. I sent them on their way. Then Burgo arrived in his jeep followed by an empty lorry.

'What a farce,' he said, 'I'm the last from the left flank. What about you?'

'X company got out complete without contact with the enemy. You seem to have taken the brunt.'

'They came out of the mist in hordes. I wasn't able to blow the bridge. We can expect their armour at any moment. It's amazing that W and Y companies got out. An umpire said we were all dead or captured but we slipped away in the dark. Where's Colonel Dennis?'

'No idea. No one was here when I arrived. I set up the check point. The three companies have gone through.'

'Time for us to get out, there's no organised body behind me. No medals in getting captured.'

'Let's just make one last call on the wireless.'

I put on my headphones, picked up my mike and signalled to everyone. W, X and Y companies all reported they were nearing the next check point. No sound from Colonel Dennis or Adam. Then Algy came on the air and asked what was happening. I gave him as clear an idea as I could. He told me to withdraw and he would meet us at the next check point. As second in command, Algy had been left in reserve in the rear.

When we reached the next river line we were checked through by a troop of the Household Cavalry, then told to get over the bridge and pull in. There we met Algy.

'Well done,' he said. 'Are you sure you're the last?'

'We're the last vehicles apart from Colonel Dennis and Adam who've disappeared,' said Burgo. 'We've withdrawn all the company vehicles bar one and quite a few men are missing.'

'There may be some stragglers. Burgo, you wait here to receive any. Keep the lorry. There's a troop out there covering this bridge. When it withdraws it will be time for you to rejoin us. It looks as though both the division's flanks have been turned. This river line will be the next to go. The battalion goes into reserve behind the next river thirty miles back. We probably need a little sorting out. Miles, you follow me.'

The battalion rested in reserve. Algy told me to return to my platoon. It had got out of the river line intact. After we had cleaned up we had a really good meal, which cheered everyone up. Later we moved back further to another reserve position where we stayed for the night and the next day. We organised games including a friendly football match with Burgo's platoon. They won. Strictly we should have kept under cover but no one knew and we wanted to keep up our men's spirits. In the evening Algy sent for me.

'Any news of Colonel Dennis and Adam?' I asked.

'Officially missing. Unofficially the colonel has been captured,

the umpires tell me. No news of Adam, though, which is curious.'

'He's probably in a *Gasthaus*,' I said.

We both laughed.

' Now, I've got a job for you to do.'

He pointed to a map in front of him.

'The enemy has halted on the third river line, here,' he said,
'probably having to wait for their supplies to catch up. The intention was to lure them on until they were over-extended so now
we've got them trapped. We are to attack at dawn and encircle
them. Now look at these.'

He passed me some air reconnaissance photos.

'The bridge at this village here doesn't appear to be held in any
strength, if at all. We've been told to secure it overnight before we
put in the main attack. Then the armour can cross it and break
through without delay. I want you to take your platoon through
this forest tonight and capture the bridge.'

He pointed to an area on the map that was green and hilly with
no roads and went on, 'It looks impenetrable, certainly to armour
and vehicles. So leave your carriers with their drivers and go on
foot. I'm giving you some men from Y company to strengthen
you. They've lost their platoon commander and serjeant. Make
your own plan. Miles, I want you standing on that bridge to greet
me when I arrive by road at dawn.'

The men from Y company were subdued and resentful. Little
Steel told them to form themselves into three groups based on
friendships, which they did and immediately cheered up. Then
we re-organised the platoon, originally two sections, into three
strong sections.

I studied the map very closely. Rides and tracks crisscrossed the
forest. I worked out a route to bring us to a point above the village
where the bridge straddled the river. We would have to march eight
miles by compass so I allowed a good four hours to be safe. We
had a meal, rested and set out just before midnight.

We marched up through the forest, climbing gently. It was very dark, the trees soaring above us. We could only just see the sky. Now and again I had to stop to check the map and the compass. Once or twice I thought we were lost. Occasionally we heard noises, only animals but eerie. I expected an enemy behind every tree but the smell of pine was comforting. When I estimated we were half a mile from the bridge we rested before going on, as I didn't want to arrive too early. As soon as we started again the track fell rapidly downhill. We were closer to the village than I thought. The track joined a main road and a hundred yards down it I saw houses. I checked the map. Surely this was the village? I lay down and studied the road and the houses through my binoculars. No one was around. The wood had been such a maze that I was still unsure whether we were in the right place so I looked at the map again. There didn't seem to be any other place we could be. Well, here goes, I said to myself. We moved on to the road by sections. Down the road we went, round a corner and there was the bridge. It was still dark.

We stopped. Little Steel took a section forward and halted on our side of the bridge. After a little he waved us on and we closed up. I studied the other side of the bridge through my binoculars. I couldn't see anyone or anything military so I sent a section across the bridge at the double. Then I doubled across with another section. We had secured the bridge. We lay there. Ahead of us no one stirred, no one fired at us, no umpire strode out of the dark to tell us we were all dead. Little Steel joined me.

'It seems deserted,' I said.

'They would have fired by now if they were going to. They may all be asleep.'

'Where?'

'Along the road. Let's have a look, Sir.'

We left the others improving their positions, with sentries posted, and walked up the road. After a hundred yards we came to a line of armoured vehicles. They were all lifeless except for the furthest one, which was showing shafts of light. We walked up to it and no one challenged us. It was a command vehicle and we could hear someone talking on the wireless.

'Dutch,' said Little Steel.

'Let's wait until they finish talking.'

The wireless crackled and buzzed. The talking stopped. Little Steel opened the door and I jumped up the steps, revolver in hand.

'You are surrounded by a battalion of the British First Armoured Division.' I said. 'You have no alternative but to surrender.'

Little Steel climbed into the vehicle pointing his sub-machine gun. Out of the haze of cigarette smoke two startled faces looked up at us. A Dutch major wearing earphones grabbed the microphone of his wireless set. Another Dutch officer, wearing an umpire's armband, leaned back wearily against the side of the vehicle. A third lay on a bench asleep. Little Steel poked his sub-machine gun into the breast of the major wearing the headphones. He dropped the microphone.

I said to the umpire, 'They have to surrender. They've no hope. They're surrounded.'

He talked to the major in Dutch. The major shrugged his shoulders.

'He agrees,' said the umpire. 'We thought you were miles away. We are waiting for fuel. We've run out. He couldn't move if he wanted to. They've been on the go for three nights now and they're dead with sleep. I suppose the sentries are asleep too. Look at him.' He pointed to the officer lying on the bench. He was still fast asleep.

'I'll have to move you off the road. You're blocking it,' I said.

'You'll have to give us fuel.'

'Surely you've enough for a few hundred yards.'

'Oh, all right.'

As Little Steel and I walked back to the bridge he said, 'I enjoyed that, Sir. Pity it wasn't for real.'

Dawn was breaking as Algy arrived with his advance guard. He stopped, congratulated us and asked some questions. Then the column of tanks and infantry motored on over the bridge.

Our carriers and my jeep came up at the end of the column. We climbed in and followed. The advance was fast. In encircling the enemy we regained much of the ground over which we had retreated and nearly reached the original river line on which we had started. Sometime in the afternoon we heard that the manoeuvres had finished. Honour had been done. We were ordered to stay where we were for the night and move back to barracks in the morning.

I found myself with my platoon in a small village. It had one street with some farms, the odd shop and a *Gasthaus*. Outside the *Gasthaus* was parked Colonel Dennis's champ, and next to it was an armoured car. Both had white flags flying from their wireless aerials. I was not sure I wanted to be the first to encounter Colonel Dennis, yet we were on the outskirts of the village and he might well find me, so in I went. There sat Adam playing gin rummy with Charles Millington of the 19th Lancers, who were acting as umpires on the manoeuvres.

Adam looked up.

'Taken your time to rescue me, haven't you? I've had to hole up in this *Gasthaus* for three nights now. Very disagreeable.'

'You look comfortable enough. Where's Colonel Dennis?'

'Dismal news, I lost him. Or, rather, he abandoned me.'

'Why's his champ outside?'

'Stop being so stern and get yourself a drink. Can't you see Charlie and I are reaching a critical moment in our game? There we are, Charlie, gin.'

He put his cards down. Charlie followed. Adam totted up the score.

'You mustn't be upset, Charlie. You only owe me twenty-seven pounds and five shillings. I'll go on playing later so you can get your own back. First I must find out what took my chums so long to find me. Well, Miles?'

'We survived and won the battle with honour despite your disappearance from the field. Where, Adam, is the colonel?'

'The early days of the manoeuvres weren't exactly "All Sir Gar-

net". Colonel Dennis had been getting very tetchy. The inactivity
had been getting on his nerves and he was getting on my nerves.
I was trying to cheer him up reciting a little Virgil, some martial
verses from the Iliad, when all hell let loose on the wireless. It
was clear to me that the enemy had broken through. "Shouldn't
we order the companies to withdraw, Colonel?" I said, "after all
we're only a screen." "No, no," he said, "we need more proof.
The companies are panicking. The enemy couldn't break through
in such numbers. I'm surprised at Burgo, not like him at all." He
rather fancies Burgo, I think. When he finally realised the enemy
had broken through and might be on our doorstep any minute, he
started to shout. My dear, the military hysteria. "Start my champ,"
he shouted. The champ wouldn't start. "What do you mean my
champ won't start? It's new." True enough, but he'd tested its
aquatic capabilities by driving it across a river. Then the wireless
failed. "I'll have to take your jeep," he said. "I must get back to
the check point. Get that champ working and the wireless. Then
you can follow me. And order the companies to withdraw." Off
he went in my jeep with all my goodies. I haven't seen him or my
goodies since.'

'What do you think happened to him?'

'The umpires tell me,' he said, looking at Charles Millington,
'that he was captured and interrogated. He was thought to be a fine
capture. You see my jeep has "intelligence officer" written on it.
For the enemy to capture a lieutenant colonel of intelligence who
must know the plans for the army was quite a coup, wasn't it?"

'And you?'

'The champ has "commanding officer" on its front. I took the
precaution of putting the colonel's greatcoat over my shoulders,
well it was cold, and flying a white handkerchief from the aerial. I
explained to the Dutch umpires that I had broken down but help
was on its way. They saluted me and left me alone. We pushed the
champ to the *Gasthaus* and made ourselves at home. The champ
won't go so we couldn't move. What else could I have done? At
least I wasn't captured.'

Adam picked up the cards and started to deal.

'I have to admit,' he said, 'that I may have had a good manoeuvres financially, thanks to Charlie here, but my days as D.P. Brown's intelligence officer are probably numbered.'

11

Last manoeuvres before winter quarters

'The wives are very much enjoying the shooting lessons, Miles. I want to thank you for running them so charmingly,' said Olivia as we walked from the indoor shooting range to the officers' mess.

'Serjeant Whettingsteel and Corporal Rothwell are doing most of the work. They're enjoying it too. Do you think Algy could persuade the quartermaster to let us have some pistol ammunition? He treats it like gold. I really think the wives should learn how to fire a revolver.'

'I'll ask him.'

'How are your other activities going?'

'The German lessons that started so popularly have reduced to a hard core of half a dozen. Ilse Hoffnung, the professor's daughter that Ivor Popham introduced, may be plain but she's a terrific instructor. And I think Harry Fox has rather fallen for her. They spend a lot of time together.'

'Where did you learn your German?'

'I did French and German at school. Then I spent a year in France and Germany before I came out. That was before the war of course. It's not perfect but I get by.'

'And the other activities?'

'Fallen apart, as I suspected they would. But it did help the wives to meet. They've made their own groups now and do things together.'

'Colonel Dennis said anything?'

'With reluctance he conceded something had happened.'

'Has he ever congratulated anyone for anything?'

'You'll have to ask Algy that. He said he'd be waiting for me in the ladies' room.'

We walked into the mess. Algy was there with Kitty and a few others. Kitty cornered me.

'Still avoiding me, darling?'

'You know we can't see each other.'

'I know it's what you think. It's awful to have no contact.'

'Have you seduced Parker Brown yet?'

'You know I'm working on Jasper first. We're getting on pretty well.'

'How well?'

'Well, Vampire's coming on a treat. Otherwise it's as you predicted. Jasper only has eyes for Vampire, not me.'

'Thank God.'

Algy joined us.

'When are you going to run Vampire, Kitty?'

'I've entered him at Hanover on Saturday week. Will you and Olivia come?'

'Yes, but isn't that the day of the mess dance?'

'It clashes but we'll get back in time.'

'Miles, Andreas von Senger has asked us shooting in three weeks' time, so we need to decide who comes. Six guns, he said. Olivia and I are going to the *Ratskeller* tonight with them. Why don't you come? What about you and Horace, Kitty?'

'You'll have to ask Horace. I'd love to come. But who's that unfamiliar face that's just walked in?'

A tall captain was kissing Olivia on the cheek.

'That's Francis Bowerman. Don't you know him?' asked Algy.

'No.'

'He was in Hong Kong for a while. He left for Staff College some time before we went to Korea,' I said.

'He arrived today,' said Algy. 'He's been at the War Office and he's going to be our next adjutant. And, Miles, while he's waiting to take up the adjutancy he's going to command your company temporarily, as you do not have a company commander at present.'

'Do ask him to dinner,' said Kitty.

'I already have.'

Francis came across to us.

'Algy, I heard you were here so I thought I'd come and say hello to Olivia. Why Miles, I'm so glad to see you. There are quite a lot of new faces I don't know.'

Algy introduced Francis to Kitty, and they fell into conversation.

'Algy, what's happening to Val Portal if Francis is to become adjutant?' I asked.

'It's time for him to move on.'

'Already?'

'Colonel Dennis thinks so and believes it would be good to have an unmarried adjutant living in the mess.'

'It'll be fun to have Francis in the mess,' I said. 'He'll be a popular adjutant, too.'

'That's not quite what Colonel Dennis had in mind, but I'm glad to hear it. Now, if we're going to dine at the *Ratskeller* we'd better get going. We mustn't be late for the Sengers. If you want to bring anyone else, do. I booked a table for ten.'

Ben and Jasper joined us for dinner; Jasper was still broke but he could just afford dinner at the *Ratskeller*. Burgo was away on a course for the day. Finbar, our doctor, was saving money. Adam was on a border patrol. After the army manoeuvres Adam had returned to his rifle company and Harry Fox had taken over as intelligence officer. Adam, we had decided, had reminded the colonel too much of his disastrous manoeuvres. Harry, as a national service officer, only had a few months left to serve. He was the new favourite at court.

The *Ratskeller* was a large cellar under the Town Hall, which served good, basic German food and wine at reasonable prices. It was jolly and lively. We had taken to using it as an easy, cheap and relaxing place for a simple evening out. The wine came in jugs and the food was piled high on the plate. It was not the kind of place in which Horace would over-indulge and have to be carried out. All the details for the day's shoot were fixed. Francis got on well with the von Sengers and spent a lot of time in conversation with Andreas. Everyone agreed to go to Hanover to watch Jasper ride Vampire at the race meeting. No one drank too much.

The next morning, after muster parade, I was in my platoon stores with my men cleaning the machine guns when Francis Bowerman and Big Steel came in.

'I don't know whether anyone has told you,' said Francis to me, 'but I'm your company commander for the time being. Serjeant Major Whettingsteel tells me the platoons are very independent, so I thought we might run an inter platoon competition. Next week we'll all be in the field. Sitting in the stores isn't soldiering. Come to my office at 1100 hours and I'll brief you. You too Serjeant Whettingsteel.'

They looked round the stores, asked a question or two, talked to some of the men and then moved on.

At eleven o'clock all the platoon commanders and serjeants assembled in Francis's office.

'The exercise,' said Francis, 'will be a test of initiative, observation, map reading, and courage. Its aim is to hone your soldiers' personal and individual skills, and identify the true soldiers and potential NCOs among them. You have all recently received new drafts of national servicemen. We need to discover who are the leaders and who the laggards. Make preparations to camp out by platoons for three nights. Personal arms only will be taken. Leave the heavy weapons in barracks with a minimum rear party organised by the serjeant major. We shall assemble at the cross roads at Kremke at 1000 hours on Monday. I will then give you further orders. I'm not telling you any more now. Any questions ask the serjeant major and he will only answer questions of fact.

The exercise will be called "Exercise Fungi".'

'Fungi?' said Little Steel as we walked back to our stores, 'what's that?'

'*Fungus*,' I said, 'is the Latin word for mushroom. My guess is that's a code for nuclear war. You know, the mushroom cloud. It must be some sort of survival test.'

'He mentioned map reading. Not many of our men can read a map. Perhaps we should give them some instruction?'

'How well do you know the intelligence section Serjeant?'

'Monty Savage? He's a mate of mine. Wasn't he your intelligence serjeant in Korea?'

'Yes. Ask him what maps Captain Bowerman has asked for and say I've asked if we can have a few in advance. At least we can teach our men not to hold them upside down.'

Little Steel returned with the maps. They covered the country round Kremke to the east of the town running to the border.

'Did you learn anything else?'

'Not directly, Sir. Only that the intelligence section rooms at the front of the building overlook the NAAFI building and that at night they can see into the NAAFI manageress's bedroom. She's got a lover and they make love with the lights on. The only part of his body they can see is his feet. He wears green socks, so it's an officer. They're saying it's Captain Wildbore as he's been seen with the manageress.'

I didn't think it could be Ben Wildbore. Regimental regulations were that officers should wear dark green socks. Some of us, including Ben, wore black socks as they were cheaper and easier to come by.

In between cleaning the guns we spent the next two days coaching the men in map reading. Once or twice Francis put his head round our door and laughed, but said nothing.

That Saturday I took Rana to the cinema. Adam and Burgo had asked me to go to Baden-Baden with them to gamble. Finbar was going. He could resist a restaurant but couldn't resist the tables. I had arranged to see Rana; I hadn't seen her for some time and I was still intrigued by her. She seemed forbidden goods, and she was a distraction from Kitty, who I couldn't get out of my mind. We sat through *Moulin Rouge*, dubbed in German. It wasn't really a film to take an Islamic virgin to, however broad-minded. Maybe that was a bad choice. I suggested we dined at the Lucullus but she said that it was too grand and expensive, and favoured the *Ratskeller*, which was not the obvious place for lovers. Perhaps that's why she chose it. She told me about her upbringing in Turkey, and I told her about mine in England. She asked me more about the army. I asked her about her father, the general, and she asked about mine. The conversation never became intimate: there seemed to be a barrier. At one stage I took her hand but she gently removed it. There was none of the zing that had seemed to pass between us before when we had met at parties, which had made me think we had clicked. I was looking for an emotional friendship, I suppose. She was looking for, and got, an opportunity to exercise her English in a civilised way. I could not navigate the gap between our cultures. When I took her back to her university lodgings, she gave me her hand and confirmed that she was coming to the races at Hanover the following Saturday, and the dance afterwards. Olivia had asked her to stay the night.

It had been a rather muddling and disappointing evening, and on the way back to the barracks I looked in at the *Junkernschenke*. In the corner of an inner room Ben Wildbore was sitting with a lovely blond whom I recognised.

'Looking for some talent?' asked Ben.

'I was interested in seeing who might be around.'

'Ben, introduce your friend.'

'Don't be silly. It's Miles. You must know him.'

'Yes, but we've never been properly introduced.'

'Oh God, the protocol in Germany. *Herr Leutnant* Player, may I present the lovely *Fräulein* Heidi von Bock, younger daughter of *Hauptmann* Baron von Bock and Baroness von Bock.'

'I'm delighted to make your acquaintance *Fräulein* von Bock. Would you honour me with the next dance?'

'I would be delighted to. Come and sit next to me until the band begins to play. Ben you can go home. I've been longing to meet *Leutnant* Player.'

'Watch out for Miles, Heidi. He's a slyboots. Behind those gentle eyes is a killer, a ladykiller. What luck tonight Miles?'

'It wasn't that sort of evening.'

'Poor boy, but you're hoping it might be? Well, you're too late. I've got the only girl worth anything round here, and I'm not sharing her.'

'Ben, there's a question I've been meaning to ask you. What colour socks do you wear?'

'Look, Miles,' he said pushing out his right leg. 'Regimental light infantry green socks. *Fräulein* von Bock is a disciplinarian. She expects her officers to be dressed properly and obey regulations.'

At ten on Monday morning we assembled, as ordered by Francis Bowerman, at the cross roads at Kremke, a tiny village to the southeast of the town. Francis's driver was standing at the crossroads and directed us down a track into a field. There, Big Steel was waiting for us. A large tent had already been pitched in one corner of the field. We were directed to pitch camp in the other corners. The men stripped off in the fine autumn day and got to work with zest, digging latrines, and erecting tents. A company notice board was erected outside the large tent, on which was pinned a large map of the area, and platoon signs marked platoon lines. It looked as though we were settling in for a month, not a few days. At midday we were called to assemble outside the large tent.

'The field in which we are camped,' said Francis, 'belongs to Baron von Senger. So does all the land hereabouts. He is a friend of the regiment and I ask you to respect his land as you would respect the land of a friend. He has very kindly agreed that we may use it.

'Exercise Fungi is a test of individual skills. By platoons, I want you to divide yourselves into teams of three. Your gun, mortar, and skills teams will provide a good basis but I want everyone to be in a team. The officers and NCOs are not to be in the teams.

'At this time of year the fields and woods abound in fungi. That is the Latin word for mushrooms. Each team is to be allotted an area in which to search for mushrooms. You may think that is easy. When your team has identified and collected at least three different types of mushroom, you are to return here to me and the serjeant major. You then have to give us the map reference of where you found the mushrooms – you'll all get maps, though I know the machine guns have already got them. Then you have to tell me the name of each mushroom and whether it is edible or not. There's a book on the table here with pictures of fungi to help you. The mushrooms you pronounce edible you must then cook in this pan on the Primus stove and eat. There will be points for the correct map reference of the position of the fungi you find, the name of each fungi, deciding whether they are edible or inedible, and for having the guts to eat those you say are edible. The team that brings in, identifies, and eats the most edible fungi wins. The winning team gets free beer and bangers at the next company smoker.

'Your officers and NCOs are there to observe. You may ask for their help in identifying the map references and the different fungi in the fields where you find them. Once you have returned to camp, they cannot help you further. You will have to identify the fungi to me, to say whether they are edible or not and eat those that you say are edible. Serjeant Major Whettingsteel will show you your areas on the map. Any questions?'

'Supposing we eat a poisoned mushroom, Sir?'

'That's the wrong question. You'll have plenty of opportunity to identify the fungus correctly from the book here.'

'Can you, Sir, tell one mushroom from another, Sir?'

'I can. And if it's edible I'll eat it too. Any more questions? No? Well, this afternoon is a practice run. As soon as you've found three different types of fungi return here. I want you all back by 1700 hours. The real competition will start tomorrow. One last rule. No one is to eat any fungi except in my presence. Got that?

Good. Now sort yourself into your teams and form up to the Serjeant Major. He'll direct you to your areas to search. Then go and enjoy your dinner, and good hunting this afternoon. Would the officers and NCOs gather round me, please?'

We gathered round Francis.

'Gentlemen, I want you to track your teams. You may help them only if they ask you, and only if you think they need help. Your main purpose is to observe them, find out who leads, who follows, how they use their initiative. This is your opportunity to assess them outside the everyday structure of platoon training and routine. Take advantage of it to get to know your men even better than you do already.'

Little Steel and I watched our platoon sort themselves into teams, and then we all ate.

Crabbe, Cookson and Catchpole had got together as a team.

'You coming with us, Sir?' asked Catchpole. 'I hope you know something about these fungi. Crabbie say he does, being a farmer's boy, and he's scaring Cookie and me to death.'

' "Send you mad," he says,' said Cookson.

'Worse'n that,' said Crabbe. ' My dad says there's some as'll kill yer. "Don't trust 'em lad," he says to me.'

'But your dad's a farmer,' I said.

'Yes, 'e knows.'

'Do you mean to say you've never eaten a puffball?'

'Course not. Mum wouldn't have one in the 'ouse.'

'But they're delicious.'

'Not from where I come from, they're not.'

'You do surprise me. When I was a boy we used to go on fungi collecting expeditions. Some of them are great delicacies.'

'Boy in our village 'ad 'allucinations from 'em. "Serve 'im right," said Dad. I'm not touching 'em.'

'I'd better come with you, then. If you go on saying this you'll never win a point. Where has the serjeant major directed you?'

'About a mile up that road, he said.'

We marched up the road, which was really no more than a track that twisted and turned between fields, until we came to a wood.

'Here we are,' said Catchpole.

'Let's all spread out and search this field and wood,' I said. 'If you see anything you think looks like fungi give a shout and we'll come to you.'

Quite soon Catchpole shouted from the wood. We all closed on him.

'There, Sir.'

'They're beautiful,' I said. 'They're chanterelles. There's a restaurant in London named after them. Well done, Catchpole. Pick some carefully and put them in a pocket. They should smell a little of apricots. Do they?'

'Not too sure.'

'You're not going to *eat* 'em?' exclaimed Crabbe.

'You bet.'

'I wouldn't if I were you, Sir. Look real poison, they do.'

'If you don't believe me, Crabbe, let's see what Captain Bowerman says.'

Crabbe grunted.

'Now let's see if we can find some other species,' I said.

'What's these?' asked Catchpole.

'Look like a fuckin' cock,' said Crabbe.

'You're right, Crabbe,' I said. 'It's a stinkhorn. The Latin name is *phallus impudicus,* which means a shameless penis. Smell it.'

'Not me. I can smell it from 'ere.'

'That's why it's called a stinkhorn. Do you see those round white things round it? They're its eggs. You can eat them.'

'Wouldn't touch 'em,' said Crabbe.

'Come on, Crabbie,' said Catchpole. 'They won't hurt you if Mr Player says so. Pick a few and put them in your pocket.'

'Not me, Poley.'

'You're not going to win us free bangers and beer at the next smoker,' said Catchpole. He picked some and put them in his pocket.

'You're doing very well,' I said. 'What about recording the map reference?'

That took a little time. Crabbe wrote it down on an envelope.

'Don't forget to record what you've found here,' I said.

'What have we?'

'Chanterelles and stinkhorns,' said Catchpole, 'here, I'll write it.'

They went on looking and found several more species. Death and doom lurked in Crabbe's every comment. Catchpole wouldn't listen to him any longer, and soon Cookson started to pull his leg. By four o'clock we were making our way back to camp with a good haul, more than they had been asked to collect, as the woods and fields abounded in fungi, just as Francis Bowerman had predicted.

As we entered the camp we smelt cooking. Francis was sitting on a campstool outside the large tent. On the tables beside him were collections of fungi, which appeared to have been labelled. All around him were soldiers sitting on the ground, tense and alert. Immediately in front of him was a soldier holding a frying pan over the Primus stove into which he was putting some fungi with his right hand. I went up to Little Steel.

'What's going on?' I asked.

'Hancock, one of our new national servicemen, has said his fungus is edible so the captain has told him to cook it and eat it. Some of the lads think Hancock's wrong. We're all waiting to see what happens.'

He whispered this, which increased the tension.

'Don't overcook them, Hancock,' said Francis. 'Fungi need very little cooking as they're mostly water.'

'I like my meat well done, Sir.'

'Do it your own way, then.'

Hancock turned the fungi over and stirred them with a wooden spoon. They looked black as a moonless night.

'He'll die,' said Crabbe, loud enough to turn a few heads.

'Please don't distract Hancock,' said Francis.

'It's murder,' said Crabbe.

'Silence!' said Little Steel.

'They're ready now,' said Hancock.

He spooned them onto a tin plate and then looked at Francis. They stared at each other.

'You still say they're edible?'

'Yes, Sir.'

'More points if you eat them, then.'

'He'll die,' whispered Crabbe.

'Shut up, Crabbie,' said Catchpole.

Everyone bent forward a little to watch Hancock more closely. Hancock picked up a knife and fork, cut a piece, put it on his fork, and raised it to his mouth.

'Stop,' said Francis. 'Are you sure?'

'Yes.'

'Eat, then.'

Hancock thought for a bit. Catchpole held Crabbe's arm to control him. Very slowly Hancock put the fork into his mouth.

'' 'e's as good as dead,' said Crabbe.

'Captain wouldn't let him die,' said Cookson.

'' 'im only just joined us,' said Crabbe.

'How do you feel, Hancock?' asked Francis.

'Fine, Sir. Aren't you going to have some? They're delicious.'

'So they should be.'

Francis helped himself to some from the frying pan.

'Not bad at all,' he said, 'congratulations, Hancock. You certainly have courage. Yes they're common ink-caps, as you said. They're a little different from the shaggy ink-caps and it's not clever to eat them with alcohol. They don't seem to mix. Otherwise they are quite harmless. Have you eaten them before?'

'Yes, Sir.'

'I thought so.'

'We call them inky caps. There're a lot about at this time of year.'

Someone shouted, 'Well done, Inky.'

Everyone laughed. Then there was loud applause.

'You and him dying, Crabbie,' said Cookson.

'Just you wait and see. They'll both die.'

After the men had had their tea meal, we all helped to mark out a football pitch in the field and erect the goal posts that the colour serjeant had scrounged from somewhere. Francis had decided that the following afternoon we would have an inter-platoon football competition: another opportunity, he said, to observe the men from the new draft, see how they performed, and sort the wheat from the chaff. When we finished it was twilight. The men dispersed to their tea in the big tent where the colour serjeant had also organised a canteen. Afterwards a few started to queue for beer. In one corner a dartboard was attracting a crowd; in another, a group had gathered to watch a chess game. Some had started to play cards. The guard had already been posted.

'Time to leave them alone,' said Francis to Burgo and me, 'and nearly time for our dinner. Andreas von Senger is joining us as our guest at the *Gasthaus* in the village, which he recommends. In fact he's the reason we are here. When we were at the *Ratskeller* last week he told me how his land was a cornucopia of fungi. He said that due to its closeness to the border it was one of the backwaters of Western Europe. That gave me the idea for this exercise and he readily agreed to let us camp and roam here. See you there in a quarter of an hour. By the way, I've asked Finbar O'Connell to join us and he should be here any minute. I thought it would be good for morale for the men to know that the doctor was around.'

Burgo and I were sharing a tent. We took it in turns to wash in a canvas bucket. We were wearing battledress. I took off my boots and put on a pair of black shoes, as did Burgo. Then we walked out of the camp to the *Gasthaus* on the other side of the crossroads. If we had gone on walking through the village and continued along that road we would have come to the border. Andreas von Senger was already at the *Gasthaus*, talking to the landlord.

'You must try the beer first,' said Andreas. 'It's the local brew and I think you'll like it.'

We were all handed mugs of beer.

'Let me tell you what the landlord has prepared. Smoked trout, which he has smoked himself, then venison stew with ceps and chestnuts. This is the best time of the year for venison. It never tastes better than in the autumn. Ah, Francis, welcome. We've started by drinking beer.'

Francis had walked in with Finbar.

'I've just walked our doctor round the camp. Everyone seems well settled for the evening. Yes, I would love a beer.'

He drained a mug down immediately.

I sat down to dinner next to Finbar.

'How was your weekend at Baden-Baden?' I asked.

'Good for me, neutral for Burgo, disaster for Adam. Hasn't Burgo told you?'

'He hasn't had time. I can't wait to hear.'

'We played roulette, which is a fool's game, but Adam insisted. By the time for dinner Burgo had ended up where he had started, I had doubled my money, and Adam had lost every Deutschmark he'd brought with him.'

'No dinner for Adam, then.'

'Not at all. He orders an expensive dinner saying, "We can't come to Baden-Baden and not have a good dinner", and goes on about how the gods will look favourably on him after a good meal.'

'So?'

'Burgo is not very happy and starts finding fault with the dinner. You know how he can behave if he wants to irritate. He says, "It's a rotten dinner, call this a first class hotel, there're better hotels in Kowloon." Adam is then very generous. You know how he can be when he's got money. He offers to pay for Burgo's dinner if Burgo stops complaining and lends Adam his money. Burgo accepts, and then tucks in and orders another course.'

'That's rather naughty.'

'Adam doesn't mind, though he's careful not to drink too much. After dinner Adam and I return to the tables. Adam loses all the money he's borrowed from Burgo and starts to borrow from me.

"My luck will change," says he. By midnight he's borrowed the rest of my money and lost that too.'

'Why did you lend it?'

'Why not? I'd doubled it. I didn't want to lose it. Safer to lend it to Adam.'

'How did you pay the bill?'

'We didn't. Adam went to see the manager who was very nice and accepted a sterling cheque Adam wrote him. After all, we'd been eating caviare and drinking champagne.'

'Giving a sterling cheque to settle a German bill is illegal. He could be cashiered for that.'

'Yes. Adam's got a month to go back with Deutschmarks to reclaim the cheque and to pay back Burgo and me.'

'Has he paid you back?'

'There's a lot of talk. "Don't be so grasping. Funds are on their way." As he seems to have sources of money I'm not worried. Burgo is delighted to have something on Adam. But Adam doesn't seem to be quite himself at present. I think that he's rather worried, and that's beginning to worry me.'

'Finbar, do you think Francis is all right? He's gone very red in the face.'

'A clear case of rubefaction, I would say. He doesn't look too good. He's been drinking a lot. I've been waiting for this. Do you know what fungi he's been eating? He told me he'd had some.'

'I saw him eat a plate of ink-caps about two hours ago.'

'Anything else?'

'Not that I saw but I suspect so.'

'That's it. It'll be interesting to see what happens.'

'Aren't you going to do something?'

'Nature will take its course. It's not dangerous. Only uncomfortable.'

Francis, red as a beetroot, got up and walked out of the room quickly. Five minutes later he returned.

'I've been a damn fool. I've drunk two pints of beer and half a bottle of wine on top of those ink-caps. I've just been as sick as a pig. Serves me right. I hope Hancock hasn't been drinking. It's bloody silly of me. I know perfectly well it's only safe to eat ink-caps at breakfast.'

Finbar turned to me.

'I hear he's a paragon of a soldier. It's good to know he's human too.'

In the morning I heard that Hancock had been fine. Some of his mates had tried to ply him with beer but Catchpole had stopped them. News got out that Francis had suffered and he got a lot of kudos. The exercise ran for another two days and was a great success. We gave Andreas a map marked up with our best finds. Every day for the next two weeks Francis got me up early to pick fungi for breakfast.

When I got back to the mess after the exercise, I ran into Adam.

'Just the person I wanted to see,' he said. 'My mother and my two sisters have just arrived in the town. They're staying at the *Junkernschenke*. I couldn't find anywhere cheaper that wasn't too tawdry. I've arranged dinner tonight in the ladies' room. Would you come? I'd like you to sit next to my mother. You're good at talking up. A suit, I think. Dressing up would embarrass them.'

At eight I went down to the ladies' room to meet Adam's family. The sisters were both younger than Adam. They were not great lookers but they shared Adam's red hair and were lively. The mother was pleasant but was preoccupied and not inclined to talk. Adam had laid on a lavish meal. Oh well, I said to myself, I can enjoy the food but I'll have to sing for my supper.

'Are you staying long, Mrs Hare?' I asked. 'There are some fine things to see in the town, and the countryside is spectacular in the autumn.'

'We're leaving tomorrow.'

'Tomorrow? So soon? What a pity. There's a dance here on Saturday that the girls would enjoy.'

'We can't stay. We have to leave.'

'On your way to Italy, I suppose? Adam didn't tell me that. The

Italian lakes will be wonderful at this time of year.'

'No, we're going home.'

'But you've only just arrived!'

'Yes, but you see, Adam has borrowed all our money.'

12

Racing days

Ben Wildbore took Burgo, Adam, and Finbar to the race meeting at Hanover. Jasper went with Kitty and Horace. Corporal O'Reilly and Whistler took the horses. Colonel Dennis went in his staff car with Francis Bowerman. Algy and Olivia came, bringing Rana and me. Rana and Kitty had become friends, for Kitty had gone out of her way to make friends with her and they rode a lot together. Olivia had encouraged it. The von Sengers came. Others came too.

There were seven races that day, two of them restricted to the British Army, the others open to all comers. Colonel Dennis was riding Red Ember in the second race, a restricted chase for British Army horses and riders only. Kitty had entered Vampire in an open novices chase with Jasper riding, the fourth race of the day.

The first race started at one o'clock so we got there early. Hanover was a medium sized course. There were plenty of facilities. We bought ourselves into the stands, had a quick lunch in the buffet and went to the paddock to look at the horses running in the first race. Adam saw us and came across.

'You couldn't lend me some Deutschmarks could you, Miles? You always seem to have some.'

'What have you done with all those you lifted off your family?'

'Burgo and Finbar demanded I pay them back and they're not in a lending mood today. I've still got to settle with the hotel.'

'I'm sorry, Adam, I'm not in a lending mood today either. I've got enough on me to put decent bets on Jasper and on D.P. Brown.'

'You'll lose your money on Jasper. It's his first time out and you've no idea what he's up against. You'd do far better to save your money and lend it to me"'

'What do *you* know about the horses running today?'

'For some time I've been betting with Karl, the mess steward. He's a keen follower of the horses and he's given me some tips for the day. I'll share them with you if you lend me some Deutschmarks.'

'I'll lend you one hundred marks on the understanding you pay me back in marks by the first of the month.'

'Thanks, Miles.'

I forgot to ask him for his tips, not that I wanted them. I was only really interested in Vampire.

'Will you see that money again?' asked Rana, who had watched the transaction.

'Yes. He has money. The difficulty is getting Deutschmarks with the currency restrictions. It means we're always limited in how much money we can spend in the town.'

'I hadn't noticed.'

'Well there are ways round it. Adam clearly thinks betting on horses will help. And it will if he wins.'

'Does he win?'

'He's inclined to. Though he had a disastrous time at Baden-Baden last Saturday when you and I were at the pictures.'

'You like gambling. Why didn't you go to Baden-Baden?'

'I wanted to be with you.'

'Thank you, Miles, you are very gentlemanly. Is Adam a gentleman?'

'Adam is a scholar, an entertainer and an adventurer. He's good company and very amusing. I'm not sure he's a gentleman, either by birth or behaviour.'

'I thought not. How did he get into your regiment?'

'You have all sorts in a regiment, even in a regiment like ours. I respect the gentlemanly code, the code of good behaviour, but, if I think about it, it is really long gone. Do you know what George Bernard Shaw said about the English gentleman?'

'Who is George Bernard Shaw?'

'He was an Irish playwright. He said, "You can trust an English gentleman with anything except women and money." '

'And you believe that?'

'There's plenty of evidence to support it. Now let's go and find a place to watch the first race.'

'You're a cynic.'

'No, just growing up.'

We watched the first race from the stands. It was a hurdle race and the second favourite won by several lengths.

'Time to go to the paddock to see Red Ember,' I said. 'On the way, let's go past the Tote to see what odds they're giving.'

Red Ember was second favourite at four to one. It was his first outing that winter, but his form was well known from the previous two seasons. I didn't think him worth a bet but Rana placed a small one. Corporal Riley was walking him round the paddock. He was beautifully prepared and as good looking a horse as any in the race. There were nine runners. Colonel Dennis mounted Red Ember and cantered him down to the start, which we could just see to the left of the stands. We would see the horses come past the stands twice. The first time Colonel Dennis was trailing the leaders, about fourth or fifth. When they came back into sight he was lying second with two fences left. At the last fence the leader fell and Colonel Dennis rode Red Ember home by six lengths.

Rana was thrilled and went to collect her winnings. She'd never bet on a horse before. She returned with Adam.

'I seem to be having luck with the second favourites,' he said. 'I hope you're winning too, Miles. Here's the hundred marks you lent me. I'll not forget that.'

'He's a gentleman after all,' said Rana, when Adam was out of earshot.

'Don't test it,' I replied. 'Let's go and watch the next race by the last fence. We can come back to watch Jasper on Vampire.'

'And in time to put my winnings on Vampire,' said Rana.

We stood by the last fence. The pounding of the horse's hooves, the heat and the swish of the horses as they raced past us, the power of their jumping and the shouts of the jockeys were a new experience for her. She took my arm.

'That was fun. I am enjoying this.'

In the open novices' chase, in which Jasper was riding Vampire, there were twelve horses. Vampire was an outsider but in the paddock he looked good.

'Why,' asked Rana, 'is he so little fancied?'

'He's an unknown and British,' I replied. 'The only money he will attract will be British Army money. Look at the crowds. Imagine how much will be going on the best German horses the crowd knows about. I expect the odds on Vampire will move out.'

'Who's the short man walking Vampire?'

'You know Whistler, the groom.'

'He's smartened himself up.'

'That's a pity. A dirty looking groom might have moved the odds out further. Let's go and put our money on.'

'And then let's go and watch by the last fence,' she said.

At the start the horses were closely bunched together. Jasper was last. We waited for them to come round. We saw them clearly as they jumped the second last fence. Two horses came over in quick succession, then Jasper. He was moving up fast. He overtook the horse lying second and came pounding up to the last fence, still three lengths behind the leader. I could see the intense concentration on his face. Rana gripped my arm. The noise increased. The leader jumped the last fence and clipped the top of it. The jockey rose above his horse's head and somersaulted on to the ground. Jasper jumped, cleared the fence, landed Vampire cleanly and galloped on. The next horse was three lengths behind. Rana gripped my arm harder and leant her head on my shoulder.

'Oh Miles, has he won? I can't look.'

She turned her head and looked at me.

'Yes,' I said, and kissed her.

She pulled back.

'Don't spoil it, Miles. I don't want to believe George Bernard Shaw.'

But she put her arm through mine as we walked as quickly as we could to the unsaddling enclosure.

Everyone had gathered there, even Colonel Dennis who was talking affably to Horace. Jasper had weighed in. Rana went up to Kitty and they hugged each other. I wondered if Rana ever kissed anyone. Adam came up looking crestfallen.

'I didn't think Jasper had a chance. I suppose you were on him? Yes? I thought all the talk was self-deception and hope. I put my money on the horse that should have won but fell at the last fence. Not all, I'm glad to say, but a sizeable sum.'

'I was at the last fence. Jasper was still making ground. He would've won even if your horse hadn't fallen. You underestimate him and the horse.'

'I'll have to think about that. Ben wants to return to barracks now to check on the arrangements for the dance, so I'll have to go.'

'Do you mean you didn't have a penny on Jasper?'

'Not a pfennig.'

'You must be the only person in the regiment who didn't.'

'Then what consoles me now is the amount of money that will be floating around in the mess tonight for a good game.'

Rana returned.

'Can we go and get our winnings? Algy and Olivia are keen to leave now that the races we're interested in are over.'

We collected our winnings. The Tote paid out twelve marks for every one bet, another reason for Rana to be pleased.

It took us two hours to get back to barracks, where Algy dropped me off at the mess. Rana was staying the night with Olivia and Algy. They drove off to get changed. We had been asked to wear fancy dress. The dance started with drinks in the mess at eight o'clock. I hurried to get ready, dressing as an effendi with a fez and a coat taken from the dressing-up box at home. My grandfather had brought them back from Egypt in the 1920s and I had claimed them for precisely such an occasion.

Where all the costumes came from I never knew. Some must have been made for the occasion; others, like mine, kept as stand-bys. Ben, dressed as a mandarin, was receiving the guests. There were several pirates, a gondolier, a ballerina, one Napoleon, two Nelsons, and a Florence Nightingale. Olivia came as Suzanne Leng-len, and Algy as Marechal Foch. Horace was one of the pirates, and Kitty was dressed as Nell Gwyn with daring décolletage. Rana was dressed as a Turkish lady of an earlier era with a hat in the shape of a spire, a long, loose, silk gown with ruffled sleeves and a mass of beads round her neck. Heidi von Bock came wrapped in a white sheet as Aphrodite. Jasper came wearing his father's double-breasted dinner jacket with a cigarette stuffed in the corner of his mouth, saying he was the Prince of Wales. Finbar O'Donnell was dressed as Pierrepoint the hangman, and Francis Bowerman came as the Prince Regent. Colonel Dennis wore a black tie, claiming dispensation due to racing.

The anteroom, cleared to make a dance floor and a sitting out area, slowly filled. The regimental dance band was already in place. When they played 'The Entrance of Queen Dido' for us to go into dinner a chattering kaleidoscope of colour launched along the corridor and burst into the dining room.

I was eating with Olivia's party.

'When are you running Vampire again, Kitty?' asked Olivia.

'Next Saturday at Brunswick. Can you come?'

'Isn't that the day we're shooting with the Sengers, Algy?'

'Yes.'

'Drat it. After that?'

'Back to Hanover. I must consult my darling jockey. Where is Jasper?'

'Talking to Colonel Dennis.'

'That's a change.'

'Colonel Dennis was delighted that Jasper won. He's been for-given,' said Algy.

'About time too. He's a prince of jockeys.'

'Colonel Dennis ran a good race,' said Algy.

'He's been doing it for long enough. And it was a restricted race. Jasper on Vampire will beat Dennis Parker Brown any day,' said Kitty.

'Will there be such a race?' asked Olivia.

'One day there will, and then just watch out.'

I turned to Rana.

'Are you racing or shooting next Saturday?'

'If you're shooting with the Sengers, then shooting, if I may.'

'Who is shooting?' asked Kitty.

'Ben, Francis, Burgo, Miles, Ivor Popham and me,' said Algy.

'At least you've left me Jasper. Who else will come to Brunswick? I must have some support.'

'I'll come,' said Adam, who'd joined us. 'I'll follow Vampire for the rest of the season if he runs like he did today.'

'It was a fluke, Adam,' said Horace. 'Keep your money in your wallet. I doubt if they'll do it again.'

'Horace, you bastard,' retorted Kitty, 'it was damned hard work and you know it.'

'The idea that Jasper on Vampire could beat Colonel Dennis on Red Ember is moonshine,' said Horace.

'I trained that bloody horse while you were playing polo and getting pissed. It's my horse. You may have paid for it, but I chose it, I trained it and I won today. And all you can do is say it was a fluke and get pissed. You bastard. Don't expect me to dance with you tonight.'

Kitty was furious. There were tears in her eyes.

'Why don't we go and powder our noses?' said Olivia. 'Kitty? Rana?'

The three of them got up. As Kitty passed Horace she said, 'Bastard. You're just jealous that I won the limelight today.' She swept out.

'After that, I'd better order a magnum of Pol Roger,' said Horace.

'Or two,' added Algy. 'You asked for it, Horace, but do try not to get pissed. Colonel Dennis is in such a good humour.'

'Are you going to play roulette?' Adam asked me.

'Maybe, but it *is* a dance.'

'I'll play roulette, Adam,' said Horace. 'Keep me a place. I'd better go and find Kitty.'

'Why does Horace behave like that?' asked Adam. 'And why did she marry him?'

'Horace prides himself on being the finest horseman in the regiment. That's one of the reasons Kitty married him. Now he recognises that Jasper is a challenge. Not for Kitty, for him. And have you noticed how D. P. Brown has been talking to Jasper most affably? Horace won't like that. He's the favoured horseman.'

'Why hasn't she got children like the other wives?'

'That's another reason Horace goes for her. She had a miscarriage and now, apparently, she can't.'

'She's looking most fetching tonight. I might ask her for a dance. Are you jealous?'

'It's all over between Kitty and me,' I said.

'Good. It's time I had a ride on the regimental bicycle.'

'Adam, you go too far.'

'I hope to. And you've got Rana.'

'I'm not too sure about that.'

We walked into the anteroom. The dancing had begun.

It was some time before Olivia returned with Kitty and Rana. As soon as she did, Colonel Dennis asked Kitty to dance. I danced with Olivia and Algy danced with Rana. Then I asked Rana for a dance.

'Is Kitty still upset?' I asked.

'Yes, but she's not showing it. She broke down and wept about everything going against her. And, Miles, she told me about you and her, that you're lovers. I had no idea. It was a terrible shock.'

'But we're not.'

'She says that you are. That she loves you above all others.'

'We had an affair in Hong Kong, years ago. I'm very fond of her. But it's all in the past. It's you I love, Rana.'

'I like you, Miles, but I'm very confused.'

'Rana, there's nothing between Kitty and me any longer. She's upset and doesn't know what she's saying.'

'She's quite clear that she's in love with you and she wanted me to know.'

'That doesn't mean to say that I'm still in love with her.'

'Perhaps not. I don't know. I'm confused.'

'Was Olivia there when she told you?'

'Yes, but she didn't hear.'

'Rana, listen to me.'

'I think I want to sit down.'

I led her off the floor and got her a drink of lemonade.

'Love is a very strong word, Miles.'

'I didn't mean to say it. But I had to.'

'I thought we could be friends. Get to know each other better. Maybe even...'

'Even what?'

'Let's go and play roulette. We're getting too serious. I'd like to see if I can double my winnings.'

Burgo was running the roulette by himself, in what he now called his *salle privée*. Only a few were playing. Horace had a chair. Rana and I sat down next to him. She won at first, then the table ran against her. Within a quarter of an hour she'd lost nearly half her winnings.

'I think,' she said, 'I'll keep the rest. I don't really understand this game.'

By then, several more had come into the room. Rana settled her losses with Burgo and stood up. Francis Bowerman asked her to dance. As I was winning, I stayed. I felt numb and cold. I just kept putting the money on and my numbers came up. I noticed that as I won Horace lost. Horace was being silly. Though he was sharing his magnum he was getting speechless. Adam joined Burgo at the bank. Jasper came in and sat next to me.

'How are you, Jasper?' I said.

'So far, one of the best days of my life. I thought I'd escape from the dancing to avoid fate turning against me.'

'You rode brilliantly. I watched you at the last fence.'

'I knew I could catch him. But I'm glad he fell, because it looks as though I was lucky and that means it won't affect Vampire's handicap too much.'

'You were going much faster.'

'You agree? Vampire still had a lot in hand at the finishing post.'

We placed our bets.

'You've just missed a spectacle on the dance floor,' said Jasper.

'What happened?'

'There was a rhumba. Ben and Heidi were dancing it rather actively. Slowly Heidi's dress - that white sheet – fell off her. As it fell it looked just as if she was rising from the foam. Aphrodite indeed. She was stark naked, not a stitch. One or two people clapped. Ben shouted, "Yippee". Not so Colonel Dennis. He looked daggers.'

'*Huit, Rouge, Manque et Pair,*' said Burgo.

'You win again,' said Jasper. 'Me too, I'm still in luck.'

'*Faites vos jeux.*'

'Let's do *rouge* and *manque* again. Well, then Ben picked up the sheet, wrapped it round Heidi and took her off. I suppose to stitch it together. That's my joke. But D.P.Brown didn't think it was a joke. Luckily the band kept playing. That's when I decided to slip away. I didn't want to get caught up in it.'

'*Les jeux sont fait.*'

'D.P.Brown probably doesn't like Ben carrying on with a German, and the NAAFI manageress at that, for all he professes the Germans are our friends.'

'*Rien ne va plus.*'

'Have you noticed that he doesn't talk to the Sengers? Did you know they weren't asked tonight on his say-so.'

'*Dix-Sept, Rouge, Impair et Manque,*' called Burgo.

'We win again,' said Jasper. 'My luck is still in.'

'Not luck, Jasper, darling,' said Kitty who appeared standing over him. 'Skill and hard work. You deserve everything. Will you make room for me? I'd like to try my hand.'

I stood up.

'Kitty, come and dance?'

'Oh, yes, darling, I'd like that.'

'Look after my chips, Jasper.'

When I'd got Kitty safely on the dance floor I said, 'Just what have you been saying to Rana?'

'I told her we were lovers.'

'That's not true, even if it was once. Why on earth did you say that?'

'I saw you at the last fence together. I saw you arm in arm. I'm jealous, Miles, and I'm in a winning mood.'

'Just because Horace is being dreadful, and he is, and everyone's on your side, there's no need to bugger up Rana and me.'

'Where are you going with Rana? Come to your senses. What do you want? A mistress or a wife? You can have both with me. You can't have either with Rana. Now I've got to know her, I like her. She's a darling. You show great taste in her. But she's from a different world. You haven't a chance with her. You have with me.'

We danced in silence for a bit.

'I'm going to divorce Horace.'

'That doesn't mean that I'm going to be part of it.'

'Don't be a fool. You love me. And I love you.'

We danced on and edged a little closer. Kitty laughed.

'Guess who's just made a pass at me?'

'Adam.'

'How did you know?'

'Did you let him?'

'Good God, no. I'm not the regimental bicycle, and I told him so. The idea. Darling, I'm going straight. It's you or nothing.'

The music stopped.

Olivia greeted us as we came off the floor.

'Kitty, Algy and I are thinking of leaving. Rana is coming with us. Would you like to come with us, too?'

'That's a very good idea. I've done everything I want to, tonight. Horace can stew. Goodnight, darling Miles. Remember what I said.'

She looked at me with love and kissed me on the cheek.

'Rana was looking for you Miles,' said Olivia. 'Ah, there she is.'

'Miles, thank you for looking after me so beautifully today,' she said as she came up to me. 'I don't think I'll come shooting with you at the Sengers next Saturday. I must think about things. I know you'll understand.'

She gave me her hand and then she left.

I wandered back into Burgo's *salle privée*.

'How's the game going?' I asked Jasper as I took the empty seat beside him.

'My luck is still in. The bank's doing all right, too. For Horace it's a disaster.'

'Serves him right. He behaved like a shit tonight.'

'So I heard. Where's Kitty?'

'Gone home with the Stanhopes.'

'Hard lying for Horace, then. Look at him.'

Horace was fast asleep in his chair, which had been pulled back from the table. He wouldn't wake up for hours.

'Burgo's just announced the last six rolls.'

'Let's play then.'

Jasper and I lost at every roll of the ball. When we cashed in our chips Adam said, 'The gods were watching over you two today. If it hadn't been for Horace, Burgo and I wouldn't have made a bean. It all balances nicely if we keep Horace out of the bridge book for everything except £5. I'm going to make Horace pay in Deutschmarks. That'll put me nearly right with the hotel.'

'How much has Horace lost?'

'Every chip he took. He's down £80.'

'How did you let him run up such an amount?'

'He was pissed.'

'Was that fair?

'Horace can afford it.'

'It's way outside the rules.'

'Who'll know?'

'It was too public. Just because you need the money there's no need to fleece Horace because he was pissed out of his mind.'

'You win a fiver.'

'And me?' asked Jasper.

'You win a fiver too. That's covered by almost everyone else losing including the divine Rana who lost four pounds and paid up in Deutschmarks, bless her.'

'Let's go and get a drink,' said Jasper. He walked over to a side table.

'Hock and seltzer do you?' He handed me a glass and lit a cigarette. We sat down in two armchairs in the corner of the room.

'Adam is sailing a bit close to the wind,' he said.

'It's very careless of him. I'm surprised Burgo let him.'

'Burgo's amused by Adam so he indulges him. I doubt Burgo knew how far Horace had plunged.'

'I hope that's true.'

'Did you have a good day like I did, Miles?'

'Rather too many puzzling portents. And it's gone out with a bang. Kitty has shopped me with Rana.'

I explained.

'Kitty talks about you a lot,' said Jasper. 'I think she really does love you. Do you love her?'

'I don't know who I love. It's all very painful.'

'Kitty generally gets what she wants. First Horace, now Vampire, you next, I expect. She's very persistent. I know her well now. She never gives up.'

'Perhaps I'd better apply for the Aden Protectorate Levies or the King's African Rifles.'

'She'll follow you.'

'I'd better finish that bottle or I won't sleep.'

We finished the bottle together and opened another. Everyone
else had left the room except for Horace who was snoring.

'What happened to D. P. Brown?' I asked.

'He was charm himself. Luckily he didn't put his head in here.
Knew better, I expect.'

'Adam made a pass at Kitty tonight.'

'What did Kitty say?'

'She told him she wasn't the regimental bicycle.'

'Adam made a pass at me earlier. He came to my room when
I was changing, with two goblets and a bottle of champagne. I
drank the champagne but declined the underlying offer. Not the
first time he's tried. Did you know he's seduced Harry?'

'I wondered. When was that?'

'After you got back from Berlin.'

'What about you and Kitty?'

'I like Kitty. She's like an elder sister to me, and she's a brilliant
trainer. She'd be just right for you, Miles, if it weren't for Horace.
Horace is tragic. And he's got no brains at all.'

'Kitty said, I think to annoy me, that she was going to seduce
you.'

'For me, Miles, it has to be perfect sympathy or perfect soli-
tude.'

'Who said that?'

'Mauriac. I'm reading *Thérèse*. Harry Fox lent it to me. He loves
Mauriac because he writes about the Bordelais, which he regards
as his country. Did you know he spent a year in Bordeaux before
he joined up? He's very interesting, Harry. He's asked me to go to
the opera in Hanover with him. You ought to come. You can do
it in an evening on the train, and get away from all this.'

'I'd love to do that.'

I poured out the last of the wine.

'Let's empty this bottle and go to bed.'

'What shall we do about Horace?'

'Horace? "Let him stew" is what Kitty said.'

Horace snored on in his chair.

At that time I was due to take the examination for promotion to captain, as were Burgo and Adam. On the Monday we went on a course and were away all week. Returning on Friday evening we were greeted by Jasper.

'You've missed more fun and games this week,' he said.

'Tell us.'

'On Monday Val bugled for me. He doesn't hand over the adjutancy to Francis until next week. Val interrogated me about the roulette game: who won, who lost, how much I'd won. "Why ask me?" I said, "ask the organisers." "They're out of barracks," was the reply. Someone had reported seeing me with a huge pile of chips. That must have been when you, Miles, were dancing with Kitty and I was looking after your chips. Horace was then interrogated. He couldn't remember anything about the game. He asked me what had happened and I said I didn't know and he'd better ask Burgo. He thought he'd lost but he couldn't remember how much. Val examined the bridge book, which appeared to be in order. It showed Horace had lost £5 along with some others. That made them more suspicious as they thought he'd lost more.'

'I'd filled it in on Sunday,' said Burgo. 'All the entries were bona fide. No one lost more than £5. The book wouldn't have revealed anything.'

'Val reported to the colonel,' Jasper continued, 'that it seemed to be above board despite the rumours. At lunchtime D.P.Brown stalked into the anteroom, picked up the bridge book and searched it. He tore it apart and threw it into the fire. Then he stumped out. He ignored me, as he has all week.

'Harry Fox retrieved the half burnt book and handed it to Ben. At that moment Algy came into the anteroom. "What's happened to the bridge book?" he said. "Colonel Dennis threw it into the fire," said Ben. "You'd better buy a new one," said Algy as he pressed the bell for the barman. Then D. P. Brown walked back into the anteroom – he must have gone to have a pee – and started accusing everyone of disloyalty, that there was something going on he didn't know about and that he was going to ban all gambling. Algy stood up to him and said no one had lost more than £5 and no one had been hurt. D. P. Brown turned on Algy and accused him of being as disloyal as the rest of us. Then he stumped out again.'

'To think we had our heads deep in the manual of military law when all this was happening,' said Adam.

'Go on, Jasper. What then?'

'Nothing really. D. P. Brown and Algy had a huge row in the colonel's office and a cloud of gloom has settled on the mess all week. But you, Burgo, and Adam will be on the mat on Monday morning. He's determined to get to the bottom of this.'

'Do you think D. P. Brown has finally gone mad?' said Burgo, joyfully.

'I wonder what set him off. He didn't come into Burgo's *salle privée*.'

'He was in a good mood,' I said.

'Until Heidi's striptease,' said Jasper.

'That didn't set him off on this witch-hunt,' I replied. 'Something must have happened on Sunday.'

'He had lunch with the Trenches,' said Burgo.

'Then Trench Foot put him up to it,' said Adam.

'Burgo, what's the position with Horace?' I asked.

'I haven't had time to talk to him yet.'

'Then you'd better write him out of the evening. Horace is the weak link. If he really can't remember anything, then don't remind him. If he suddenly admits to losing £75, that's all the evidence D. P. Brown needs to show we've flouted the rules.'

'I need that £75 in Deutschmarks to settle with the hotel in Baden-Baden,' said Adam.

'You'll have to find it elsewhere,' I said. 'Now let's go through exactly what happened very carefully.'

On Saturday morning Ben Wildbore took me to the shoot at the Sengers in his Talbot.

As soon as we got out of the town Ben said, 'I must talk to you about an investigation Colonel Dennis has asked Val and Francis to conduct into the roulette game last Saturday night.'

'We heard about this when we got back to the mess last night. I don't understand.'

'It is thought that the losses were larger than those written into the bridge book. Algy and I have said that is nonsense, but neither of us was in the room or playing. There appear to be people who were in the room who report much larger sums were being won and, more importantly, lost.'

'Who were these people?'

'I'm not sure. But be warned. Algy and I are on your side. Algy has asked me to enquire whether you've been following the rules. Have you?'

'Yes.'

'If there is anything you want to tell me, tell me now. Algy wants to know the truth. He can't defend you otherwise. He doesn't think you would flaunt the rules. But you might have bent them a little.'

'What is in the bridge book is accurate. There is one entry missing. The bank let Horace run up a debt of £80. They gave him credit in the hope of his winning it back, but he was so pissed and didn't know what he was doing. In the circumstances we thought it best not to collect from him. Horace, being Horace, has always been considered to be outside the rules. If the bank had refused him credit he would have made a scene. You can't limit Horace to £5. There was enough trouble that evening as it was.'

'I understand. Who else was playing?'

'The usual crowd. Val played for a bit. So did Jack Trench.'

'That's the problem. Val and Jack Trench don't approve of the bachelor mess and its ways. Jack Trench particularly dislikes Adam and has got it in for Jasper. You should warn them.'

'Nothing is going to change Adam or Jasper.'

'Tell them not to be so blatant in Jack and Val's presence.'

'They only do it to tease.'

'Teasing majors like Jack Trench will only end in tears.'

'Val leaves next week. Surely things will change under Francis as adjutant?'

'That's what we all hope. But no one can change Jack Trench except the colonel.'

'And the colonel likes Jack's sneaky ways?'

'I'm not answering that. So, apart from Horace's debt, the bridge book told the whole story?'

'Yes.'

'Good. I'll tell Algy. On Monday, when Francis sends for you, stick to the story that Horace only lost £5 and that the bridge book is correct. You can say that Horace asked for more credit and that the bank refused it. Be sure that Adam and Burgo stick to the story too.'

We motored on.

'Isn't all this gambling a little silly?' asked Ben. 'I enjoy it now and again. Adam and Burgo seem to be making it a way of life. You are senior subaltern. It's not in your interests to let it get out of hand.'

We sat in silence while I thought about that.

We got to the Sengers at ten o'clock. In the morning we shot pheasant. After four drives we'd shot twenty-six brace. Andreas was pleased and, producing a bottle of cherry brandy to start the lunch, he said it was a good bag for the land we had shot over. After lunch it was ground game. Andreas stationed us on two edges of a large, sprawling wood. A team of beaters worked the wood from the far sides, walking casually and silently. He'd told us this was the best way to get the game moving in our direction without disturbing them too much. We stood and waited. I was alone again and could only think about Kitty and Rana. Everything was quiet around us. We waited. Suddenly a deer ran out of the edge of the wood across me. I fired too late and missed. Algy, twenty yards to my left, shot the deer cleanly. There was some shooting on the other side of the wood, then silence, and the beaters emerged from the wood. No one saw a boar.

As we counted the bag, Algy said, 'Your shot alerted me, Miles.

I didn't expect to get a chance next to you.'

'I just wasn't expecting the deer at that moment.'

'It's always difficult first time, Miles,' said Andreas. 'Perhaps I should have explained that you have to have enormous patience and attention. If the beaters make a noise then the deer rush out of the wood at speed in all directions. If the beaters walk casually and noiselessly, then the deer nose their way out and only start to run when they see a human. I probably placed you too far in the open. But now you've tried it, you must come again.'

I thought if Rana had been beside me I would have paid more attention. Or, I had to admit, if Kitty had been.

In the car on the way back, Ben said he had discussed the roulette issue with Algy. He was grateful to have been told the truth. We were to stick to the story we'd agreed and Algy would support us. Back in the mess we were having a drink when Adam came in.

'Jasper was inspired,' he said. 'He pulled it off at Brunswick at ten to one. I've won enough Deutschmarks to settle the hotel and,' he went on, looking at me, 'to take Jasper, Kitty and Rana to the Lucullus for dinner. I'm just going to have a bath and get changed.'

13

More racing days

Later I learned from Jasper that Adam had been teasing me. He had won enough money to pay off the hotel and take everyone to dinner at the Lucullus; it was Horace who proposed dinner and footed the bill in an attempt to placate Kitty. Rana was there, as she had gone with Kitty to the race meeting. So were others. They sat down, so Jasper told me, ten to dinner. I had a dreary meal in the mess, played backgammon with Francis, lost, and went to bed.

At half past six on Sunday morning I was woken by knocking on my door. It was Francis.

'Mushrooms and bacon for breakfast, Miles.'

I threw on some clothes. We motored to the fields near Kremke and collected enough fungi for breakfast for everyone in the mess.

'You seem a little unhappy, Miles. It's not about the roulette, is it?'

'My problem, Francis, is love.'

'Oh dear.'

'Am I, or am I not, in love? And with whom?'

'I can't help you there.'

'No one can except those involved and they're either giving me too much help or too little.'

'How many might you be in love with?'

'Only two.'

'Joint favourites?'

'I hadn't thought of it like that.'

'Always calculate the risk. Much of life is about risk taking.'

'Both, on reflection, are outsiders with long odds against. I haven't a chance with either.'

'Neither sounds a good bet to me.'

'You're right. I feel ready for breakfast now.'

'It's always good to get up early.'

It was our custom on Sunday to have drinks in the mess after church. In those days most of us went to church, to matins followed, once a month, by Holy Communion according to the Book of Common Prayer. The Roman Catholics went to a church in the town, but most of the officers and their wives attended morning service at the chapel in the barracks, as did quite a few soldiers. As we were all congregating in the mess Kitty came up to me.

'Darling,' she said, 'I'm so sorry you couldn't come racing at Brunswick yesterday. Jasper and Vampire were stars. I do hope you can come next week to Hanover. We're on a winning streak.'

'I'm so pleased for you both,' I replied.

'I want you, darling, to be part of this. We can't talk now but do come riding next week. I need your support.'

She turned away to talk to Jack and Julia Trench.

On Monday Francis, now adjutant, sent for me.

'I am uncomfortable having to do this,' he said, 'but I've been asked to investigate an allegation that excessive sums were gambled at roulette in the mess on the Saturday before last. It has been suggested that the sums won and lost were far greater then those put in the bridge book and that you, Jasper, Adam, and Burgo came to an agreement to disguise the figures. Is this so?'

'No.'

'That's all I want to know. Thank you, Miles.'

He talked to the others and upheld Algy and Ben in finding that nothing had been untoward. Colonel Dennis had to accept it but he didn't like it.

Later in the day I went to the stables with Jasper. Kitty was already there, and the three of us rode into the forest, Jasper ahead.

'I'm so glad you've come riding today, darling,' she said. 'I want to talk to you so badly. I've written to Daddy to say that I want to divorce Horace. Horace is frightened of Daddy and he'll do what Daddy tells him. I haven't mentioned you and it's best if we're not seen alone. Someone like Jack Trench will smell a rat and sneak on us. I want you kept out of this. As it is, Horace suspects I'm having an affair with Jasper. He's such a fool.'

'Kitty, you must divorce Horace. You can't go on as it is. I'm thinking of volunteering for the King's African Rifles in Kenya, and go and fight the Mau Mau.'

'That's a marvellous idea, darling. When I've got my divorce I can come and join you. I'd love to live in Kenya. We'll have a wonderful time there.'

We rode on in silence.

'Yes,' she said, 'we'll have a wonderful time in Kenya. That's something to look forward to at last. Oh darling, I nearly forgot to tell you. Rana's leaving us at the end of the term. Her father thinks it's time she returned home and got married.'

She rode off to ride beside Jasper leaving me to think about the letter in my pocket that I had received from Rana that morning.

Dear Miles,

My father has written me a long letter about my future. I had written to him about you, told him some of the things we had done together. I had said that I liked you. He warned me not to get emotionally entangled with a foreigner in Germany. He said we came from different worlds, that however much we might be attracted to each other now, in time our different worlds and beliefs would separate us. He said we had no future, that it was time for me to return home and get married. I think he has someone in mind for he is a wise man, has always guided me well, and I owe him everything. I must marry one of my own

countrymen and I know Daddy is right. I have never been out
alone with a man before you. I have often thought that, as well
as you and I get on together, there is something in the way. I
now know what that is and my father has made me see it. Also,
I have thought a lot about what you and Kitty have told me. I'm
still puzzled by it but I do hope life gets better for both of you.
    With fond thoughts, dear Miles,

                                                    Yours, Rana Selzuk.

I re-read the letter in my mind. Those two girls, I thought, are
deciding my future for me. I'm not in control. And what's all this
talk about marriage? I can't marry anyone. Then and there I decided to go and see Francis and apply for a transfer to the King's
African Rifles.

Kitty and Jasper decided to put Vampire into an open chase restricted to British horses only. This was to be at Hanover. Colonel
Dennis was also riding Red Ember in it. There were only nine
horses running but they were the top British horses in Germany.
I had stayed away from the racecourse not wanting to confuse
Kitty's life; nor had we been alone together again. Jasper reported
to me on all the races and brought messages. No news had leaked
out about divorce and I wondered what steps Kitty had taken.
Maybe her father had dissuaded her though I doubted anyone
could, once she had made up her mind. Everyone knew that Kitty
and Horace were at loggerheads. There were strong rumours, too,
about Kitty and Jasper.
    The day of the big race I went shooting with Francis at the
Sengers. When we got back to the mess in the evening Adam and
Burgo were drinking Bollinger and preparing to spend more of their
winnings at the Lucullus. They asked us to go with them. Adam
told us that Red Ember had started favourite, Horace having put a
sizeable amount on him. Vampire was third in the betting at keener
odds than before but still worthwhile. The mess had been evenly
divided about who would win, the junior officers mainly favour-

ing Vampire and the senior Red Ember. I had given my money to
Burgo to back Vampire for me. There was no question in my mind
that he was the better horse, Jasper the better rider, and Kitty a
talented trainer. Adam told us that D. P. Brown had led for most
of the way, Jasper lying well back. Then, at the fourth last fence,
Jasper began to make his way forward, caught Red Ember at the
last, where D. P. Brown fell, and won by three lengths.

'Come to the Lucullus,' said Burgo.

'Will Jasper be there?' I asked.

'He promised to join us. So did Finbar and Ben.'

'Would he have won if D.P. Brown hadn't fallen?'

'Yes.'

'What about the Belchers? Are they coming?'

'They said they'd try. But they were quarrelling. Kitty said she
wanted to look after the horses and damn D. P. Brown who'd just
sworn at Horace for asking him how he was. Rather bruised in
fact, physically and mentally. Horace had been drinking and had
lost seriously, even for Horace.'

Despite an excellent meal, we had a rather empty evening at
the Lucullus. Jasper, Finbar and Ben never appeared. Nor did
the Belchers.

Ben was waiting for us when we got back to the mess.

'I've only just got back here myself. I've got bad news. Horace
was killed on the autobahn on the way back from Hanover. Kitty
is in the British Military Hospital at Hanover, critically ill.'

'Will she live?' I asked.

'Finbar is with her. I can't tell you more than that.'

'What about Jasper?'

'Jasper's fine. I've sent him to bed. Luckily he was travelling
with me.'

'How did it happen?'

'We left the racecourse before them. Horace caught up and
overtook us. He was driving very fast, weaving in and out of the
traffic. Kitty appeared to be asleep. I put my foot down to keep
up with him. He was following a lorry that had overtaken another,

and he started to overtake that one on the inside. The lorry pulled over, squeezing Horace off the road. We stopped immediately. It wasn't a pretty sight. Horace must have died instantly. Kitty was lying there like a sack. I thought she was dead but Finbar said unconscious. Her face was untouched but Finbar thought she'd broken a lot of bones. The police came. He went in the ambulance with her to the hospital and we followed. Finbar's still at the hospital. He said there was nothing we could do but that he wanted to stay with her in case she came round. They were operating on her when we left. Jasper wanted to stay too, but Finbar told him to go back to barracks with me.'

Ten days later we buried Horace with full military honours. As I knelt during the funeral service in the great Protestant church in the town, the memories of others we had buried in Korea without any panoply and grandeur overtook my thoughts: those who had been killed in great acts of courage or merely by chance, and those whose bodies we never found and might still be lying rotting and unburied on the battlefield. Today, I thought, we were burying a man with all the splendour the regiment could muster, whom Colonel Guy Surtees refused to take to Korea, a man whom Colonel Dennis Parker Brown had tolerated because of his prowess on the polo field but had harassed to the point that Horace had been fighting for military survival, with his final recourse the bottle and his victim his wife. I thought of Kitty lying in the hospital at Hanover, conscious now but still critically ill. The tears that I had been holding back began winding their way down my cheeks. I was angry at the incongruities of life and the hypocrisy of the occasion. I was angry with Colonel Dennis for ordering so grand a funeral. Was this how he was exculpating his guilt over the way he had driven Horace to his death? Was I going too far now?

The last hymn had begun. Vaughan Williams' magnificent 'For all the saints who from their labours rest' was filling the church. I sang the line 'O may thy soldiers, faithful, true and bold'. Yes,

Horace was faithful: faithful to his colonel. He, unlike the rest of us, never questioned him. Yes, Horace was true. He never dissembled or pretended to be anything he was not. He did his duty. Yes, Horace was bold. No one was bolder on the polo field. I must give the man his due and show compassion to one so insecure that he had to compete so disastrously with his wife. I remembered what Little Steel had said to me. 'Pity about Major Belcher, Sir. He was a great character and a great horseman. Of course we all thought him a little mad.' Perhaps Horace was a little mad. Perhaps that is what had once attracted Kitty.

The buglers sounded the last post, and the family followed the coffin out to the burial ground.

Afterwards we gathered in the mess.

Kitty's father, old General Fisher, came across to me. He was wearing a regimental tie, red with blue and green stripes, with a regimental tiepin.

'Well, Miles, this is a rum do'

'I'm terribly sorry about Kitty, Sir.'

'No one more than me. She should never have married that man. All Sonia Blessington's fault. I let Kitty go out to Hong Kong to stay with her godmother Sonia to get over some silly engagement she'd insisted on. Blow me, Sonia lets her go and get married almost immediately to the first man she meets. Sonia's your cousin isn't she?'

'She's my mother's first cousin.'

'What's her other name?'

'Blessington'

'No, no. I know that. Her other name. Wasn't Ivan Blessington made a peer when he gave up being governor of Hong Kong?'

'Yes. He's called Cathay now.'

'Ah, yes. Haven't they got a daughter?'

'Phyllida. She's much younger than Kitty.'

'Belcher, over there, Horace's elder brother, has been very decent. He's said Kitty will benefit from all the trusts that Horace had. She's a rich girl now. That is, if she lives.'

'How is she?'

'Very weak. Great spirit. Looks fine. Heaven knows what's happened to her body. I could kill Horace if he wasn't already dead. Suppose I shouldn't talk like that. Go and see her. You're an old friend. Cheer her up.'

'I'll do that, General.'

'Where's Brown, your colonel?'

'Talking to Sir Jeremy Belcher.'

'If I'd been colonel of the regiment I wouldn't have accepted him. Calls himself Parker Brown now I hear. Where did the Parker come from?'

'I've never heard.'

'If I were colonel of the regiment now I wouldn't have him as commanding officer.'

'You are talking very loud, General.'

'Am I? Ah, there's Algy Stanhope. Want to talk to him.'

As he left me Sonia Blessington, now Viscountess Cathay, came across. She kissed me.

'Darling Miles. All this is so terrible. I feel so guilty about it.'

'Why, Cousin Sonia? It was Horace at the wheel.'

'I just feel I could have done more for Kitty. Her condition is terrible.'

'You couldn't have done more than you have. She is so strong willed. No one has been able to steady her.'

'I think you did once, Miles. Go and see her. She's been asking after you. And come and see us when you're next in London. We don't see enough of you. It's time we had a good chat. I've got to leave after lunch.'

She gave me another kiss.

As she left me, Olivia came across.

'Oh Miles,' she said and she hugged me.

'Don't make me cry again,' I said. 'You're wonderful to have spent so much time with Kitty. How is she, really?'

'She's had your letter. She wants to see you. And she wants to see Jasper. When can you go?'

'We could go after lunch.'

'I'm going back after lunch. Come with me.'

'Thank you, Olivia. We'll have to square Francis.'

'Algy will fix that. I saw you talking to Kitty's father. He's staying with us. Isn't he wonderful?'

'I've known him all my life.'

'Tell me about him. I've always admired him.'

'He's 75. He won his first DSO when he was 23 in the Boer War. When the Great War started he was a major. He finished it a major general. He won two more DSOs. He never got any further as he was too outspoken. A great horseman of course. He's always rather looked down on the Belchers. The Fishers were among the first baronets in the seventeenth century. The Belchers are late nineteenth century baronets, industrialists. It's an interesting conceit.'

'You can see where Kitty gets her spirit and her horsemanship from. How did your cousin Sonia come to be Kitty's godmother?'

'She was Kitty's mother's great friend. Kitty's mother was much younger than her father. When she died Sonia tried to keep a close eye on Kitty but, what with the war and following Ivan round the world, not as close as she would have liked.'

Algy joined us.

'I hear you've volunteered for the King's African Rifles in Kenya,' he said.

'I've asked Francis if it can be arranged.'

'Francis thinks it a good opportunity for you and so do I. Colonel Dennis was impressed by your spirit in wanting to go and fight the Mau Mau. Now, with Horace's death, he says he can't afford to lose two officers. He's vetoed it. I can understand why. I'm sorry but I'm glad you'll be staying. I'm telling you this off the record. Be surprised when Francis tells you.'

After lunch Olivia drove Jasper and me to the hospital in Hanover. She talked to the nurses and went in to see Kitty, alone. She wasn't long.

'You go in first, Miles. But don't stay more than five minutes.'

Kitty was lying flat on her back looking at the ceiling, with a huge cage over her body and lots of tubes. She didn't look at me. I don't think she could turn her head.

'Hello, darling. Thank God you've come. I've been miserable without you.'

She took my hand and held it. I bent down and kissed it.

'Kiss me, darling.'

I kissed her on the cheek and looked into her eyes. All love was there.

'No. On the lips.'

I kissed her very softly on the lips.

'This is a rum do.'

'That's what your father said.'

'How funny. Haven't things changed? I'm a rich widow now. We're going to be so happy. I can't wait to get out of this place. You did bury Horace this morning didn't you?'

'We buried him with full military honours.'

'He didn't deserve that but he would have wanted it. He'll be happier where he is.'

She paused. She was finding it hard to speak for long.

'I don't think we should get married immediately,' she said. 'That would seem improper. But soon and we'll be so happy in Kenya. I'm thinking so much about it. We are going to get married, aren't we darling?'

'Yes, we are.'

'Better for you to marry a widow than a divorcee. Your mother would prefer that.'

'Yes, darling.'

'I loved your letter. Did Olivia tell you? Please write again soon.'

'Did Olivia read it to you?'

'Oh don't worry. Olivia knows. She always has. You will write, won't you? A proper love letter. I will write you one when I can.'

'Of course, darling.'

'Darling, you'd better go now. Kiss me again on the lips.'

I left. Olivia made Jasper wait a few minutes before he went in.

He came out quite quickly, looking grim.

'Will she live?'

'She will, if it's possible,' said Olivia. 'She wants to so much. She's very knocked about. What did she say to you?'

'She wants me to go on running Vampire in races. And she wants to enter him for the Grand Military at Sandown. We've discussed it before. She says she'll be well enough by then to take him back to England and train him at home for it. She's going to buy more horses for me to ride.'

Olivia went in to see Kitty for a minute. Then we drove back to the barracks.

Two days later Kitty died. Jasper and I were standing in the ante-room when we heard.

'No more racing now,' said Jasper.

'She wanted you to go on,' I said.

'Look out of the window.'

I looked out and couldn't see more than a hundred yards. Great flakes of snow were tumbling down the sky. Suddenly I began to shiver uncontrollably but it wasn't because of the snow.

Months later, after the snow had gone and the reality of Kitty's death had sunk in, a few of us went to a small ceremony to conse-crate the headstone that had been placed on her grave.

'Almost her last words were about her headstone,' said Olivia. ' "You'll have to bury me next to Horace," she said, " but on my headstone I want to be described as the only child of General Fisher with all those grand letters after his name." '

I looked at the stone.

In loving memory of
Katherine Sophia Belcher
beloved only child of
Major General Sir George Fisher Bt
CB CMG DSO
1929 - 1953

'And her last words, Olivia?'

'She was holding your last letter in her hand. I had just read it to her. She said, "Tell Daddy I'm sorry to have been such a trouble to him. And bury me with Miles's letter in my hand." '

14

Some home truths

'Congratulations on your majority, Ben.'

'Thanks, Miles. I'm sad it had to happen the way it did.'

Ben had been promoted and taken over Horace's company.

'I've got to go to London,' he said. 'Why don't you take some leave and come with me? It's time we had a break from this place. I don't think I can stomach another row over gambling or watch another race.'

We were sitting in the anteroom alone after dinner.

'That's a good idea. Why've you got to go?'

'My aunt has died and left me everything. I've got to go and see the lawyers and sort it all out. She had a house in Harrington Gardens, which she'd turned into flats. There're some shares and money in the bank, too. My mother is furious.'

'I'll have to ask Francis.'

'I'm sure he'll think it a good thing.'

The following morning I went and asked Francis if he thought the colonel would grant me a week's leave. I said I wanted to have a week's shooting. He thought the colonel would approve of that, so I wrote my name in the leave book and gave my address as care of Lady Cathay in Herefordshire, though I intended to stay in London with Ben most of the time. I thought the colonel would find it difficult to deny me a week with the Cathays.

'You'll need ration cards,' said Francis. 'There's still some rationing in England, especially butter. Get them from the chief clerk. There are some errands you can do. Most of the Belchers' stuff has been packed up and sent back to their families. There are still some personal things that can only go by hand of officer. I take it you're travelling with Ben? His leave has been approved for the same dates.'

'Do you think we should go and see General Flaxman? He always says he likes to see his officers when they are in England.'

'Yes, he does. Ben should write to him to say you'll be in London and then ring him when you get there. He's not at all well. You might cheer him up.'

Ben and I left for England the following week in his Talbot. He had arranged to get rid of it; it was becoming a vintage car. He was going to buy a new Sunbeam Talbot that could do 100 mph. He had been asked to return some of Horace's personal possessions to his brother. I had been given Kitty's jewel case and a bundle of papers to give to General Fisher.

We motored, in uniform, through Belgium and France to Calais. We had no difficulty with the customs though Ben did have to show a carnet for his Talbot when we passed the frontiers. The car was loaded on to the ferry by crane. We got to Folkestone in the morning, reaching Ben's house in Harrington Gardens in the afternoon. It stood five stories high. We walked down the area steps and rang the bell of the basement flat.

'Good afternoon Mrs Pooley,' said Ben to a middle-aged woman who opened the door.

'Oh, Major Benjamin, I got your telegram. Everything's ready for you. I've made up the beds. Otherwise it's just as Lady Rooke left it, except your mother's been round and removed all her lady-ship's clothes. I hope that was all right?'

'I hope she didn't remove anything else?'

'Oh no, I was with her all the time. Only the clothes. I'll get the key now and open up for you.'

Ben's aunt had lived in a self-contained flat she had made out of the ground and first floors of the building. The main staircase now served the three flats that had been created at the top of the house. We entered what was now Ben's flat.

'I hope you'll be comfortable. I've lit a fire in the sitting room.'

The flat was bursting with furniture and carpets, mainly from the East.

'I've been wanting to talk to you,' she went on. 'I want to know what's expected of me. It hasn't been an easy time with your aunt and I'm concerned about the future.'

'Mrs Pooley, you're not to worry. Tomorrow I'm going to see the lawyers. I'm going to tell them that I want you to stay on and look after the flats as you did for my aunt. I don't want anything to change. I won't be here much, but I want you to know that your job is secure. Some of my friends may use the flat, like Mr Player here, but I'll always let you know.'

'Oh, Major Benjamin, you are kind. I was hoping you'd say that. I do appreciate it. Now I'll make you some tea. Would you like me to cook you some dinner?'

'Tea would be wonderful. Dinner we'll go out for. Mr Player has got some ration cards that you might find useful.'

'Oh, I could use those. How thoughtful you are.'

She scurried away a much happier woman.

'I always thought your name was Benedict?'

'It is.'

'And Lady Rooke?'

'She was my father's sister. Her husband was governor of an Indian province. Isn't the furniture ghastly? I'll have to do something about that. I can see why my mother only took the clothes. Luckily, the lawyers have got the jewel case.'

I had written to General Fisher asking if I could deliver Kitty's jewel case, and he had invited me for a night, and a day's shooting. My programme took shape round that. The following day, after Ben had seen his lawyers, we were to meet at the military club in Pall

Mall we both belonged to, a grand nineteenth-century building modelled on a palazzo on the Grand Canal in Venice. We thought we might run into some regimental chums there. In the afternoon we arranged to have tea with General Flaxman. The evening we were to spend with the Cathays in London, before I went to stay with General Fisher the following day. I then arranged to go and see my mother, and later, Jasper's mother. With any luck the Cathays would ask me to Herefordshire for a weekend's shooting before we returned to Germany. Ben said I could use the flat as a base and gave me a set of keys.

When we had made all these arrangements we changed into suits, climbed into the Talbot for the last time together and drove to the Aperitif Grill in Jermyn Street for dinner.

'It's time,' said Ben, 'we treated ourselves to a bit of London crumpet after that farce in Berlin. We'll go on to the Astor Club. There'll be no nonsense there.'

In the morning I was woken by the crackle of burning wood and the smell of coal. Mrs Pooley was making a fire in my bedroom. It reminded me of my childhood before the war when every morning in winter a maid had come and made a fire in my room before I got up. I haven't been spoilt like this for years, I thought.

'Breakfast will be ready at eight thirty,' said Mrs Pooley. 'Have you anything you want pressing? You gentlemen did come in late. I suppose you went to a nightclub. I didn't know they stayed open that late.'

There were bacon and eggs and butter for breakfast. Mrs Pooley must have acted quickly with the ration cards.

I went to Duke Street, had my hair cut and washed, which made me feel better and encouraged me to walk up to the regimental tailor in Sackville Street and order some clothes. At half past twelve I met Ben at our club. Two generals in our regiment asked us searching questions about battalion life in Germany. They seemed disbelieving when we reported that life under Colonel Dennis was 'All Sir Garnet'.

'What else could we say?' said Ben, over a moderate lunch. 'Don't you think this stuff is muck compared to what we eat in Germany?'

'They should employ Mrs Pooley. Breakfast was excellent.'

'Don't you suggest it. Where did you end up last night?'

'Somewhere off the Edgware Road. And you?'

'Rather too near Harrington Gardens. I could've walked home.'

'Have fun?'

'Rather. And you?'

'Yes. But I couldn't stop thinking about Kitty.'

'You'll get over that. How much?'

'Fifteen oncers.'

'Snap.'

We went to see General Flaxman. He lived in a flat on the top floor of a 1930s block in Princes Gate. A male servant opened the door, took our hats and umbrellas and showed us into an exquisitely furnished room at the back of the flat, overlooking gardens. General Flaxman was in his mid sixties but he looked much older. He was sitting in a heavily cushioned *bergère* chair, with two sticks beside him. His beautifully tailored clothes sagged round him emphasising his thinness. His voice was thin too.

'How civil of you to come and see me,' he said. 'I can't get up. Come and shake my hand. Goodness, you both look well. Life must be treating you well in Germany. I remember we had a fine time there after the First War. You must tell me all about it. I'm too halt to come and see you. The quacks won't let me travel. Morris, bring some tea for the young gentlemen. Biscuits too. And anchovy toast.'

Morris served tea and left us.

'Miles, you're looking after the shooting since Dermot Lisle resigned, aren't you? That was terrible, losing the divisional small arms meeting like that. I don't know what could have got into Dermot. I always had such high hopes of him. Do you know his father wrote to me complaining how badly the regiment had treated Dermot? I didn't reply. Dermot had become so disloyal. Colonel Dennis said he'd had too much success too early. So how is the shooting team doing now?'

'We're doing well but we were very sad to lose Dermot, General,' I said. 'He was a brilliant team captain.'

'Not what I heard, Miles. You can't have seen everything that was going on. We can't afford scandals in the regiment. It's fortunate Dermot resigned before there was a scandal. Now Ben, you're PMC aren't you? I hear you've a fine mess. I was delighted to get this revision of my monograph on the mess possessions.'

He picked up a book from a side table. It was bound in dark green leather with gold lettering beneath a regimental crest.

'Dennis Parker Brown sent it to me. I don't know how he had the time to bring it up to date himself. He said you were giving some much-admired parties. Which reminds me, I hear you gave Horace Belcher a fine funeral. Just what I would have expected. Sir Jeremy Belcher wrote to me to say how much he appreciated everything the regiment had done for his brother. Tragedy about Horace. Such a fine polo player. Pity about Kitty. The Fishers are a wild family. Let her racing successes go to her head, I expect. I hear Jasper Knox is a fine horseman, but I didn't like the rumours I heard about them.'

'Jasper is a fine horseman, General, the finest we have, better than Horace,' said Ben. 'Kitty Belcher excelled as a trainer. There was an entirely professional relationship between them.'

'Not what I heard, Ben, but then why should you know? He wasn't in your company was he? Miles, as senior subaltern, it's your job to keep the subalterns under control. But I'm not your commanding officer and I hear good things of you both.'

Morris returned to the room and drew the curtains.

'Time for your rest, Sir John. You know what the doctors have said.'

'Yes, Morris. These gentlemen are just leaving. Thank you so much for coming to see me. I'm sorry I can't come and see you in Germany. The quacks won't let me at the moment. Just remember, the regiment must avoid a scandal. So good of you to come and see me.'

Ben and I got up, shook his hand and left.

As soon as we were out of the building Ben said, 'Let's find a pub. We need a drink.'

'Better to walk to the Hyde Park Hotel. It's not far.'

'That man's gaga.'

'Worse than gaga. He's brainwashed by D.P.Brown.'

'What the hell has D.P.Brown got on him? It's a disaster. We must find out.'

'He's dying. He can't last much longer.'

'Another day's too long.'

'What was all that about the regiment must avoid another scandal?'

'And Dermot resigning before there was a scandal?'

'No wonder D.P.Brown gets away with everything.'

'Yes, but why?'

We both shook our heads and walked on to the bar at the Hyde Park Hotel. Two whiskies restored our morale.

'How did your visit to the lawyers go?'

'Fine. I'm quite well off, but don't tell anyone. Otherwise people will start touching me. Adam has already. He seems to have money and then he doesn't. I can't make Adam out. Where does his come from?'

'His grandfather made a packet in silk stockings, or socks or gloves or something. There's not all that much left. Every now and again his mother wheedles a bit out of his father and hands it on to Adam, or so Adam says.'

'Lucky to have a mother like that.'

'I've got to go and see my mother and I'm not looking forward to it.'

'You've got all those fairy godmothers. Sonia Blessington, Olivia Stanhope, how many more?'

'Time we went to the Blessingtons. Sonia asked us to be early.

We're going out to dinner.'

We got a taxi, drove in a thickening fog to Eaton Terrace and rang the bell. A Chinese manservant opened the door and showed us up to the sitting room on the first floor where Sonia greeted us.

'Darling Miles, dear Ben, how lovely and early. I was afraid you were going to be late in this smog. We're going to the Berkeley rather than the Savoy. It's nearer and if the smog gets worse it will be easier to get home. Ivan will be here shortly, and Phyllida. They've gone to see the Diaghilev Exhibition. I've been. You must see it. Now, what would you like to drink? Miles, why don't you make us some martinis? It's all there on the drinks trolley.'

We were chatting away drinking martinis when the Chinese servant came in.

'Yes Chang?'

'Lord. He telephoned. You meet him Berkeley. I take in motor.'

'When Chang?'

'Soon.'

He withdrew.

'Good. Miles, your martinis are delicious, much stronger than Ivan makes.'

As I shook the shaker again I said, 'If he calls Ivan "Lord", what does he call you?'

'Nothing. I don't exist. He's Ivan's, heart and soul.'

'Do you take him to Herefordshire?'

'Good heavens, no, it's bad enough having him here. In Herefordshire we'd be a laughing stock.'

'How do you get to Herefordshire then?'

'We go by train and are met.'

'I've got to take some of Kitty's things to General Fisher tomorrow. I'm to be met at Basingstoke.'

'Oh, Kitty, Kitty, Kitty, what a tragedy. It makes me cry talking about Kitty. Miles, I know Ivan wants you to shoot this Saturday. Come on Friday, and we can have long talks about dearest Kitty.

Will you come Ben?'

'No, Lady Cathay. Thank you, but I've been asked by Jeremy Belcher to spend the weekend and he's promised some shooting too. Like Miles I have to deliver some things.'

Chang appeared at the door.

'Time go meet Lord.'

'Quite so,' said Sonia.

Ivan and Phyllida were waiting for us in the bar at the Berkeley. When I had last seen Phyllida in Hong Kong she'd been a girl. Now she was a woman, a younger version of her mother and as good looking.

'Cousin Miles,' she said, giving me her hand.

'Phyllida,' I said, kissing her on the cheek, and added, 'you're ravishingly beautiful. How fortunate I am to have so lovely a cousin.'

'You didn't come to my party,' she said, a slight blush softening the reprimand.

'I couldn't get leave. You know what the army is like.'

'I don't, but I forgive you.'

'I think we should go in,' said Sonia. 'Miles made us some martinis and they're much stronger than yours, Ivan. Let's sit down and order.'

We were shown to a table in a corner.

'Ben, you sit on my right between me and Phyllida,' said Sonia. 'Miles will see a lot of Phyllida at the weekend. That's right. Now what are we going to have? Where's the waiter?'

Sonia proceeded to give us the benefit of her considerable experience of the place. Ivan handed me the wine list saying, 'I suggest a bottle of white burgundy and a magnum of claret. Choose something decent.'

We ordered. Then Sonia and Phyllida talked to Ben, pumping him to tell them all about his inheritance.

'How are you enjoying the army in Germany?' Ivan asked.

'Not as much as I'd hoped, and certainly not this afternoon.'

'What happened this afternoon?'

'We went to call on General Flaxman, the colonel of the regiment, and found him gaga and totally under the thumb of Dennis Parker Brown, our commanding officer.'

'I hear he's dying. He won't be with us much longer.'

'Serving under Parker Brown is difficult to say the least. He's getting away with murder.'

The wine waiter brought the wine.

'That's a good choice,' said Ivan looking at the bottles and the decanted magnum of claret. 'That should be enough for you.'

'Aren't you going to have some?'

'No. I'm happy with this.'

The waiter put a silver tankard in front of him. It was full of champagne.

'It's best in silver,' said Ivan. 'It keeps cold that way. It's very good to have you with us. We see too little of you nowadays.'

He raised his tankard. I raised my glass.

'You could always join the Colonial Office. They're looking for people like you.'

'I thought the empire was contracting?'

'Not at all. India was a special case. There are great opportunities all round the world. People seem to think we are on the decline. Far from it. We're living in a new Elizabethan age. Life is changing for the better, both in this country and the world. I saw a fine French film the other day called *La vie commence demain* about all the opportunities opening up for mankind. We have to take advantage of those both here and in our colonies. We need people to help develop those countries.'

'I wasn't actually thinking of leaving the army. I'd been thinking of the King's African Rifles in Kenya, but Parker Brown vetoed that.'

'We're going to need a big army for a long time. All these bush fire wars around the globe. The empire needs policing, and we must keep a modern army in Western Germany as a bulwark against communism. That's why your regiment still has two battalions. We may have to increase our forces, not reduce them.'

'I thought with the armistice in Korea the army would be cut back.'

'Too great a commitment to NATO and too many small wars going on for that.'

'What about the cold war? Isn't that a stalemate because of nuclear weapons?'

'We need to maintain enough conventional forces to prevent Russia walking through Western Germany. Wars arise from weakness. Look at the experience of the 1930s. We have to be strong and be seen to be strong. That was the reason for fighting in Korea. Stalin saw that we were prepared to fight. The United Nations and NATO are powerful forces for maintaining the status quo.'

'And America?'

'We have a special relationship with America. Winston is close to Eisenhower. You've got the two most important world leaders seeing eye to eye. We can rely on the Americans to help us.'

'I think I'll stay in the army. Stationed in Germany one feels a little out of things. It's very helpful to have that all so clearly explained.'

'The army is always a little out of things, as you put it. And so it should be, outside politics. Your role is to carry out the needs of the politicians. The politicians' job is to give you the wherewithal to do what they ask.'

'We don't think much of the new jeep the government has given us - it's called the champ - to do the job. It's so complicated it breaks down all the time.'

'Who breaks down all the time?' asked Sonia.

'Miles is talking about a new vehicle the army has,' said Ivan.

'You *are* being serious. I hoped you were talking about that dreadful colonel of yours, Dennis Parker Brown. How do you put up with him? He was so pompous and awful at Horace's funeral.'

'Sonia!' Ivan remonstrated.

'Well he was. I was there and you weren't. I think these boys deserve better. Now Guy Surtees, there was a soldier. You could see that at a glance. But Parker Brown, he looks like a small stuffed prick. All pretence.'

'Mummy, if I had said that you would have scolded me.'

'So I would but he does.'

'Have you heard what we call him?' I asked.

'No.'

'We call him D.P.Brown.'

'Dennis Parker Brown. So what?'

'No. Down Penis Brown.'

Sonia screamed with laughter. Phyllida giggled. Ivan looked disapproving.

'You'll encourage these boys to acts of disloyalty if you go on like that, Sonia.'

'These boys, as you call them, are quite old enough to look after themselves. You are being batey tonight. You used to enjoy a good joke. It seems to me they're having fun in Germany whatever they say and whatever Down Penis Brown does.'

She screamed with laughter again.

'I thought,' said Ben, 'we all might go round to Hatchett's after dinner. It's only next door. My treat.'

'What a lovely idea. How generous of you, Ben,' said Sonia.

'You go with Phyllida,' said Ivan 'I must go home and study some papers. I'll send Chang back to wait for you.'

So Sonia, Phyllida, Ben and I went to Hatchett's and danced.

'It's fun being in London,' I said to Sonia.

'I think so too. But Ivan's bored and has got mixed up in politics, which is very dull. I suppose I'll have to become a political hostess. I had hoped all that was over.'

The next day I took a train to Basingstoke where I was met by Mr Bradley, General Fisher's man. He was wearing a bowler hat and, below his black coat, breeches and leggings. He doffed his hat and took my cases, putting them into the boot of a 1930s Rolls Royce. We drove for about five miles along country roads, turned through some gates, up a short straight drive and stopped before the portico of a Palladian house. It was dark but I recognised it well.

'I'll look after your bags and your gun, Mr Miles,' said Bradley and opened the door of the house.

Inside Mrs Bradley came bustling out of nowhere and curtsied.

'Welcome, Mr Miles,' she said. 'The general's in the library waiting for you.'

I took off my overcoat, took Kitty's things out of its deep pockets and walked across the black and white tiled hall to the library.

'Miles, how very good to see you', said General Fisher. 'Have a whisky after your journey? Good. Now what have you there?'

I handed him the jewel case and the bundle of papers.

'Poor Kitty,' he said, 'she had such life in her.'

He opened the case and frowned.

'I thought it would just be some of her mother's jewellery. Kitty had left most of that here, including her tiara. Horace seems to have given her a lot.'

He put the case back on the table, opened the bundle of papers that Olivia had thought should be returned and looked through them.

'Poor Kitty,' he said again. 'It was very difficult trying to bring her up alone. I didn't know how to do it. The only thing I had any success at was making her into a fine horsewoman. I gave her too much head and spoilt her. Sonia tried, I know. But she was always abroad. I was too old too. I was more like a grandfather to her.'

'I found myself closer to my grandfather than my father, and loved him dearly.'

'That's because your father was away so much.'

'Perhaps. But Kitty loved you very much. She often told me so.'

'Did you know she wanted to divorce Horace?'

I didn't reply.

'You should have been older Miles. You should have married her. She always liked you. I could never understand why she married Horace.'

There was a long silence while he looked through the papers.

'Thank you, Miles, for bringing these. Look, have the other half and take it with you to change. We'll eat early. I don't like to keep the Bradleys up late. They're the only indoor staff I have now, and we're shooting tomorrow.'

The General led me up the great staircase and showed me to my room. My clothes were already laid out for me on the bed and a hot bath had been drawn.

'Come down as soon as you're ready,' he said. He had already changed.

We sat down to eat in the small red dining room.

'We'll have a good day tomorrow,' he said. 'Six guns and we'll shoot the Sherborne coverts. Pheasant, so we're eating partridge tonight. They're excellent this year. I've still got a gamekeeper. Do you know before the war we had nine servants in this house? And the house and land were worth nothing? Today I've just got the Bradleys. The war saved the house and the land because it rescued agriculture. Before the war arable land was worth £5 an acre. Now they tell me it's worth over £100.'

'How much land have you got?'

'Five thousand acres. I couldn't get rid of it when I wanted to. Now I don't want to. Kitty would have had it all. I'm glad Horace won't get it. I would have liked Kitty to have had it - yes Kitty and you.'

I don't think he had an inkling about Kitty and me. He just liked to think it might have been possible. He'd always liked me. We had been his neighbours, on a much smaller scale, and my mother still lived only five miles away.

'I've a cousin in Rhodesia. I don't see why he should have it. Anyhow I hear he likes Rhodesia so he'd never want to come and live here. I'm thinking of giving it to the National Trust. Had a fellow down here the other day talking about it. A tall, thin fellow, and shrewd - wanted all the land as an endowment. He knew a bit or two about the house too. He liked the gallery especially.'

'How long have the Fishers had the house?'

'About three hundred years. That's the life of most families in the male line I'm told. Father to son for most of it, too. No, we're finished. Except for the chap in Rhodesia.'

We had started with vegetable soup and were now eating partridge.

'Of course, England, as we've known it, is finished too. The empire's gone or going.'

'I had dinner with the Cathays last night, you know the Blessingtons. Ivan Cathay was full of a new Elizabethan age and its opportunities.'

'Don't you believe him. He's so close to this fantasy that he believes it. I hear he's dabbling in politics now. Even more reason not to believe him. New Elizabethan age, indeed. Delightful and dedicated young queen maybe, but what can she do? The trade unions have too much power. The new conservative government doesn't dare undo anything Atlee did, though not everything he did was wrong. Manufacturing industry is in desperate need of investment. Most of the wartime controls are still in place and the government interferes in everything. It'll get worse too. Worst of all, we're broke.'

'I thought the Americans were helping us get on our feet?'

'Don't trust the Americans. They're only propping us up – and Western Europe – as a bastion against communism so they can get us to carry most of the burden. This special relationship Winston goes on about only started in 1940 when France went to the wall. Winston started it. No wonder he goes on about it. His mother was American. I saw the Yanks walk away from the Versailles Treaty after the Great War. They're powerful, they're rich, but they're only interested in themselves and taking over the world.'

'Taking over the world?'

'We built the empire on trade. The more we traded the more we grew and the more those we traded with grew. The navy was there to protect trade. We didn't interfere with cultures. Look at India, look at Hong Kong. The Yanks are building their empire on business. Businesses grow by taking over other businesses and spreading their business cultures. The Americans have the most powerful business culture in the world. As soon as their interests divide from ours, they'll drop us.'

'What about France and West Germany?'

'The French can't form a government for more than a week. The Fourth Republic is a farce. Now the Germans, they'll grow. It's a pity we had to drop the Germans for the French, all the Kaiser's fault. Take my younger brother who was killed on the Somme. Guess where he went after Winchester and Cambridge? Heidelberg, not some Frog university. The Germans will recover. The French won't until they get a strong leader. I like Paris, though, but I'm talking too much. How's Germany?'

We had got to the savoury and drunk a pint of claret each. I was thinking what to reply.

'Half a bottle of claret isn't enough for a chap, and a bottle is too much,' he said. 'I've always bought pint bottles. They're becoming difficult to find. If you see any, let me know.'

'I can see what you mean about Germany growing,' I said. 'In the short time we've been there I've watched some of the towns that were destroyed by our bombing beginning to spring back up. In London one is hardly conscious of any building. There's war damage everywhere still.'

'Is there? I don't go to London much, and then only to Brooks's.'

'Soldiering in Germany could be enormous fun, but Dennis Parker Brown is very difficult to serve.'

'The man's outrageous. Kitty wrote to me about some of the asinine things he'd been doing. Trouble is he has something on that fool Flaxman. They tell me he's dying. I won't be sorry.'

'Ben Wildbore and I went to see General Flaxman yesterday. He's not well and he's almost gaga. We also thought he'd been brainwashed by Dennis Parker Brown and completely under his thumb. We couldn't understand why. He kept on saying the regiment must avoid a scandal.'

'Did he? Avoid a scandal? That's rich. The scandal is Flaxman and Brown. Brown was a very handsome young man when he joined the Second Battalion. Flaxman was commanding and he was an unhappily married man. Flaxman fell for Brown and Brown encouraged him. I don't know exactly what happened. I wasn't there. Something sexual, I was told. Brown has held that over Flaxman ever since. Flaxman is terrified that if he doesn't do what Brown wants, Brown will expose him. The fact is Brown probably wouldn't dare. Flaxman is surprisingly weak. Very few know about this. I don't see any harm in your knowing. In six months time you'll have a new colonel of the regiment who Brown won't be able to control. You've not long to wait for Algy Stanhope to command, and then the future of the regiment will be looking rosier than the future of Britain.'

'If the future of Britain looks glum doesn't that mean the future of the army is too?'

'Yes it does. We won't be able to afford an army the size we have today. When you've stopped having fun in the regiment it will be time to get out.'

'What do you suggest I do then?'

'Do? Why, go to New York. That's the new centre of the universe. If you can't beat them, join them. You'll make a fortune.'

He roared with laughter.

At breakfast the General said, 'I've been looking through the papers you brought me. There's a question about what should happen to Vampire. I gave up hunting years ago. What do you think I should do with him?'

'Give him to Jasper Knox. He loves that horse.'

'I hoped you'd say that. I'll arrange it.'

Then we went shooting.

After tea, the general asked Mr Bradley to take me to my mother's where I would be staying the night. I thanked the general for my stay and he thanked me again for bringing Kitty's things.

Then he said, 'Give my love to your mother. I'm afraid I don't see much of her. She rather keeps to herself. Your father and I were great friends. We served on the boundary commission together after the Treaty of Versailles. I was a major general and he was a lieutenant. He spoke French and German. He was a great help to me. That's how we got to know each other and why, when he married your mother, he came to live near here. I found them your house. Come and see me again, my boy, any time. You're most welcome and you bring back happy memories of Kitty. If you see any pint bottles of claret, let me know.'

My mother lived in an Edwardian house that was too big for her. She sometimes talked about moving but she had lived there, when not in India or in army quarters, for over a quarter of a century. She found it too difficult to tear herself away from the house or the neighbourhood and couldn't see a house nearby that she wanted.

My mother was a Victorian, born in the last decade of the nineteenth century. I am sure she loved me, but she had always been strict with me, and she rarely discussed anything about herself with me. She never talked about money. Since I reached manhood she had kept me on a shoestring. I'd never known whether this was because she had little money or because she felt I should not have any, and I was determined on this visit to find out. Life was quite expensive in the regiment. Gambling didn't help though I was not short because of that. I was one of the few who had not been burnt. But I had exhausted the money I had saved in Korea and I wanted a car and a horse of my own. I just couldn't afford them on a lieutenant's pay.

I had not seen her since going to Germany, so there was a lot to talk about over dinner. When we had finished I said, 'Mummy, can we talk about money?'

'Why?'

'I'm broke.'

'Is that the reason you've come to see me?'

'Oh, Mummy, can't we have a proper grown up conversation?

I'm twenty five. What is the situation about grandpa's money and the trust funds? I was wondering if it's possible to have some money of my own. I hate asking you for money. You've been very kind with presents and I've got Daddy's guns and some of his things. If I could have something on a regular basis it would be much easier to plan. You know how little we get paid. I know grandpa and his father were rich men. There must be a lot left.'

'If you can't make ends meet in the army perhaps you should go into the city.'

'That's not an answer to my question.'

'I don't see why I should answer your question. I find it a little impertinent.'

'Mummy, I know there's money in trust for me. I know you've got your own money. Is it possible for me to have some?'

'I can only just afford to live in this house. I know it's too big but I don't want to move. Your trust fund comes to you on my death and until then the income is mine. As to all the money you think I have of my own, I did have some. Your grandfather settled some on me when I married your father and your father spent it freely. When he was killed he had massive debts which I felt obliged to pay. He had such charm he could borrow from anyone. I've been dreading this conversation. It makes me so unhappy to talk about these things.'

She began to cry.

'Mummy, if there isn't any money I understand, but why couldn't you have told me this before?'

'I loved your father. I still do. But he was such a spendthrift and he used to get drunk, as well as going off with other women. It was unbearable.'

'I know about that, I saw the rows. I'm so sorry. I don't want you to cry but I just wanted to know the situation.'

'I could let you have something now and again.'

'What do you mean by now and again?'

'Oh, how I hate talking about money. Your father made it all so awful. I'll have to look at my accounts and talk to the lawyers.

Perhaps I could let you have £100 a quarter. I'd have to move.'

'I don't want you to move. I only want the money if it's there. You've told me it's not, so that's the end of it. General Fisher suggested I leave the army and go to New York to make my fortune.'

'Miles, please don't do that. You've no idea how unhappy I've been over money. I used to argue with your father over it. "What about Miles?" I used to say. "It's as much his as yours." He just laughed and spent it, saying there was going to be a war. Sonia Blessington has still got her money and more. She married Ivan and he was clever with it. Look at them now. House in Eaton Terrace and the estate in Herefordshire she got from her father.'

'Yes, but look at what a bore Ivan has become. Sonia is fed up to the teeth. As far as I can see she only sticks with him because of Phyllida. He's so pompous. At least Daddy was fun.'

'Daddy was fun. He was such fun in India when he was still under control in the regiment. He went off the rails when we came back to England. I left him alone too much. I was here and he was in London. I've never enjoyed London, but he did. I wanted to make a home for you here. It's all my fault he went off, which makes it worse.'

'Tell me about India.'

'What do you want to know?'

'What you did? How many tigers did Daddy shoot? Did he play polo? Who commanded? Were you there when John Flaxman commanded and Dennis Brown arrived?'

'Why do you ask that?'

'Curiosity.'

'What do you know?'

'I know that something happened between them and that Dennis Brown has held it over General Flaxman ever since.'

'It was filthy and I'm not going to say any more.'

'Oh Mummy, I'm grown up. I'm twenty-five.'

'Your father was amused by it when he told me. He said they were behaving like a couple of schoolgirls with crushes. I was shocked. I didn't know such things went on.'

'Is that all you can say?'

'Miles, I'm tired. I think it's time we went to bed. Are you staying tomorrow?'

'Tomorrow I promised to go and see Jasper's mother in London and on Friday I'm going to Herefordshire to shoot with the Blessingtons.'

'Why are you going to see Jasper's mother?'

'To tell her Jasper's fine but lonely and that he needs money too. His trustees withheld his trust fund from him.'

'Do you have to go and see that woman?'

'Yes, Mummy, I do.'

'I wish you didn't,' she said as she went out of the door.

At breakfast she said, 'I'm sorry about the way I behaved last night. I hate talking about money. It reminds me of all the awful talks I had with your father. I so hope you stay in the army, darling. A regiment is such a lovely life and good discipline for you too. I'll do what I can to let you have an allowance on a regular basis and I should have done it before. I was just so worried you'd behave like Daddy and spend it all and more. I've kept you short. Here's something for you now.'

She handed me an envelope. When I said goodbye, she cried in my arms.

In the train I opened the envelope and found a cheque for £100. I would be able to stay in the army after all.

Jasper's mother lived in a flat in a mansion block off Kensington High Street. She had asked me to lunch. She opened the door herself.

'Goodness, Miles, how like your father you look. It's quite unnerving.'

She kissed me. Verity Knox was elegant, and she led me into an elegantly furnished small sitting room where she gave me a glass of sherry, sat me down, and asked about Jasper. I told her, as evenly as I could, everything that had happened to Jasper since

she had last seen him. Most of it was new to her. Jasper clearly
didn't write much.

'Oh dear, Miles. I suppose I mishandled the trust fund. I still
think I was probably right not to hand it over but I can see I did
it in a rather heavy-handed way. The trouble was Dennis Brown.
I had thought they got on and that Jasper admired him for his
horsemanship. How wrong one can be? There's always trouble
when Dennis Brown is around. I should have guessed.'

'Tell me more about Dennis Brown as you call him. Why does
he call himself Parker Brown?'

'That's easy. His mother was a Miss Parker and she had a rich
bachelor brother. Dennis added Parker to his name in the hope
of inheriting, and he did. He's always out for the main chance, is
our Dennis.'

'Were you in India when he arrived in the second battalion?'

'You mean when John Flaxman fell for him? I thought that was
rather funny ridiculous. No one outside the regiment knew and not
many in the regiment. We were in a station by ourselves. Luckily
John Flaxman was promoted to be a brigadier, moved on, and it
all blew over.'

'No it didn't. Dennis Brown has blackmailed him with it ever
since. That's how he gets away with everything he does in the
battalion. John Flaxman is protecting him.'

'That I didn't know. Oh, dear. We'd better have lunch and you
can tell me more.'

When we had eaten she asked me if I thought there was anything
else she could do.

'I don't think so,' I said. 'I just wanted you to know what was
going on. Jasper is rather exposed. We're great friends and I try
to help him.'

'You are very like your father, always helping people. He was
a great help to me after Jasper's father was killed. Do you know
about that?'

'Yes I do. There's no need to talk about it if you don't want to.'

'Thank you Miles.'

I spent the weekend with the Blessingtons in Herefordshire. There was good shooting with Ivan, and lots of laughter with Sonia and Phyllida. On Monday Ben drove us back to Germany in his new motor car. We had a lot to talk about. Ben had been to a nightclub every night until he went to the Belchers. We did 100 mph on the autobahn, much to his satisfaction.

When we got to the mess everyone came out to admire the car. I took Burgo aside and gave him a résumé of what I'd learned.

'So now we know,' he said. 'How long have we got to stick it out?'

'About another six months.'

'I wonder whether we can all wait that long?'

15

Disloyalty at Christmas

'Colonel Guy is coming for Christmas,' said Burgo.

'That's unbelievably good news,' I said. 'Who's he staying with? Algy?'

'No, D. P. Brown.'

'You're teasing again.'

'Big Steel told me. You know how the serjeants' mess knows everything before we do. I asked Francis and he confirmed it.'

'When does he arrive?'

'Tomorrow.'

We were sitting in the anteroom. It was the week before Christmas. The first heavy fall of snow had melted. The locals didn't predict snow again until the New Year, so Christmas was not to be white, and racing had not been abandoned. Jasper was to ride Vampire again at Hanover in two days' time. Several of us were going to support him.

'We should ask Colonel Guy if he'd like to come to Hanover,' said Burgo.

'You were closest to him, Miles, and you're the senior subaltern. Write him a letter of welcome and invite him to Hanover.'

'From the little I remember of him from England,' said Jasper, 'he'll come. But if he's staying with D.P.Brown, won't D.P.Brown have planned something else? He's not running Red Ember and he won't want to come and watch me.'

'Write all the same,' said Burgo. 'We must try. Fancy having Colonel Guy here for Christmas.'

'What about taking him to Kremke?'

'He'll want to ride.'

'He'll want to ride Vampire. He rode in the Grand Military before the war.'

'No one ever told me that.'

'Shooting at the Sengers on Boxing Day?'

'From all I hear and know,' said Adam, 'it's bound to end in tears.'

'Adam has a point,' I said. 'If there's one person D. P. Brown would be unlikely to ask for Christmas it has to be Colonel Guy. Exciting as it all is, I think I'll discuss it with Francis before I put pen to paper.'

After lunch I found Francis alone in his office. Francis said he thought Colonel Dennis would welcome having Colonel Guy taken off his hands. He said Colonel Guy had proposed himself, asking if he could stay with the Stanhopes. Algy had wisely discussed this with Colonel Dennis who had said that Guy should stay with him. I suspect D. P. Brown believed he could control Guy better that way. 'I can't allow,' he must have said to himself, 'Guy and Algy to get together and plot behind my back.'

Francis disappeared into the colonel's office and came back almost immediately.

'Colonel Dennis says it's an admirable idea to take Colonel Guy racing and to take him on to dinner afterwards. If you've got any other ideas, let me know. Well done, Miles.'

We set out for Hanover in several cars. Ben drove Colonel Guy in his Sunbeam Talbot with Heidi and me. Finbar took Adam, Burgo, and Charlie Chance. Charlie was a new national service officer who'd been riding with Jasper and was dying to see the race. He was clever, short and excitable. Harry Fox, who sold his car to Finbar, had left us at the end of his national service and returned to London to work in his father's wine business. Jasper went with Algy and Olivia. At the end of the day we had arranged for everyone to dine at Kremke.

Corporal O'Reilly and Whistler had left early with Vampire. This was our first outing since Horace and Kitty died and, in spite of my week in England, I still felt an emptiness. When Rana had left so abruptly I'd hardly felt a pang. My grief after Kitty's death had been unbearable and I was not the only one to have felt it so strongly. Jasper was distraught, not that he showed it. I just knew he was. Others, too, were stunned and sad. Horace's death had been taken as a matter of course, one of the inevitable events of life, another officer gone. Kitty's death had affected people deeply.

When we got to the racecourse Jasper and I went to check up on Vampire. The others made for the bar.

'How is he?' asked Jasper.

'Vampire's in good shape,' said O'Reilly. 'We'll get him into the paddock early. Whistler will walk him.'

'They've made him favourite,' said Whistler, looking pleased.

'I thought they might,' said Jasper, 'but we mustn't let that concern us. Mrs Belcher was never interested in the betting. She wanted him to do his best, and loved watching him run. She'll want him to win today. She never had a bet.'

'I could never understand that,' said O'Reilly. 'Whistler and me, we've done nicely on him.'

'I would have thought you would have backed Red Ember, Corporal.'

'Red Ember's a good horse and I've won a bob or two on him in my time, but Vampire's the better horse. Always was. He's got more stamina.'

I left Jasper with them and, making my way to the stands, ran into Adam.

'What do they say about Vampire?' he asked.

'Whistler says he's in good shape. He'll be disappointed if he doesn't win.'

'Wretched odds. I don't like backing favourites. Will it make a difference Kitty not having trained him?'

'I doubt it. He's as fit as he's ever been. He's won over the distance. Jasper is determined to win. Vampire is his horse now.'

'I'm sorry about Kitty, Miles. It was cretinous of Horace to drive like that. She was a delightful girl and great fun. The gods will be looking after her. What you need is pleasure. Pleasure is the great cure all.'

'Thank you for saying that. Where are the others?'

'In the buffet.'

'This cold makes me hungry.'

'I could do with a drink, too.'

The buffet was crowded and there were friends from other regiments. As I pushed my way through the crowd Major Skidmore, a questionable friend who had commanded the engineer squadron in the river crossing exercise, stopped me.

'Vampire going to win?'

'He's the favourite.'

'The tote's giving rotten odds. Your colonel run the tote?'

'You know our colonel disapproves of gambling.'

'Damned shyster. They've rumbled him at division. You know I'm at division now? They're saying there could be no battalion in the division better than yours if it weren't for your colonel. When are you going to get rid of him?'

'Perhaps you could tell me that?'

'I've heard rumours.'

'Anything specific?'

'Between you and me and anyone else you want to tell, they're trying to find a way of unseating him and putting your second in command in his place. Parker Brown's fighting a rearguard action. I understand the general wants it to happen but someone higher up is stopping it.'

I pushed on through the crowd. Charles Millington stopped me.

'That was terrible about the Belchers. We're all so sorry.'

'We're all very unhappy about it.'

'They're saying your colonel drove him to it.'

'Who's they?'

'We've all seen Horace being hounded by your colonel. He's one hell of a martinet.'

'Horace was under pressure and it would be wrong to say that he didn't deserve it. But it's wrong to say that he was driven to it. It was a most unfortunate accident. Horace had been drinking and was driving too fast.'

'I'm not surprised. Your colonel, after he'd fallen, gave Horace one hell of a dressing down in front of everyone. Horace should have asked for a transfer. We'd have had him.'

'Horace loved the regiment. He also, curious to say, loved his colonel.'

'Poor fellow.'

I reached Burgo at the bar.

'Get me a double.'

'A double what?'

'A double anything. A double horse's neck.'

'You won't get that here. Have my schnapps and beer while I order some more. Where've you been?'

'Getting the gossip.'

'I'm all ears.'

'Not here, later. Where are the others?'

'In the far corner. They've got the food.'

After lunch we watched the first two races with muted interest. Adam bet on both, winning on the first and losing on the second. Then we all went to the paddock to see Vampire.

'Beautifully built horse,' Colonel Guy said to me. 'Of course, you can never tell just by looking at them. There are so many elements that combine to make a winner. If I bet I would be betting in ignorance.'

'When we were in England after we got back from Korea and you went racing nearly every day did you bet?'

'Not on every race like Adam Hare. He's a gambler, a plunger I should say. Even if he's got a lot of money he'll get himself into trouble sooner or later. I used to follow a short list of horses that I'd selected and just bet on them. I didn't worry about the odds. I bet on a horse if I thought it would win, irrespective of the odds.'

'Did you win?'

'Towards the end of the season I began to win but the bookies won early on. You have to pay for your pleasures. I really just like to watch horses race. Betting is secondary for me.'

'Kitty Belcher never bet.'

'She's a great loss. I could never understand why she married Horace.'

'She thought she could change him.'

'That was a bad bet, one I wasn't prepared to take.'

We returned to the stands to watch the race. There were twelve runners. As they came past the stands for the first time Jasper was keeping Vampire well in hand, behind the leaders but up with them. I had lent Colonel Guy my binoculars so I couldn't follow the horses round. Colonel Guy said Jasper was keeping his place. Four fences from home he started to move up and at the second last fence he went into the lead. He won by two lengths. How that would have delighted Kitty, I thought.

We got to Kremke in time for an early dinner, which suited everyone as we had only had a snack lunch. The landlord welcomed us with a huge fire. We had got to know him well since Exercise Fungi. He chose what we should eat so there was no agonising over the menu. The food just arrived and was always good.

As we stood around, warming up and having our first drink, Colonel Guy said to Jasper, 'Vampire is an exceptional horse and you rode well.'

'Thank you, Colonel. I'm entering him in the Grand Military but, without Kitty, I'm not sure how I'm going to get him to England and train him there.'

'I wonder if I could help,' said Colonel Guy, and they discussed this.

Burgo nudged me.

'When are you going to tell me the gossip?'

'There are strong rumours that the general, that is the divisional commander, wants to replace D. P. Brown with Algy but that someone higher up is stopping it.'

'We know who that is.'

'There're rumours, too, that D. P. Brown harassed Horace to his death.'

'Juicy. Shall I spread them?'

'You didn't get them from me.'

'What are you two scheming now?' said Algy. 'The landlord wants us to sit down. He's ready to serve dinner. Guy, come and sit next to Olivia. Heidi, come and sit next to me. Sort yourselves out.'

I found myself between Adam and Charlie Chance.

'Swap places,' said Adam.

'Why?'

'I want to sit next to Charlie.'

'If you must.'

We changed seats and I had Burgo on my left.

'As senior subaltern it'll be your duty to protect young Charlie from the lascivious Adam,' said Burgo.

'Will I have to?'

'Adam seems hell bent on a conquest.'

'He seems quite discreet about it.'

'He offers inducements.'

'What inducements?'

'Lucre, filthy lucre. He favours the new national service officers, fresh from public school, impecunious and as yet uncorrupted by women.'

'Is he successful?'

'Less often than he would like.'

'Do you find him a moral danger?'

'I find him entertaining.'

'Francis tells me D. P. Brown regards him as a moral danger and corrupting influence. That's over gambling. I don't think they know about the other thing.'

'I gather D. P. Brown once quizzed Horace about it.'

'What did Horace say?'

'He said he didn't feel he had to stand with his back to the wall when Adam walked by.'

'Typical Horace.'

The next course came.

'Did you make money today, Adam?' I asked.

'Not as much as I should have. I backed all the good-looking jockeys. Except for Jasper, the ugly ones won. Though I won on Jasper I also backed a Lancer friend of Charlie Millington in the same race. I couldn't resist his legs in the paddock.'

'You could have put a tidy sum on Jasper with little risk.'

'Not my style, I like tidy sums at long odds. You win more.'

'And you lose more.'

'I'm cross with young Jasper. He's being difficult to get, resists all my advances.'

'Adam, for most of us the camp talk is just words. We don't lust after each other.'

'What was good enough for the Greeks is good enough for me.'

You've said that before.'

'And I'll say it again.'

'What do you see in boys?'

'I prefer bedding women but they're so complicated and cause such trouble. All boys ever ask for is money. You know where you stand with them.'

'Maybe you are a moral danger to the rest of us, Adam.'

'How could I be? I have no morals.'

Another course came.

'I was wrong to say he's discreet, Burgo,' I said. 'He's blatant and I hadn't noticed.'

'You've been preoccupied. He's been blatant for some time.'

'He made a pass at Kitty.'

'He made a pass at me.'

'At you?'

'Yes, me. He offered me a pony.'

'And?'

'I just laughed at him which annoyed him.'

'Has he made a pass at a soldier?'

'Not that I know.'

'That could lead to trouble.'

The evening was noisy. On the far side of the table Olivia was deep in conversation with Finbar O'Donnell, and Heidi was chatting away with Ben. Between Olivia and Heidi, and exactly opposite me, were Algy and Guy.

'What happened to your brevet lieutenant colonelcy?' I heard Colonel Guy ask Algy.

'Never heard any more.'

'I thought it was decided weeks ago?'

'So did I. You know Dennis Brown has given me an adverse report?'

'An adverse report?'

'He said I was disloyal.'

'He's given *you* an adverse report?'

'Not too loud.'

'What have you done about it?'

'I've complained to the brigadier who supports me and has taken it up with the general.'

'And what has he done?'

'The general has ordered Dennis Brown to withdraw the report and rewrite it.'

'Has he?'

'He's refusing to.'

'That's monstrous. Have you written to General Flaxman?'

'He's in Dennis Brown's pocket. I sometimes wonder if Dennis Brown has something on him.'

'What does he mean, disloyal?'

'At one time or another Dennis Brown has accused almost every officer of being disloyal. He ruined Dermot Lisle's career accusing him of disloyalty, and prevented him from going to Staff College,

which is why Dermot resigned. He was unnecessarily harsh on
Horace Belcher who was defenceless, fool as he was. I'm thinking
of resigning.'

'You can't do that. You're the next commanding officer of this
battalion. You'll go a long way in the army, Algy, much further
than me.'

'Not if Dennis Brown has anything to do with it. I've never had
an adverse report and I'll never live this one down.'

'The man's demented.'

'Paranoic, I think. You wait and see. There'll be some fireworks
before Christmas is over.'

Adam, who had been deep in conversation with Charlie Chance,
nudged me and said, 'Charlie is asking what are the plans for
Christmas?'

'Very few,' I replied. 'Christmas Day is devoted to the soldiers.
First of all the serjeants challenge us to hockey in front of the battalion. Then the officers and the serjeants serve the soldiers their
Christmas dinner. After that, the serjeants try and get us pissed
in their mess. In the evening, the married officers entertain us to
dinner and we close the mess. Charlie should have had an invitation by now. Then on Boxing Day, being a bank holiday, there
are no parades and traditionally we hold an inter company knock-
out competition. This year it's to be hockey as we can play it on
both parade grounds. Each company enters a team. Headquarter
company, as it's so large, enters two, and Algy, as second in command, enters one, recruiting whomever he can. That makes eight
teams. In the evening we have a feast in the mess with the wives.
Dancing afterwards, too.'

'Plenty of spare time, then?'

'What are you thinking of?'

'We could have a game of chemmy on Christmas afternoon?'

'I expect you'd get some takers for that.'

'I'll organise something. Charlie wants to play.'

'I might too.'

'We might have a game of something tonight. It's quite early.'

'Not for me.'

We were breaking up. It had been a good dinner. Ben was asking everyone for ten marks, a little under a pound. But it had been another empty day without Kitty.

The following day, Colonel Guy came to have a drink in the mess before lunch. He was quickly surrounded by officers who had been with him in Korea. D. P. Brown came and stood in a corner talking to Adam and Charlie Chance, furtively eyeing the group round Colonel Guy where there was much laughter. After one loud eruption D. P. Brown left abruptly.

'It's very good to be with you,' said Colonel Guy, 'but I must go. I'm having lunch with the Stanhopes and Colonel Dennis is taking me.'

'He's already left.'

'Oh, he said he would take me.'

'He left a few minutes ago,' said Ben. 'I'll drop you at the Stanhopes. It's not far.'

They left.

'Let me tell you what I heard last night,' I said to Burgo, and I told him what I had overheard at dinner the previous evening and swore him to secrecy.

'Algy guesses something but doesn't know. Should we tell him?'

'How can we? This has to be played out. We can't interfere.'

We went into lunch and stayed remarkably sober.

Christmas Day came. In the morning the whole battalion turned out round the upper parade ground to watch the officers beat the serjeants four goals to two at hockey. Hockey was the great regimental sport that nearly everyone played. Much ribaldry from the touchline accompanied the game. We changed back into uniform and got ready to serve the men's Christmas dinner.

Burgo and I, with Big Steel and our serjeants, paraded at the upper cookhouse, which our company shared with headquarter company. At 12.30 Colonel Dennis arrived with Colonel Guy and were greeted by acclamation. Colonel Dennis gave a short speech followed by applause. Then the officers and serjeants began to serve the men their dinner. Colonel Dennis, the great administrator, had ensured a superb dinner: turkey, of course, with the full works including beer, crackers, flaming Christmas puddings, mince pies, and ice cream. This took time to serve. Some of the men called for more and got it. Colonel Dennis and Colonel Guy went round the tables shaking hands and wishing everyone a merry Christmas. Francis, as adjutant, kept on trying to talk to Colonel Dennis. Colonel Dennis was not to be stopped and went on round the cookhouse until he had talked to almost everyone. Then Francis forcibly directed him to the door. They left amid more applause. Colonel Guy stayed on for a bit. When the men started to sing he left to follow Colonel Dennis down to the lower cookhouse. Burgo and I stayed on, chatting to some of our men until Big Steel said it was time for us to join him and the serjeants in their mess.

As we passed the lower cookhouse shared by the rifle companies, Adam came out with some other officers and serjeants, and joined us to walk down to the serjeants' mess.

'Quite a caper, that was,' said Adam.

'What happened?'

'I thought the men would mutiny.'

'Sounds exciting.'

'The men were all sitting down by twelve thirty but D. P. Brown had given orders for dinner not to be served until he arrived. He didn't appear until nearly one o'clock. By then the men were hammering on the tables with their eating irons shouting, "Where's our Christmas grub?" Truth to tell, their phraseology was more explicit. No one could control them. They only stopped when D. P. Brown finally appeared. When he spoke to them, they listened in silence, icy silence. The moment we started to serve the food a great shout went up, and at the same moment Colonel Guy entered the cookhouse. You would've have thought that the shout was for Colonel Guy, not the food. D. P. Brown did. He looked daggers at Colonel Guy and ordered Francis to take him down to the serjeants' mess instanter. He then walked round the tables with the RSM. He got a cool reception, barely polite. They had been waiting for half an hour. I'm glad to get away.'

We crowded into the sergeants' mess. At one end of the room I could see a bar massed with bottles of every denomination: not just brandy, sherry, gin, whisky, vodka and rum, but bottles of pastis, aquavit, green chartreuse, Benedictine, Grand Marnier, Strega and many others glinting and jostling for space on the shelves. From these bottles the barman was making lethal mixes. In a corner of the bar Charlie Chance, hedged in between two serjeants, was drinking a rich looking brew. Well, I thought, I did warn him. Big Steel appeared with glasses of beer for Burgo and me.

'Happy Christmas, gentlemen,' he said.

We drank carefully. The beer was unadulterated.

'How's the serjeants' mess enjoying Germany?' I asked.

'Good enough station,' replied Big Steel. 'We live better here than we could in England. Good quarters, too. Some of the wives moan about being so far from their mums but they'll complain anywhere. In one way better than Hong Kong as our money goes further here. What about you, Sir?'

'We've settled in well. Plenty of things to do and fortunate that we're the only battalion for miles so that no one's breathing down our necks.'

'Good to see Colonel Guy, isn't it Sir?'

'Splendid. We miss him.'

'So do the serjeants. We were lucky to have him commanding us in Korea,' he said. 'The serjeants were talking about giving him a Christmas stocking but the RSM vetoed it.'

'He got one, don't worry,' said Burgo.

'How do you know?' I said.

'I gave him one. I gave them both stockings. At two o'clock this morning I climbed up a drainpipe, got in through a window that was open and put stockings at the bottom of both their beds. I'm still waiting to hear the reaction.'

'What did you put in them?'

'Anything to hand, a Deutschmark in the toe, toothpaste, miniatures, some chocolate. Not very imaginative but thoughtful. I would have been pleased to get it.'

'Happy Christmas, Whettingsteel.' Colonel Guy had joined us. 'All well with you, I hope?'

'Fine, thank you, Sir.'

'This is a little different from Christmas in Korea,' said Colonel Guy.

We all laughed. On Christmas Day in Korea the cookhouse had caught fire.

'Still time for something to happen,' said Big Steel. 'Did you get a Christmas stocking, Sir?'

'Funny you should ask. When I woke up there was a stocking at the bottom of my bed. Unlike Colonel Brown to give me a stocking, I thought, so I took it down to breakfast with me. First thing he said was "Did you give me this?" He was holding up a stocking. It was a regimental football stocking like mine. Some wag must have climbed in at night. I can't imagine who it was,' he said, looking at Burgo. 'We unpacked the stockings. miniatures, toothpaste, chocolate, that sort of thing and very useful. Trouble was, mine had a bottle of whisky in it and his didn't. I don't think he liked that. Careless of Father Christmas.'

Charlie Chance's eyes were beginning to roll. I'd been watching him. He'd managed to drink two pint glasses of the vicious brew he had been given, an accomplishment in itself. I thought it time to rescue him. I broke off, took him by the arm and got him back to the mess.

'What you need is food, my boy,' I said. He dashed, goggle eyed, to the lavatory and was violently sick. We didn't see him again that day.

'Why on earth,' I asked Burgo as we sat down to lunch, 'did you put a bottle of whisky in Colonel Guy's stocking and not one in D.P. Brown's?'

'I thought Colonel Guy deserved something special,' said Burgo, 'I love that man.'

'Maybe, but you aggravated D.P.Brown unnecessarily.'

'That's not difficult.'

'All the more reason not to.'

'May I join you?' said Colonel Guy standing in the doorway of the dining room.

'Come in, Colonel, come in,' said Ben. 'We've only just started.'

'I've lost Colonel Brown.'

'He drove out of the barracks some minutes ago. Eat with us. I'll run you back to the colonel's house afterwards,' said Ben.

Colonel Guy sat down.

'We're going to play cards this afternoon,' said Burgo. 'Care to join us, Colonel?'

'What are you playing?'

'Adam had proposed chemmy but I thought, for nostalgic reasons, a game of poker would be fun on Christmas Day.'

'Poker would be great fun. I'll join in. There was nothing planned for this afternoon. The Pophams have asked me to dinner. I've nothing till then.'

After lunch we called for brandy and cigars. Then Ben, Adam, Burgo and I sat down to play poker with Colonel Guy.

'House rules,' said Ben.

'What are they?' asked Colonel Guy.

'Chips are worth a shilling each and no one can lose more than a fiver.'

'Fair enough.'

It was a predictable game to start. Burgo played carefully following the old maxims. Adam bluffed but not all the time. This fooled the rest of us but not Colonel Guy, who was the best player. The chips on the table showed it. As it got dark and the lights were turned up, Colonel Guy began to lose. When it was time for an early drink no one was up or down much.

'I enjoyed that,' said Colonel Guy. 'How do we settle?'

'I'll put it in the bridge book,' said Burgo picking up the new bridge book that had arrived from London.

'A new bridge book?' said Colonel Guy. 'You must have been playing a lot to have filled up the old book. Where is it? It would be interesting to look back in it. We had it in India before the war.'

No one said anything.

'You haven't lost it have you?'

'It was burnt,' said Burgo.

'I hadn't heard that you'd had a fire in the mess.'

'Colonel Dennis burnt it as he disapproved of the stakes that he thought we were playing for,' Ben said.

'Threw it into the fire,' said Burgo.

'Were you playing for high stakes?'

'Not really,' said Ben. 'One or two people, like Horace and Adam, had won or lost sizeable amounts but no one had been hurt.'

'It's best not to play for high stakes in the mess,' said Colonel Guy. 'If you want to play high go to a casino.'

We broke up. Ben took Colonel Guy away.

'What a wretched game,' said Adam, 'we could have played chemmy and abandoned house rules if you hadn't invited him to join us. And did you see how he lost those last hands he played on purpose?'

'Yes, clever of him,' said Burgo. 'Now let you and I have a game of picquet until we have to change for dinner. No house rules and I'll take you to the cleaners.'

At breakfast on Boxing Day Adam sat down opposite Ben and me.

'I hope your Christmas dinner was as amusing as mine at the Trenches,' he said. 'Charlie Chance didn't show, Trench Foot gave us bugger all to drink, and Julia got pissed all the same. I kissed her under the mistletoe. Then we had to play charades afterwards. Today I'm going to have my revenge on Burgo at picquet. He won a pony off me before dinner.'

'God, your gambling bores me,' said Ben. 'Can't you do anything else? That cannot go in the bridge book,' said Ben.

'It hasn't. He demanded a cheque. I have to win it back.'

Ben rolled his eyes in boredom.

'What happened at the Pophams?' I asked.

'Rather lively,' said Ben. 'Colonel Brown, as Colonel Guy calls him, asked Guy what he had done in the afternoon. "Played poker in the mess," he says. "You'd have enjoyed it. We had a good game." "You played *poker* in the mess?" said D. P. Brown, "who with?" "Don't know all the names. Won a small fortune but I let them win it back." "My God," said D. P. Brown, "you encouraged them to gamble while I'm trying to stamp it out. Is there no end to your chicanery?" "Now, now Dennis. No one won or lost more than a pound. That's fair isn't it?" "I don't believe you," said D.P. Brown. "Don't be silly, Dennis," says Colonel Guy, "it was a harmless game. You should play with them yourself if you want to control the stakes. It's no good throwing the bridge book into the fire." '

'What did D. P. Brown do then?'

'Choked. Brigadier Popham slapped him on the back, and by the time his choking fit subsided the conversation had moved on. What time does the hockey start?'

'The first two games are at 0930. Colonel Guy's playing. Algy has got him to keep goal for the second in command's team.'

'That should be worth watching.'

It was. Algy had selected some good players. Besides Colonel Guy, he'd also enrolled Finbar, who was a talented inside forward, the padre who was a county player, and one or two others from the battalion team including Serjeant Feard. The battalion, with nothing else to do, turned out in force to cheer on the teams. Algy's team got through to the final without conceding a goal. The support company team, which I captained, was the other finalist. We met after lunch and it was a fast game. Whenever Colonel Guy saved a goal he got a great cheer. At the final whistle Algy's team had won 2-0. Both teams lined up to be congratulated by D. P. Brown. After presenting the cup to Algy he shook hands with the members of both teams. When he shook Colonel Guy by the hand the spectators gave an almighty cheer.

That evening, thirty officers and eight wives gathered in the ante-room for the Boxing Day Feast. The wives wore long dresses, regimental brooches flashing on their shoulders. The officers wore uniform, mess kit with miniature medals or number one dress. The Duchess of Richmond's ball before Waterloo came to mind as we gathered and then walked along the corridor to the dining room. Candles alone lit the room. The silver glittered in the candlelight, reflected in the patina of the table. This is regimental grandeur, I said to myself. Can the evening live up to it?

D.P.Brown, as colonel, sat in the middle of one side of the table with Olivia, the senior wife, on his right; Algy, as second in command, sat opposite him and Ben Wildbore, as president of the mess committee, sat at the end of the table. He had placed Colonel Guy on his right, as far from Colonel Dennis as possible. Charlie Chance, looking cherubic and as if he had never had a sore head in his life, sat at the opposite end of the table, as vice president. I sat next to Julia Trench.

'Adam reported he had a fine time with you last night,' I said.

'Just what did he say?'

'He said he had a good dinner and he enjoyed himself,' I lied.

'I can't remember much about last night but I do remember I let him kiss me under the mistletoe and it wasn't just an ordinary kiss.'

'Were you high, Julia?'

'Yes, just a little.'

'Are you high now?'

'Miles, your questions! Yes I am. I've been looking forward to tonight but I had to steel myself. Jack and I never go out now. We used to see something of you when we first arrived. Now all we see is Dennis Parker Brown. You bachelors are very exclusive. I've been meaning to complain to you for months.'

'We bachelors think you are the stand-offish ones. We rely on the married officers for our social life outside the mess. So I should complain to you. When did you last invite any of us?'

'I'm grovelling in shame.'

'I forgive you. Algy says we are selfish and intolerant. I suppose that's because we value our independence and are rather bent on pleasure.'

'So I've heard.'

'What have you heard?'

'Well I know about the bachelors and Kitty. I shouldn't have said that. I'm sorry Miles. That was awful of me.'

'There were a lot of unfounded rumours about Kitty. She attracted talk. Don't say you were jealous of her?'

'Jealous? I was furious no one paid any attention to me.'

'But you're just married.'

'I've been married over a year now.'

'And you want attention?'

'Yes, I do. Jack is only interested in what Dennis Parker Brown thinks of him. I'm secondary baggage. I merely exist as Frau Major Trench. Julia Trench doesn't exist.'

'Why are you telling me this?'

'I don't know. I suppose I'm pissed and I've got to tell someone.'

'We thought you and Jack were thick with Colonel Dennis.'

'Jack would like to think so. I don't think anyone is. The man's a monster. He just uses people.'

'Why don't you ride? You used to.'

'Perhaps I should. Jack warned me off riding with Kitty because he thought the Belchers were on a collision course with Dennis Parker Brown. Perhaps now I should for the sake of Jack's career.'

The meal was half way through. I noticed Algy get up and leave the room. He didn't return until the port and the Madeira were going round. By this time Julia was almost in my lap and I was getting embarrassed about what to do with her. When Olivia got up to withdraw with the ladies, Julia gave me a kiss.

'You were getting on rather well with my hostess of last night,' said Adam.

'She's anyone's tonight,' I said.

'Yours?'

'Don't be silly.'

'What riches. And just as I've got Charlie in my sights.'

'Julia is an unhappy wife and half pissed. Don't do anything caddish.'

'Seems a perfect opportunity. Maybe, even, *à trois*.'

I found Olivia and asked her to dance.

'Oh, Olivia, how I miss Kitty.'

'That why you were getting close to Julia at dinner?'

'It was Julia trying to get close to me.'

'Don't tell me. Another unhappy wife.'

'An unhappy, unsatisfied, and slightly drunk wife. It seems Jack Trench is so set on pleasing Colonel Dennis that he pays her scant attention.'

'Don't tell me any more. I can't take it. Not after tonight.'

'What do you mean?'

'Didn't you see what happened tonight? Didn't you see Algy leave?'

'What was that about?'

'In the middle of dinner there was a great commotion around Guy Surtees. He was laughing his head off, as was everyone round him. Dennis Brown – as Guy Surtees calls him – was bridling all evening. This was the last straw for him. He shouted across the table "Major Stanhope, I order you to go to my quarters, pack Colonel Surtees' bags and remove them".'

'Goodness. What did Algy say?'

'Algy said, "In the middle of our Boxing Day Feast, Colonel?" And Parker Brown replied, "That's an order, Stanhope." Algy then said, "And what, Colonel, would you like me to do with his bags?" To which Parker Brown replied, "Anything you like. I don't want to see him, or his bags, or his bloody Christmas stocking ever again in my life." '

16

Movement Orders

On New Year's Day snow fell again and this time it stayed on the ground. In anticipation, on the Sunday after Boxing Day, Francis had driven me to the Harz Mountains where there was a ski resort. He wanted to have a look at the facilities. He said Colonel Dennis wished to make arrangements for the men to ski and was thinking of sending a platoon at a time. Immediately after the war the army had commandeered some chalets to do this, somehow still had them, and D.P.Brown had made a bid for them. He also wanted to have a battalion skiing competition and then enter a battalion team into the divisional championship. So we had to look at the hotels too.

After we had walked round the ski resort and Francis had had his questions answered, we found the grandest hotel where we sat drinking chocolate.

'Delicious chocolate,' I said. 'I've never drunk anything so rich and creamy.'

'A speciality of ski resorts.'

'I don't remember. We only went skiing once before the war when I was ten.'

'You'll love it. It makes you feel on top of the world. I'm hoping it will take everyone's mind off what's being going on lately.'

'Jasper's good on skis.'

'I'm worried about Jasper.'

'Me too.'

'Have you noticed he's started to drink rather heavily? You know him well. Is there anything you can do?'

'Jasper misses Kitty. He called her his elder sister. She was wonderful with him. She picked him up after Colonel Dennis dropped him. There was nothing sexual, just horses. He admired her knowledge and the way she trained Vampire. She admired his horsemanship.'

'Everyone misses Kitty,' said Francis.

After a little he said, 'Why did Colonel Dennis drop Jasper?'

'He was involved in a fracas in London at the end of his equestrian course. Colonel Dennis accused him of disloyalty. After that, he interfered with Jasper getting his trust fund, which was unfair. Jasper won't forgive him.'

'I didn't know about the trust fund.'

'What set Colonel Dennis off at dinner on Boxing Day? I couldn't understand why he exploded then.'

'Apparently Ben told Guy Surtees that you called Colonel Dennis 'D. P. Brown' and explained what it meant. Guy couldn't stop laughing and everyone round him joined in. Some instinctively looked at Colonel Dennis who then knew they were laughing at him. It's a tragedy Colonel Guy ever came.'

'Does Colonel Dennis know he's called D. P. Brown?'

'He knows he's got a nickname but doesn't know what it is or what it means. And I'm not telling him. Back to Jasper. I'm even more worried about him, now. What can we do?'

'Can't you get Colonel Dennis to be gentler with him, to make it up?'

'He's smarting about Jasper winning that race.'

'Why did he have to give him an adverse report?'

'He wanted to dock him six months' seniority and I stopped that. I try to stop the excesses but I'm not able to stop them all.'

'What about Burgo? He seems to be in the doghouse.'

'Colonel Dennis resented the Christmas stockings. He wanted me to give Burgo a week's extra orderly officer. I told him everyone would ask why and that it would make him look foolish. Burgo was a fool not to put a bottle of whisky in both stockings.'

' "Careless" is what Guy Surtees said.'

'It's the same thing. Colonel Dennis's trouble is his loneliness. He's isolated himself in his house and thinks everyone is scheming against him.'

'Adam once said what he needed was love. But he hasn't accepted it from anyone. Certainly Adam failed.'

'Adam is too louche. He worries me too.'

'He's an asset in the mess. From the little I've seen of him outside the mess he despatches his duties well and the men like him. But he's only really interested in pleasure.'

'Yes, he amuses the men. I've seen that. What sports does he play?'

'He's an erratic, occasionally brilliant, batsman.'

'I thought we didn't play cricket here?'

'We don't.'

'Worse than I thought.'

'I wish Colonel Dennis had let me go to the King's African Rifles. I need a change.'

'You're getting one. The colonel wants to see you on Monday. He wants to tell you himself.'

Francis wouldn't tell me what was in store for me, just that it was to my advantage. I puzzled about it for the rest of the weekend.

'Ah, Miles,' said Colonel Dennis when he summoned me. 'Your keenness to volunteer for the King's African Rifles in Kenya to fight the Mau Mau impressed me. But I couldn't let you go. I need you here and I'm promoting you Captain.'

'Thank you Colonel.'

'No need to thank me. I want to see what you can do. Support company needs a company commander and I'm giving it to you to command. I know you will have to command old friends of yours. That may be difficult. On the other hand you know the company and I think you can do it.'

'We'll need someone to take over the machine gun platoon. May I propose Jasper Knox, Colonel?'

'Jasper Knox? I don't think he's ready for that yet.'

'He needs help and a change. I think I could guide him.'

'No, he must prove himself where he is. I'm giving you Adam Hare to command the machine guns. He's clever and has ability. But he's idle and needs stretching. You'll have to push him. I'm sending him to England for the next machine gun course at Netheravon but I want you to train him first.'

'I'll do my best, Colonel.'

'I'm sure you will. I'm relying on you to lead these officers and I know they can be headstrong. You are one of my company commanders now, Miles. I expect absolute loyalty.'

I saluted and went into Francis's office.

'I told you it would be to your advantage. Pleased?' asked Francis.

'With the promotion, yes, but is the appointment a late Christmas present or a poisoned chalice?'

'A poisoned chalice, as you put it, is not intended. He thinks you will be able to command the support company officers better, be more acceptable to them than Jack Trench, for example. I think it's an inspired appointment.'

'What I don't understand is how, as the most junior captain, I can command a company, even if it is support company?'

'Colonel Dennis is having some difficulty attracting senior officers. Several who should be here have found cosier billets. We're short of a major and two captains. And that's why in two rifle companies we've got national service subalterns acting as company second in commands.'

'I feel better. By the way, I asked for Jasper for the machine guns. The colonel said Jasper had to prove himself where he is.'

'That won't have done you any harm. Asking for people, choosing your own, is the mark of a good commander.'

'When can I put up my new badges of rank?'

'Now. Your promotion and appointment will be published

in today's orders. Congratulations, Miles. And get Adam word perfect on the machine gun so that he doesn't disgrace us at Netheravon.'

Algy's office was the other side of the corridor to Francis. I knocked on the door and went in. Algy was there with Olivia.

'Congratulations, Miles,' said Algy. 'It's well deserved and long overdue.'

'I'm so pleased,' said Olivia, and kissed me. 'Now, I've got some news for you. Your cousin Phyllida is coming to stay. Sonia wrote to me to say that Phyllida is going skiing in Austria. She's asked if Phyllida could stay with us for a week or so on her way through. I've written to say yes. We'd like that and I thought you would, too.'

'I'd like to see Phyllida again. She's great fun. Can she ski?'

'Sonia says she loves skiing.'

'Couldn't be better. Jasper can look after her and take her skiing.'

'Can't you ski, Miles?'

'We went once before the war when I was ten. As soon as I was commissioned I went to Hong Kong. Tell me, has Colonel Guy left?'

'We put him on a train on Sunday,' said Algy. 'No one came out of his visit very well though it beats me how it could have been avoided.'

When I got back to my room in the mess Catchpole was there. He had placed all my uniforms in a pile on the bed.

'What are you doing, Catchpole?' I said.

'Serjeant major says to have your new badges of rank sewn on pronto, so I'm taking these to the tailor. You'd better give me the jacket you're wearing now. You wait here and I'll get him to do it immediately. Congratulations, Sir. Can I stay on as your driver?'

'Of course you can. How long have you got to do now?'

'Twenty six weeks and three days to Blighty, Sir.'

'Do you all count it by the day?'

'Most of us have calendars and strike it off day by day.'

'Is it that bad?'

'No. It's not bad at all. But we conscripts want to get back to our trades. Now I must get going. Off with that jacket.'

Captain Player, I thought to myself. Captain Miles Player, officer commanding support company, 2nd Battalion The Prince Regent's Light Infantry. It was incredible. I had given up thinking about promotion and now I was a captain and a company commander. A month or two ago, I had been a lieutenant trying to escape the impossible situation of being in love with Kitty. Now I had stepped, almost, into Horace's shoes to become a company commander. I knew it was partly due to Horace's death that I owed my promotion. But I didn't get Kitty. What were the gods up to? Why? Now I had been dealt a new hand of cards. I just hoped that it would be possible to play it better than the last hand. That is what life seemed to be about: playing the cards in your hand as best you can. Then along comes fate with a trump card, and there is nothing you can do but hope you get dealt a new hand that has got some possibilities. But I no longer had a card with Kitty on it. I couldn't help thinking about that.

Catchpole returned with my jacket. I stepped out for my new office as Captain Player.

'Congratulations, Sir,' said Big Steel. 'We're all very pleased with your promotion and appointment. I see Catchpole has acted swiftly.'

'Thank you, Serjeant Major. And thank you for sending Catchpole across to the mess to get my uniforms changed. I'd like to keep Catchpole as my driver.'

'I'll fix that. Mr Hare was up here a moment ago asking for you. I sent him along to the machine gun platoon stores. Everyone knows. He'll go down well with the lads.'

'Let's go and see the machine gun platoon. Then I'd like to look at the other platoons. Tomorrow we'll hold a company muster parade. I can inspect all the men and they can see me. We'll have a company muster parade once a week on Saturdays. On the other days platoons can muster individually. I don't want to change things. Inter-platoon rivalry is good. But everyone needs to understand this is a company not just a handful of private fiefdoms.'

Big Steel liked that. We went to the machine gun platoon stores to arrange Adam's instruction in the arcane mysteries of the Vickers machine gun. Adam was already sitting on the floor behind a machine gun with Little Steel explaining the parts to him.

'I think I'm going to like the machine guns,' Adam said without looking up, 'especially as I'm going to have my own jeep again. Oh, by the way Miles, congratulations.'

'It's incredible,' said Jasper in the mess at lunchtime after he had congratulated me. 'I've been told I'm skiing officer. I'm to take my platoon and Colour Serjeant Crum and run a ski camp. I can't believe my luck.'

'When are you off?'

'Tomorrow. I'm to run the camp and instruct. Colour Crum can run the camp and I'll do the instructing. There're to be competitions. The battalion is to come one platoon at a time.'

'Did D.P. Brown tell you?'

'No, Francis did. But he said it was Colonel Dennis' decision. I can't believe it.'

'Now's your chance. Don't do anything rash.'

'No fear.'

'If I come at the weekend will you teach me?'

'If I can't do it I'll find you an instructor.'

'By the way, my cousin Phyllida Blessington is coming to stay with the Stanhopes. She skis.'

'Bring her.'

The day Phyllida arrived the Stanhopes asked me to dinner. The Sengers were there. They had a chalet at the ski resort. The Stanhopes were taking Phyllida to stay with them that weekend. Duties prevented me from joining them. I had, too, to see Adam was up to scratch on the Vickers machine gun as he had been found a place on the very next course at Netheravon. He was an able and receptive pupil, was soon adept in the skills necessary to fire the Vickers, and mastered much of the theory merely by reading the machine gun manual. Little Steel was astonished at his proficiency.

After the weekend, I took Phyllida to dinner at the *Ratskeller*.

'How was the skiing?'

'The slopes are quite simple but it was fun. Jasper skis like a dream.'

'Jasper is a good friend of mine. I'd hoped you'd get on.'

'We did. He's a love. He took me to the casino. I thought we were going to dance. I'd never been to a casino before. We went into the *salle privée* and I played roulette with his help.'

'Did you win?'

'Yes. Beginner's luck, Jasper said. He didn't play. He does seem a little preoccupied.'

'He misses Kitty Belcher. They were like brother and sister. They used to ride every day. I thought the ski slopes would occupy him.'

'Oh they do. It's just the way he behaves. And he drank a lot. Do you miss Kitty?'

'Why do you ask?'

'Mummy told me what happened between you and Kitty in Hong Kong.'

There was a long silence.

'Yes, Phyllida, I miss Kitty. I loved Kitty. Have you ever been in love?'

'Me? A few crushes. But I've not been mad about anyone for longer than a few weeks. I'm a virgin, Miles.'

'So I should hope.'

'I'm not so sure. Mummy says keep it for my wedding night, for heaven's sake. My friends who've done it say it's such a relief to get it over with and it's fun. I'm curious and I want to grow up. It's an awful thing, being a virgin.'

'You should be proud of it. Most men want to marry virgins.'

'Was Kitty a virgin when she got married?'

'No.'

'There you are, you see.'

'Look what good it did her.'

'That was bad judgement on her part and bad luck. Poor Kitty.'

We ate on in silence for a bit.

'I loved seeing you in London, Miles. We had fun didn't we? And in Herefordshire?'

'It was wonderful.'

'You loved seeing me too?'

'Of course.'

'I hoped you would say that. Miles, will you deflower me?'

'Will I what?'

'Deflower me.'

'Phyllida, I will not.'

'What's wrong with me? I'm not bad looking. Some say I'm good looking, even beautiful. I've always liked you. I'm your cousin. It's your duty to help me.'

'Phyllida, it just doesn't happen like that. I can't possibly "deflower" you as you put it. One goes to bed with someone as a result of sexual fire. You're my little cousin. I'm here to look after you, not to take advantage. Is that why you came to Germany?'

'Yes. I want to get it over. I can't in London, everyone would know. I thought it would be much easier to do it abroad. What could be sexier than skiing? Then I thought, "Cousin Miles will be just the man, he'll be experienced". You're quite sexy too.'

'No, I'm not.'

'I don't believe you.'

We looked at each other, not believing a word either said.

'I'll have to ask Jasper, then.'

'Jasper's only interested in horses and skiing.'

'I'm not so sure. I just wonder how experienced he is, though. I want someone with experience. Anyhow, I'm going to do it while I'm out of England.'

'What about contraception?'

'That's up to the man. That's his responsibility.'

'Where and when are you planning your defloration?'

'I'm going on to Kitzbühel where I'm meeting some friends. We're staying at the *Weisses Rossl.* Why don't you come? We could do it there. Much easier and more fun in a hotel.'

'Phyllida, you don't know what you're saying.'

'Yes, I do.'

'Phyllida!'

'All right, I will ask Jasper.'

'He won't get leave while he's skiing officer.'

'You're a great disappointment, Miles. You're letting me down and I was looking forward to comforting you after Kitty.'

The next weekend Francis took me skiing. We stayed at the grandest of the hotels. Phyllida and the Stanhopes were staying with the Sengers again. While I tried to get to grips with my skis on the nursery slopes, they all went off on the high runs with Jasper, and had a lot of fun.

After dinner Phyllida said, 'I'm so glad you're here, Miles. I hope you've come to tell me you've changed your mind.'

'I've come to tell my little cousin to think again.'

'I'm quite determined. I shall ask Jasper. He's such fun on the slopes.'

'Where is Jasper?'

'He's gone to the casino. Let's join him.'

Jasper was in the *salle privée* sitting at the roulette table with a concentrated look. He'd been having modest success but soon his chips began to dwindle. He put the last one on zero. It didn't come up.

'That's that. I'm cleaned out.'

'Come and dance,' said Phyllida. 'I've a proposition to make to you. It'll cheer you up.'

'I'd like to hear the answer,' I said. 'I'll stay here and play.'

For once my luck was in. When you don't need to win you do.

When you're desperate to win you always lose. I played for nearly an hour and couldn't stop winning. I made two hundred and fifty Deutschmarks. I went to look for Phyllida and Jasper to tell them my good luck but I couldn't find them. Everyone seemed to have gone to bed.

The next day I found Phyllida in a corner of the refreshment chalet drinking hot chocolate and smoking a cigarette.

'Well?' I said.

'Well what?'

'Are you still a virgin?'

'Jasper was not receptive to my caresses and found an excuse to go back to his camp. He seemed to have something on his mind.'

'He's been at the tables all week, I hear. He's broke. He said so'

'I think it's more than that. Look, here he is.'

Jasper came in from the slopes. I had seen him look more cheerful.

'Miles, I need your advice. I've a problem. Sorry, Phyllida, it's military. It'll bore you.'

We walked outside so no one could overhear us.

'Colour Crum has been on the fiddle,' he said. 'I was given a wad of Deutschmarks to buy fresh food, a mark per head per day. We only brought tins from the barracks. I gave it to Colour Crum. After all, he's running the camp while I'm instructing all day. I checked the accounts at the beginning of the week and found he'd spent it all. "How come it's all gone already, Colour? It was meant to last two weeks." "Things are expensive here," he says, "look it's all accounted for." Well it wasn't. He'd fiddled the books. "Where's it all gone, Colour?" I asked. "I got a little carried away," he says. "There's an afternoon game at the casino. While you was all on the slopes I nipped down and had a punt. I lost it all." I got him to promise not to go near the casino or any gambling joint again. I told him to correct the accounts and I'd put the money back. It was my fault because I shouldn't have given it to him in the first place. We were short of two hundred and fifty marks. I hadn't got that amount so I punted every night and you saw me lose my last mark last night. I'm skint till payday. Francis is staying over tomorrow. He's bound to check the money as he's going to give us more. No one's had any fresh food for a week and they're complaining. What am I going to do?'

'Luckily, Jasper, I have two hundred and fifty marks. Here, take them and tell Colour Crum to keep his mouth shut. Can you fix it now?'

'I'll pay you back.'

'Forget it. Fix it.'

'Thanks, Miles.'

'Did Phyllida proposition you?'

'Yes. She's asked me to join her and her friends at Kitzbühel. She said the skiing was magnificent. I said I'd ask for leave to go.'

'Is that all?'

'Isn't that enough?'

The next morning, I accompanied Francis to Jasper's ski camp. Everything we saw was 'All Sir Garnet'. Francis congratulated Jasper and Colour Crum. He checked the accounts and handed over more Deutschmarks. Jasper asked for leave to go to Kitzbühel for a few days. Francis thought that would be all right but he would have to get Colonel Dennis's approval.

Motoring back to barracks, Francis said he considered Jasper was doing a great job, and that we had to return the next weekend to enjoy the skiing. All week I looked forward to it. I could now see why people spoke so highly of skiing, and I was determined to master it. Perhaps, I thought, I should go to Kitzbühel for a few days to get better slopes and better instruction. But my new appointment kept me occupied, Adam had gone on his course and it would have been difficult at that time to have got away for a week.

One day the following week, I was sitting in the anteroom alone in the early evening when Jasper walked in.

'On your way to Kitzbühel?'

Jasper looked furious. He pressed the bell for the barman.

'May I ask what brings our ski master to barracks?'

'To take a hiding from D.P. Brown.'

'Whatever for?'

Corporal Cheke came into the room.

'Good evening, Mr Knox, Sir.'

'Good evening Corporal Cheke, would you bring me a double brandy and ginger?'

Corporal Cheke nodded and left the room.

'You remember how Colour Crum fiddled the books and you helped me put it right? The bloody fool told his serjeant major how decent I had been not to make a fuss and how grateful he was, the serjeant major told the RSM and the RSM told D.P. Brown. I think they were all trying to compliment me. D.P. Brown went mad.'

Corporal Cheke entered with the double brandy and ginger. Jasper drank it down and asked Corporal Cheke for another.

'D.P. Brown screamed at Francis saying how could Francis keep such a thing from him. I was sent for. I've just spent an hour with them arguing about it. I kept you out of it. Colour Crum never knew where I got the Deutschmarks. Francis took my side. Said he couldn't see anything had happened contrary to military law. No money was missing.'

Corporal Cheke returned with a double brandy and ginger.

'Maybe,' said Francis, 'I had been over trusting to start and then shown too much forbearance, but I'd behaved as any good officer would over a slip by a senior NCO with an unblemished record, and that I was to be congratulated not reprimanded. Apparently the RSM was of the same opinion. D.P. Brown recanted a little but he was still bloody. I'm on my way back to ski camp where, frankly, the skiing has become rather boring.'

'Well you've got Kitzbühel to look forward to.'

'D.P. Brown has cancelled that. It's bloody unfair. I was so looking forward to skiing with Phyllida.'

A month later Francis, Ben, Jasper and I did go to Kitzbühel. We had a high time. But Phyllida had long left.

The battalion enjoyed its skiing. Now there were signs of spring, Jasper and I were riding every day. We were closer than ever because of Kitty. Jasper was keen to race again, but he was drinking a lot, too. One evening I came into the anteroom to find Adam, with a Campari and soda in his hand, talking to Burgo and Jasper. He had just returned from his course in England.

'It's disgraceful,' said Burgo. 'Adam says he got an "A" grade. I don't believe him.'

'It's true,' I said. 'I read his report in the orderly room this morning. He did get an "A". Remarkable, Adam, and congratulations. How did you do it? You were expected to get a "B", but getting an "A" is a little excessive, almost ostentatious.'

'Little Steel was an exemplary instructor so I arrived more proficient than anyone. Starting in the lead I thought I'd try and stay there. The machine gun school commandant asked me to stay on and become an instructor. Promotion to captain and the extra loot were tempting but I thought it better to return to my chums and our civilized town than rot in the English countryside.'

'How was London?' asked Burgo.

'I had a few nights at the Gargoyle and made a conquest, or two.'

'Girls or boys?' asked Burgo.

'Both.'

'We must celebrate your return,' said Burgo. 'We've been a dull lot without you.'

'Except for skiing,' said Jasper.

'I'm glad I missed that,' said Adam.

'There was a casino.'

'I'm sad to have missed that.'

Karl, our mess caterer, arranged a decent dinner. Caviare to start, then veal escalopes, followed by angels on horseback.

'*Burgunder* wine,' Burgo had instructed in the anteroom beforehand, 'with a glass of vodka to start, but only one, Karl.'

'*Herr Leutnant*, this I have anticipated.'

'Be sure to keep the vodka to one glass.'

'One glass, *Herr Leutnant*.'

'Oh Burgo, stop being such a nanny,' Jasper said.

'You know you're drinking too much, Jasper. You'll spoil the evening if you go on.'

'I shan't.'

'You're a little pissed already, aren't you?'

'And why not? And who are *you* to reprimand me?'

Jasper was not really drunk, just very touchy. After that skirmish we went into dinner and the air cleared. Adam told us some stories about what he had got up to in London. Then the talk turned to racing. Jasper had entered Vampire for the Grand Military at Sandown, and was due to take Vampire to England and finish his training there. Algy and Francis had made it difficult for D. P. Brown to deny Jasper this chance. We discussed what odds Jasper was likely to get. Most of us thought he would be an outsider as he had no form in England; he would, though, be a strong contender to win on his German form. Few punters would rate this so he would attract little money. Jasper was not concerned about the odds. He was concerned about winning, was adamant that he could, and drank a lot of burgundy as if to prove his ability. We all drank a lot of burgundy.

'That,' said Adam, 'was a passable dinner. Good as any I had in London. Karl is to be congratulated. Francis, you're not going to leave us so soon? Won't you join us for a game of cards to celebrate my return?'

By this time only Ben, Francis, Burgo, Adam, Jasper and I were still sitting at the table. We'd all settled at one end round Ben. The others had left as they probably hadn't wanted to go on drinking or be lured into a game of cards with Adam on his return.

'I can't tonight. You ought to know that the Colonel inspects the bridge book regularly. He knows you are playing a lot. "What else," I say to him, "would you expect your officers to do in these long winter nights?" He's puzzled it seems so above board.'

'That's because Adam has been away,' Ben replied. We all laughed.

'Now Adam's returned let's keep it above board.'

'Hear that Adam?' said Ben.

'Yes, Uncle Ben.'

'How does he know we're playing a lot?' asked Jasper.

'Probably because you Jasper, as you order your double gins before lunch, have been overheard swanking about how much you won or lost the previous night. A certain company commander looking for favour with the colonel has long ears and is, I tell you again, no friend of yours.'

'Trench Foot still up to his old tricks?' said Adam.

'There's a rumour being spread by the serjeants' mess that he may be leaving us at last,' said Burgo.

'That's so,' said Francis. 'His posting order has come through.'

'Where's he going?' we all asked in one voice.

'Back to the paras. Let's say both he and the colonel have seen the light,' said Francis.

'Bravo,' said Burgo.

'I'll miss Julia,' said Adam.

Jasper tossed back his port and filled his glass from the decanter standing in front of him. 'Best news I've heard for months,' he said.

Adam pushed the decanter past Jasper and said, 'But Francis, why can't you stay and play tonight. You will see how I observe the rules. Do we perceive a flap is on? Is there a little military hysteria in the air? I noticed you didn't get back to the mess until the first mess call for dinner.'

'No flap. We don't flap, Adam. Just work to be done.'

Francis had dined well. He must have drunk a bottle of burgundy, let alone anything else, though he hadn't had time to drink much before dinner. He was in a relaxed, happy, knowing, almost confiding mood.

'Well,' he said, 'you'll all learn tomorrow so there's no harm in telling you tonight. The serjeants' mess probably knows already. The colonel will bugle for the company commanders after muster parade tomorrow to brief them. I've still got some details to tie up, which is why I must return to the orderly room. Perhaps, Karl,' he said raising his voice, 'you could recharge the decanters and then leave us. And would you be so good as to close the door. It was an excellent dinner.'

What is Francis going to tell us now, I wondered. Even Jasper had a rare look of curiosity.

'In a word it's Kenya. We're ordered to Kenya, instanter.'

Jasper was the first to open his mouth.

'Kenya? Kenya? No one's ever talked about Kenya. We're meant to be here for another year. I've got races to win and Vampire is entered in the Grand Military.'

'No more racing for you in Germany or England, Jasper. I could barely stop from laughing when everyone was discussing the likely odds of backing you. The general in Kenya has asked for more troops and he's got us. We are to return to England and those charming Victorian barracks we all know, go on embarkation leave, and then three weeks on one of Her Majesty's cruise ships will see us in Mombasa ready to frighten the Mau Mau.'

'Goodbye, civilisation,' said Adam.

'Hello, jungle,' said Burgo. 'Now for some real soldiering.'

'Will Algy command?' I asked.

'Well, er, Colonel Dennis will take us to Kenya and hand over once we're operational.'

'Will Algy take over then?'

'Not decided.'

He stopped and thought. Then he said, 'You might as well know this too but don't say I told you and don't let on you know when you hear from someone else. Promise?'

Francis looked at each of us.

'Promise?'

We nodded in turn.

'You too, Jasper.'

'Promise, Francis.'

Francis cleared his throat.

'Algy has resigned. He resigned yesterday. I'm surprised the news hasn't got out, but Algy was at Brigade today so he hasn't had time to tell anyone. He told me he would never live down the adverse report Colonel Dennis gave him, whatever the brigadier and the general and the colonel of the regiment said. One day some smiling shit in the War Office would turn it up and use it as evidence that Algy wasn't sound. So he's resigned. The colonel doesn't want it known yet. The orders for Kenya only arrived today but I think he's known about it for some days. Someone he knows at division or GHQ told him. He's always on the telephone to them. Tomorrow he'll tell the company commanders that Algy has resigned and that he, Colonel Dennis, will take the battalion to Kenya. He'll say it in such a way that it will sound as if Algy resigned after he knew about Kenya, and will put him in a bad light.'

We all looked at each other horrified.

'Whatever happened,' I asked, 'about Algy's brevet lieutenant colonelcy? We all know he was thinking about resigning, but he said to me if he got his brevet that would encourage him to stay on, implying it would be one in the eye for Colonel Dennis.'

There was a long silence. We all looked at Francis.

'Look, you've really got to promise again. If this gets out it will be traced back to me. I'll be for the chop and I won't be able to do anything to help any of you any longer. Promise?'

Francis looked at each one of us in turn.

'I promise, Francis,' said Ben, followed by Adam, Burgo and me.

'Promise, Jasper?'

'I promise, Francis, darling.'

'The letter from the War Office confirming Algy's brevet came through three weeks ago. Colonel Dennis said he thought it best to put it in a drawer for a bit.'

There was a long silence. Finally Jasper broke it.

'When we get to Kenya,' he said, 'the first chance I get I'm going to shoot D.P.Brown.'

There was another long silence.

Then Francis, Ben, Burgo, Adam and I slowly got up from the
table and left the room. Jasper sat on, glowering at the decanter
of port in front of him.

'You know,' Burgo said to me as we walked through the door,
'I think he's perfectly capable of doing it.'

Yes, I thought, he is.

17

All at sea

'Have you heard, Sir? The Colonel of the Regiment is dead,' said Tom Body as I came into the mess in the barracks in England where we had arrived a few days previously from Germany.

'It's not unexpected,' I replied. 'He's been ill for months. How do you know?'

He followed me into the anteroom.

'Officers are to wear uniform at the funeral. I've been told to find mourning bands for you to wear.'

We had been sad to leave Germany. We had come to love our university town and the barracks that overlooked it, whatever tribulations D.P.Brown had put us through. It had been the best of peacetime stations. Now, the opportunity to see action in Kenya had re-invigorated the battalion. We had a new purpose and the excitement was palpable. A rush of events had enveloped us. General Flaxman's funeral would now be seen as one more thing to do, one more event in preparing for Kenya. We would bury him with pomp and honour, and bury with him our time in Germany. We all knew General Flaxman had been eking out his life; perhaps we had been eking out our own lives, wasting them in Germany. The interesting question now was who would take his place, who would now look after our interests and guide us when we were in Kenya? The colonel of the regiment had great influence, especially on officers' careers. One life and one tour end. A new life and a new tour begin.

'When is the funeral?' I asked.

'Tomorrow week.'

Tomorrow week we were scheduled to go on embarkation leave. We would go a day late now. That is, the officers would and those of the warrant officers and serjeants who would want to attend, together with the cortège party. More tangible and of much greater concern was the departure of Algy Stanhope. The War Office had finally accepted his resignation. Who would replace Algy? We recognised that he had tempered D.P.Brown's worst excesses. We wondered if anyone else would be able to do this half as well. Certainly none of the senior officers serving with the battalion at present could.

'One other thing, Sir,' said Tom Body. 'Major Bulman arrives this afternoon. I'm to find him a good room and there isn't one fit for a second lieutenant let alone a new second in command. I'll have to move someone.'

So it was to be George Bulman. That was good news. George had been my company commander in Hong Kong and Korea and we'd been close. Wounded in an early engagement in Korea, he had been evacuated home to recover. It was then that Dermot Lisle had taken over the company. George was unusual, almost eccentric, and different from Algy. He had a strong character. If anyone could stand up to D.P.Brown he could. And he was a friend.

'You are dining out Major Stanhope on Wednesday,' said Tom Body. 'I've been ordered to produce as good a meal as I can. Tragedy we didn't do it in Germany. I could have produced an excellent meal there for nothing. It's going to cost a bit here.'

'I don't think anyone is going to object to that,' I replied.

'I've heard the commanding officer is to be away that night,' said Tom with a knowing look.

'Ask Corporal Cheke to bring me a goblet of beer, Colour.'

'Very good, Sir,' said Tom and he walked off.

Gone were the days of duty free gin and champagne. The reality of living in England was already hitting our pockets, which was another reason to be looking forward to Kenya.

I flopped into an armchair. Gone too was the beautiful mess with all our possessions. We had chosen some pieces of silver and a few pictures to keep with us, some of which were in the anteroom now, for we would have a base camp in Nairobi where we could have an officers' mess. Most of the possessions had been boxed and sent to the regimental depot where they would be stored. Living in this half-furnished mess added to the unreality of everything else that was happening.

Burgo came into the anteroom, followed by Corporal Cheke with goblets of beer for us.

'Have you heard?' I said. 'George Bulman arrives this afternoon.'

'Big Steel told me a moment ago. He said the serjeants' mess would be pleased. I came here as fast as I could to share the news.'

'It's wonderful news for everyone. Have you heard that John Flaxman has died?'

'Has he now?' He stopped and thought. 'Does George's arrival mean that he'll take over command?'

'I haven't heard that. Maybe in time. There's no doubt that D.P.Brown will command at first in Kenya.'

'That man is getting worse. At the inspection this morning he was only interested in bootlaces. He didn't look at the weapons.'

'We're to leave all our weapons here. You'll get new ones in Kenya.'

'Maybe, but bootlaces! It's an insult.'

The last few days had been taxing. Everyone was under pressure. We were having to do things we were not used to and having to find our way all the time. New drafts of soldiers had arrived to bring our numbers up to war establishment, so we now had to train them in record time. We had lost many of our trained national servicemen who hadn't enough time left to come to Kenya. There were some new officers too, but not in my company.

'Have you seen Adam?'

'He's still at the quartermaster's stores fitting new uniforms.'

We were being fitted out with jungle green clothing, and both long and short trousers. We had puttees instead of gaiters and everyone had to learn how to put these on. There were inoculations and a hundred other administrative chores.

'Any absentees today?' asked Burgo.

'None, thank God.'

While we'd been in Germany, the soldiers had been largely untroubled by their families, most of whom had been resigned to their absence. Now that most of the soldiers were within easy travelling distance of their homes they were continually being badgered to return home and help out. Every day a soldier came to me with an excuse for immediate compassionate leave. One said his father, a farmer, was ill and couldn't look after the animals; another that his mother, a widow, had broken her leg and couldn't cope. I had to look into every case. Most were inventions. A few were real and leave was granted.

One or two soldiers went absent without leave. This worried me most. Going absent when under orders for active service was a serious offence. I talked to the whole company about it. I got my platoon commanders to talk to each of their soldiers to ensure everyone understood this and that none had problems we didn't know about. All the same one soldier went absent. The colonel blamed me. In Germany few soldiers ever went absent. It was too difficult for them to go anywhere, especially to get home. In England it was too easy.

'Anyone up for commanding officer's orders?' asked Burgo.

'Not today,' I said crossing my fingers.

Most of the soldiers had been well behaved in the town in Germany. They had found bars and places where they had been made welcome. They had also had a good canteen in the barracks and there were regular company smokers, evenings when the company as a whole entertained itself and the officers joined in. In England we didn't have the same facilities in the barracks, nor did the soldiers want them. They wanted the fleshpots in the garrison town, where we were one of several battalions. The men ran into groups from other regiments, and there were brawls. We had to help mount a garrison patrol every night to ensure law and order.

'I wish,' said Burgo, 'that we'd gone straight to Kenya from Germany.'

'So do I but I doubt if we could have organised it properly from there.'

This was a difficult time. Everyone was bored or frustrated and longing to slip the leash.

Jasper joined us.

'God, I need a drink,' he said as he rang the bell. 'Do you know what D.P.Brown was interested in this morning? Bootlaces. We have a commanding officer who's only interested in bootlaces. Can you believe it?'

'At least he's consistent,' said Burgo.

Corporal Cheke entered the room.

'Any of my duty free gin left?' asked Jasper.

'An amplitude, Sir.'

'Then I'll have a double gin and tonic.'

Jasper had returned early from Germany to run Vampire in the Grand Military. Algy had ensured this. Jasper had hidden a case of gin and a case of whisky in the horsebox. Those who knew about this rather admired his daring, though it had been foolhardy.

'How's Vampire?' asked Burgo.

'Vampire is a happy horse with his new commanding officer, Colonel Guy.'

'Have you sold him then?'

'I couldn't take him with me. Colonel Guy offered me a decent price. I think Kitty would have liked him to come home and win races here. He will. I'll have another go at the Grand Military after Kenya.'

Jasper hadn't won the Grand Military. In a close finish he had been placed fourth out of fourteen runners. He'd had little time to prepare Vampire, who had not shown the finishing speed we knew him capable of. None of us had been able to watch the race, but

Adam had backed Vampire heavily and was still to recover from his loss. Everyone blamed D.P.Brown for not supporting Jasper and not giving him enough time to prepare.

Others came into the anteroom. The conversation was more about George Bulman's arrival than General Flaxman's death.

The dinner to say goodbye to Algy was a suppressed affair. It little resembled the night we had dined out Dermot Lisle in Germany. We all felt weakened by Algy's departure. Everyone sensed this; no one spoke it. Algy seemed sad too. We drank a lot. It was not a happy evening.

George Bulman had come and gone. Leading the advance party, he had set off on the long flight to Nairobi via Malta, Benghazi, Khartoum, and Entebbe.

A few days later we buried General Flaxman. As we stood in the graveyard at the end of the service, Ben asked me what my plans were.

'I was wondering if I might come and stay with you for a few days in London?'

'Of course. Do you know what the others are doing?'

'Adam is going home to see if he can raise some money for a trip to the south of France with Finbar and Burgo, who leave at the end of the week. They'll be in London for the first few days, as will Jasper who's staying with his mother. Jasper's then going on to Colonel Guy's.'

'We could all do something together in London.'

'Sonia Blessington is giving a party and has asked me to bring you and the others. We could have a lot of fun. Then I must go and see my mother. I thought I'd go and see General Fisher too. He's always got news.'

'Harry Fox told me to look him up. He wants to show us his cellars.'

I went to stay with Ben.

We all met up at Sonia's, where we were treated like heroes on our way to war. We knew little about what we were to do in Kenya but we were soon enlightened. Many of those at the party were politicians or diplomats. A few were businessmen. Some knew Kenya well and most knew someone in Kenya. We were given a number of introductions that were to prove very useful. Sonia had clearly arranged the party for this purpose.

As the party thinned Sonia said, 'Don't go, we'll go out to dinner. Ask Ben and Jasper too. Phyllida likes Jasper. We'll go to the Allegro, we can dance there. Phyllida will bring a friend. It's time we had some fun together again. Ivan will pay but I don't think he'll come as he always has papers to read.'

'You are an angel to arrange this party. We've got some wonderful introductions.'

'I'm so glad. I've always felt very close to your regiment, what with your mother and father and Hong Kong. I wanted to do something for you.'

The six of us went to the Allegro, had dinner, and danced.

'Well, Phyllida?'

'Well, Miles?'

We were dancing quite close.

'Are you still a virgin?'

'Yes I am. And no thanks to you.'

'I'm glad to hear it.'

We danced on.

'Why do you ask?'

'Just curious.'

'Don't tell me you've changed your mind?'

'I just want to know who I'm dancing with.'

'Do you now? I've been watching you all evening watching me. Shall I tell you who *I'm* dancing with? A soldier on his last leave, going to the front and looking for a bang. You're wondering if you could take me to bed, aren't you?'

'You're very beautiful.'

'That's not enough.'

'What is enough?'

'Helping me out when I wanted you to. Do you think I'd do it now, in London, under my mother's eyes, with you?'

'You've changed.'

'No, circumstances have changed.'

'You've got a boy friend?'

'No.'

'You're in love with someone who doesn't love you?'

'Wrong again.'

'Well?'

'I want it to mean something. You told me that. It can't if you lay me and then immediately disappear to Kenya.'

'I thought you just wanted to be deflowered, the burden of virginity being too much.'

'I may do. The circumstances just aren't right. There, Miles, don't be upset. Now's not the time or place. I do like you a lot.'

The music stopped. She kissed me on the cheek, and we returned to the table.

I danced with Sonia.

'You and Phyllida looked very intense. She likes you a lot. Sometimes I think she might even love you. I don't blame her. What do you think of her?'

'The more I see her the more I like her. She's become very beautiful.'

'Yes, she has. She worries me. She says she wants to lose her virginity. I tell her to wait until she's married. She says, "Why Mummy? Did you?" That was difficult to answer.'

We went on dancing.

'Do you know who I lost my virginity to?'

'How could I?'

'Guess.'

'Ivan?'

She laughed.

'Guess again.'

'I've no idea.'

'Your father.'

She laughed again.

'He was such fun, your father. I was silly enough to tell Phyllida. She was shocked. "Mummy," she said, "how could you? Do you mean that Miles' father is my father?" I replied, "Of course not darling, it was long before I married your father." '

'That,' I said, 'explains something about Phyllida that's been puzzling me for some time.'

'I shouldn't have told you.'

'I'm glad you did. Does my mother know?'

'I've never known. Ever since we were children she's always been rather distant with me. It was your grandfather who kept us together. How is your mother?'

'Being very decent to me. She's just started to give me an allowance.'

'Just? She's got enough money.'

'Yes, just. Since I came home on leave last year. She said she could only just afford it as my father spent most of her money.'

'He spent a lot but don't you believe that. There's money in trust for you, I know. She's just being careful, like I hear Verity Knox has been careful with Jasper.'

When I went to bed that night I fell asleep wondering how many more revelations were still to come.

Leave raced away. It was not until we had embarked on the troop-ship and were at sea, steaming across the Bay of Biscay, that we all had time to take stock and get into a new routine. We were back under the direct rule of D.P.Brown who daily, as we sailed closer to Mombasa, the port in Kenya where we were to disembark, became more manic.

The ship was overcrowded. When I went below decks to visit my men's quarters I was embarrassed by their lack of space. There wasn't much room for anyone. I shared a cabin with Burgo and Jasper. Burgo, to relieve boredom, would lie on his bunk reciting the farewell address given by the new colonel of the regiment, who was a sleek lieutenant general with a quick eye, a lively step, and a word for everyone.

' "And now that you sail away," ' recited Burgo, ' "to engage in the operations against the Mau Mau in Kenya, I know that you will not only maintain but enhance the great reputation of the regiment". It's always "maintain and enhance". Do you remember that when we returned from Korea we had "maintained and enhanced" the reputation of the regiment? And when we went to Germany we were "going to maintain and enhance"? Do you think colonels of regiments are appointed on their ability to memorise and adapt "maintain and enhance" to any situation?'

'If they are, you're qualified.'

'Did you notice that D.P.Brown didn't look too comfortable? He was jumping around like a paranoid monkey trying to please the new colonel of the regiment who took little notice of him.'

'You're not the first to make that observation.'

'In the long term that may be a good thing. In the short term I smell fireworks.'

Burgo was right. D.P.Brown put fireworks under everyone to get activities going. Left to their own devices, the company commanders would have organised training and interests to have kept everyone fit, instructed, and occupied. With the second in command, who was responsible for training, already in Kenya with the advance party D.P.Brown took it upon himself to direct everything. He was like a circling shark, appearing from nowhere to pounce upon a squad or group of soldiers. He would stand there fiddling with his signet ring and looking at them, ready to intervene, reprimand, or worse, steal away without a word. We settled into a routine of events that relieved boredom but did little to inspire.

There were lectures on Kenya, jungle warfare (Francis Bowerman had fought in Malaya and one of the company commanders had been with Orde Wingate in Burma), the history of the Mau Mau insurrection, health in the tropics, and camp discipline. Equipment and uniform inspections were frequent. When, as we steamed into the Mediterranean, we changed into our jungle green uniforms, D.P.Brown's favourite routine was to inspect whether the men had put on their puttees correctly.

'Do you think,' said Burgo lying on his bunk between reciting permutations of the colonel of the regiment's speech, 'do you think that our secret weapon to defeat the Mau Mau is the puttee?'

A ship's concert, produced by Ben and directed by Burgo, Jasper and Charlie Chance, with a lot of input from the serjeants' mess, livened things up, as did a deck hockey league and competition, a series of boxing evenings, and a canvas swimming pool rigged amidships when the temperature rose. We steamed past Gibraltar and Malta, refuelled at Suez where the gully gully men entertained everyone and made a good sum for themselves by diving for coins thrown overboard, dazzling the soldiers with their magical tricks, and selling strings of beads that the soldiers said they were buying for their wives and sweethearts and wore themselves.

The heat of the Red Sea then paralysed everyone. Boredom, so long held at bay, and ennui took charge.

'If I could have a pint of lemonade,' said Burgo lying naked on his bunk exhausted by the heat, the colonel of the regiment's speech laid to rest, 'for every glass of wine I drank in France, I would pledge never to drink wine in Kenya.'

'There won't be any wine in the jungle.'

'Not what I've heard about Nairobi.'

'How much did you drink in France?'

'We ended strictly rationed. Adam came after all. He had raised some loot from his parents, so he said. He lost it all at Cannes.'

'Why Cannes?'

'He brainwashed us. All the way down he sang:

> Menton's dowdy,
> Monte's brass.
> Nice is rowdy:
> Cannes is class.

All the way back we had to buy him a meal and a bed. He always went for the expensive menu. "Won't be able to eat like this in Kenya," he would say. By the time we reached Dover we were all broke. Haven't you noticed he's been trying to get a high stake chemmy game going? No one's taking. He's had to be content with small stake *vingt-et-un*.'

We had drunk little because of the heat. There was mild card play. D.P.Brown's presence in the mess had overshadowed it. For a time he had held a bridge four after dinner. That had stopped. Steaming through the Red Sea the only entertainment that held its attraction was the sweepstake on the ship's daily run for which some hardened punters were still prepared to climb off their bunks.

'To think,' said Burgo still naked on his bed, 'that my grandfather used to pay good money to cruise on a ship. Heigh-ho! Jasper and I have got to go to a meeting with Ben who's putting on another concert to amuse the men. In this heat! We're writing some skits with Jasper and Charlie. Charlie's got some rather good ideas for songs. Do you know "How much is that doggie in the window"?'

'The one with the curly tail?' I responded.

'Charlie is going to dress up as a lieutenant colonel with a big blond wig and an enormous signet ring and sing:

> How much is that Mau Mau in the window?
> The one with the fuzzy wuzzy head.
> How much is that Mau Mau in the window?
> I do hope that Mau Mau's quite dead.

What do you think?'

'Excellent. Why don't you do "Daddy wouldn't buy me a Mau Mau" too?'

'I like that. We're working another up to the tune of "Oh dear, what can the matter be, six old ladies locked in a lavatory?" It starts:

> Oh dear, where can Kenyatta be?
> Is it true he's locked in the lavatory?

It gets worse. Far worse.'

'You'll bring the house down'

'Ben's a little concerned about D.P.Brown's reaction.'

'Why should he be? Think of all those songs about Hitler and Goebbels.'

'That's what Charlie and Jasper say.'

'We're also working on a finale based on "We do like to be beside the seaside". It's a glorious spoof of life on board ship.'

The next day we escaped the oven of the Red Sea and steamed into the Arabian Sea, south-east of Aden. The concert, to be held on deck, was to start at half past six when it would be dark but still hot. The first half was a great success. In the interval D.P.Brown could be seen in a huddle gesticulating with Francis Bowerman, Ben Wildbore, and the regimental serjeant major.

As the curtain, so to speak, was about to go up on the second half, Ben Wildbore appeared on stage.

'We are delighted you have enjoyed the show so far.'

There were shouts of approval.

'We think that the heat is too great for the show to continue and we have decided to close the show now. Thank you all very much for coming. Please give the cast a big hand.'

The cast came on stage. It included those who been expecting to appear in the second half. There were whistles, catcalls and some applause. Someone shouted, 'What about the heat in the jungle?' which attracted more whistles and shouts. Slowly the din died down and the audience dispersed.

'What happened?' I asked Ben when I met him in the mess.

'I can't decide what D.P.Brown objected to. He wasn't coherent. It could have been the lewdness of some of the skits. It could have been something else. All he could say was "It's a disgrace. A scandal. To think that the battalion has come to this. We'll be in Mombasa any day and we're fiddling around at sea. It can't go on." He went on and on. He was adamant. Francis and I thought it was best to finish immediately before he jumped on the stage and said something. The men were enjoying it so much I thought there might be a riot. I'm surprised at how well behaved they were. I didn't like having to stand up and close it down. I just made up all that about the heat. Colonel Dennis was not coherent.'

'I could murder D.P.Brown,' said Burgo who joined us. 'All that effort and all D.P.Brown could say was he wanted it stopped. Charlie nearly wept he'd put so much into it. Jasper's in a murderous mood too. And we never had the glorious finale. We couldn't keep it from Big Steel and Little Steel that it was the colonel who had closed it down. They can't understand it. No one can. There's an ugly mood in the serjeants' mess. I'm glad I'm not the RSM.'

We had dinner. D.P.Brown did not appear. Afterwards a few of us sat down to play cards. No-one really wanted to play; we were discountenanced. The game broke up and the players drifted away. I picked up a pack of cards and started to play patience. Francis came and sat next to me.

'Are you good at getting it out without cheating?' he asked.

'Francis, I haven't had to cheat yet.'

'Everyone does, once in a while.'

I went on playing.

'That was a puzzling fracas tonight,' I said.

'The heat has been too much for some people. The sooner we get to Mombasa the better.'

'Isn't Kenya going to be hot?'

'Not like this.'

'There you are,' I said as I played the last card. 'It came out.'

'Do it again,' said Francis.

I shuffled and started to play again.

'There's an ugly mood tonight, Francis.'

'You don't have to tell me.'

'I hope you've got your ear to the ground.'

'I try to have.'

'It's not just the officers. I wouldn't want the colonel coming near my company in the jungle. Someone might be trigger-happy.

I've overheard some of my NCOs asking each other if they think Colonel Dennis is fit to command in action. And that was before tonight.'

'They actually said that?'

'Yes. And they knew I could hear.'

'With Algy gone, and George Bulman on the advance party, I've no one I can talk to. I had hoped Colonel Dennis would relax on the boat but he's gone into overdrive. He seems to have a lot on his mind.'

'Do you think he's in his right mind?'

'I'm not sure.'

'There's always the doctor.'

'Yes, I'll have a word with the doctor tomorrow and see what he thinks. I wish I knew him better.'

Finbar had left us in England to return to civilian life. None of us had yet got to know the new doctor.

My cards started to slide across the table. Slowly, one by one, they slid onto the floor.

'What's happening?' I said.

'The ship's leaning over.'

'Why?'

'Curious. It's normally steady as a rock.'

Some of the chairs had begun to slide across the room. Francis was leaning away from me. Then I noticed that I was leaning towards Francis.

'The boat's listing.'

'I can see that,' said Francis.

'Do you think it's going to turn over?'

'Unlikely.'

The boat was definitely listing.

'It doesn't seem to be getting any worse,' said Francis.

'Perhaps it's not going to turn turtle after all.'

'Perhaps, if we can stand up, we should find out what's going on.'

The duty officer, one of the new national service subalterns that had joined us in England, came into the room, leaning against the list. He was in uniform and wearing a fore and aft hat. He hesitated and then saluted.

'There's a man overboard, Sir,' he announced. 'The ship is turning round.'

'Do you know if the ship's captain is on the bridge?'

'Yes, he is.'

'What does he want us to do?'

'He wants the battalion to muster and have a roll call. He wants to know who's missing.'

'Muster the battalion on deck at its muster stations. Tell the RSM. The officers are to muster with their companies. I will set up battalion headquarters here in this saloon. Ask all company commanders to hold a roll call and report to battalion headquarters when they've done it. Is that clear?'

'Yes, Sir.'

'We're not on the parade ground.'

'No, Sir. I mean Francis. '

'Report back to me when you've done that. I'll need you.'

'Yes, Francis.'

I went to my company muster station. Slowly the company formed up. The ship was upright again, steaming back north. Big Steel called out all the names. Everyone was present. Officers too. I told Big Steel to keep everyone together and returned to Francis in the saloon. Half the company commanders had reported. No one was missing yet. It took some time to get the final reports. Being a hot night the men had been all over the ship. When all the reports had been made everyone was found to be present. Francis went to report to the captain on the bridge, and then returned to the saloon.

'The captain is adamant a man fell overboard. The lifebuoy sentry in the stern said he distinctly saw someone and heard a cry. He threw the lifebuoy and sounded the alarm immediately. The captain is determined to find him. Even though it took some time to start turning the ship round, he said that if the person can find the lifebuoy we've a very good chance of rescuing him. The water is warm so he won't suffer from hypothermia and there's a full moon. The only problem is sharks, as there are quite a few in the Arabian Sea. He wants to know who's missing. It's not one of the crew, so I want all companies to do a double count and report back to me.'

The double count over, we all came back to Francis. One by one we reported no one missing, and Francis went back to the bridge, baffled. He returned and ordered us to do another count.

Before I left the saloon I turned to Francis.

'Have you told the colonel?' I asked.

'I don't want to wake him up. He needs sleep, not another headache.'

'Perhaps you'd better now. He won't thank you for not waking him.'

Francis turned to the duty officer.

'Go and wake the colonel. Be gentle. Tell him from me that there is a man overboard and ask him, with my compliments, if he would join us in the saloon.'

I returned to my company. As Big Steel called the roll I checked every man myself to ensure no one was doubling up. Everyone was present, and I returned to the saloon, as baffled as Francis.

'Where's the colonel?' I asked.

'He wasn't in his cabin,' said Francis. 'The bunk hasn't been slept in. The duty officer thinks he's on the bridge with the captain. Obvious place for him to be but he wasn't there when I was.'

The company commanders re-assembled. All reported their companies present and correct. The duty officer returned from the bridge.

'The colonel's not on the bridge. The captain says he hasn't seen him all evening.'

'Have you checked his cabin again?'

'Yes. He's not there.'

'Has anyone seen the colonel?'

There was a long silence.

Then Ben said, 'Oh, my God.'
We all looked at each other.

The ship found the lifebuoy, its light blinking away in the dark on
a flat calm sea, exactly where the captain had estimated it would
be. A boat was lowered and we waited while the boat's officer
retrieved the lifebuoy and brought it back on board. A hand was
clutching one of the lifebuoy strings. There was no body. On the
little finger of the hand was Colonel Dennis's signet ring.

Main Characters

Characters who appeared in *On Fire* are marked (OF)

Horace Belcher	Major, company commander. Married Kitty Fisher in Hong Kong. Posted to staff in Singapore and did not serve in Korea (OF).
Kitty Belcher	Wife of Horace, daughter of General Fisher, god-daughter of Sonia Cathay. Unofficially engaged to Miles Player in Hong Kong (OF).
Phyllida Blessington	Daughter of Lord and Lady Cathay.
Heidi von Bock	German NAAFI manageress.
Tom Body	Colour Serjeant, MM. Commanded Assault Pioneer Platoon in Korea (OF).
Francis Bowerman	Captain. Takes over from Val Portal as adjutant.
Dennis Parker Brown	Lieutenant Colonel, OBE. Takes over command of battalion from Guy Surtees in Germany.
George Bulman	Major, MC. Commanded a company in Korea where wounded early on (OF).
Dick Catchpole	Private, national serviceman and driver/ soldier servant of Miles Player.
Ivan Cathay	Viscount, formerly Ivan Blessington, GCMG, GBE. Past Governor of Hong Kong (OF). Now active on fringes of government.
Sonia Cathay	Viscountess, wife of Ivan, godmother of Kitty Belcher, cousin of Miles Player. Was in Hong Kong (OF).
Charlie Chance	2nd Lieutenant, national serviceman.
Sam Cheke	Corporal, officers' mess barman.

'Cookie' Cookson   Machine gunner.

'Crabbie' Crabbe   Machine gun platoon storeman.

Ernie Croucher   Lance Corporal, national serviceman, motor cyclist.

Bert Crum   Colour Serjeant. In Hong Kong and Korea. (OF).

Desmond D'eath   Lieutenant, 5th Hussars.

'Geordie' Feard   Provost Serjeant.

George Fisher   Baronet, Major General, CB, CMG, DSO. Father of Kitty Belcher. Served in regiment in Boer War and WWI. Owner of Sherborne Court. (OF).

John Flaxman   General, GCB, GBE, DSO, MC. Colonel of the regiment.

Harry Fox   2nd Lieutenant, national serviceman. Son of a wine merchant.

'Inky' Hancock   Private, national serviceman.

Adam Hare   Lieutenant. Oxford graduate and late entry.

Ilse Hoffnung   Daughter of Professor and Frau Hoffnung.

Burgo Howard   Lieutenant, MC. Fought in Korea (OF).

Karl   German, Officers' Mess caterer.

Jasper Knox   2nd Lieutenant. Scion of a regimental family.

Verity Knox   Mother of Jasper. Husband killed at Dunkirk with regiment.

Dermot Lisle   Captain, DSO, MC. Fought in WWII and commanded a company in Korea (OF). Now intelligence officer.

Charles Millington   Lieutenant, 19th Lancers.

Finbar O'Connell   Captain, regimental medical officer.

Patrick O'Reilly   Corporal, head groom.

Emily Player   Mother of Miles and widow of Lieutenant General Fred Player CB, CBE, DSO, killed in WWII. First cousin of Sonia Cathay.

Miles Player	Lieutenant. Son of Fred and Emily Player. Was aide-de-camp to Ivan Blessington in Hong Kong where unofficially engaged to Kitty Fisher. Platoon commander, then intelligence officer in Korea (OF).
Victor Popham	Brigadier, CBE, DSO, retired. British Resident in town.
Val Portal	Captain and adjutant.
Rod Rothwell	Corporal. Member of battalion cricket and shooting teams.
Monty Savage	Intelligence section serjeant (OF).
Rana Selzuk	Turkish student at university.
Andreas von Senger	German landowner and panzer officer in WWII.
Elisabeth von Senger	Wife of Andreas.
Alec Skidmore	Major, Royal Engineers.
Dwight Smiley	Colonel, 101st US Armored Cavalry.
Algy Stanhope	Major, DSO, MC, battalion second in command. In WWII commanded battalion aged 28.
Olivia Stanhope	Wife of Algy.
Guy Surtees	Lieutenant Colonel, DSO, OBE. Commanded battalion in Korea with distinction (OF). Hands over command to Dennis Parker Brown in Germany.
Jack Trench	Major, company commander. Took to whisky in Korea (OF).
Julia Trench	Young wife of Jack.
Ben Wildbore	Captain. Fought in Korea (OF).
'Big Steel' Whettingsteel	Miles Player's platoon serjeant in Korea (OF). Now company serjeant major.
'Little Steel' Whettingsteel	Younger brother of 'Big Steel' and corporal in Korea (OF). Now Miles's platoon serjeant.
Dick Whistler	Private, groom.

A Note on Ranks and Organisation

For those unfamiliar with army ranks and the organisation of an infantry battalion such as the 2nd Battalion Prince Regent's Light Infantry (2 PRLI) in the British Army of the Rhine (BAOR) in the early 1950s, here is an outline.

Battalion headquarters consisted of:
Commanding Officer *(Lieutenant Colonel)*
Second in command *(Major)*
Adjutant *(Captain)*
Intelligence Officer *(Lieutenant or Captain)* i/c Intelligence Section
Regimental Serjeant Major *(Warrant Officer I)*
Provost Serjeant *(Serjeant)* i/c Regimental Police
Bugle Major *(Bugle Major)* i/c Bugle Platoon

There were **four rifle companies** each consisting of a **company headquarters**:
Company Commander *(Major)*
Company second in command *(Captain)*
Company Serjeant Major *(Warrant Officer II)*
Company Quartermaster Serjeant (CQMS) i/c company stores
(Colour Serjeant)
Runners, soldier servants, storemen

and **three platoons**, each of which consisted of a **platoon headquarters** and **three rifle sections**, about 40 in all:
Platoon Commander *(Lieutenant or 2nd Lieutenant)*
Platoon Serjeant *(Serjeant)*
Wireless operator
Rocket Launcher operators
Runner/soldier servant

Section Commander *(Corporal)*
Section 2IC *(Lance Corporal)*
Riflemen
Light Machine Gun group

A rifle company consisted of about 130 in total, and the four rifle companies were about 520 in strength.

There was also a **support company** consisting of a company head-quarters similar to a rifle company headquarters and four platoons:

> **Assault Pioneer Platoon**, who were the engineers of the battalion commanded by an officer or a serjeant, and manned by men with specialist skills.

> **Anti-Tank Platoon**, commanded by an officer, with three sections, each of two 17 pounder anti-tank guns commanded by a serjeant.

> **Machine Gun Platoon**, commanded by an officer, with three machine gun sections each of two Vickers medium machine guns commanded by a serjeant.

> **Mortar Platoon**, commanded by an officer, with three mortar sections, each of two 3-inch mortars commanded by a serjeant.

The officers commanding support platoons were the more experienced lieutenants or sometimes captains.

Finally there was a **headquarter company** concerned mainly with administration. It had a company headquarters, and the company commander *(a major)* was often the President of the Regimental Institute (PRI) and Band President as well. In the company were:

> **Motor Transport Platoon** responsible for all the vehicles in the battalion staffed by drivers and mechanics of various ranks, commanded by an officer *(Lieutenant or Captain)*

> **Signals Platoon** responsible for wireless and line communications within the battalion staffed by specialists of various ranks, commanded by an officer *(Lieutenant or Captain)*

> **The Band**, about 30 strong, under command of a Bandmaster *(a Warrant Officer I)*

> The personnel of battalion headquarters for administration

> The **Quartermaster** *(Captain or Major)* with his Regimental Quartermaster Sergeant *(RQMS - Warrant Officer II)* responsible for the provision of victuals, ammunition, clothing, stores, petrol, oil and lubricants, and their accounting.

In the BAOR of the 1950s most units were under strength, some quite seriously so. The establishment strength of an infantry battalion was between 700 to 800. In reality many battalions were only 500 to 600 strong. This resulted in there being only three active rifle companies, the fourth company being a training company. Platoons might be only 20 to 30 strong. If a battalion were seriously under strength, some of the rifle companies might only be able to muster two, not three, platoons. Similarly the support weapons platoons might be reduced to two sections. This was sometimes the case with 2 PRLI as drafts of national servicemen came and went.

The rifle companies in 2 PRLI were named W, X, Y and Z to differentiate them from the rifle companies in 1 PRLI, named A, B, C and D. 2 PRLI was proud of this arrangement, which was not usual in the army as a whole.